LOVE
AND OTHER
LOST
THINGS

BOOKS BY MELISSA WIESNER

Her Family Secret
The Girl in the Picture
Our Stolen Child
His Secret Daughter
It All Comes Back to You

LOVE
AND OTHER
LOST
THINGS

MELISSA WIESNER

bookouture

Published by Bookouture in 2024

An imprint of Storyfire Ltd.
Carmelite House
50 Victoria Embankment
London EC4Y 0DZ

www.bookouture.com

ISBN: 978-1-83525-677-0
eBook ISBN: 978-1-83525-676-3

This book is a work of fiction. Names, characters, businesses, organizations,
places and events other than those clearly in the public domain, are either the
product of the author's imagination or are used fictitiously. Any resemblance to
actual persons, living or dead, events or locales is entirely coincidental.

For Kaia and Tess.
Thank you for all the beautiful energy you put into the world.
You deserve every happily ever after.

AUTHOR'S NOTE

This book contains scenes of domestic violence and abuse which may be triggering for some readers. If you would like some resources, I've included them in the reader letter at the end of the book.

PROLOGUE

TEN YEARS AGO

The minute the front door slammed shut, Jane McCaffrey peeled herself off the floor of her bedroom and clambered unsteadily to her feet. Every muscle protested, begging her to lie back down on the soft carpet until the pain in her body eased. But she didn't have time to wait for the pounding in her head or the throbbing in her bones to subside. And as for the deeper ache in her heart...

That would *never, ever* heal.

From between the slats in the window blind, Jane watched the sedan back out of the driveway and accelerate down the street. Mom and Dad were off to a fundraiser for the Linden Falls Police Foundation, and they'd taken the patrol car. Normally, Jane wouldn't have paid attention to the vehicle they drove but, as she watched the taillights round the corner and disappear from sight, the loss threatened to overwhelm her.

Her guitar was in the back of that car. Last night, Jane had watched Dad toss it inside like it was nothing more than a rag doll. She'd heard the thunk of the case as it bounced on the leather seat and slammed into the opposite door. Felt the thrum of the strings vibrate across the instrument. A jangling, dissonant E minor chord. She'd never know if the force had damaged the body, cracked the neck. Either way, that guitar was lost for good.

Jane pushed away from the window, and the motion sent a shooting pain from her collarbone to her sternum. Fleetingly, she wondered if one of her ribs was cracked. In the mirror over the dresser, Jane caught a glimpse of her reflection. A reddish contusion marked her cheekbone near her left eye where blood had pooled under her skin. The image was sadly familiar and foreign at the same time. Years of experience watching similar discoloration form on Mom's face told Jane that, by tomorrow, the bruise would be an ugly tie-dyed design of dark purples. But Jane had never seen those marks on her own face before.

And I will never see them again.

Her body vibrating to its own off-key melody, Jane turned away from the mirror and raced out into the hallway as quickly as her unsteady legs would allow. She yanked open the closet door and reached for Dad's old camping backpack, ducking to avoid the swinging nylon straps as she slid it off the upper shelf. He was going to be mad when he went to pack for his next fishing trip and found it missing.

Jane hesitated. She'd be long gone by then, but Dad would take out his anger on Mom. He'd do that anyway when he found *Jane* missing, though, and there was nothing she could do to stop it. Jane had never been able to protect Diane McCaffrey from her police-chief husband.

All she could do now was protect herself.

And Nik.

With that thought, Jane's body went limp, and she sagged against the wall, dropping the backpack to her side. "Nik," she whispered. Could she really leave him behind after everything that had happened between them? All their plans, all the promises they'd made.

All the love they'd shared.

Jane took a shaky breath, closing her eyes and allowing herself one last memory of his hand sliding under her dress, hot against her thigh. His lips pressed to her neck. The absolute rightness of being in his arms.

But if I stay, it will destroy us both.

The thought sliced through her like the splinters from the stair railing had cut into her skin the night before. Jane's eyes flew open.

Dad hated the police foundation fundraisers. He would put in an appearance and make the rounds, joking with the donors and complimenting their wives like he was the good guy everyone believed him to be. But as soon as Dad could get away, he would head home to where Jane and Mom knew the truth about what kind of guy he was. Jane calculated she had two hours, maybe three.

Clutching the strap of the backpack, she dragged it into her room and tossed it on the bed. She had no idea what to pack. No idea where she was going except that it was somewhere far away from here. Somewhere they'd never think to look for her.

Jane threw in jeans, T-shirts, underwear. She was probably going to need to find a job, so she stuffed in a couple of dresses, a pair of black trousers, and a white blouse. And then she gazed around the room. The bulletin board above the desk was a tribute to a life that was already long gone. Dances and band concerts and smiling selfies with Hannah, Ali, and Nik.

Her college acceptance letter from Cornell.

Some other student would be taking her spot. Dad had already withdrawn Jane's enrollment that morning. He'd spoken to the woman at the registrar's office in that same tone he used to charm the donors at the police foundation fundraiser. Kindly, like he had his daughter's best interest at heart. The registrar woman couldn't see his vicious grin through the phone, but Jane saw it. He'd made her sit on his recliner in the living room and watch him make that call.

Jane set her phone on the desk and then scrawled a quick message on the flowered notepad next to it. *I'm leaving. Don't bother looking for me.* Hopefully, they wouldn't see it until morning. She was eighteen, and legally allowed to move out if she wanted. But this way Mom would know she hadn't been kidnapped or something. And maybe they truly wouldn't come looking for her.

Jane lifted the backpack and settled it as gingerly as possible on her back. And then she limped down the stairs, keeping her eyes on the wall in front of her so she wouldn't have to think about what those steps had looked like when they'd come hurtling toward her face.

She exited through the kitchen, out the back door. It would be a short walk through the woods to Route 8, the winding two-lane highway that would take her to the bus station in West-brook. From there, Jane could go anywhere.

Anywhere but here.

ONE

PRESENT DAY

The first thing Jane noticed as she steered her sedan off the highway onto the winding country road leading to her hometown was the crows. A massive flock of crows flitting through the ominous gray sky like flecks of pepper spilled across the kitchen floor. A shiver slipped up her spine as that image called to mind another one—over a decade old now but still fresh—the fear in Mom's eyes as she rushed to get the broom and hide the broken salt and pepper shakers in the garbage before Dad got home.

You never knew. Dad might have laughed affectionately and made a joke about Mom's clumsiness. Or he might've—

Jane shook her head, focusing on the double yellow line bisecting the road in front of her. The only thing predictable about men like Dad was that you could never really predict anything. There might be long stretches where everything seemed like it was going to be okay. So, you'd get comfortable, let your guard down for just a moment, and start to believe that they really intended to change.

And that's when they would hurt you the most.

Jane peered into the growing darkness down the road

ahead. Nobody would be bracing themselves for Dad's reactions ever again. It was the only way she'd been able to come home, back to the blustery Western New York town where she'd spent her childhood. Back to these old stone farmhouses, the skeleton trees stripped bare of their leaves by the lake wind, and those crows.

If Jane were the superstitious sort, she'd think those crows were an omen, but what she had no idea. Hannah would know. Hannah, who used to flip to the last page of the local newspaper every day at the school lunch table and read their horoscopes aloud over their trays of cafeteria pizza. Hannah would've spotted those crows and grabbed Jane's arm in excitement.

Jane, do you know what this means? Crows are a symbol of good fortune. This is a very auspicious sign.

But Jane hadn't talked to Hannah since the day she'd taken off, down this same country road over a decade ago, on her way out of town. She hadn't talked to any of her old friends—Hannah, Ali... Nik—and the chances of that changing on this trip were non-existent. No, Jane would be here just long enough to figure out what to do next. There was nothing *auspicious* about it.

Jane glanced in the rearview mirror to check on her sleeping daughter in the back seat. This trip had been hard on Scarlett. In a lot of ways, Scarlett had been forced to grow up faster than other kids her age. She'd understood why they had to go. But still, she was only nine. Packing up everything that was important to her—and leaving some things behind so it wasn't obvious they weren't coming back—would be terrifying for any kid.

Jane had been there once.

She slowed the car as she approached the same old sign that had welcomed people to Linden Falls for her entire life. It looked a little worse for wear—the blue faded to more of a dull gray now—but then again, maybe it had always looked like that.

Everything lacked a certain luster compared to the artificial gleam of Los Angeles.

Jane's car coasted down Spring Street past the Grassroots Café, the coffee shop where she used to play her guitar and sing in the Saturday open mic nights. A sign in the window told her that Pete, the café's owner, still hosted those music showcases, but Jane looked away before she could see the name of whichever musician would be featured. She didn't want to know if she knew them, didn't want to know who'd replaced her.

Next up on Spring Street was the library, where Jane had spent more hours of her life than she could count. It was the sort of place you could hide out without anyone knowing that's what you were doing. Dad had certainly never set foot in there. He'd tossed an occasional police thriller into his bag for fishing trips, but books hadn't really held his interest.

Jane kept driving, her gaze slowly oscillating from the store fronts on one side of the street to the other. Except for the displays in the windows and a new sign on the dry cleaners, Jane could have been looking at the town on the day she left a decade ago. Another contrast to LA, where the restaurants and shops came and went so quickly nobody ever got too attached. Nobody got attached to much of anything in LA.

When the town's municipal building came into view, decked out with a two-story Christmas tree, twinkling lights, and a life-sized nativity scene, the realization sank like a stone in Jane's gut.

Christmas is in a few days.

How could she have forgotten? *I might be the worst mother in the entire world.* Glancing into the back seat again, Jane's gaze traced her daughter's face, from her long eyelashes fanned out against her flushed cheeks to the well-loved stuffed elephant tucked under her chin. When Scarlett was asleep like this, she still reminded Jane of a tiny baby passed out on her chest, little mouth working on an invisible bottle in her dreams.

Jane wished she could go back to those days, when everything still felt full of possibility and hope. The days when she'd still believed Matteo would be a good partner and father. Before she knew who he really was. Or at least when she'd still been able to convince herself otherwise.

Scarlett hadn't reminded her about the upcoming holiday. She'd never really believed in Santa—Matteo had disabused her of that notion when she was practically a toddler. And back in LA, the holidays were usually more stressful than festive. The club where he worked was busy, crowded, and Matteo had to juggle all the regular patrons plus private parties. It left him tired, cranky, and—when he got home after a long day—ready to pick a fight.

Jane eased the steering wheel to the right and pulled up next to the curb in front of Ford's Hardware and General Store. Scarlett didn't even stir when Jane engaged the parking brake and turned off the engine. Jane considered waking her daughter, but then she wouldn't be able to buy her a present in secret. So instead, she climbed from the vehicle, careful to close the door gently. Then she circled the car, checking the locks. It was silly, Linden Falls was the safest place on Earth, and she'd managed to get a spot right in front. The car would be visible through the wide window the entire time.

Still, Jane hesitated on the sidewalk. She'd been hoping to avoid downtown Linden Falls entirely, to head straight for Mom's house and hide out until she could make a more permanent plan for her and Scarlett. Past experience had taught her that it would be nearly impossible to move through this town without running into someone she knew. But her desire to give Scarlett some semblance of a normal Christmas outweighed her fear of being spotted by an old acquaintance. Besides, it had been a decade. Maybe nobody would remember her.

Jane took a deep breath before pushing the door open. She was greeted by the cheerful jingle of the bells attached to the handle and the smell of cut wood, paint, and a mix of holiday spice. A quick glance at the cash register had her shoulders relaxing. It looked like a high school kid was working today, and he wouldn't have been more than five or six when she'd left town. Maybe she'd get out of here unnoticed after all.

Jane's gaze skated past the pile of snow shovels, an aisle full of kitchen gadgets, and a display advertising jars of local honey. It was a mystery how this place hadn't been run out of business by the Walmart out on Route 8.

Jane made her way down an aisle displaying holiday candles in scents like *Sugar Cookie* and *Pine Bough*, and then up another lined with an assortment of toys. Her eyes were immediately drawn to an enormous box with a blond character standing in front of a Victorian house in various shades of pink. A Lego set of the Barbie Dream House. Jane ran a hand along the edge of the box. Scarlett would *love* this. But then Jane looked at the price and audibly gasped. *A hundred and twenty-four dollars?*

She backed away slowly. A hundred and twenty-four dollars was a huge chunk of the meager savings she had in her purse. The money she'd managed to wheedle from Matteo and squirrel away for this trip. *All the money I have in the world.* Exhaling a shaky breath, Jane turned to the other side of the aisle. Who wanted a gaudy cotton-candy house with a skinny blond doll anyway? She grabbed a sketchpad and a pack of colorful pens. Total: $26 plus tax. Still a significant amount of money, but it was Christmas, and Scarlett deserved it.

Jane spun on her heel to find the wrapping paper aisle, and in front of her stood a sixty-something woman wearing an unironic holiday sweater and a disapproving expression on her face. Edna Swanson, the receptionist at the police station where Dad had been chief for over two decades. She'd put on a few pounds and her hair was grayer than the last time Jane had seen her, but Jane would recognize that scowl anywhere.

Mrs. Swanson looked her up and down. "Jane McCaffrey. What a surprise to see you here."

"Oh, hi, Mrs. Swanson. It's—uh." Jane shifted the gifts in her arms. "It's good to see you." She forced a smile to cover up the lie.

"I suppose you're here to see your mother."

"Yeah. Just for—probably for a week or so."

Mrs. Swanson's lips twisted with displeasure. "We were surprised that we didn't see you this fall for the funeral. But your mother said you were busy with work."

She did? Jane wondered what other stories her mother had been telling about her for the past ten years. Anything so people wouldn't learn the real reason the great Chief McCaffrey's daughter had taken off without a word.

Mrs. Swanson shook her head. "It was very hard on your mother, you know. Such a tragedy." She pressed a hand to her heart, face crumpling. "Your father in the prime of his life."

Jane stood back while the older woman dabbed at her eyes, knowing that anything she said would only prolong this.

Finally, Mrs. Swanson's face folded back into a scowl. "Your poor mother couldn't eat or sleep for weeks. She's lucky she had the town to rally around her since her own daughter was too busy."

Jane's chest began to burn. *Oh, yeah?* Where had the town been all those years when Mom had shown up with another cast on her arm or bandage on her hand? Were they rallying around her when their eyes darted over Mom's shoulder to avoid looking at the bruises on her face? How many ladders did they really believe Mom had fallen from?

But before Jane could let her anger spill out, a tall, dark-haired man carrying a shopping basket turned the corner at the end of the aisle and began making his way toward them. Jane moved to the side to make room, but before he could pass, Mrs.

Swanson beamed and fluttered her eyelashes. "Hello, Nikolas. It's lovely to see you."

Jane barely heard what the man said in return because she was busy stumbling sideways into the Barbie Dream House.

Did she say Nikolas?

Her gaze whipped in the direction of the man, and she had to tilt her head back to see his face. The last time she'd laid eyes on Nik, he'd been a skinny teenager with messy hair, glasses slightly askew, and a pair of headphones permanently stuck to his ears with the tinny sound of Radiohead playing through the speakers. He couldn't have been more than a few inches taller than her own five-foot six frame, and he'd practically lived in a worn flannel button-up.

This Nikolas was well over six feet tall with dark hair carefully styled back off his bronze forehead and a close-cropped beard on his handsome jaw. Under his Patagonia puffer jacket, Jane could make out broad shoulders and a pair of light blue scrubs. This guy looked like he'd fit right in on the set of any network hospital drama.

This couldn't be the same Nik, could it?

But then his dark eyes met hers and, for a moment, Jane wondered if she were back on the Southern California fault line because the earth shifted beneath her feet. There was no mistaking those eyes.

Jane knew the moment he recognized her because his head jerked back as if she'd slapped him. Keeping his eyes on her face, he slowly lowered his shopping basket to the floor. "Mrs. Swanson, can I carry your packages to the register for you?" he asked the older woman.

"Aren't you sweet? Here you go, young man." Mrs. Swanson handed over her wrapping paper and hand cream, shuffling down the aisle.

Nik adjusted the packages in his arms, all the while keeping his gaze glued to Jane's. Her heart pitched and she struggled to breathe air into her lungs. Finally, he turned and followed Mrs. Swanson.

As soon as Nik rounded the corner, Jane took off in the opposite direction. Of all people, Nik was the last person she'd expected to see. She never would have stopped at this store if she'd had even an inkling that he'd be here. She never would have stopped in this *town*. They'd always talked about getting out of here for good, but his scrubs and local hospital ID badge implied he was on his way home from work, not just here for a weekend to visit his mom.

How did Nik end up living in Linden Falls, a good Samaritan carrying old ladies' packages and working at the local hospital, while Jane was that selfish McCaffrey girl who'd abandoned her family and didn't even bother to come home for her own father's funeral?

Jane did her best to shrug off that thought. It was infinitely better if she let them all believe that. And best if she and Scarlett hid out at Mom's for the next few days and then got the hell out of town for another decade. Or forever.

But if Nik came looking for her, it was going to be a lot harder to pull that off.

She'd have to run past the register to leave out the front door, so instead, she made her way to the far side of the store, ducking into the feminine hygiene aisle. Through a space between shelves, she spotted her car parked by the sidewalk, the top of Scarlett's sleeping head pressed against the window. Could Jane duck out the back door and run around the building? Or was it better to wait it out here and not risk running into Nik again out on the sidewalk?

As she debated her options, a blur of dark hair and blue jacket flashed at the end of the aisle. Refusing to look up, she picked up a box of tampons and examined it closely. Maybe he'd keep walking. What man would stop to talk to a woman in the tampon aisle?

But then: "Jane."

She picked up another box and kept reading. *Organic cotton—interesting.*

"*Jane.*" Now he towered over her, less than an arm's length away. "Can we talk for a minute?"

His voice vibrated through her, as familiar as her own. She'd been hearing that voice in her dreams for a decade.

Releasing a shaky breath, she slowly lowered the box and looked up. "Oh. Hey." She forced a lightness into her tone, like they were nothing but two high school acquaintances home for the holidays. Like she wasn't crumpling the box in her hands to keep them from shaking.

Nik shifted his weight. "What are you doing here?"

Jane blinked. "Uh—" She curved her mouth into a rueful smile as she waved the tampon box at him. "You know. Just some shopping."

He didn't even glance at the box, his dark eyes stayed laser-focused on her. "What are you doing *in town*?"

"Oh. Right." Jane tossed the tampon box back on the shelf. "I—uh." She probably should have thought up a good story in advance in case anyone asked. But she'd been in survival mode since they'd left LA, and she hadn't been able to think further ahead than the next truck stop. "I—just came home to help my mom with some of my dad's stuff," she improvised. "The will and death certificates. Sorting the mess in the basement. All that stuff."

If Nik still lived here, he'd have heard about Dad's passing. Chief McCaffrey's death had made the front page of the local newspaper, and so had the funeral. Jane had googled it just to be sure he was really gone.

Nik's brown eyes softened. "I'm sorry about your dad."

Jane looked away. "Yeah, well, that makes one of us."

"Jane, listen—"

She cut him off. "It was nice seeing you." Her attention

snagged on the ID tag with his photo hanging around his neck. *Linden Falls Hospital, Nikolas Andino, MD.* So, he *did* live here in town. Jane wasn't sure what to think about that. She'd always imagined him somewhere new. Not spending his days in all the places they used to spend their days together. "*Doctor Andino,*" she couldn't help but add.

Nik glanced down at his ID tag, and then back to her face. His gaze roamed over her, and then he flinched. The next thing Jane knew, he was reaching out, sliding his palm under her chin, taking it in his hand. She sucked in a breath at the heat of his touch. How was it possible he left her feeling so shaken, all these years later? Why wasn't she stepping back, away from him? Instead, she found herself leaning in. Nik angled her face so he could get a better look at her left side, and then Jane remembered.

The cut under her eye, and the purple bruise radiating from it.

"Are you okay?" Nik's thumb stroked her cheek. "That's a pretty nasty bruise." His voice was so caring, his touch so gentle, and inexplicably, she was tempted to open her mouth and spill her secrets.

What is the matter with me?

She jerked away, pressing a palm to her cheek. "Oh... this is nothing," she said, forcing her voice to sound casual. "We have this—cabinet that hangs at a weird angle and I'm always running into it." It was the same story she gave the trucker in Kansas, and the waitress in Indianapolis.

But Nik tilted his head and stared for a beat too long. Could he see right through her? He'd always been able to before. She held her breath. Finally, he nodded slowly, face skeptical, but at least he didn't ask any more questions.

Jane exhaled.

"I'd heard a rumor you live somewhere out in California," Nik said, stuffing his hands into his pockets.

"Yeah. Um. Los Angeles." Though Jane had cut ties with everyone in Linden Falls, she'd kept in touch with Mom. They talked a few times a year, usually when Dad was on one of his fishing trips and there was no danger of him walking in and finding Mom FaceTiming with Scarlett. But this town was full of gossips, and there had to be speculation about Chief McCaffrey's only daughter, and why she never came home. What had Mom told them? What had Nik heard about her?

The silence stretched between them, unbearable and awkward. There was so much unsaid but, somehow, they had nothing to say. They used to talk endlessly all afternoon and then go home and text each other all evening.

"Well... I should be going." Jane took a couple of steps backward down the aisle. "Tell your mom I said hi."

"Sure." Nik nodded, and if he was sorry to see her leave, he hid it well. She had no right for that to bother her. "You too."

With that, Jane turned and fled.

She'd made it to the end of the aisle when Nik called out to her. "Jane, wait."

Jane pretended she didn't hear him, hurrying to the register to drop some cash on the counter for Scarlett's gifts and run for the door. She needed to get as far away from Nik as possible.

Because she might have been away for a decade, but all it took was five minutes in his presence and a gentle hand on her cheek for him to burrow through her defenses. If she kept this up, it would only be a matter of time before he figured out why she'd really left this town.

And why she could never stop running.

TWO

Jane McCaffrey was back.

Nik stared at Jane's retreating form as she hurried down the aisle, around the shelving unit, and back out of his life. For a moment, he was tempted to follow her. To grab her arm, whirl her around, and demand to know where the hell she'd been for the last decade. But that would require touching her again, and just that brief brush of his hand on her cheek a moment ago had sent him far more off-balance than he wanted to think about.

He almost hadn't believed it when he'd turned the corner and seen her standing there like a beautiful ghost. Talking to Mrs. Swanson like she hadn't disappeared into thin air with no explanation. On first glance, Jane hadn't changed at all. She still had the same long, wavy blond hair that tempted him to tangle his hands in it, the same arch in her eyebrow, the same ability to make him feel like someone had reached into his chest and yanked out his heart.

And she still had that same guarded look in her eyes. The difference was that he used to be someone she trusted. The last time he'd laid eyes on her—a decade ago—he'd never felt closer to another person in his life. It hadn't only been physical, though there was that, too. Hands and mouths colliding, clothes peeling off sweat-soaked bodies, heavy sighs mingling in the back seat of that old sedan. But it had been so much more than that. It had been souls converging.

Nik raked a hand through his hair and slumped back against the shelf of tampons. *What the hell?* "Souls Converging" sounded like the title to one of the dozens of three-chord emo songs he'd listened to the summer she took off, holed up in his childhood bedroom feeling like he might die without her. It was *not* the sentiment of a successful twenty-eight-year-old man who'd moved on with his life.

Which he was. And he had.

At least, he had before she'd walked back into this damn town.

"Can you believe it?" hissed a voice from the end of the aisle.

Nik pushed himself to a standing position and turned in the direction of the person hurrying toward him. Mrs. Swanson again. Damn it, he was not in the mood for the local gossip. But he reminded himself that he wasn't a sullen teenager anymore—he was a respected member of this community, and being rude probably wouldn't go over well if it got back to his supervisor at the hospital.

"Can you believe that girl has the nerve to stroll back into Linden Falls like she hasn't been gone a decade?"

Nik's breath hitched. No. No, he couldn't. But he wasn't about to get into it with Mrs. Swanson. "Well, her mother still lives here. So, I guess she has just as much right to be here as anyone."

"Well, if you ask me, she lost that right when she abandoned her mother. And her poor father, too. That man was never the same after she left. I'm sure that's why his heart finally gave out."

As an ER doctor, Nik knew Chief McCaffrey's heart attack

had nothing to do with Jane taking off, and likely everything to do with the fact that he'd smoked two packs a day and had a diet straight out of a college tailgate party.

The man might have been the head of the police department, but he'd left the heavy lifting to his deputies. Chief McCaffrey had liked to drive around in his fancy department-issued SUV casting threatening glances at teenagers, giving approving nods to the law-abiding citizens whose taxes paid his salary, and silently letting it be known he'd had his eye on everyone and everything. The older residents of the town had loved him, and even Nik had to admit that there hadn't been so much as a vandalized car or break-in at a shop on Spring Street while Chief McCaffrey was in charge.

But while the town saw a protective cop keeping them safe, Nik's friendship with Jane had given him a peek into the other side of Chief McCaffrey. The side that had caused Jane's shoulders to hunch to her ears when he walked in a room.

And in the past ten years, nothing about Chief McCaffrey had shown him to be heartbroken over the loss of his daughter. If anything, the man had only gotten meaner.

It had been an ordinary Tuesday in the Linden Falls ER when Diane McCaffrey had come in, and he was treated to a front-row seat of exactly what mean really looked like. It was obvious that her broken bones and split lip had nothing to do with a slip and fall down the porch steps, especially when Nik took in how her voice shook and her eyes darted over his shoulder. But Mrs. McCaffrey had begged him not to intervene. And then Chief McCaffrey had died of a heart attack on a fishing trip before Nik could do anything at all.

For a moment, when he'd been patching up Mrs. McCaffrey's cuts and setting her broken wrist, it had occurred to Nik that maybe this was the reason Jane had fled Linden Falls a decade before. Except she would have told him. Aside from the steamy night in the back of his car, and the... *souls converging,*

Jane had been his best friend for his entire life. They'd shared everything. If she'd taken off because of her father, Jane would have told Nik, and he would have gone with her, no question.

If there was one thing she must have known, it was that.

So, the only explanation that made any sense to him after years of searching was that none of it—that night, their friendship—had meant to her what it had meant to him.

She'd always said she'd get out of this place, and she'd made good on that promise. And if she'd set fire to the other part of her promise... the part that included *him*... well, that was her choice to make.

Mrs. Swanson's voice dragged him back to the general store aisle. "I hope that selfish McCaffrey girl isn't planning to prance back in here so she can grab a piece of Chief Swanson's hard-earned pension." She sniffed. "Her mother is going to need every penny now that she's on her own."

"I'm sure she's not here for the pension," Nik said, an edge creeping into his voice. Jesus. How long would it take Mrs. Swanson to spread that little tidbit around?

But—

Why *was* Jane back in town all of a sudden? His thoughts flitted to that gash on her cheek, the bruise under her eye. She'd said she'd accidentally bumped the corner of a cabinet. Nik didn't believe it for a second. For one thing, it was the exact same excuse her mother had given him that day in the ER —at least until he'd pressed further and she'd admitted Chief McCaffrey had knocked her into a doorframe. And for another, that haunted look in Jane's eyes told an entirely different story.

Who had knocked Jane into a doorframe? The thought of that gash bisecting her perfect cheekbone, of somebody violently putting his hands on her, had Nik's own hands shaking with rage. He shoved them in his pockets, or Mrs. Swanson would soon be telling the entire town that Nik

Andino had lost his shit over Jane McCaffrey right there in the middle of Ford's General Store.

"You two used to date, didn't you?" The older woman eyed Nik with interest, the pension forgotten. Looking for a bigger scoop, maybe.

"We were friends," Nik managed to reply, his voice curt.

"My memory is that you were more than friends. Always hanging out together, day in and day out."

"That's right," Nik answered slowly, like he was talking to a toddler. "That's what friends do."

"Hmm. Well, I heard she did a real number on you when she left. And I wouldn't get too attached to her now that she's back. She won't be sticking around. Selfish girls like that only look out for themselves. She'll be off again as soon as she gets whatever it is she came here to get." Mrs. Swanson shook her head, muttering something that sounded like, "...*stayed away for an entire decade*" but Nik didn't care enough to try to decipher it.

"Have a good holiday, Mrs. Swanson. I've got to get to my shift at the hospital." Nik turned on his heel and headed for the door before he said something he'd regret. He couldn't stand there and listen to this for another second. Especially because while Mrs. Swanson might be an insufferable gossip, there was one thing she was right about. Jane wouldn't be sticking around. He knew it the minute his eyes met hers. She already had one foot out the door.

THREE

We'll go inside as soon as this song is over.

That was what Jane had been telling herself for the past fifteen minutes. Instead, she sat in the driveway of her parents' white Victorian-era farmhouse—well, it's *Mom's* house now— while Scarlett napped in the back seat.

If Mom had noticed them pull up, she hadn't come to the door. Blue light flickered from the front window into the growing darkness of the yard. The local news was probably on, and then *Jeopardy* after that. Dad used to watch it with a beer after work, and old habits probably died hard.

Jane took in her childhood home. That old crabapple tree that Mom and Dad had planted their first spring in the house had finally succumbed to some sort of disease, and all that was left was the trunk and a few drooping branches. The paint was peeling off a patch of wooden siding on the house, and the downspout had detached from the gutter over the porch. Back when Jane lived here, Dad would have spent a fall weekend cutting down that tree, scraping the peeling paint, and fixing the gutter before the first snow of the year. But Dad hadn't been here this fall to do any of those things, and the maintenance on that big house had to be too much for Mom to handle.

For a moment guilt stabbed her, but Jane shook it off. This wasn't a house where happiness echoed in the halls, and she didn't know what Mom was still doing here now that Dad was gone.

The only memory that didn't leave Jane flinching had played out right here in this driveway. She closed her eyes. It had been a sedan just like this old Toyota, except, back then, Nik had been driving. He'd leaned across the center console to kiss her goodbye. It was a chaste kiss. Innocent. Sweet. And then his tongue had brushed her lip, dipped into her mouth for just a second, a brief reminder of the passion they'd shared just an hour earlier. Jane had reluctantly moved away from Nik, back to her side of the car. She hadn't wanted Dad to peek out the window and catch them making out.

If only I'd known.

With that, Jane's mind inevitably shifted to Nik and the heat radiating from his tall frame as he moved closer to her in the store aisle. The warmth on her skin that had nothing to do with his hand resting there. And, just like that, it had all come rushing back like no time had passed.

Maybe she should have anticipated seeing him back here in Linden Falls. It was the holidays after all, and people came back for the holidays, didn't they? But Jane had put Nik out of her mind a decade ago and had doggedly beat back any thoughts of him that had tried to creep in. It was the only way she was able to keep moving forward.

Jane paused to send Matteo a text, letting him know they'd arrived safely. To her relief, he replied with nothing more than a thumbs up emoji. Hopefully, he'd be so busy with holiday parties at the club that he wouldn't want to talk much this week. She was probably just being paranoid, but ever since he'd agreed to let her and Scarlett take this trip, she'd lived in fear that an expression on her face or the waver in her voice might give her away.

Sighing, Jane hauled herself out of the car, slung her backpack on her shoulders, and then pulled a sleepy Scarlett from the back seat. Jane's knees creaked under her daughter's weight, leaving her feeling ages past her twenty-eight years. These opportunities for Scarlett to still be her little girl were few and far between. In another year, her daughter would be too big to carry at all.

At the front door, Jane hesitated with her hand outstretched. This place hadn't been her home in a decade. Was she supposed to knock? Before Jane could make up her mind, the door swung open.

"Mom." Jane stared at the figure in the doorway, heart pounding. Her first urge was to stumble across the threshold and throw herself into her mother's arms. *Mommy*, she wanted to say, burying her face in Mom's neck and inhaling her familiar scent. She wanted Mom to rub her back, just like she used to do, and make all the nightmares go away.

Even after everything she'd been through, everything she'd navigated on her own, she still wanted the comfort of her mother.

But instead of giving in to her longing, Jane took a step back, steeling her heart. This woman wasn't the same person who used to care for her when she was young, who Jane thought would care for her forever. That woman didn't exist, and this woman was a stranger. She'd proven that when Jane had needed her most, and Mom had abandoned her.

When Mom had chosen Dad instead of her own daughter.

"Please..." Mom stepped back and waved stiffly into the house. "Come in."

Jane eased past the older woman into the entryway. She even *looked* like a stranger. Mom was only forty-eight, but the exhaustion on her face had aged her at least a decade more.

Deep lines crisscrossed her forehead and extended from the dark circles under her eyes. One of Dad's old sweatshirts swallowed up her thin frame, and she wore a brace on her left wrist.

Since Jane had been gone, they'd only FaceTimed a few times a year, and usually Jane handed the phone to Scarlett. When had Mom gotten so old? Did she look this tired the last time they'd talked a couple of weeks ago? Jane had still been processing Dad's death and wanted to tell Mom her plan to leave LA before Matteo got home. Maybe Jane had been too distracted to notice.

Mom closed the front door. It stuck a little and she had to give it an extra shove with her shoulder before she clicked the lock shut, wincing at the effort.

Another unwanted stab of emotion pierced Jane's heart. "How are you?" she asked, trying to keep her voice from shaking. "You're not sick, are you?"

"No, I'm fine. Just a little tired. It's been a long couple of months... since your father..." Mom pressed a hand to her abdomen as if it physically pained her to think about it.

Jane tried not to resent the grief on Mom's face. The woman had lost her husband of three decades to a heart attack, of course she felt some sort of sorrow over his death. But Mom didn't *miss him*, did she? Over Mom's shoulder, Dad's smelly, beat-up recliner was still taking up space in front of the living room window, the coaster where he used to set his beer on the table beside it. His boots were still lined up on the floor mat in the hall. It had been months since his death. Why hadn't Mom gotten rid of those reminders of him?

She couldn't possibly long for the days of flinching when the front door opened in the evening, of tiptoeing around, wondering what Dad's mood would be like, of living life as the punching bag for a relentless bully. And Jane would have never in a million years come home if Dad were still around. Never in a billion years would she have brought Scarlett. Did Mom feel any sort of gratitude that she was finally able to meet her only grandchild in person? Her gaze slid to Mom's arm. The brace she wore there was just as familiar as this old house. But shouldn't Mom's injuries be in the past now?

"What happened to your wrist?"

Mom adjusted the Velcro on the brace. "This is just an old injury. It acts up sometimes, especially in the cold weather."

So, it wasn't just Dad's emotional scars that would linger forever. Jane shuddered at the memory of Mom holding her broken wrist with the opposite hand. *I slipped on the rug, that's all.* Her voice had cracked, belying her claim that it didn't hurt that much. It flooded back to Jane as if the incident had happened a few months ago instead of decades, along with that same tightening in her chest.

And along with a similar ache in her own wrist that acted up when the temperature dropped.

Jane never thought it would happen to her, never thought she'd end up like her mother. But here she was. This was why she had to run. Because if she didn't, it would only be a matter of time before Scarlett ended up like both of them.

Jane's arms were starting to shake under Scarlett's weight, so she gently eased her to her feet. Scarlett stirred, rubbing her eyes with a palm, still clutching her elephant in the other hand.

"Oh." Mom froze, staring at Scarlett as her eyes filled with tears. "Oh, Scarlett. It's wonderful to see you in person." Her gaze flew to Jane's, roaming over her face. "It's wonderful to see you both. I'm so glad you could come." She reached out a palm to touch Jane's cheek, but something hard must have flashed across Jane's face because Mom dropped her hand at the last second.

Jane wasn't here for hugs and tearful reconciliations. She was here to protect her daughter, something her mother hadn't done for her. Jane bent her head, focusing on helping Scarlett out of her coat to hide the moisture welling in her eyes.

"She's—she's so *big*." Mom stood back, gaping at Scarlett.

Jane nodded. "She's nine."

"I know... I just... I guess I was still imagining that little baby in the photo. And then on FaceTime, it's hard to see how tall she's gotten."

Jane had mailed a single picture right after Scarlett was born, but Mom had asked her not to send any more. She was afraid Dad might find them and know they'd been in contact. Eventually, Jane and Mom had settled into their routine where Mom would call every six months or so, but only when Dad was away on his fishing trips. Jane only answered when Matteo was at work. So maybe she and Mom weren't so different after all.

"Scarlett, say hi to Grandma." She cleared her throat and did her best to sound upbeat for Scarlett's sake. "We'll be staying with her for a little bit."

"Hi," Scarlett said shyly, hiding her face part-way in Jane's jacket.

"You must be hungry," Mom said, awkwardly leaning down to Scarlett's level, standing back up, and then leaning down again as if she didn't quite know where to land. The effect made her look like a turkey crossing the road. "Would you like some soup?"

Scarlett shook her head.

"We stopped at McDonald's about an hour ago," Jane explained.

Mom pressed her lips together, most likely in disapproval. Jane did her best to shrug it off. Mom had given up her right to express her opinions on Jane's parenting choices long ago. "We're still on California time, and it's past bedtime. I think I'll take Scarlett upstairs to get settled."

"Oh." Mom looked from Scarlett back to Jane. "Okay. I made up the bed in the guest room for you two. It's a queen, so you'll both fit. I wasn't sure if you'd want to sleep in your old—"

"The guest room is fine." Jane took her daughter's hand. "Come on, honey."

Jane led Scarlett upstairs, where they stopped briefly in the bathroom and then headed into the guest room. Jane hesitated for just a second in front of her old bedroom. Was her guitar in there, the one Nik had given her for her fourteenth birthday? Or had Dad made good on his promise to burn it? With a shudder, Jane backed away from the door. She wasn't ready for that assault of old memories.

Scarlett climbed into the bed—it was far more comfortable than any of the cheap motel mattresses where they'd slept on their trip across the country—and immediately fell back asleep. Scarlett had grown up in an apartment over a nightclub, so she'd learned to sleep through anything. It was unlikely she'd wake up before morning, but Jane flipped on a nightlight just in case.

Jane found her mother in the kitchen, and she settled into a chair at the old oak table. Back in high school, this kitchen had looked typically middle-class—similar to all the other kitchens in these old houses—and she'd never paid much attention to it. But now with time and distance, it looked dated, too dark, with yellowing appliances that had seen better days, and a dripping faucet. More house repairs that Mom wasn't equipped to deal with.

Mom stirred something on the stove and then ladled the contents into a stoneware bowl. The faucet released its slow drip again, and it plopped into a mug in the sink. Mom sprinkled cheese on top of the soup. "So, how long are you staying?"

Jane hesitated. "Just a week or so."

Mom looked up from the bowl. "That's it? A week?" She frowned.

"Matteo was unhappy about us going at all," Jane said. "If it weren't for Dad's death, and the fact that he would have looked like a jerk if he'd said no, he would have put up more of a fight about us coming here." Matteo didn't care much about *being* a jerk. But he didn't want to look like one. "He thinks we'll be back in early January, by the time Scarlett's school break is over."

"And you won't be."

"No, we won't." Jane's chest squeezed. God, she hoped not. "I have about a week to figure out how to..." She trailed off.

How to disappear.

The unspoken word settled around them.

There would be no more phone calls, no checking in. These few days in Linden Falls would be the last time she'd ever see or talk to Mom again. Matteo's power over Jane couldn't be broken by mere miles between them. She and Scarlett had to truly *disappear*. It was the only way they'd finally be free. If there was any way for Matteo to find them... a postmarked letter, a traced phone call to Mom...

She didn't want to think about what he'd do.

Jane shook her head as if that would wipe those dark thoughts from her mind. *We're going to get away.* There was no other choice. "Anyway," she said, doing her best to keep the waver out of her voice. "While I'm here, I'll help you get things packed and organized. Get as much settled as possible before we go."

But that change of subject didn't offer any comfort. Jane dreaded sorting through the fragments of her life, dreaded what she'd find—*or wouldn't find*—in those piles of memories in the basement.

Especially one memory in particular.

She wasn't sure what would be worse: To dig up that old guitar that Nik had scoured pawn shops to find and then present to her on her fourteenth birthday. Or to finally accept that it was lost to her forever.

Just like Nik was lost to her forever.

She had a flash of him from earlier today. Those dark eyes searching hers, the lock of deep brown hair falling across his forehead, the heat building as he closed the space between them. She'd worked so hard to stave off memories of Nik, and all it took was ten minutes in this town and one look in those eyes to bring them all rushing back.

"Well." Mom cut into her thoughts. "I'm not sure there's much to do. The lawyer is helping with the estate paperwork. He says everything automatically goes to me, so it's not very complicated. And your father's old tools and things are fine where they are in the basement for now. I can invite that high school boy from down the street to come and take what he wants in the summer."

Jane's head jerked up. "Summer? I thought we talked about you selling this place this spring? Getting an apartment in town. What about that retirement building with the pool and exercise classes?"

"I'm not sure I'd fit in at a fancy high-rise like that." Mom placed a mat in front of Jane and set the bowl of soup on top, even though Jane had told her she'd already eaten.

"High-rise? Mom, it's five stories."

"Still, I'm comfortable where I am." She followed the bowl with a napkin and a spoon right in the middle.

Steam rose from the bowl. It smelled delicious, but Jane didn't think she could choke down a bite. Knowing Mom would be out of this old house and safely settled in a retirement community in town had helped Jane to come to terms with her own plans to move on. "You can't take care of this place all by yourself. I counted about eight different things that need repair just from the front door to here."

"Well, there's that high school boy. I can ask him to help out. He'll be happy to make some extra money." Mom picked up a pot and began scrubbing it in the sink.

Once again, Jane was struck by the lines on Mom's face. The circles under her eyes that looked darker under the overhead light. "What's really going on here? Why are you so determined to stay in this house?"

"Despite what you think, there were a lot of good times here." Mom's gaze skated around the kitchen. "Birthdays... holidays."

"What, like the Christmas Dad kicked the tree over because he thought you spent too much money on presents? Or the day he threw my birthday cake in your face because you left the oven on?" Jane shook her head. Sure, there were plenty of holidays and birthdays that weren't blighted by Dad's anger, but the possibility had always hung over this house like the smoke from Dad's cigarettes. *What would be the next thing that would set Dad off? What would have him kicking in the drywall or backhanding Mom across the kitchen?*

Mom swiped at the pot with a dish towel. "That birthday—I should have remembered to turn the oven off—"

"Just stop it!" Jane slapped her hands on the table, and Mom flinched. *Old habits again.* "Do you really not see who he was?"

Mom stared down at her hands. "He was your father."

They were the same words Mom had used to justify his behavior a decade ago.

He's your father.

Didn't she see that made it *worse?*

"How can you *still* be defending him?" Jane shoved the bowl of soup away, and a few drops splashed on the placemat. She immediately grabbed the napkin to clean it up. Even now, even knowing he was gone, that old anxiety and fear had seeped back in the moment she'd set foot in this house. Her eyes darted to the doorway, waiting for him to come charging in, angry at the mess she'd made.

Jane crumpled the napkin, leaving the spilled soup on the mat. And then she stood up and marched out of the kitchen. Had she really believed she could come back to this house without talking to Mom about the day she'd left? They always managed to avoid that subject on their phone calls, focusing on Scarlett, and Jane had told herself she was over it.

Clearly, she wasn't over it. She hadn't even made it an hour in Mom's presence, and the pain of betrayal was as sharp as ever.

In the hallway, Jane grabbed her jacket and yanked it on.

"Where are you going?" Mom called from the kitchen doorway.

"For a walk," Jane muttered, hopping on one foot as she pulled on a shoe.

"It's dark out."

"I don't think anyone would have the nerve to mess with the daughter of the late Chief McCaffrey, hero of Linden Falls, do you?"

"What about Scarlett?"

"Scarlett will sleep until morning. I won't be long." Without waiting for an answer, Jane swung the door open and headed out onto the porch, pulling the door shut behind her.

FOUR

TEN YEARS AGO

Jane slowly limped down Route 8, her heavy backpack cutting into her shoulders, ribs aching with the effort she needed to expend to stay upright. An occasional car sped past, the whoosh of the engine startling her as the tires kicked dirt and gravel in her direction. But so far, she hadn't recognized any of the vehicles, and nobody pulled over to ask what the teenage daughter of the police chief was doing out here alone.

That was a miracle in a small town like Linden Falls. Jane knew the risks of walking the main road leading out of town. Anyone could come by and recognize her, but she didn't have any other choice. If she wanted to get to Westbrook in time to catch an overnight bus, the two-lane highway heading out of town was the fastest route. And walking was the only way she could think to get there. Linden Falls didn't have a taxi service, and Jane certainly couldn't ask any of her friends to drive her. Not in her condition, which no amount of make-up could hide, and not if she hoped to make it without her parents or Nik finding out.

Thankfully, the dusk was doing a pretty good job of

concealing her, and so was the small hill she'd slid down into the ditch by the side of the road.

Jane squinted in the dim light at the road sign ahead. One mile to go. Every part of her body protested, begging her to lie down in the weeds and rest. But if she did that, Jane was pretty sure she'd never get up again. So, she put one shaky leg in front of the other, and she kept moving.

She'd made it another quarter mile when a car rounded the bend up ahead, its headlights shining in her eyes as it came closer. Jane held her breath, willing it to keep going like the others had, but instead of speeding past, the vehicle began to slow. Jane didn't recognize it—a huge black SUV with tinted windows—and her heart began to hammer as it pulled up beside her.

She'd spent so much of the walk worrying over people she knew coming along that it hadn't occurred to her to worry about someone she *didn't* know. A strange man might be very interested to find a teenage girl walking alone at night. And she was in no condition to run or fight back.

Jane gripped the straps of her backpack. Would the adrenaline come to her aid, even with her bruises and what she suspected was a cracked rib? She wasn't that far from town. Maybe there was a house over the hill where someone might hear her scream?

Jane stood frozen, debating what to do, when the car window began to slide down, and a deep, throaty female voice said, "Jane McCaffrey, is that you?" An overhead light switched on in the car.

Jane sagged with relief and slowly made her way up the embankment toward the driver's side window, where a woman with cropped strawberry-blond hair and piercing blue eyes peered out into the dusk. Kait Butler, the owner of the autobody shop in town. Jane didn't really know the older woman, but despite what Dad used to say, Jane was pretty sure Kait wasn't someone she had to fear would hurt her. Or rat her out.

Dad refused to service the family car or the police vehicles at Butler's Garage, even though it was right in town. Instead, he used a business over in Glendale for repairs. Dad made it known that he wasn't a fan of Kait Butler. He used to complain that she was running an illegal racket out of the back of her shop, selling stolen car parts. But despite his suspicions and investigations into the matter, he could never prove it.

When he'd complain about it over dinner, Jane secretly wondered if Dad hated Kait because she was breaking the law or if it was because she was a woman. According to Dad, women didn't belong fixing cars. *Or walking around looking like a man and doing God-knows-what with other women*, he'd grumble. *It's not natural.*

For her part, Jane had always secretly admired Kait.

Tall and lean, with her hair shaved on the sides and tattoos covering her from wrist to shoulder, Kait always struck Jane as someone who didn't give a shit what Dad—or anyone—thought of her. And she certainly didn't seem desperate for his business or concerned that she might get arrested. She moved around town with a confidence that Jane could only imagine, smirking at the haughty looks from judgmental people like Mrs. Swanson. But Kait had always been friendly to her and Nik, giving them a nod and a smile when they stopped in the minimart attached to the autobody shop to buy snacks and drinks.

Now as Jane approached the car, Kait gave her that same nod, though in place of the smile, her face was creased with concern. "What are you doing out here all alone at night?"

Jane stopped just outside the pool of light spilling from the car onto the roadside berm. Maybe the darkness would hide the worst of her bruises. Kait gave her a long stare, her mouth hardening. But to Jane's relief, she didn't comment.

Jane hesitated. The more she interacted with people from

town, the more likely it was that it would get back to Dad. But it was getting dark, her shoulders were killing her, and her ribs felt like they were rattling with every step she took. "I'm heading to Westbrook," she said, shifting the heavy bag on her back.

Kait nodded slowly. "Yeah? You want a ride?"

"That would be great. Thanks." As gingerly as she could, Jane shrugged off her backpack, and the weight of it nearly knocked her sideways. She was used to carrying her guitar in a backpack case to school, and over to the Grassroots Café for Saturday evening open mics. The bulk of Dad's old camping backpack felt completely wrong in comparison.

Jane ran her thumb over the calluses on her fingertips that had built up over years of playing the guitar. The loss of that instrument was so small after everything else that had happened. But somehow letting go of that gift made it all feel so final.

"Where can I drop you off?" Kait's voice cut into her thoughts.

Jane reached for the car door. *Home.* For a moment, she considered asking Kait to take her back to Linden Falls. Maybe, in a couple of days, Dad's anger would cool, and he would change his mind about college and the rest of it. Maybe if she apologized and behaved perfectly, she could smooth it all over.

But the thought of it made Jane's stomach churn. She'd been acting like the perfect daughter and smoothing things over for her entire life. She'd gotten good grades, sang in the church choir, and kept her room clean. Most importantly, she'd stayed out of the way. Jane knew other kids sometimes defied their parents, talking back or staying out past curfew. But not Jane. Never, ever Jane.

And still it hadn't kept Dad from pushing her down the stairs the moment she'd stepped out of line. If she went crawling back now, he'd only use it against her.

Jane had only been about nine at the time, but could still

remember the day Mom had asked Dad to let her take a trip to
Canada to visit her hometown outside of Ottawa. An old friend
was getting married and had invited Mom to be in the bridal
party. Mom's fatal mistake was revealing how badly she wanted
to go. Letting the longing flash across her face, the pleading
creep into her voice. Not only did Mom miss that wedding, she
never went back to Canada again. Dad derived a sick pleasure
from withholding the things Mom wanted most.

Jane had no doubt he'd do the same to her. He'd ruin her
life, and Nik's right along with it.

She yanked the car door open and set the backpack on the
backseat of the SUV. Then she slid in next to Kait. "The bus
station, please."

Kait flipped off the overhead light and shifted the car into
drive. "So, you're heading to New York City?"

Jane blinked. "Um." She hadn't gotten as far as to figure out
where she was going.

Kait gave Jane one more long look. "Only bus heading out
of town this time of night is going to New York."

It occurred to Jane that she shouldn't say any more. If Dad
came looking for her, the fewer people who knew anything, the
better. But maybe it was the darkness that enveloped her, or her
relief at not having to limp along at the side of the road, because
the next thing she knew, the words, "Yep. I'm going to New
York," popped out. *New York doesn't sound so bad.* She could
blend in in New York City. She could hide there. Maybe she
could even start a new life.

"You and your friends just graduated, right?" Kait tugged at
the steering wheel and pulled the car into a U-turn on the road,
accelerating in the direction Jane had been walking. "I saw the
signs all over town. *Congratulations, graduating class of Linden
Falls.* Are you headed to New York for college in the fall?"

Jane thought about that acceptance letter to Cornell that
had been hanging on her bulletin board since the day it arrived

in the mail this past February. It was supposed to be her ticket
out. *Their* ticket out. Nik had a matching one hanging in his
bedroom next to the letter about the full scholarship the Linden
Falls town committee had granted him thanks to his excellent
grades and community service.

His mom was a single mother who'd started working as a
house cleaner to stay afloat after his dad passed away years ago.
Nik would never have been able to afford to join Jane at Cornell
if Mrs. Andino had to pay for full tuition. When the news came
in about the scholarship, they almost couldn't believe how well
it had all worked out.

Until it hadn't.

"No. I decided college wasn't a good fit." Jane could barely
choke out the lie. Had her dream to study music really just
vanished into thin air?

Kait stopped her SUV at the red light on the edge of town
and gave Jane a sideways glance. "So, what's in New York?"

"Eight million people."

Kait nodded like she understood that and, briefly, Jane
wondered why the other woman had stuck around in Linden
Falls for all these years. Kait looked to be in her early thirties,
and she'd been running the autobody shop since Jane was a kid.
Why did she put up with people like judgy Mrs. Swanson and
Dad harassing her? Surely there was a more accepting place
than this.

Kait hit her turn signal, coasting off Route 8 and onto the
main road leading to Westbrook, a slightly larger town than
Linden Falls, but not by much. Maybe it had two stoplights
instead of one. And the bus station, of course.

"Thanks for going out of your way," Jane said.

Kait laughed. "Half a mile out of the way isn't going to make
much of a difference to me. I'm just grabbing some things from a
friend's house and then heading out to Los Angeles."

"Tonight?" Jane blinked and turned to look at Kait. Her

reddish hair glowed crimson in the traffic light. "You're driving all the way to California?"

"Well, I'm not going the whole way tonight. I'll probably make it about as far as Toledo, Ohio tonight, and then grab a motel room until morning."

"What's in Los Angeles?" It was none of her business, but an idea was slowly starting to form in Jane's head, and she couldn't help herself.

"A buyer for this car."

"All the way out in LA?"

"We find them cheap and fix them up. If someone in LA wants it, I'll deliver it for the right price," Kait said, with a smirk. "We're a full-service garage."

Jane wondered if she was sitting in one of those stolen cars Dad used to rant about. But what did Jane care? The car was on its way to LA, and it wasn't like Dad had a stellar track record of tracking down Kait's vehicles. Hopefully, he wouldn't be very good at tracking down missing people, either. "How will you get back here?"

"I've got a plane ticket for Tuesday."

The light turned green, and Kait accelerated through the intersection. They rode the next block in silence as Jane turned over this new information in her head. New York City was huge, but it was still only a couple of hours away from here, and even closer to Cornell. But Los Angeles... She could be truly anonymous in Los Angeles. She could start a brand-new life, away from Dad's control, and Mom's betrayal, and...

Her heart stuttered.

Away from memories of Nik.

Nobody would *ever* think to look for her in Los Angeles.

They coasted down another block, past a sign directing them to the bus station. Jane peeked through her lashes at Kait. She didn't know Kait at all, but she had a feeling she could trust her. By the long looks Kait had been casting her way, slowly lingering on her bruises, Jane had a feeling that Kait knew exactly what had happened—or close enough that she wouldn't rat her out to Dad. And she'd shown genuine concern when she'd picked Jane up on the side of the road.

Jane took a deep breath. "Can I come with you?"

Kait's eyebrows shot up. "You want to come to LA with me?"

"Yes."

"Why?"

Jane was eighteen. Technically, she could go anywhere she wanted. Do anything she wanted, and Dad would have no say about it. But it didn't mean he wouldn't try. "Because nobody would ever think to look for me there."

Kait parked the car in front of the bus station and turned in her seat to face Jane. "Are you in some kind of trouble?"

"No." Jane shook her head. "No. I just need to get out of this town. And away from..." She pressed a hand to her face, wincing as her fingers slid over the lump that had formed on her cheekbone.

Kait nodded. "Yeah. I get it." Her hands tightened on the steering wheel. "I've seen your mom around town with bruises that matched yours. Always wondered if I was the only one who suspected. I even approached her once when she came into the minimart, offered to help, but she told me to mind my own business." Her eyes darkened. "I guess he's been treating you the same."

"He didn't..." Jane said. "Not for a long time. And then—" She closed her eyes and saw the stairs coming fast, felt the splinters dig into her palm as she grasped at the railing to slow her fall, the pain in her shoulder as her weight propelled her forward anyway. "And then he did."

Kait cursed under her breath.

Jane sensed her opening. "So, can I come? Please? I can pay you gas money."

Kait waved her off. "Keep your money. You're going to need it in LA. It's a hard city."

Los Angeles couldn't be that much harder than what Jane was leaving behind. At least in LA she'd be in charge of her life. She had a little over a thousand dollars zipped into her pocket, most of it graduation gifts or money she'd earned babysitting. She wasn't dumb enough to think it would get her very far. But she'd find a job. Maybe she'd even find a thrift store guitar and start playing gigs—*real* gigs—and not just the open mic at the Grassroots Café.

It wasn't what she'd planned for her life. But maybe this wasn't a disaster. Maybe it was actually an opportunity. Anything could happen in Los Angeles. Dreams could come true.

And with me out of the picture, Dad will leave Nik alone.

At the thought of putting three thousand miles between her and Nik, Jane's heart faltered. Maybe once he got out of Linden Falls, she could reach out to him, and Dad would never know. Maybe their love wasn't truly lost forever, just for a little while. She had to believe that this wouldn't be the end. But for now, Jane had to keep going, keep moving forward, just like the car Kait was steering back onto the highway.

FIVE

PRESENT DAY

Jane stomped down Mom's porch steps and took off down Lancaster Road without a destination in mind, needing to get out of there, to move after her long drive and... everything that had happened that evening.

It must have snowed recently because the drifts shoved up against the edge of the yards were still fluffy and white, not dingy with dirt and pollution from the road. The crunch of salt under her shoes was the only sound other than the occasional bark of a dog inside one of the houses. Those dogs probably weren't used to strangers walking on these roads, and she was a stranger in this town now.

Jane continued down the street, taking one turn and then another, more by muscle memory than conscious plan. At each corner, the neighborhood made a slow transformation. Large Victorians with sprawling yards became smaller cottages and then double wides parked on modest lots with varying levels of upkeep.

Soon, Jane found herself standing in front of a small bungalow set back off the road behind a sprawling maple tree. The house appeared to be in good repair, with freshly painted wooden siding and dormant flower beds that would be bursting with color in spring. A light glowed by the front door, reflecting off the snow and illuminating a porch swing that wobbled gently in the breeze.

How many hours had Jane spent on that swing with her shoulder bumping up against Nik's as they shared a set of earphones and a plate of Mrs. Andino's cookies? How many conversations had that old swing heard about their plans to break free of this town? How had it never once occurred to them that their futures would be anything other than intertwined?

Jane jumped at the whoosh of a car approaching and the glow of headlights cutting across the darkness. She shoved her hands into her pockets, put her head down, and kept walking, but the car slowed as it drew nearer. When it was right beside her, the window rolled down.

"Jane McCaffrey, is that you?"

Jane squinted into the darkness of the car at a woman with a wide smile and Nik's dark eyes. "Mrs. Andino?"

The woman shoved the car into park and flung the door open, and before Jane knew it, a wool coat scraped against her cheek and the smell of vanilla surrounded her as Mrs. Andino wrapped her in a hug. "I had no idea you were in town!" She stepped back, still clutching Jane's shoulders. "Look at you. You're gorgeous."

Despite herself, Jane smiled. "Look at *you*. You haven't aged one bit." It was the truth. Unlike Jane's mother, Mrs. Andino seemed frozen in time. Her long, black hair only held a touch of gray and her face was as unlined and youthful as the last time Jane had seen it. But more than that, Mrs. Andino's smile radiated the same warmth and welcome it always had, and Jane didn't deserve it. Her heart tilted as she swiped at her eyes, hoping the darkness would mask the tears there.

"How are you?" Jane asked in a wobbly voice.

"Busy with the holidays right around the corner. Everyone wants a clean house for their holiday parties. I'm only getting home now."

Jane was surprised that Mrs. Andino was working as late into the evenings as always. Her job was to clean the McMansions that developers had built on the old Baker farm out on Route 8. Part of Nik's motivation to become a doctor had been that his mother wouldn't have to scrub rich people's toilets anymore. Jane did some quick math in her head. He was probably a resident at the hospital now, which meant he was in training and wouldn't make a high salary for another couple of years.

"I imagine you're here to see your mother," Mrs. Andino asked. "She's had a hard time of it."

Jane nodded, waiting for the condolences about her father to follow, but Mrs. Andino remained silent. Had she known he wasn't the man everyone in this town built him up to be? It was a subject Jane had never broached with anyone. But Mrs. Andino was more observant than most.

The older woman rubbed her hands together. "What are you doing out here in the cold, and the dark, too?"

Jane shrugged and gave a vague wave of her hand. "Oh, just out for a walk. Enjoying the snow. We don't get much of that in California."

Mrs. Andino didn't look surprised by that statement. So, she'd heard the rumors that Jane was in California. Or Nik had told her.

"You didn't walk over here looking for Nik, did you?" Mrs. Andino asked. "He has his own little place out on Sand Hill Lane now."

Jane shook her head. "Oh—no. No, of course not. I—uh, I saw Nik earlier today."

Mrs. Andino clutched her hands to her chest. "Oh, I'm so glad to hear the two of you reconnected. Nik was absolutely devastated when you left. I tried to tell him that sometimes young people need to spread their wings, but there's no talking sense into a teenage boy in love." She shook her head with a laugh. "I'm happy to see you two moved past all that."

In love? Nik had been her best friend in the world. For one beautiful—*terrible*—night, he'd been so much more. But then Jane had left, and she and Nik had lost the chance at love. In the decade that followed, she'd shoved that night—and Nik— into a dark corner of her memory, just like everything else about her past. But being here in Linden Falls, with Nik's presence everywhere she turned... with the heat of his hand still lingering on her cheek... with words like *love* hanging in the frozen air...

How did he still have the power to affect her like this? To fill her with this old longing?

Jane straightened her shoulders and turned to Mrs. Andino. "I won't keep you standing here in the cold. But it's lovely to see you. Truly."

"Oh, you too, honey." Mrs. Andino wrapped her in one more hug and hopped back into her car. "Stop by before you head back to California if you get the chance."

Jane nodded, knowing she wouldn't. She couldn't afford to get mired in memories, in wishes, in words like *love*. Not after everything she'd done to get this far. And not when her survival —and her daughter's—was on the line.

SIX

TEN YEARS AGO

Kait hadn't been kidding when she'd warned Jane that Los Angeles was a hard city.

As Jane opened her motel room door and stepped into the dim hallway, she was immediately hit with a now-familiar cacophony of sounds: the cry of a baby down the hall, the raised voices of two people fighting, the electronic crashes of a video game, the low moans of the couple who always seemed to be having sex. Nobody in the building besides Jane seemed to mind that the walls of this rundown motel were paper-thin or that she was an unintentional observer of their constant chaos.

Jane coughed as pot smoke wafted out from under the video-gamer's door and quickly hurried along so it wouldn't seep into her department-store blouse and trousers.

When she had wandered in looking for a cheap place to stay, the woman at the front desk had offered her a long-term lease. "Twenty percent off," she'd offered. But Jane had opted for day-to-day. She didn't have the money to pay upfront, and she'd hoped to be able to move somewhere nicer once she found a job. But now Jane wasn't sure if that was going to happen. Los Angeles was so much more expensive than she'd imagined, and she'd never had to think about things like rent or the cost of food before.

Two weeks had already gone by since Jane arrived in Kait's SUV, and the only work she'd managed to find was a job standing on the edge of a strip mall holding up a sign advertising a car wash to people driving past on the main road. Mostly, it seemed like her role was to stand on the corner and put up with the constant catcalls from people zooming by. Nobody seemed interested in the car wash, a fact that increasingly angered the car wash owner when each day passed without any new customers.

Jane's hands shook each evening as he handed over the paltry roll of bills he owed her for her work. The job paid cash under the table, and cash was something she desperately needed to pay for her never-silent motel room and the packets of ramen noodles from the minimart on her way home at night.

She'd gone on a handful of job interviews, mostly for entry-level office positions, but so far, nothing had panned out. There must have been hundreds of girls like her in LA, maybe even thousands. Girls who'd moved out to California in search of a better life and who were looking for something to pay the bills in the meantime. Jane had encountered them in insurance office elevators and law firm waiting rooms. Many of them had been cobbling jobs together for years, and most had far more impressive resumes than she did.

As Jane made her way down the motel hallway, past the room with the fighting couple and wailing baby, she winced as the voice of a man behind the door grew louder, more aggressive. The woman was crying along with the baby now. A tiny part of her considered calling 911, but Jane knew it would likely only make things worse, so she put her head down and kept moving.

Outside the motel, the clamor of her neighbors was replaced by the chaos of the busy four-lane road that cut through the center of the neighborhood. When Jane had imagined Los Angeles as a kid, she'd pictured palm trees and Malibu beaches and the Hollywood sign. She hadn't been prepared for freeways and strip malls, gas stations, and seedy nightclubs with bouncers posted outside, who glared at her as she hurried home from work in the evenings.

Jane passed one of those clubs now, marked by an imposing black door in an otherwise nondescript warehouse building. At 9:15 a.m. there were no bouncers outside, and the neon sign with the name of the club had been switched off.

For the first time, however, Jane noticed a hand-written sign taped to the door.

Help Wanted: Server.

Jane paused on the sidewalk and eyed the sign. She'd never worked as a server in her life, and it seemed like a steep learning curve. To be honest, she'd never really had any kind of job in high school other than volunteering at the library and hosting the open mics at the Grassroots Café, because Dad had never allowed it. But it seemed easier to fake experience filing paperwork and answering a telephone than it did balancing cocktails on a tray and weaving through a crowd of drunk people.

Jane headed down the sidewalk, picking up her pace so she wouldn't be late for her interview—a law firm this time. She found the building—a storefront in the far end of a strip mall situated between a dry cleaner and a Nepalese restaurant. Her stomach growled as the spicy scent wafted down the sidewalk, and Jane squeezed her eyes shut. *Please God, let this job work out.* She didn't know how much longer she could live on microwave noodles. The waistband of her dress pants was already fitting looser than the last time she'd worn them to church in Linden Falls just a few weeks ago.

Jane paused in front of a sign in the storefront window that matched the one she'd seen on the bus stop a few blocks back. It depicted two middle-aged white men in suits helping a third, older and infirm white man limp toward a hospital bed. The tagline across the top read, *Injured? We've got your back.* And across the bottom, *Morgan and Morgan, Attorneys at Law. Free consultations.*

Jane pulled on the glass door, and it opened with a jingle. She stepped into a waiting area where a bored-looking receptionist barely glanced at her before she went back to typing.

Jane stepped up to the desk. "Hi, I'm Jane McCaffrey. I'm here for my nine-thirty interview for the administrative assistant position."

The receptionist's fingers continued to tap across the keys. "Have a seat."

Jane sank down in one of the worn upholstered chairs lined up in front of the window and checked the clock on the opposite wall. 9:20. The receptionist kept typing. Jane took in the cheap office furniture, stained carpeting, and slight buzz of the fluorescent lights overhead. This was not one of those high-powered law firms where she'd interviewed earlier that week. But it was a job, and maybe here the competition wouldn't be as stiff. She sat back to wait.

The clock slowly ticked. Jane shifted in her seat, looking from the receptionist to the closed door behind her, and then back to the clock.

Her interview was scheduled for 9:30. Jane had been hoping that if she showed up early, they might have the interview over in time for her to get to the car wash for her scheduled 10 a.m. start, or maybe only a few minutes late. Or even better, maybe they'd offer her the job, and she wouldn't have to worry about the car wash anymore.

The clock ticked again.

At 9:50, she was beginning to sweat. Finally, the door behind the receptionist opened and a man stepped out. Jane recognized him as one of the Mr. Morgans on the storefront and bus stops. Today, he wore a polyester polo shirt and a pair of wrinkled khakis. He looked younger in his photo standing next to the other Mr. Morgan. In person, his hair was thinning and his blond comb-over had streaks of gray.

The receptionist looked up. "Interview for you. Jane McCaffrey."

Mr. Morgan blinked at her for a second and then hitched his chin for her to come into the office. Jane said a silent prayer and headed across the reception area. Once they were inside, Mr. Morgan slid behind his desk. Jane perched on a chair across from him.

Mr. Morgan looked at his computer monitor, clicked around a few times, and then he said, "Sorry, we filled that position."

"You—" *No.* She needed this job. At least, she needed *a chance.* "But I have an interview scheduled."

"My partner liked the woman who interviewed at 9 a.m. better."

"But he hasn't even met me yet."

Mr. Morgan glanced up at Jane then, his gaze slowly drifting from her face down to her white rayon blouse and back up. Then he turned and picked up a small pile of papers next to his keyboard. After a moment of sorting, he pulled Jane's resume from the middle of the stack. "You're Jane McCaffrey?"

"Yes."

Mr. Morgan peered at the paper in his hand. "And your experience is working in the Linden Falls public library?"

Jane nodded. She'd considered fabricating an entirely new resume, but what if they asked her for references? So, instead, she'd stretched the truth as much as possible. Technically, she'd only been a volunteer at the library. But Mrs. Lui had always liked her, and Jane hoped that if the law firm wanted to check up on her, she could ask the librarian for this little favor. It was risky, but she didn't have much of a choice.

"Yes, I did all sorts of administrative work while I was there. Answering the phone, filing paperwork. I can use Excel and..."

She trailed off when Mr. Morgan gave her a bored, "Uh huh."

Jane pulled her shoulders back. *She needed this job.* "Look, I promise I'm a hard worker. If you'll just give me a chance..."

Mr. Morgan pulled the top paper off the stack. "Jessica Bartlesman has five years of experience working in law firms." He picked up the next one. "Alice Silver has worked reception at a doctor's office for almost a decade." He tapped a finger on the stack of papers. "Do you want me to go on?"

Jane's heart began to pound. Her job at the car wash had started at 10 a.m. She'd taken a risk with this interview. "Please," she whispered. "I know my experience doesn't seem like much, but if you just give me a chance to tell you what I'm capable of and meet with your partner..."

Mr. Morgan sighed. "Listen, Jane. Do you want my advice?"

"Yes. Please." Jane nodded eagerly. She'd take any help she could get.

He swiveled in his chair and slowly dropped Jane's resume into the trash can by the desk. "My advice is to go back to Linden Falls."

Jane jumped to her feet and backed away slowly, her eyes filling with tears. "I can't. I can't *ever* go back there."

He just shrugged.

Before she burst into tears right there in the office, Jane turned and ran out the door, past the receptionist, and then, giving the glass doors a shove, stumbling out into the parking lot. She dug her prepaid cell phone from her bag and checked the time. It was ten fifteen. She was late for work, and now she needed that car wash job more than ever. Jane took off down the sidewalk, her purse thumping at her hip with each step, one hand clutching the waistband of her pants in case this was the moment they decided to slide down her legs.

Jane sprinted the five blocks to the car wash, her heels

bruising on the hard pavement in her flimsy flats. The door to the office was on the side of the building so, to save time, Jane headed directly through the car wash garage, hugging the wall to avoid puddles.

"I'm here," Jane heaved, once she was inside the office, bending over to catch her breath. "I'm sorry I'm late."

"You're not late," the car wash owner, a middle-aged white man named Duane, said mildly.

Jane stood, still breathing hard. "I'm not?" The bottoms of her feet were really starting to burn now, not to mention her aching ribs from her injuries back in Linden Falls. She didn't know how she was going to stand out there on the street corner all day. But like everything else in her life, she didn't have much choice. "Oh." Maybe she'd gotten the time wrong?

Duane crossed his arms over his barrel chest. "You're not late because you don't work here anymore. You're fired."

"What? No. I can't be fired. I'm only—" She fumbled in her bag for her phone. *Twenty-five minutes late.*

"You're fired because you're terrible at your job."

Jane felt a flare of anger. The last place wouldn't even give her an interview because she didn't have the experience, and now this guy was telling her she wasn't good enough to stand there grinning stupidly and holding a cardboard sign? "How can I be terrible at it? How would someone be more skilled?"

Duane hitched his chin at the empty garage. "Where are the cars? Where are the customers? This is the slowest week I've had all year."

"But—" Jane could not lose this job. She had exactly enough money to pay for one more night in the motel and one more pack of ramen noodles. After that, she'd be—

Over Duane's shoulder, out the window, a homeless man wrapped in a grimy gray blanket slept on a bench next to a bus stop sign. His meager belongings were tucked into a blue plastic bag under his head like a pillow.

"You're a distraction," Duane muttered. "Too pretty. People look at you instead of the sign."

Jane held back an incredulous laugh. She'd never been less attractive in her life. Thanks to the constant noise in the motel, she hadn't slept in days, and permanent dark circles hung beneath her eyes. She was sunburned from standing on the corner in the hot sun all day, and though she'd managed to cover the bruises on her face with thick make-up, her left cheek was still a little swollen, giving her face a lopsided look.

"I can wear a hat. And sunglasses. And a heavy sweatshirt." She'd roast out there in the California sun, but at least she wouldn't get sunburned. "People won't even be able to see what I look like."

Duane stroked his goatee, considering her proposal.

"Please?"

"Well. I would take you up on that. But there's the matter that you were late." He smirked. "So. Sorry. No go."

"Sir, please—" Jane could hear the desperation in her voice.

Duane hitched his chin toward the car wash garage. "Door's that way."

Jane limped slowly back to the motel, her body growing heavier with each step. How was she so naive to think that she could do this on her own? That her money would last more than two weeks in a city like LA? That she would be able to find a job without any experience?

And what was she going to do now?

Every part of her longed to call Mom and ask for plane fare home. But would Dad let Mom send it? Or would he refuse so he could punish her? And if he *did* let Jane come home, what would the punishment look like then? Her stomach lurched. Jane had defied Dad in every way possible. She'd taken away his control. And she had no doubt her disappearance had humiliated him in front of the entire town. He would never let her get away with it.

And even worse, what would he do to Nik?

If she went back to Linden Falls, Nik would throw his whole life away before he'd accept that Jane couldn't see him again. She couldn't do that to him, which meant she could never go back.

Jane was halfway down the block in front of her motel when she noticed a commotion in front of the building. Two police cars and an ambulance both blocked the entrance to the parking lot, their lights flashing.

Jane picked up her pace, ducking between the cars to survey the scene. She spotted a toddler in the arms of a police officer, wailing at the top of his lungs and flailing to be put down. The police officer gripped the toddler tighter as he lunged sideways, straining toward the woman Jane assumed was his mother.

But the mother ignored the child, reaching for a second police officer instead. Blood poured off her cheek and dripped onto the tight white T-shirt that hugged her enormous breasts, but she didn't seem to notice. Tears followed the blood as she clutched the other officer's arm.

"Please," she pleaded. "Please let him go."

Are they going to take the toddler away from his mother? But no. Jane froze as she spotted the man in the back of the police car. With a sinking heart, she realized he was the same man she'd seen going in and out of the room down the hall, the one with the screaming and fighting.

The man glared at Jane through the police car window, and she took a startled step backward.

"Please." The woman shook the police officer's arm. He was tall, muscular, and probably had a hundred pounds on the woman, but in her desperation, she managed to nearly knock him sideways. "Please let him go. He didn't mean to do it. I'm fine. Really."

"Ma'am," the police officer said, finally managing to wrench his arm away, "you're fine this time. But what about next time? What about the baby?"

"The baby needs his daddy."

Jane's stomach curled and every part of her wanted to scream: *This is your chance. Don't choose him.*

But the woman kept ignoring her child to plead for her abuser's freedom.

Jane couldn't stand here and watch for another moment. But if she went back in that motel room, the chaos and noise might finally break her. Slowly, Jane turned and limped down the sidewalk with no real destination in mind. About a block away, she passed a terracotta-tiled building with a flashing red sign that said *Fernanda's Tacos.* There was only a man sitting at the tables out in front, probably because it wasn't quite eleven in the morning and the lunch rush wouldn't start for another hour. On a tray in front of him sat a burrito and a bag with grease stains that probably held tortilla chips.

Jane tried not to think about her empty stomach as she pulled a free neighborhood bulletin from the dispenser on the sidewalk and sat on a bench to flip to the *Help Wanted* ads. She knew most of the desirable jobs would be advertised on the internet, but apparently Jane wasn't qualified for the desirable jobs. She scanned a couple of administrative assistant positions at law firms that sounded similar to the one who'd just rejected her. She could swing by and drop off her resume, but at this point, she'd seen her competition, and she didn't hold out much hope.

Jane kept reading. It seemed that there were a lot of clubs looking for strippers. Duane's voice echoed in her head. "You're too pretty."

Jane's nausea had nothing to do with her empty stomach. Could she possibly do this? It would be better than ending up on the street. But she shook her head, crushing the corner of the newspaper in her fist. She didn't know the first thing about being a stripper, and she'd probably stand there shaking and die of embarrassment before she even got her shirt off.

So, she kept looking—a few fast-food jobs looked promising, but they were all the way across town, and the thought of navigating the complicated bus system to a far-away neighborhood was intimidating. And then her finger slid to the next listing. *Help Wanted. Server.*

The name of the club looked familiar. It was the place down the street—the one she'd passed on her way to her job interview. *Maybe it's a sign.* And while she'd never worked as a server, she'd eaten out at restaurants plenty of times. Could she fake it? Worst case, they'd figure it out in a few days and fire her, but that was a few days' worth of tips that would be in her pocket first. Her gaze lingered on those stripper ads. What did she have to lose?

Nearby, the man outside the Mexican restaurant crumpled up the empty foil that held his burrito. He stood, picking up his tray, and Jane's stomach growled again as she followed it with her eyes. The bag of chips looked untouched. *Is he just going to throw them away?* The man carried the tray to the garbage can and tipped it inside. Then he headed down the sidewalk.

Before Jane could talk herself out of it, she was on her feet, running toward the garbage can. Reaching inside, she felt for the crinkle of paper and the crunch of chips. Her hand closed around the bag, right on top, and she pulled it out with a cry of happiness. The waxy paper would have protected the chips from anything in the garbage, right?

At this point, she was too hungry to care. She yanked the bag open and plunged her hand inside, shoving two chips in her mouth at once, and then two more.

When her hunger had finally abated, she stared at the greasy bag, horror heating her body. She was supposed to be packing for college right now, hanging out with Nik and Ali and

Hannah. Instead, she was in a strange city, broke and alone, and she'd just eaten a stranger's food out of the garbage can.

Was this really her life now?

She crumpled the neighborhood bulletin in her hand and started down the sidewalk in the direction of the club. Halfway there, she stopped in front of a thrift store. If she didn't want to be treated like a girl from Linden Falls, she needed to stop acting like one.

Ten minutes later, Jane stepped out of the shop wearing a pair of sky-high heels, a short skirt, and a tight white tank top. She was going to land that server job if it killed her.

SEVEN

PRESENT DAY

The morning after Jane returned to Linden Falls, she opened her eyes and stared up at the unfamiliar light fixture hanging from the ceiling. It was a little dusty, a little dated—one more thing that would look glaringly out of place in LA. She supposed the light fixture wasn't completely unfamiliar—it had probably been hanging there when Jane had last been in this house—but that was a decade ago, and she didn't remember it. There were a lot of details of this house she'd forgotten.

And then there were some she never, ever would.

Jane rolled over to give her daughter a squeeze. All of that would be behind her soon. This house, the memories, and Los Angeles, too. Soon, she and Scarlett would start their new life, safely away from all of it. She had a week to put her plan into place.

When Jane reached for Scarlett on the other side of the bed, her hand fumbled in the rumpled sheets. She sat up abruptly. Scarlett was gone.

For a moment, panic seized her. What if Matteo had come in the night and—

Before she could get carried away with that train of thought,

Jane heard voices drift up from downstairs through the old heating vents: Mom's chuckle, followed by a giggle from Scarlett.

With a relieved sigh, Jane slumped back against the pillows. Matteo hadn't snuck in last night and kidnapped their daughter. Of course he hadn't. He'd even approved this trip—albeit grudgingly.

"You told me you don't get along with your parents," he'd said, when Jane had broached the subject. She'd waited until he was in a good mood, right after he'd come home from his weekly poker game. He'd won. If he hadn't, Jane would have given him a wide berth. "You haven't seen them in ten years. Why would you bother to go now?"

Because it's my only chance.

She'd told Matteo about Dad dying, that Mom needed help packing and moving into the retirement community in town. Matteo would check up on her—google Dad's obituary and make sure she wasn't lying or using it as an excuse to have an affair. Jane didn't even go out with friends, let alone another man. Still, he liked to throw around accusations that left her defending herself.

"My mom is old and frail," Jane had argued, knowing that Matteo would prefer that. Old and frail were no threats to him. "She doesn't have anyone else to help her move."

Matteo's mouth had twisted up on one side. He was thinking about it.

Jane's chest had filled with hope, but she'd done her best to smooth her face into a neutral expression. "We'll drive and stay in hotels. Scarlett will get to see a little bit of the country."

She'd held her breath then. Driving would buy her a couple of extra days if she needed them. She could tell him a fabricated story about a blown tire or dead battery and say they'd be a few days late coming back. He'd be angry about it, blame her poor driving or accuse her of leaving the headlights on all night. She'd pay for it later when they got home.

Except she'd never be going home again.

"Please, Matteo?" she'd whispered, and then flinched. *Never let him know how badly you want it.*

But Matteo had just smirked. He'd liked it when she begged, when he could exert even more power over her. Finally, he'd peeled off a wad of bills from his poker winnings and tossed it in her direction.

Jane had grabbed the cash and clutched it to her chest.

The minute he'd left the room, Jane had counted it. *Two thousand dollars. Oh, thank God.* If she and Scarlett stayed in the cheapest motels and brought their own food in a cooler, it was more than twice the amount of money they'd need to get to New York State.

Of course, Matteo had believed she'd use the other half to get back again. But with any luck, she and Scarlett would be long gone before he even knew to look for them.

With that thought, Jane climbed out of bed—and was hit with a wave of cold air coming from the direction of the drafty window with its peeling paint on the wood frame and latch that didn't close completely. It was ridiculous that Mom thought she could stay in this big, rambling, old house all alone. It was surprising that she'd *want* to. It wasn't just the upkeep. Didn't Mom want a new start, too?

Jane threw on a cardigan over her T-shirt and pajama pants and headed down the stairs that creaked with each step. At the bottom, she heard voices from down the hall punctuated by the occasional giggle.

Jane entered the kitchen to find Scarlett standing on a step stool in front of the stove. Mom leaned against the counter next to her, holding a bowl with one hand and the handle of a sizzling pan with the other. Scarlett reached into the bowl, scooped some batter with a measuring cup, and carefully drizzled it into the pan. She looked up when Jane stopped in the doorway. "Mommy! Look, I'm making pancakes!"

Jane forced a smile and nodded in acknowledgment. Part of her wanted to run over and snatch Scarlett's hand away from the hot pan before she burned herself. Scarlett had never learned to cook at home. It opened up too much possibility for chaos and mess. Matteo hated chaos and mess. But the pride on Jane's daughter's face stopped her. "I can't wait to try them. I bet they'll be delicious."

Mom reached an arm around Scarlett to give the pan a shake, a smile lighting up her face and smoothing out the hard lines around her mouth. For the first time since Jane arrived home, Mom looked her own age instead of decades older.

A long-buried memory flashed in Jane's head. Mom pulling a tray of cookies out of the oven, giving Jane that same easy grin. They'd dug in before the gooey discs had even cooled, melted chocolate smearing on their hands and mouths. Then they'd left the dirty bowl in the sink all afternoon while they spread a puzzle out on the coffee table, with no concern for whether they'd be in the way.

Jane had lived for those weekends when Dad took his fishing trips. When it had been just her and Mom at home, and nobody had to hold their breath or tiptoe around him. When Mom's smile had come readily, and her shoulders hadn't tightened in fear.

"Can't he move out?" she'd asked Mom on one of those magical weekends. "Can't he get one of those apartments in town and we can live here alone?"

Mom had sighed. "No. He doesn't want to move out."

"Well, then we can leave."

"It's not that easy."

Something about the sadness in Mom's eyes had told Jane to stop asking questions like that.

So, late at night, when she was supposed to be sleeping,

Jane used to imagine something happening to Dad—an accident on the boat, maybe. There'd be a solemn knock on the front door, and then Mom would swing it open, her face going pale. On the step would stand two officers from the police station, their eyes darting over Mom's shoulder when they broke the news that Dad would never be coming home.

It had been a shocking, terrible thing to wish for. What ten-year-old relishes the image of their father suffering such a terrible fate?

But then Dad would come home from his trip, and the cloud of fear would settle back over the house. It had become harder and harder for Jane to muster up much guilt over her secret fantasies for it to be just her and Mom, forever.

Jane watched Mom hand Scarlett a spatula and help her flip the pancakes. It looked like Jane had gotten her wish after all. Something had happened to Dad on one of those fishing trips. The police officers went looking for him when he didn't come home on Sunday night, like he usually did. They'd found him alone in the boat, the fishing rod and cooler of food Mom had packed on the seat next to him. The thermos of chili half-eaten. They suspected he'd died on Friday. A sudden heart attack.

The doctors had told Mom that even if Dad had been in town, just minutes from the hospital, they didn't know if they could have saved him. Smoking two packs a day for decades had taken a toll. He'd been on medication for his blood pressure and cholesterol for years. Dad's heart had just given out. They'd assured Mom that he hadn't suffered.

Jane had to admit she was a tiny bit sorry about that last part.

And now, Mom was finally free.

And Jane...

Somehow, she'd ended up living her own version of Mom's story. But soon, she'd be free, too.

"After breakfast, maybe Scarlett can open one of her presents. Santa came early!" Mom said in an upbeat tone, for Scarlett's benefit. And then, quieter, to Jane: "In case you won't be here for Christmas."

Jane felt a stab of guilt as Mom's smile faltered. But Mom knew that Jane was in Linden Falls just long enough to figure out how to leave. It had been the plan from the moment Mom had called to say that Dad had passed. Mom hadn't protected her when Dad was alive, but this temporary sanctuary would be her parting gift to Jane for the start of her new life.

Scarlett nodded eagerly, clapping her hands, and Jane gave her a sideways smile when Mom wasn't looking. A little thank you for playing along with the Santa story. That could be *their* parting gift to Mom: a handful of special moments with her only grandchild before she and Scarlett disappeared into thin air. It wouldn't make up for the decade Mom had missed. But it was something.

Jane peeked into the living room where Mom had set up a small, plastic, table-top Christmas tree decorated with lights and all the handmade elementary-school art class ornaments Jane had made throughout her childhood. Jane's gift to Scarlett —the sketch pad and pens—was tucked under the tree in its simple star wrapping paper. Next to it sat a much bigger box encased in sparkly silver paper tied with a giant red bow. Santa's gift, most likely.

They took their plates into the living room, something they never would have done if Dad were still here. Jane was grateful to focus on the gifts because she wasn't up for making chit-chat with Mom over the breakfast table. It wasn't like they could talk about life back in LA—she wouldn't be going back there and there was no use pretending—or Jane's plans for the future, since she didn't have any plans without a thousand holes. And Jane really didn't want that last fact to become glaringly obvious to Scarlett.

Up to this point, she'd been able to pass this trip off as an adventure, but Jane knew her daughter suspected more than she was letting on. For now, it was Christmas—an early one, anyway—and maybe, for once, Scarlett could just be a kid.

Scarlett looked genuinely happy about the sketch pad and pens, giving Jane a wide smile, and Jane's heart squeezed. She had so little idea of what would be next for them. But Jane vowed that by this time next year, they'd be settled, safe. Not just physically away from Los Angeles and all the trauma they'd endured, but finally on their way to healing and putting it behind them.

Mom placed her pancakes on the side table and bent over to pick up the large, wrapped box. She pressed a hand to her back as if the effort pained her, and Jane set aside her own plate and jumped up to help. "You have back pain, too?"

Mom shrugged. "I'm getting older."

"You're forty-eight."

"I pulled a muscle climbing out of the rowboat at the lake. The last time Dad wanted me to go with him. It acts up sometimes."

Jane huffed. Mom hated the lake. Hated boating and was afraid of the water. Dad usually let her stay home, said he couldn't relax with her shaking like a dying fish on the bench next to him. But every once in a while, he used to drag her along. Jane knew it was to prove to Mom that he was in charge. That he had the power to make her go. And maybe he liked watching her shake like a dying fish on the bench next to him.

Jane pressed a hand to her temples, surprised by how quickly the bitterness rose up in her, eclipsing any compassion she might have felt for Mom's pain. It was just more proof that Jane was doing the right thing, leaving Matteo like this, even if it felt daunting, and terrifying, and sometimes nearly impossible. She never wanted Scarlett to look back on her childhood the way that Jane did. To remember that her mother got in that boat, even though she couldn't swim, because Dad told her to.

She never wanted Scarlett to think that was what love looked like.

Jane had already given too many years of her life, too many years of her daughter's life, to a man just like her father. She set Mom's gift in front of Scarlett and watched her daughter's eyes light up. Maybe for today, they could just enjoy this. Pancakes and presents and Scarlett being a kid.

Scarlett tore off the shiny silver paper, revealing the gift beneath. The Barbie Dream House Lego set. "Oh, Grandma, I love it!" Scarlett clambered to her feet and threw herself in her grandmother's direction. "Thank you!"

"Careful, Grandma has a bad back," Jane called, but half-heartedly, because Mom's face was shining as brightly as Scarlett's as she wrapped her arms around the girl and pulled her in tightly.

"Can I put it together now, Mommy?" Scarlett asked, jumping up and down.

Jane nodded, but as Scarlett turned back to admire all the colorful photos on the side of the box, her heart twisted. They might not be able to take a Barbie Dream House with them when they left. It was too big, and it would draw too much attention. Jane didn't know yet if they'd have a car.

But she'd face that soon enough. For now, she'd let Scarlett enjoy the moment.

Scarlett tore into the box, and soon she was blissfully buried in a pile of tiny plastic blocks and miniature Barbie figurines. Jane was just finishing her pancakes when Mom reached under the tree and produced a small red envelope. Wordlessly, she passed it to Jane.

"Oh," Jane said, turning the folded paper over in her hands. She should have thought to pick up something for Mom when she'd stopped in Ford's last night. One of those pine-scented candles. Or a card, even.

Jane trembled at the memory of those brief moments in Ford's. She'd barely been able to remember her own name when Nik had walked in. And then he'd cornered her in the far aisle of the store, towering over her like a California redwood, all broad shoulders and long limbs. His hand sliding across her cheek had haunted her dreams last night. Jane couldn't remember the last time a man had touched her like that. With such gentleness and care.

The last time might have been the last time Nik had touched her.

Jane dragged herself back to Mom's living room. When she looked up, Mom was watching her, head cocked. "Are you okay?"

"I'm fine." Jane sat up straight. "I'm sorry, we left LA so quickly, and I didn't bring you anything..."

Mom waved it off. "You did. You brought—" Her attention shifted to Scarlett on the floor and her lips tugged into a wistful smile. "And you. You're the best gifts I could ask for."

Jane didn't answer, sliding a finger under the flap to open the envelope instead.

Inside was a basic Christmas card with a photo of Santa sitting next to a tree, the kind printed on slightly flimsy card paper that comes in a multi-pack. Mom used to buy piles of those cards to send to their neighbors and acquaintances in Linden Falls. She'd tuck a family photo inside with the date scrawled on the back. On the card, she'd print, *Love from Chief McCaffrey and family*. Jane and Mom didn't even get to have their full names in that card. It was all about Dad.

It was always all about Dad.

The inside of this card was blank, though, other than the printed *Merry Christmas* sentiment. But a slip of paper slid out and fell into her lap. Jane picked it up. A check with Jane's name printed on the top line. *Pay to the order of.* Then she focused on the amount.

Five thousand dollars.

Her gaze flew to Mom. "What?"

"For you. And Scarlett."

"I—" Jane opened her mouth to say she couldn't accept it. That she didn't need Mom's money. But the words would be a lie. She desperately needed every dollar that would help her escape Matteo. But— "I can't." Jane held the check in Mom's direction. "You'll need this to fix up this old house. If you decide to move—"

Mom folded her hands in her lap. "Your dad had a good pension and some retirement savings. I'll be fine."

Jane stared down at the check. Before she could answer, Mom continued. "You could use it to hire an attorney. Someone who specializes in cases like yours. They could help you to leave Matteo and take full legal custody of Scarlett."

Jane peeked at Scarlett who was engrossed in the Lego instructions and didn't seem to be paying any attention. "We shouldn't talk about this here," Jane murmured.

Mom stood and picked up her coffee mug. "Why don't we go and clean up the breakfast dishes?"

Check in hand, Jane followed her down the hall.

"You can't be serious about this," Jane said, when they were safely in the kitchen. She set the check on the counter. "Matteo would never let us go like that." Jane grabbed the pan off the stove and ran a sponge over it. "You of all people should know that."

In the sunlight streaming through the kitchen window, the lines around Mom's eyes looked deeper than they had last night. "Do you remember Martin Lefkowitz from high school? He just took over his father's family law practice, and he handles divorces and custody cases. He's handling Dad's paperwork, and everyone says he's really smart. He went to Harvard Law and then practiced in New York before he—"

Jane cut her off. "All the Harvard lawyers in the world aren't going to stop Matteo if he wants to come here and drag us back home again." She scrubbed harder at the pot. "He won't care that they practiced in New York."

"The police, then."

Jane's eyes widened. "The *police*?" She banged the pot onto the drying rack on the counter and grabbed a mixing bowl. "You really think the police are going to help me? The police in *this* town?" A wave of anger washed over her. "They can't get involved in a little domestic dispute, remember?"

Jane's body tensed at the decades-old memory. Dad in a rage about something. She couldn't even remember what it was now, but she knew it was something that wouldn't even register in a normal family. Dad's rages were always over some small infraction, that's what made them so dangerous. You'd never know if the wrong toothpaste or a pair of shoes in the hall would set him off. It was part of how he exerted his control. By leaving you constantly afraid.

Jane also couldn't remember why Mom had finally called 911 on that particular day. Had she feared for her life? Or was it that she'd finally had enough? But Jane's memory was clear on one point. In her hiding place under the porch, she'd watched Officer Wylie pull up in his patrol car and climb out slowly. Almost reluctantly. From inside the house, Jane could still hear Dad yelling. Mom crying.

Why aren't the police officer's lights flashing and his siren on?

Mom had run out onto the porch, her bare feet thumping on the wood slats above Jane's head. Jane had heard the tears in Mom voice, the desperation as she'd begged the police officer for help. "He did this to me," Mom had said.

Later, Jane would see the full extent of what Dad had done.

The bruises, the fractured wrist. But at that moment, Jane could imagine. She'd seen it before.

Officer Wylie had cleared his throat. "Uh, sir..." He'd trailed off then, one black sneaker kicking at a stone on the path leading up to the porch, not meeting Dad's eyes.

Dad had descended the steps. Put a fatherly arm around the young officer, and calmly explained that he and Mom had been having a little argument when she'd slipped on the bathroom rug. "There's no need for you to get involved in our silly domestic dispute."

A moment later, Officer Wylie had been back in the patrol car on his way down the street. It had always struck Jane that he drove faster on his way out than he had on the way in.

She would never, ever trust the police to help her.

"It would be different with you," Mom cut in. "You're Chief McCaffrey's daughter. If you tell them Matteo is threatening you, those officers will protect you."

Jane turned away to grab a dish towel and vigorously swipe it over the mixing bowl. "I'm Chief McCaffrey's daughter, who took off and *abandoned* him." Mrs. Swanson had made that clear last night in Ford's. "I think I'll take my chances with my plan." Even with all its flaws, it had to be better than going to the police.

Mom sank down on a stool across the counter and absently straightened the placemats piled there. "Jane," she whispered. Her hands were shaking. "I'm just saying that there are options. There are other ways to protect yourself and Scarlett. You don't have to run. You can stay here and give your daughter some stability. You can fight for the life you want."

Was this why Mom didn't want to move to that retirement home in town? Because she imagined that Jane and Scarlett would move into this old house? Jane's first instinct was to shudder at the thought and open her mouth to refuse. But as she gazed around the kitchen, something held her back.

Last night, in the dim light, the room had looked shabby, rundown, an aging monument to all her worst memories. But now with the sun shining in, Jane could see subtle changes. Mom had set flowers in a mason jar on the island and hung colorful curtains in the window. There were rainbow sprinkles in the spice rack and a set of pink butterfly cups in the china cabinet. Was all of this for Scarlett?

And for Jane, too?

It was only nine in the morning, and already this had been Scarlett's best day in years. Chocolate-chip pancakes and Barbie Legos spread across the living room floor. Earlier, Jane had heard her talking about building a snowman. Linden Falls had four seasons, good schools, and speed limits that people actually respected. In a house like this, Scarlett could have her own room where her friends could come over. A backyard where she could play with the local kids. A neighborhood she could roam without worrying about drug dealers or traffic.

This would be Scarlett's Dream House.

Jane's heart tugged with longing.

But she knew how the system worked. She'd talked to a lawyer once, just like Mom had suggested. *There are laws*, she'd thought. Mechanisms in place to help women.

A protection from abuse order.

A piece of paper signed by a judge. It told the abuser to stop the abuse, to stay away from the victim or face serious legal consequences. If the judge was involved, signing a paper, shouldn't the abuser *already* be facing serious legal consequences?

It doesn't work that way.

A protection from abuse order from a judge wasn't going to stop a man like Matteo. Jane knew he'd show up and promptly step right on it, grinding in his heel along the way. If Matteo was told to do something, he took it as an invitation to do the opposite. A PFA wasn't worth the paper it was written on.

Matteo would never let her go. Mom had to understand that better than anyone.

"At least meet with Martin," Mom urged. "See what kind of advice he gives you."

Jane shook her head. "I can't. It would never work." There was no sense in entertaining these wild ideas that she could ever come home, ever live a normal life, ever stop looking over her shoulder.

"Think of Scarlett—" Mom began, but Jane cut her off.

"Stop." Jane whirled on her. "Just stop." The last thing she needed was Scarlett overhearing them and getting her hopes up. In the midst of pancakes and Legos, she'd only have her heart broken. "Did *you* try to leave Dad? Did *you* fight for the life you wanted? No." Jane slapped the dish towel down on the counter. "At least I left. You stayed. You chose *him*."

When I desperately needed you to choose me.

At age eighteen, scared and alone, all she'd wanted was for her mother to protect her. To save her. *That's what mothers are for.* But Mom had said no.

"Everything I'm doing is for my daughter," Jane snapped. "Which is more than I can say for you."

And with that, Mom's shoulders hunched, her head hung, and her arms wrapped around her midsection as if that would protect her from Jane's words. It was as if she made herself smaller, maybe she'd become invisible.

Jane felt a shudder go through her. That posture was so familiar. She'd seen Mom shrink into herself just like that every time Dad had berated her for something. But this time it wasn't Dad's fault—it was Jane, and her self-righteous anger, who'd caused Mom to look like that. Anger that wasn't justified. Because what right did she have to blame Mom for staying when she'd waited a decade to leave Matteo? Waited for the right moment, for it to be easier.

Waited to stop being so afraid.

To have something to do with her hands, Jane yanked open a drawer to look for a dry dish towel but, finding silverware instead, she slammed it shut and pulled open the drawer next to it. Two cartons of cigarettes slid to the front. They were the kind Dad used to smoke. The tobacco scent drifted up, taking her back to her childhood.

Jane remembered the faded square on Dad's pants pocket, where those cigarettes had permanently lived. The way he'd slap them against his palm to pack the tobacco to one end. It used to make her jump, that sound.

"Why do you still have these?" She glanced up at Mom, who seemed to be turning an unnatural shade of red. "Don't tell me you can't even get rid of his cigarettes." Jane slammed the drawer. "He was an abusive asshole. And he's dead. How can you ask me to stay here when you can't even get rid of his old cigarettes? He's like a ghost, still lurking around here. You're even holding on to his old things. The recliner in the living room and now these…"

Jane turned to look out the window. It had snowed again last night, and the sidewalks were covered. She couldn't even flee like she had yesterday. But she couldn't stay here, mired in all the pain in this house's walls.

Jane pushed away from the counter. "I'm going to shovel the walk." One more task Mom would have to handle on her own once she and Scarlett took off. Because Jane sure as hell wasn't staying.

EIGHT

Nik didn't know what he was doing, driving down Lancaster Road at nine in the morning. It was completely out of the way of his route from the hospital to his house on Sand Hill Lane. But when he'd pulled out of the hospital parking lot after his overnight shift in the ER, his hand had wrenched the steering wheel to the left instead of right, almost like it had a mind of its own. And before he knew it, Nik was cruising toward the west end of town.

Before I knew it.

Please.

Nik knew exactly what he was doing. He was heading to the McCaffreys' street, and when he got to their house, he was probably going to slow the car and do a shady drive-by. Because that's what Jane had reduced him to all those years ago when she left with no warning. A creeper on her life. And not even a very good one, because he still didn't know shit about her.

How many times had he googled her, only to come up with nothing? How many times had he trailed her mom on the sidewalk or in the grocery store, hoping for the right moment to casually ask about Jane. Mrs. McCaffrey never had much to say.

"Jane is just fine." Nik didn't know if that's all she knew or if it was just all she'd been willing to share. One distracted day in the checkout line, when Mrs. McCaffrey couldn't get her credit card to work properly, she'd muttered something about Jane and California. That was it. *California.*

Adding the state to his Google searches hadn't helped.

Jane had disappeared.

Luckily, it had been a slow night in the ER because Nik hadn't been able to stop thinking about the fact that suddenly, unbelievably, Jane was only a couple of miles away. She owed him an explanation. He *deserved* an explanation. But what would be the point in pursuing this? Nothing she could say would ever be good enough.

So, when he'd finally handed his patient files over to his colleague on the day shift, Nik had gotten in his car, fully intending to go home and sleep. Fully intending to put her out of his mind for good.

Except now, here he was. Coasting down Jane's street, his foot gently tapping the brake.

Halfway down the block, he spotted a figure on the side-walk in front of the McCaffrey house, snow shovel in hand. Slowing the car even further, he squinted to get a better look. Her enormous maroon parka and plaid pajama pants practically swallowed her up, obscuring the curves he'd spotted beneath the leggings and cropped sweatshirt she'd been wearing last night. She'd shoved her feet into a pair of oversized boots that probably used to belong to her dad, and she wore a pair of thick gloves on her hands. He'd never seen a more ridiculous outfit in his life.

And still, he couldn't keep his eyes off her.

Jane shuffled forward awkwardly, likely from her choice of footwear, but also because it looked like she'd never held a snow shovel in her life. Which probably tracked if she'd spent her entire adult life in California.

Nik brought the car to a stop next to the curb, rolling down the window.

Jane looked up, surprise registering on her face as her eyes swept across him. "Nik," she finally said, a little breathlessly. "What are you doing here?"

"I was"—he gave a completely ambiguous wave that could have indicated any direction—"in the neighborhood."

"Oh." She reached up to tug her knit Buffalo Bills hat down on her forehead. The royal-blue band matched her eyes. Her cheeks and the tip of her nose were flushed pink from the cold, full lips parted slightly from exertion.

And, just like that, Nik was seventeen years old again, and the two of them were running across the baseball field behind the high school. It had started snowing that morning, falling steadily all day long until the grounds were transformed into a magical wonderland by the time their last class of the day had let out.

Or at least it had felt magical to Nik. Everything had been magical when Jane was around.

Jane's cheeks had glowed pink, eyes bright as she half laughed, half shrieked in mock fear, dodging the snowball Nik lobbed in her direction. She'd come to a stop and bent over, her blond hair falling around her face as she scooped up a handful of white powder and tossed it in his direction.

Snowflakes had drifted over him like frozen bits of confetti, landing in his hair, clinging to his eyelashes, and sliding down his neck. "Damn, that's cold!" Nik had pulled at the collar of his coat, trying to shake the snow loose while Jane cackled beside him. He'd spun slowly in her direction, one eyebrow raised, a half-smile tugging at his lips. "Is this funny to you?"

"No." Jane had stood up straight, attempting to smooth her features into a serious expression and failing miserably. She'd pressed a gloved hand to her mouth to hide the grin still lingering there. "Not at all."

He'd moved quickly, shifting his weight forward and wrapping his arms around her. Before Jane had been able to react, she'd tumbled backward into a thick snowbank. He'd landed part-way on top of her, their arms and legs entangled. A puff of white powder had settled around them, giving the world a misty quality. Or maybe that had been Jane again.

He'd leaned back to look her in the face. "How do you like the snow, now? A little cold?"

She'd shifted under him but hadn't moved away. "I'm not cold at all," she'd murmured. "You always keep me warm."

As their eyes had met, all humor gone now, something had stirred in his chest.

Nik had never been sure of the exact moment he'd fallen for her. Their mothers had enrolled them in the same preschool when they were three and, apparently, they'd been inseparable from the very first day. NikandJane. One word. He couldn't remember a moment from his childhood that Jane hadn't been right next to him. He'd always loved her, and that fact had been as much of a part of him as his dark hair and sense of humor and desire to be a doctor. It just existed.

But that day in the snow, with her blue eyes shining up at him with so much trust, that was the day it had occurred to him that maybe she could feel the same way. That was the day he'd decided he was going to tell her. Before they went away to Cornell together, he was going to take the leap and bare his soul and let her know that he wanted to start their new life together as so much more than friends. That he wanted to start their new life as... everything.

It had taken him a while to work up to it, but he'd finally told her on graduation night. And for one amazing moment, he'd believed they could have it all.

Right before she'd disappeared into thin air.

And now he was idling in his car in front of her house, still unable to quite convince himself she was real.

"Are you on your way home from work?" Jane asked, her voice wary, eyes darting to his and then away, like she wasn't quite sure where they should settle. A little part of him was glad that he'd left her feeling as off-balance as he'd been since the moment he'd spotted her in the aisle last night.

"Yeah, night shift." He put the car in park.

Jane turned away from him and focused her attention back to the sidewalk and the snow shovel she held awkwardly in her hands. Nik watched her scoop up a small, ineffective pile of white fluff and attempt to tip it onto the grass. Before she could make it there, the snow slid off the shovel and over her boots. She huffed and tried again, with the same result.

Nik climbed out of the car. "It looks like you could use a little help."

"I'm fine," Jane snapped. "I just—" She gave her shoulder a couple of shrugs, like she was trying to shake off the soreness.

He eyed the mark on her cheek where she said she'd run into a cabinet. It would have been quite a feat to injure her shoulder the same way. The rage from the night before ignited in his gut. *Had* someone hurt her?

"It was a long drive. Days in the car," she finally mumbled, defensively. "I'm just a little stiff."

Nik stepped closer, so near he could reach out and pull her against him. For a wild moment, he considered it. Last night, he'd barely brushed a hand against her cheek, and it was like someone had set his palm on fire. What would it feel like to have her back in his arms after all these years?

Jane's eyes widened, almost like she knew what he was thinking. But she didn't step away. Her tongue flicked out to nervously wet her bottom lip, and somewhere buried beneath the surface of her unease, he saw a flash of desire that mirrored his own.

What the hell am I thinking?

Before he could do something epically stupid, Nik grabbed the shovel from Jane's grasp and got to work on the snow drifts.

"I can do that," she called, but he was already halfway down the sidewalk, taking out his frustration on the piles of snow, filling the shovel and heaving the contents onto the lawn, giving a stubborn piece of ice a kick with his shoe. At the edge of the neighbor's yard, he finally stopped, breathing hard, sweat beading on his forehead and beneath his scrubs. Shifting the shovel to one hand, Nik yanked off his coat and gave a sigh of relief as the cold air seeped into the flushed skin of his bare arms and the V at the neckline of his scrub shirt.

He turned in Jane's direction. She stood at the edge of the driveway, clutching one hand with the other, her eyes roaming over his shoulders, his chest, and down to the stomach he kept flat with his daily runs up the mountain, where he'd bought a cabin last fall.

He'd give a year of his hospital salary to know what she was thinking.

"Thank you for shoveling," Jane finally murmured. "And for stopping by while you were in the neighborhood." Her lips curved upward with a smile that displayed absolutely no sentiment. "It was nice to see you." She said it with a note of finality, like they were acquaintances who'd bumped into each other on the sidewalk, and this conversation was over.

And suddenly, his anger was back.

He didn't want her thanks, didn't want her fake smiles and small talk. He wanted to know where *the hell* she'd been. And why she'd left. In ten seconds, he was in front of her again. Nik took a breath, the questions forming on his tongue, but before he could speak, Jane's gaze darted from his toward the house and then back.

"Jane..." Nik began, but her eyes shifted away again. It reminded him of when they were teenagers, and her dad was still around. Almost like Jane was afraid they'd get caught doing something that would get her in trouble. And then a slight movement from the house caught his attention. A curtain moving, a figure framed by the window. But it was only Mrs. McCaffrey. Nik gave the older woman a wave. She lifted a hand in return and then disappeared back in the house.

Why was Jane so nervous? Her dad was gone, and she was an adult who could talk to whoever she wanted. Unless...

That bruise on her cheek. The soreness in her shoulder.

Was there someone else in there? Someone who might object to seeing her talking to a guy out on the sidewalk? Nik's hands tightened on the shovel. If the person who'd hurt her was inside he'd...

He'd what?

Nik stopped, briefly closing his eyes.

Storm into the house? Beat this imaginary person with a shovel? He dropped the tool on the lawn. Seeing Jane again had thoroughly sent him off the deep end. And now he was inventing stories about her. For all he knew, she really *had* run into a cabinet. And if not... Well, she certainly hadn't asked him to swoop in. In fact, she hadn't asked him to come around at all.

Jane had returned to town after a decade and hadn't let a single person know she was coming. When she was done helping her mom sort through her dad's belongings, she'd head back to—wherever it was she lived. Her obligation would be over, and another decade would go by without a word or a trace of her.

Just yesterday, he'd told himself he wouldn't spend another minute on Jane McCaffrey.

But somehow, he couldn't let it go. She might be a stranger to him now, but she'd been more important to him than anyone... once. How could he turn and walk away without making sure that she was safe?

Jane glanced at the house again. "I really should be going."

"Jane," Nik said, shifting his body into her line of sight. "Can you meet me for coffee later today?"

In a matter of seconds, an entire encyclopedia of emotions crossed her face. A surprised blink, an uncertain bite of her lip, and that apprehension again. "I don't know..."

"Just to catch up," he cut in. "As old friends."

Her eyes darted over his shoulder to whatever was worrying her inside the house. "Sure. Okay. But I really need to go now." Before he could react, she was heading up the porch steps. "Thanks for shoveling."

"Grassroots Café at seven?" Nik called up to her.

She nodded and then slipped into the house.

Nik stood on the sidewalk, gaping at the McCaffreys' front door. If you'd told him twenty-four hours ago that he'd be meeting Jane for coffee tonight, he never would have believed it. But the question was: would she actually show? If Jane left him sitting at a café table alone, it wouldn't be the first time she'd disappeared without a word. But at least now he knew where to find her.

NINE

Through a break in the curtain, Jane watched Nik climb into his car. For a moment, she was tempted to take it all back and tell him that she couldn't meet tonight. What had she been thinking, saying yes to a date with Nik Andino?

It's not a date. He's just an old friend.

An old friend who'd stood so close, she could feel the heat radiating from him.

Jane closed her eyes. Despite his transformation into a *Grey's Anatomy* extra, everything about Nik was achingly familiar. The way he shifted his weight to one foot and stood with his hands in his pockets. The slight tilt of his head, the vulnerability in his eyes. That was her best friend since she was three, the boy who'd once known her better than anyone. The boy who—apparently—could still make her heart rattle in her chest.

This trip to Linden Falls would be the last she'd ever see of Nik Andino. Who could blame her for wanting one more hour with him, even if it was an agonizing one? Still, she should have said no. She *should* have turned and left the minute he'd pulled the car up instead of standing there, staring at the blue cotton clinging to his muscular chest in sweaty patches. Jane had less than a week to figure out how to disappear, and Scarlett to worry about.

And then Jane's attention swung from wiping her boots on the entryway mat to the movement on the living room floor. Her heart rattled for a different reason. Thank God Scarlett was still there, putting together her Legos. When Nik had invited Jane for coffee, it was right after she'd spotted Mom peeking out the window. What if Scarlett had appeared there next? Jane had panicked and agreed to go. Better to meet somewhere neutral than have Nik hanging around here.

It would only complicate things to have her daughter interacting with people from her old life in Linden Falls. Scarlett knew they had left Matteo and wouldn't be going back—Jane could never keep something that important from her—but she was only a child. What if she slipped and told someone their plan? What if she mentioned Canada? Jane's entire future hinged on Matteo having no idea where to look for them.

Jane had hoped that she could keep Scarlett entirely hidden from the people of this town. A busybody like Mrs. Swanson would probably take perverse pleasure in giving them away when Matteo came poking around. And as for Nik...

She should have considered Nik before she came back to Linden Falls.

When Mom had called to say that Dad had died and asked her to come home to help sort his things, Jane felt like the universe had handed her an incredible gift. It was the chance she'd been searching for and had almost despaired of ever finding. And it had all worked out perfectly... until she ran into Nik in Ford's General Store. It had never occurred to her that he might still live in this town, but she should have known better.

Nik could never know about Matteo, or Scarlett, or anything about her life in LA. The chances were too great that he'd ask questions, that he wouldn't be satisfied with vague answers and attempts to change the subject. There was that moment in Ford's yesterday when he'd taken her chin in his hand to get a better look at her bruised and battered cheek. She'd sensed his concern and had known he suspected there was more to her story than an accident with a cabinet.

If Nik ever knew how much more to the story there really was, would he want to get involved? Outside on the sidewalk, he'd seen her struggling and taken the snow shovel from her. Last night in Ford's he'd immediately offered to carry Mrs. Swanson's packages. Nik had been a volunteer emergency medical technician, and now he was a doctor. He was the kind of guy who stepped in to help. She'd always loved that about him.

But there was no helping her out of this situation. Jane had to do that on her own.

She kicked off her snow boots as Mom came down the hall to greet her.

"Was that Nik?"

"Yeah." The remaining bits of snow on her boots landed on the wood floor and started to melt. Jane focused on the mess, using her foot to nudge the doormat over the boards to soak up the puddles. "Sorry."

Mom didn't even glance at the floor. "What did he want?"

Jane pulled off the coat she was wearing. It had looked warmer than the jacket she'd brought from LA, so when she'd headed out to do the shoveling, she'd grabbed it off the hook. The minute she'd slipped it on, Jane had realized it was Dad's old coat. The stale scent of burned tobacco had wafted around her, reminding her of Dad, of Matteo, of the smoke that used to seep into their apartment from the club below. When she'd reached her hand into the pocket, it had closed around the crumpled cellophane of a half-used pack of Marlboros. Jane had shoved the cigarettes deeper into the folds of the coat with a shudder.

"Jane?" Mom prompted. "What did Nik say?"

"He just..." Jane lifted her shoulders in a shrug. "Wanted to say hello."

"Well, that was nice of him, especially after all this time. He took it hard when you left."

Jane's head swung in Mom's direction. How could she know that? Were she and Mrs. Andino talking again?

When Mrs. Andino had started cleaning houses to pay the bills after her husband passed, Mom had convinced Dad to hire her. *If the leaders of this town support a struggling family, others will follow.* Dad had cherished his reputation as the town's protector and all-around good guy, so he'd agreed. Mrs. Andino had started coming once a week to clean the house. She'd bring Nik to hang out with Jane, and after her work was done, she'd sit in the living room drinking tea and talking with Mom.

As the police chief's wife, Mom was friendly with everyone in town, but Helen Andino had been the first and only real friend Jane could remember her having. And those Tuesday afternoons had been the first time she'd seen Mom smile, relax... even laugh. Looking back as an adult who understood a little bit about loneliness and isolation, Jane could imagine what a relief it must have been to finally make a real connection with someone.

And then one day, maybe a year later, Dad had come home early and found the two women giggling on the couch. Jane could still remember the way the entire house had suddenly filled with tension. Mom's spine stiffened and her laughter died in her throat, and Mrs. Andino immediately began gathering up the mugs and plates to carry into the kitchen. That night, over dinner, Dad had asked Mom when she was going to start cleaning the house herself again. *How long are we supposed to support that family?*

"Just a little longer," Mom had insisted. "I can't fire her on the anniversary of her husband's death. It won't look good to the rest of the town."

Dad had just grunted and gone back to his potatoes.

The next Tuesday, one of Mom's gold necklaces had gone missing. Dad had discovered that it wasn't hanging on her jewelry stand when he went upstairs to bed that night. "It was here this morning," he'd grumbled. "Helen must have taken it."

It had been easy for him to get rid of Mrs. Andino after that.

Jane wasn't aware that Mom and Mrs. Andino had talked in years, outside of exchanging polite hellos around town. "How do you know Nik took it hard when I left?"

"He used to approach me at the grocery store and ask about you."

Jane's eyes widened. "What did you tell him?"

"I never told him much. I didn't *know* much." Mom hesitated now, as if she were weighing whether to say the next thing. "After Dad died, Nik stopped by a few times, just to check in and see if I needed anything."

Jane's heart pitched. Of course he had.

"I'm sure that had more to do with you than it did with me," Mom mused. "That boy never got over you."

Jane gave her a long stare. Mom had been there the day it had all come crashing down. She knew what had happened with Nik, and she knew what Dad had done. And she hadn't done anything to stop it from happening.

But that was a decade ago.

"Of course he got over me." Jane tossed her scarf on the bench. "I mean, you've seen him around." She pictured that patch of golden skin exposed by the V-neck of his shirt, and the way the lines of his muscles had contracted when he tossed the snow shovel aside. "Nik probably has people of all genders throwing themselves at him." Jane bit her lip. "He probably has a girlfriend."

Mom nodded. "Oh, I'm sure he does."

Jane hated the way that simple sentence seemed to stab her straight in the heart. *Did Nik say he has a girlfriend?* Well, if he did, and if it hurt to hear, it was Jane's own fault for bringing it up.

"But that doesn't mean he ever got over you," Mom continued.

"Who's Nik?"

Jane whirled around to find Scarlett standing in the doorway of the living room. When Jane was Scarlett's age, Nik had been the most important person in her life. Jane had been sure she was going to marry him. Hell, almost ten years later, she'd *still* been sure she'd marry Nik. And now, ten years after that... "He's nobody."

Mom cleared her throat, giving Jane a stern look. "That's not a very nice thing to say."

Jane sighed. "He's not nobody. He's an old friend from when I was a kid. He stopped by to say hi."

"Your mom and Nik were the best of friends. They were so inseparable, they used to finish each other's sentences. And then when they got older, I'm pretty sure they spent every single day together after school."

Mom didn't mention the part about how Jane had always gone to the Andinos' because she didn't want Dad to come home early and find Nik at their house. Just in case Dad tried to drive Nik away—the same way he'd done to Mrs. Andino.

Jane used to leave Nik's house and hurry home each evening before Dad got off work, making sure she was in her room studying before his patrol car pulled into the drive. She'd brace herself, listening for signs of his mood. If he rapped on her door to say hello, it meant he'd had a good day. If he went in the kitchen to yell at Mom... not so good.

But none of that was something Scarlett needed to know about. She had her own experiences of tiptoeing around someone else's moods.

"Was Nik your boyfriend?" Scarlett asked.

Jane felt her face flame, even all these years later, at the memory of Nik's mouth on her neck, his hands sliding across her heated skin. "No. Just friends," she said, in a quieter voice.

"So, Daddy was your only boyfriend?"

Jane hesitated. Though she'd been with Matteo for a decade, and they'd never married—*thank God*—it sounded odd to call him her boyfriend. At Scarlett's age, Jane had imagined that a boyfriend would hold her hand, take her out on a date, buy her flowers. Matteo had done some of those things, at first. But it was hard to remember them now. "I guess you could say that."

"Were you and Daddy inseparable?" Scarlett asked. "Did you finish each other's sentences?" She looked down at the Ken and Barbie Legos in her hand, her face shining and hopeful. "Were you in love?"

TEN

TEN YEARS AGO

Jane grasped the handle beneath the *Help Wanted* sign duct-taped to the door at eye level. She could do this. She *had* to do this.

Teetering on her high heels, Jane stepped over the threshold, out of the California sun and into the shade of the club. The door swung shut behind her, and Jane was plunged into darkness. At just past eleven in the morning, the place was empty, the only illumination coming from the emergency signs marking the exits and a glowing blue lamp hanging over the bar.

She'd never been in a place like this in her life. The only bar in Linden Falls was the Harp and Fiddle, but since she was only eighteen, she'd never been allowed inside. Still, from the few glimpses she'd caught walking past the window, it was more of a small-town pub, with a scratched wooden bar and worn leather couches.

Jane blinked to adjust her eyes, gazing from the row of tufted-velvet booths to the shiny line of liquor bottles on the shelf, and then the DJ booth suspended above the dance floor.

The Harp and Fiddle was nothing like *this*.

Jane straightened her mini skirt. Linden Falls was a world away, and here in LA, she was no longer that girl whose dad would lose it if she was caught with a beer in her hand. Here in LA, she could be whoever she wanted.

Jane made her way across the empty dance floor, the tap of her heels echoing around the cavernous room. "Hello?" she called tentatively, looking for signs of a bartender, or maybe one of those bouncers who usually stood out front. At the long chrome bar, Jane paused, peering over the side, but all she found were rows of glasses and mini fridges holding champagne bottles. Maybe nobody was here? It *was* early for a club to be open. What if the door was left unlocked by mistake, and now she was breaking and entering? If she ended up in jail, nobody was going to bail her out.

But then again, she wouldn't have to pay for her cheap motel room tonight either. How bad had it gotten that this fact felt like a silver lining? Jane breathed out a half-laugh.

"Can I help you?"

Jane pushed away from the bar, spinning around to find a man in a doorway under the sign leading to the bathrooms. Though he stood across the room, Jane could see that he was tall and muscular by how well he filled out the doorframe.

"Uh, hi," she said, straightening her skirt.

The man wore a tight white T-shirt that stretched across his broad chest and a pair of jeans that hugged his trim thighs. In the dark, blueish light, his hair looked almost black, curling from under the edges of a beat-up LA Dodgers hat, and over the nape of his neck. He reached up to brace himself in the doorway, and the muscles in his biceps contracted.

Jane's breath hitched. He was without a doubt the most attractive man she'd ever seen. Though she'd always thought Nik was good-looking, he was a boy, and this... Well, this was a man. He was probably at least thirty.

Jane was left momentarily speechless. "I—" she stuttered.

The man let go of the doorframe and crossed the room to where Jane stood gripping the back of a barstool for balance. "Are you lost?"

"No." Even in that one syllable, Jane heard her voice shake. "No, I'm, uh..."

Get it together. This is your chance. The thrift store clothes hadn't been expensive, but she was dead broke so they might as well have cost millions. She wasn't here to stare at a beautiful man with her mouth hanging open. She *needed* this job.

Jane let go of the barstool and stood up straight. "I'm here for the server job."

The man stopped in front of her, and Jane had to tilt her head back to look up at him. A slightly amused smile slanted across his face. "You are, huh?" He had smooth bronze skin, high cheekbones, and inky lashes a mile long.

"That's right." She wobbled on her heels, undermining the confidence in her voice.

"Have you ever worked as a server before?"

Jane was tempted to stare over his shoulder but forced herself to look him in the eye. "Of course I have."

"How old are you?"

"Twenty-one," she said without hesitation, glad she'd practiced that on the way over.

The man's gaze swept over her, heating every part of her it touched. "What's your name?"

"Jane McCaffrey."

"Jane, I'm Matteo." He held out his palm, and she slipped her hand in his. It was warm, strong, reassuring somehow. "I'm the club manager. Why don't you have a seat, and we'll talk about your experience?"

The way his eyes lingered on her mouth made her feel like he was asking about more than just her previous serving jobs.

Jane slid onto a stool while Matteo rounded the bar and stopped opposite her. "Tell me about where you've worked as a server."

Jane cleared her throat. "It was an Irish bar called the Harp and Fiddle in a small town you've never heard of."

"Try me."

Jane hesitated. The more honest she was, the less likely she was to mix up her story. Besides, what did this guy care about the middle-of-nowhere town where she'd grown up? What was he going to do, call her dad? "Linden Falls, New York."

"Yeah." He cocked an eyebrow. "Never heard of it."

"Consider yourself lucky." Jane felt a smile tug at her lips.

Matteo leaned an elbow on the bar. "So, Jane McCaffrey, what brought you to LA from..." He waved a hand like he'd already forgotten the name. "...East Bumfuck...?"

Jane shrugged. "You know. The usual things that bring people to LA."

He ran a hand over his chin, stroking the hint of razor stubble. "You're pretty enough to be an actress."

Jane blinked at that. This beautiful man thought *she* was pretty? Suddenly, she was glad she'd ditched her too-big trousers and splurged on this tank top and skirt.

He shook his head. "But I don't get the actress vibe from you."

"I didn't come to LA to be an actress." Jane took a breath. "I'm a musician. A singer-songwriter."

"Yeah? Are you any good?"

"Of course I am," she said, with every bit of self-assurance she could muster. *I got into every music school I applied to, didn't I?* But she'd just spent two weeks sitting in waiting rooms with dozens of aspiring stars who were only applying for office jobs until they got their big breaks. She'd learned pretty quickly that nobody gave a damn if you got into music school. They only cared about the clubs you'd played, which, for Jane, were none at this point.

Matteo confirmed this by asking, "Where are you playing these days?"

Jane bit her lip. "Uh, well, nowhere yet. I had to leave my guitar back in... uh... East Bumfuck. But I plan to buy another one soon and start booking some gigs."

Matteo nodded like he believed it, and Jane wasn't sure if he was humoring her or if she'd actually managed to pull off a little bit of confidence.

"What about you?" Jane changed the subject. "Where are you from?"

"LA, born and bred."

"And you didn't want to get out of here? Go someplace new?"

He raised his eyebrows, and Jane immediately realized she might have insulted him, implying he was somehow stuck in this club. "I mean... I didn't mean that you need to..."

Matteo laughed. "I don't need to get out of LA to go someplace new. I can just drive across town."

"I guess that makes sense." Apparently, it could take hours just to get from one end of the city to the other. Not that she'd had any chance to explore any part of LA that wasn't within a square mile of the motel. But someday she would. If she managed to land this job, maybe she really *would* buy that guitar and start playing gigs all over town.

She'd been in this club for ten minutes and Matteo hadn't kicked her out yet. In fact, he seemed to like her. Her confidence kicked up another notch. Jane flashed her most charming smile. "So... about the job..."

At that moment, a stocky, thirty-something man carrying a bucket of ice under each arm walked in. He gave Jane a nod as he crossed behind the bar to open a cooler and dump it in.

Matteo turned away from Jane to address the man. "Hey, did that tequila order arrive yet?"

The man set the ice buckets on the floor and ran a hand through his hair. "Nope. I called and they said it might not be delivered until tomorrow."

"Goddamn it." Matteo slapped a hand down on the bar, causing Jane to jump. "I've got a party coming in who specifically requested that brand." His jaw clenched and eyes narrowed.

"I told them you need it tonight," the stocky man said. "But they're understaffed and can't get someone to the warehouse until tomorrow." He held up his hands in an *I'm just the messenger* gesture. "Sorry, man."

Matteo pushed away from the bar, his face turning red. "*Fucking hell.*"

Jane shrank back against her chair back. He was on the other side of the bar, and she didn't really feel threatened. But experience had taught her to tense up when a man was turning red with anger.

But then Matteo's shoulders relaxed, and Jane felt hers do the same.

"It's okay," he said, with a sigh. "I'll call them later."

The stocky man picked up his buckets and headed back the way he'd come.

Matteo turned to Jane with a shrug. "Sorry about that. This vendor has been screwing me over for weeks now."

"I'm sorry," Jane said. It was probably difficult to run a bar and try to meet so many customers' demands. "Is there anywhere else to get that tequila? A liquor store or... I don't know. Another bar, maybe?" And then her face heated up. She'd told him she'd worked in a bar before, so shouldn't she know something about how to buy tequila? There probably wasn't another way or he wouldn't be so upset about it.

But a grin slowly spread across Matteo's face. "You know

what? Maybe there is." He reached under the bar to pull out a phone, hitting a few buttons and pressing it to his ear. "Hey," he said, when someone on the other end had answered. "How's it going?"

There was a pause where the other person was clearly speaking, and then Matteo continued: "Listen, any chance you have an extra bottle of Jalisco Tequila? I have a customer who requested it and a supplier who's pissing me off." Another pause, and then, "I'll pay you double, and I won't call the health department and let them know your bathroom is a fire trap."

The person on the other end said something, and Matteo tossed back his head and laughed.

Jane eyed the strong cords of his neck, the stubble on his jaw. And then she felt her cheeks turn crimson.

Matteo was staring back at her with heat smoldering in his dark eyes. He muttered something into the phone, and then something else, but she missed it entirely. Finally, he promised the person on the other end that he'd send someone over to pick up the bottle, and then he hung up the phone. "Well, Jane McCaffrey from East Bumfuck," he murmured, his voice low and gravelly. "It's a good thing you walked in here today. You saved my ass."

Jane's pulse picked up speed. "So, about the job. Does that mean..."

Matteo gave her a nod. "You're hired."

She breathed out a sigh. "Oh, thank you." *Thank God.*

"You can work the party for the customer who requested the tequila tonight. That should earn you some big tips."

"Great," she murmured, hoping she sounded confident and not terrified.

Matteo smiled, half amused and half like he wanted to know what she had on under her tank top. "It looks like you're my lucky charm."

Jane forced a smile. She hoped so. She hoped she could pull

this off, and earn enough that this would be the start of her new life in LA.

She hoped Matteo, this bar, and this new job would be her lucky charm, too.

Jane was a much better server than she'd expected. It wasn't that hard, really. Since Matteo had assigned her to a private table, she didn't have to worry about wading through the crowd on the dance floor. All she had to do was put in the drink orders with a red-haired bartender named Yolanda and carry them on a tray to the table.

Matteo roamed the club, slapping people on the back, laughing, charming everyone sitting at the private tables. Jane was drawn to him every time he walked by. He'd ditched the Dodgers hat and changed from his jeans and T-shirt into a pair of black pants and a fitted button-up shirt with the sleeves rolled up. If she'd thought he was attractive before, he could pass for a movie star now. She expected him to ignore her while they worked—he was the manager of the club, and she was just a small-town server after all—but when she passed near him, he met her eye, gave her arm a squeeze, held her gaze for an extra beat.

The club cleared out around 2 a.m., and Jane was finally able to get a minute to run to the bathroom. When she returned, she found Matteo alone behind the bar.

"Where is everyone?" Jane asked, as she piled glasses on a tray.

"The DJ had an after-party to work, and I sent Yolanda and the servers home." Matteo wiped the counter with a rag. "They have to get up early to get their kids to school."

"That's nice of you."

Matteo shrugged. "It means it's just you and me cleaning up, though. I hope you don't mind."

"I don't have anywhere to be." She set the tray on the bar and unloaded the glasses so Matteo could wash them.

"No?" He reached for a glass, his hand brushing hers. "No boyfriend waiting for you at home? Or back in East Bumfuck?"

Jane shook her head, shoving all thoughts of Nik out of her head. She couldn't think of him now. This was her new life, and today had gone better than she could have hoped. Maybe everything would turn out okay.

They finished cleaning up, and Matteo handed her a roll of cash. "Great work tonight."

Jane clutched the bills in her hand. She didn't want to count it in front of him, but it looked like it was all twenties, and there were at least ten or fifteen of them. Had she really made over two hundred dollars? She stuffed it in her purse, a wave of relief washing over her.

Matteo put two shot glasses on the bar and poured in a pale gold liquid, sliding one in her direction. "Our lucky tequila."

Jane had never had a drink before. Sometimes Nik, Ali, and Hannah would steal bottles of wine from their parents' stash and drink it by the lake in Randall Park, but Jane stayed away from it. She couldn't take the chance that Dad would catch her sneaking home smelling like alcohol. She'd always been a rule follower, had always done everything she could to keep Dad happy, to keep the peace in her house.

But look where it got her.

Jane picked up the glass. Matteo held out his in a toast and then tossed the liquid back. She mirrored his motion. Immediately, her throat ignited, and her chest felt like she'd swallowed acid. She gagged and tried not to choke. Thankfully, she managed to breathe through the pain and gulp down the drink without humiliating herself. A moment later, a warmth began to spread over her.

Matteo poured another shot, and this time she drank it without flinching. By the third, Jane felt positively giddy. She slid onto the bar stool, patting the pocket of her purse that held the money she'd earned. Hundreds of dollars in a single shift. That money would pay for at least a couple of nights in the motel, plus some real food. And if this kept up, maybe she could find her own little apartment somewhere.

Her attention turned to Matteo. *God, he's beautiful. Does he really think I'm pretty?* Her head spun.

Matteo caught her watching him, and he set his shot glass down on the counter. A moment later, he'd rounded the bar and was standing in front of her. "You're adorable, Jane from East Bumfuck."

Jane flushed at that. She didn't want to be adorable. She wanted to be sexy. Like the women who came into the club.

But then Matteo took a step closer, sliding his thigh in between her knees to spread them apart. Her skirt was so short it gave little resistance, and he settled there between her legs, staring into her eyes, mouth inches away. "The women who come in here are usually so jaded. But you... my lucky charm..." He leaned closer. "You're so refreshing."

And then he was kissing her, tangling his hands in her hair, sliding his tongue into her mouth. Jane had never kissed someone who wasn't Nik before. Matteo's thick razor stubble scraped her face, and his arms felt like tree trunks wrapped around her. He tasted like alcohol and a hint of tobacco. She kissed him back, lightheaded, holding on partly so she didn't fall off the stool and onto the floor in a puddle of tequila and exhaustion.

"Come up to my place." Matteo's lips slid to her neck, and she felt herself melting. "I live upstairs."

It was so appealing. Her feet were absolutely killing her in these heels. If she left the bar now, she'd be alone on the streets of LA at three in the morning. And when she got back to the motel, there would be the noise, the fights, the police cars zooming by with their sirens on.

Matteo's hand slid beneath her shirt, slipping under the lace of her bra. He thrust his hips forward, his erection straining against his pants and pressing toward the center of her. He was the most attractive man she'd ever met, and he wanted her. Her head spun from the tequila and his nearness. She was so tired of feeling alone. "Okay," she whispered.

He took her hand and led her up the steps to his apartment.

ELEVEN

PRESENT DAY

"Mommy, did you love Daddy?" Scarlett repeated.

Jane's heart squeezed at the hope shining on her daughter's face. Matteo was Scarlett's father, and Scarlett loved him. And at the same time, Matteo was a violent man, and she and Scarlett weren't safe with him. Jane understood that both things could be true at the same time, but Scarlett was only nine: it was hard to see the world in shades of gray.

Mom turned away to straighten the coats hanging in the hallway. Jane reached for her daughter's shoulder, steering her to the couch in the living room. They sank down into the cushions and Jane turned to look at Scarlett. "I cared about your daddy a lot. When I met him, he was handsome and charming, and I thought we'd be happy together."

"Was he always so mad?"

"No, he wasn't always so mad." If he had been in those early days, Jane wanted to believe she would have left. "I was all by myself in LA, and he gave me a job."

Scarlett nodded. Jane had shared a little about how she'd left Linden Falls to pursue a music career in LA.

"At first, your dad made me feel safe."

That apartment above the club had been a sanctuary in those early days. Sure, there'd been noise from the club, but that had been nothing compared to the loud sex, the fights, the screaming babies at the motel. That first morning after she'd slept with Matteo, he'd woken her up with coffee and a croissant from the café down the street. When she'd reluctantly climbed out of his bed to go back to the motel to shower, he'd drawn her a bath in his oversized tub and then climbed in beside her.

A couple of weeks later, Matteo had surprised her with a guitar. With tears welling in her eyes, Jane had picked it up. Her left hand had automatically formed the shape of a chord as her right hand reached for the strings. She'd tentatively strummed a few times, getting used to the feel of the instrument in her hands, savoring the notes vibrating in her chest. The guitar had been heavier, the body smoother than the vintage one Nik had gifted her.

"I have a couple of friends whose bars book live music," Matteo had told her.

Jane had looked up from the shining maple of the brand-new instrument, unmarred by bumps or scratches or band stickers.

"I can talk to them about getting you on the schedule," he'd said.

"Really?" Jane had asked breathlessly.

"Sure." Matteo had given her a half-shrug like it was no big deal. And then he'd leaned closer. "Play me something." His voice had dipped low and raspy, as if hearing her sing would be the most erotic thing in the world.

Jane had chosen a folk ballad with a complicated chord progression and finger picking pattern. She'd wanted to impress him. To show him she was worthy of playing his friends' clubs.

At the end of the intro, she'd taken a deep breath and opened her mouth to sing. But the words had died in her throat as her gaze had locked on Matteo's whiskey-colored eyes, hot and full of desire. He'd leaned in to kiss her then, taking the guitar out of her hand and setting it on the floor. As he'd slowly eased her back on the couch cushions, the possibility had hovered at the edge of her consciousness.

Maybe I could be happy with him.

But Matteo's temper had unraveled slowly, like a sweater with loose threads that gradually become a hole.

Jane remembered that first day when his jaw had tightened, and the annoyance had flashed in his eyes. But then he'd reined in his anger, and Jane had believed everything was fine. Growing up in this house with Dad, Jane hadn't learned how to gauge a normal, healthy reaction to an inconvenient problem. She'd had no experience with following her instincts. When Matteo had snapped at a clumsy server at the club, his tone was mild compared to what she was used to. When he'd punched a bartender for stealing from the cash drawer, she told herself he was under a lot of pressure.

And it wasn't like he'd hit *her.*

Maybe she'd been too desperate and too alone to expect much more than what she'd ended up with. Maybe it had seemed better than where she'd come from.

Jane focused on her daughter. "It's been hard for you to leave Los Angeles and know we won't be going back, hasn't it?" she asked. "I'm sorry that we were so busy before we left that I didn't have a chance to explain it all to you as well as I should have."

Scarlett held Ken and Barbie in one hand, and she picked up her stuffed elephant from the couch and clutched it in the other. "Are we really never going to see Daddy again? Because he hits you sometimes?"

Jane hesitated. She'd always tried to be as open with Scarlett as was age-appropriate. But the questions were getting harder. "Yes. Nobody should ever hit someone. And we shouldn't live like that anymore. Do you understand that?"

Scarlett nodded. "I'm glad we left. I'm tired of being scared. But..." Scarlett's eyes darted to Jane's, and then back down to the toys in her hand, as if she didn't want her mother to see the doubt there. "... won't Daddy be lonely without us?"

Jane's chest squeezed. So many of the stories and messages aimed at children were told in such simple terms. There were good guys and there were bad guys. Parents were supposed to love you. Families didn't hurt each other. But what were you supposed to do when real life didn't look anything like that? When you were nine years old and you loved your father, and you also wished he would go away so he could never hurt your mom again? Nobody was stocking the library with books about the kids whose childhoods were spent hiding in a closet while their father sent their mother to the ER.

"He might be lonely, sweetie. I'm sure he's going to miss *you* a whole lot. But hurting someone is never okay, and I don't want you to grow up thinking that it is."

Scarlett absently rubbed her stuffed elephant's ear, a habit that had started when she was a baby. "I don't want to go to Canada. It seems so far away. It's a *foreign country*."

"I know, but it's really not that far. Just a few hours north. And it's just like the United States, really. Your grandma is from Canada."

Scarlett looked up. "Maybe Grandma wants to come with us? Then at least we'll know someone there."

Jane shook her head. If Mom had wanted to go to Canada, she would have done it when Jane had begged her ten years ago. But she couldn't say that to her daughter. "I think Grandma needs to stay here. But we'll meet new people."

Scarlett nodded. "Can I bring my Lego Barbie house?"

Jane hesitated. Scarlett was already losing so much. She didn't want to take this from her daughter, too. Which meant she'd need to get moving on her plan. *Today.* "Yes. Yes, I'll make sure you can take your Lego Barbie house."

Scarlett went back to the floor to assemble the Dream House kitchen, and Jane stood. When she turned, she found Mom standing in the doorway with tears in her eyes. As Jane moved past her into the hallway, Mom whispered, "You're a good mother."

Jane kept walking. She didn't know what else to do.

TWELVE

An hour later, Jane pulled her old Toyota into the alley behind Butler's Garage. She and her friends used to stop by the mini-mart where they'd stock up on snacks before lying by the lake at Randall Park. But now Jane avoided the front of the store and entered the garage through the back door. She'd learned a lesson running into Mrs. Swanson at Ford's, and the fewer people who might spot her on this particular errand, the better.

Jane stepped into the building, which somehow managed to be dark and blindingly bright at the same time. A dim fluorescent bulb flickered on the ceiling, casting only the barest light into the corners of the vast room. But scattered through the middle was a variety of cars, some suspended on lifts with mechanics in coveralls working on them from below, and others parked on the greasy ground with their hoods open and bright work lights shining in. Jane jumped at the sudden buzz of a welding machine starting up entirely too close for comfort, its sparks bouncing in all directions.

All around her hung the sharp scent of gasoline and tire rubber. Jane hovered in the shadows, scanning the room for a familiar sleeve of tattoos and a head of short, reddish hair.

"Miss, you can't be in here." A tall woman with long dread-locks and a pair of blue coveralls appeared from behind a high-end SUV, waving a wrench toward the door Jane had entered through. "You need to leave."

"I'm here to talk to Kait. Is she available?"

The other woman tucked the tool in her pocket and hitched her chin in the direction of the minimart. "If you're here to have your car serviced, go through the front and leave your keys with the attendant."

Jane shook her head. "I don't need my car serviced. I need to talk to Kait. Please? It's important."

The woman eyed her for a moment, and then turned in the direction of a Mustang parked a few vehicles away. "Hey, boss."

"Yeah?" To Jane's relief, a familiar figure stood up from under the hood. Kait's hair was still short, still reddish blond, though in the gleam of the work light, Jane spotted a few streaks of gray.

"This woman is here to see you."

Kait squinted across the garage, and Jane gave a nervous wave. Surely Kait would remember her. It had been a decade, but they'd spent almost four days in a car together. Jane had a feeling that despite whatever kind of excitement came with Kait's line of work, it wasn't every day that she drove fugitive teenagers to the West Coast.

Kait wiped her hands on a dirty rag and crossed the garage, giving her employee a nod. "Thanks, Piper. I've got it from here."

"Okay, boss." Piper shrugged and went back to the car she'd been working on.

"Jane McCaffrey," Kait said, with a raise of her eyebrows. "This is a surprise. I never expected to see you back in this town."

"Me either." Jane shoved her hands in her jacket pockets. "Believe me."

Kait's gaze roamed over her. "You look exactly the same. Even that black eye hasn't changed a bit. Why is that?"

Jane pressed a hand to her cheek. She'd hoped it would have started to fade by now. "Just bad luck, I guess."

"More like bad company."

"That, too," Jane acknowledged with a nod. Kait had been the one person Jane could be honest with all those years ago, and she had a feeling that hadn't changed. "Is there somewhere private we can talk?"

Kait hitched her chin at a door in the back corner of the garage. "My office."

Kait's office was a small, cluttered room with two chairs and a desk piled with unsteady stacks of paperwork, paper cups of old coffee from the minimart next door, and grease-stained tools. Jane sank into the first chair, a gold-upholstered relic from another era.

Kait moved a file box from the desk chair and sat down. "So, what's it been? Nine or ten years?"

Jane nodded. "Ten and a half."

"Are you still out in LA?"

Jane shook her head. "I'm... in transition."

Kait leaned back in her office chair, waiting for Jane to elaborate. She'd never been the kind of person to pepper someone with questions or push them to talk if they didn't want to talk.

Jane and Kait had formed a sort of tentative friendship on their drive across the US but hadn't kept in touch after Kait had dropped Jane off in the motel parking lot all those years ago. For one thing, Jane hadn't had a phone number to give Kait. And she'd gotten the feeling that Kait was someone who would help you with a ride, but she wasn't going to call you for a chat. Plus, Jane had been trying to cut ties with Linden Falls.

Jane rubbed her sweaty hands on the fabric of her leggings. She never would have imagined herself asking for another favor when Kait had already done so much for her, and for nothing in return.

Jane had little to offer in return now, too. But she also had few options. "I hoped you could help me with a car."

"What kind of car?"

"An old one. Junky, but not too junky. Something extremely unmemorable."

Kait nodded like she was thinking it over. From out in the garage, Jane could hear metal clanking against metal, drills whirring, and the steady puff of air from a hydraulic lift. Kait ran a bigger operation here than Jane had imagined. Hopefully that meant she'd be able to help, and quickly. Jane's only plan B was Greyhound, but a bus full of strangers meant there could be dozens of witnesses.

"I don't have a lot of money. But I have that Toyota out there." Jane waved her hand at the grimy window behind Kait's desk that opened to the alley in back. "It's an older model, but it runs well. You could have it."

"So, you want to do a trade?"

"Yes." Jane let out a slow breath. "Except there's just one other thing..."

On their drive out to Los Angeles ten years ago, she and Kait had mostly listened to country music and news on NPR. Other than their initial conversation where Jane had begged for a ride, they hadn't talked about Jane's home life or Kait's business or anything personal at all. Jane certainly hadn't asked if Dad's suspicions about Kait's illegal side business were true. Kait had been doing Jane the biggest favor of her life. Jane hadn't wanted to know if her getaway car was stolen.

But there was no getting around it now. If Dad had been wrong, and everything about Kait's business was on the up and up, Jane was about to offend the last person who deserved it.

"What is it?" Kait prompted.

"The Toyota needs to disappear. Forever."

Kait's eyebrows rose.

"And nobody can trace the car you give me," Jane continued.

Kait's attention shifted to the spot below Jane's eye where she'd done her best to cover the yellowing bruise with make-up. The other woman cocked her head. "Because *you* need to disappear, too."

Jane nodded. "Yes. And I need your help."

Kait stared at her, as if considering Jane's words, and Jane held her breath. After a moment, Kait nodded. "Alright. What's the plan? How is this all going to work?"

The less information anyone knew about where she was going, the better. But like she'd said to Mom, Kait was the one person she'd ever been able to trust. "My mom grew up in Canada, in a small town outside of Ottawa. She was in her first year at the University of Toronto when she and a couple of girlfriends took a trip to Niagara Falls. It was the same weekend my dad and his buddies had driven up from Linden Falls for a bachelor party."

Kait's lip curled up in disgust, but she nodded at Jane to keep talking.

"My dad was more than ten years older than my mom, handsome, charming, and had a good job on the Linden Falls police force. It didn't take long for him to convince her to drop out of school and marry him." Jane shifted in her seat. "Mom got pregnant on their honeymoon. A month before her due date, she went to visit her parents in Ottawa, and that's when I decided to make an early appearance. I have dual US and Canadian citizenship. It's not something most people know about me."

Kait nodded slowly. "Including the guy who put that mark on your face, I'm guessing."

"No, he doesn't know." Even before Jane had discovered the full extent of who Matteo really was, some part of her had known to keep that secret to herself, just in case she needed it someday. "If I use my Canadian passport to cross the border, Matteo—my... ex—might have a harder time tracking me down."

Since Scarlett was a minor traveling with her mother, all she'd need was her birth certificate to cross the border. But even Kait didn't need to know about Scarlett. Nobody in this town did. "Once I'm safely in Canada, I'll head west and look for a town to settle in. Somewhere that I can blend in and find work as a server or house cleaner. If Matteo doesn't know I'm a Canadian citizen, he won't think to look for me there."

"And if I tear your car down and sell it for parts, and give you an old beater, he could spend ages looking for the wrong vehicle."

"Exactly. He'll still think I'm driving the Toyota he gave me." Jane wasn't nearly as confident as she sounded. There were so many things that could go wrong. But going back to LA with Matteo wasn't an option. Jane wasn't sure if she'd survive it. And then what would happen to Scarlett? Jane clutched her abdomen as nausea rolled over her. So far, Matteo had never been violent with Scarlett. But then, for most of Jane's life, Dad hadn't been violent with her. Until one day that had changed.

"Are they going to run some kind of check on your vehicle plate and registration when you get to Canada?" Kait asked. "Will this car need to be registered to you? I don't want you to get held up at the border."

"It would be best if it was registered to me, but they probably won't check unless I look suspicious."

Kait nodded. "Okay. It's going to take me about a week, maybe a little longer. I can get you a car pretty easily, but I'll need to call a guy I know to expedite the paperwork. Can you work with that?"

If everything went smoothly with Kait's guy, it would be

fine. And if not—well, Kait's guy would just have to come through. "Matteo is expecting me back in LA by New Year's."

"Okay. We'll make it work." Kait gave a curt nod of her head, a gesture that reassured Jane. If Kait didn't think she could do it, Jane knew she'd be blunt enough to say so. "Leave me your phone number." Kait pulled a Post-it note and pen out of the drawer, but hesitated instead of handing it over.

Jane's pulse picked up speed. *Please don't let her change her mind.*

"Listen, Jane." Kait clicked the pen. "Are you sure you want to do this? Sure you want to keep running?"

"I don't have any other choice."

"You always have a choice." Kait cocked her head. "You think it's easy being a lesbian car mechanic in a place like this? I've been threatened, I've had my shop vandalized more times than I can count."

Jane's stomach churned. She had no doubt that some of those threats had come from Dad.

"But I decided a long time ago that I wasn't going to let them drive me away. This is my home. So, I stay, and I keep fighting."

Jane shook her head. "You don't know what Matteo is capable of. If I leave him, and he finds me..." Jane closed her eyes, remembering the one time she'd tried. The worst week of her life. "It's not just me I have to think about."

Kait paused but didn't ask Jane to elaborate. She just slid the pad and pen across the desk. "I'll be in touch as soon as I have something for you."

Jane took the paper and scribbled down her number. "Don't you want to see the Toyota? To make sure it's worth your effort?"

Kait shrugged. "Whatever the value of the Toyota, I'm sure it's worth my effort."

A wave of emotion crested over Jane. For the second time in

her life, this almost-stranger was helping her. Saving her, with nothing in return. Jane wished there was a way she could properly thank her. To promise to make it up to her.

But if everything went to plan, Jane would never see Kait, or anyone in this town, ever again.

THIRTEEN

Jane McCaffrey actually showed up.

From his seat at the table across the room, Nik watched as Jane paused to scan the small café crowd. He hadn't realized just how much he'd been bracing himself for her to be a no-show until he saw her familiar figure appear in the doorway. After all, how many hours had he spent staring at doorways waiting for her to walk in? Practicing what he wanted to say to a voice that never materialized on the other end of the phone?

He took a moment to watch her before she noticed him. In high school, the sight of her used to have his pulse quickening, but now it was hammering so loudly he was afraid it would drown out the music coming through the café speakers. Everything about her was familiar as she stood there scanning the room for him. It felt like a week since they had last been in this café together, sitting at their usual table in the corner, planning their future. College at Cornell, then they'd move to a city with a music scene where she could play gigs and he could go to med school.

It had all sounded so easy. Their whole lives ahead of them, anything was possible.

But ten years had passed, and they were strangers now. He eyed the bruise on her cheek, the tiny lines of fatigue around her eyes. Those were only physical changes, but they hinted at a whole world beneath the surface that he had no part of.

Jane's gaze lingered on their old table in the back corner. It had been empty when he got here, but Nik had intentionally chosen to sit in the middle of the room instead. Jane's head swung in his direction, and Nik could tell the exact moment she spotted him because her eyes softened and her lips curved into a hint of a smile, almost as if she couldn't help herself.

His heart tightened in his chest.

Jane made her way over, and he stood. If she were anyone else—Hannah or Ali or someone he was dating—he would have greeted her with a hug. Instead, he helped her with her jacket, taking care not to brush her neck with his hand. Underneath, she wore simple black leggings and a dark green T-shirt that slid off one shoulder. Nik dragged his attention from the line of her collarbone, trying not to think about the last time he'd seen that expanse of skin.

"Hi," she said nervously, once she was seated across from him.

"Thanks for coming."

"Sure." Jane picked up her menu and looked it over. "Oh, they still have those peanut butter brownies," she said, her eyes lighting up.

At that moment, a plate with a brownie landed in the middle of the table, followed by two napkin rolls of silverware.

"Thanks," he said to the server who had delivered the dessert, and then he gave Jane a rueful smile. "Order whatever you want, but I thought this might interest you."

Smiling, Jane grabbed a fork, carving off a bite of gooey chocolate and sliding it into her mouth. "Mmmm," she murmured, closing her eyes in happiness, and something in Nik's abdomen clenched. He really was a glutton for punishment. Why hadn't he ordered the plain scone instead? But then Jane opened her eyes and grinned at him, and he was tempted to call the server back and ask her to put the whole damn pan of brownies on his tab.

"I can't believe you remembered," she said, already digging in for another bite.

"Seriously? Of course I remembered. The crime scene in my mom's kitchen?" Nik prompted.

In the last quarter of their senior year, Jane had begged Pete, the café's owner, to share his brownie recipe so she could take it to college with her. Pete had good-naturedly refused, claiming it was his mother's secret recipe and he wasn't at liberty to give it out. So, Nik had stocked up on baking supplies and printed out a dozen different recipes. They'd spent an entire rainy Saturday attempting to recreate Jane's dream brownies, recipe by recipe. By the end of the day, the kitchen counters, the oven, and both Nik and Jane were covered in more melted chocolate and peanut butter than they'd stirred into the brownies. They never did figure out the recipe, and it took them two hours to clean up, but Nik still looked back on it as one of those perfect, sepia-toned days when every moment felt like a beginning.

Jane's shoulders shook with laughter, obviously remembering at least the mess, if not the rest of it. "I don't think I ate brownies for a month after that chocolate bloodbath."

"Who are you kidding? It was a week."

Jane took another bite of brownie. "Fine, it was a week." She looked from the brownie, half-eaten now, to Nik. "I'm hogging the whole thing. Here. You should have some."

He leaned back, holding up his hands. "I can have one of Pete's brownies whenever I want. This is all you." Nik hitched his chin at the plate. "Though say the word and I'll send you some whenever you want."

Her smile dipped slightly, and she shrugged. "We have some pretty good bakeries in LA."

Los Angeles. Nik could have sat there all day questioning her about that one topic alone... *Why did you move there without telling me? How could you let ten years go by before you came back?* But there was a wariness in her eyes that told him he shouldn't cross those lines. It needled him, her caution where he was concerned, because they'd always been so open with each other.

He felt like a circus performer perched precariously on a tightrope, suspended between the burning desire to interrogate her about everything she hadn't told him and the fear that it might send her running for another decade. Nik could recognize that simply getting her to meet for coffee was a win, and he should approach cautiously. But at the same time, he might not have another chance.

"So, how did all of that turn out for you?" he asked.

She blinked, momentary confusion crossing her face. "You mean—"

"Los Angeles." He cocked his head. "I always assumed you headed out there to make it in the music business."

"Oh." Jane took her time setting the fork down on the plate. "Yeah. I did. I mean, LA is the place to be for the music business, right?"

"Is that what you're doing out there?" He'd googled her, obviously, but hadn't found a website, any social media, or evidence of upcoming shows. But that didn't mean Jane didn't have those things. Maybe she played with a band or used a stage name.

"Um." Jane reached for her napkin and absently folded it into smaller and smaller squares. "I'm still working on it, I guess you could say." She pressed her lips together as if she were choosing her words carefully. "LA is a hard place. I don't think I had any idea when I left here." Her cheeks flushed pink.

Did she regret going and leaving everyone behind?

He shoved that thought away. Maybe she just felt uncomfortable talking about it because she hadn't made it in the music industry yet. Could that be why she hadn't reached out for all these years? She'd taken off to follow her dream, it hadn't materialized yet, and she thought people in this town would judge her?

Some would. He remembered Mrs. Swanson's criticisms in Ford's General Store yesterday. But those were the grumpy old timers and people like her dad. Jane couldn't think that Nik would be one of those people, or any of their friends, like Hannah and Ali.

"Jane," he said. "I think you were brave to leave this town and go for it in LA."

She looked up sharply. "You do?"

He settled back in his chair, feigning a nonchalance he absolutely did not feel. "I mean, I admit I don't completely understand why you decided not to go to Cornell." *Or why you didn't ever reach out*, he thought to himself but sensed he shouldn't say. "But if LA was what you wanted, it took a lot of guts to go out there and make it on your own."

Something about that had her swallowing hard. Nik hated every minute that he didn't know what was putting that sadness in her eyes. That she didn't trust him enough to share her real life. "I just want to know one thing," he continued.

Jane nodded.

"Are you happy?"

She blinked rapidly, staring down at the napkin she was now squeezing the life out of. Who was he kidding? Nik was the complete opposite of nonchalant. He leaned forward, reaching across the table to still her nervous hands. As soon as their skin brushed, an electric current shot up his arm.

Her gaze flew to his and something like longing... something like that *desire* he'd seen on her sidewalk today, mirroring his own emotions... crossed her face.

His chest filled with a warmth he hadn't felt in... *ten years*.

When his last girlfriend had broken up with him a couple of months ago, she'd accused him of being cold, detached. *I can't get close to you,* she'd told him with regret. Those words had lingered because his girlfriend in college had said a version of the same thing. Nik had never thought of himself as *cold.* He was still close with Hannah and Ali and had built new friendships with his coworkers at the hospital. His patients loved him.

But sitting here, a connection stretching between them that had survived a decade of time, three thousand miles of distance, and so many unanswered questions, he suddenly understood what his former girlfriends were talking about.

This.

He hadn't been able to give them *this.*

"Happy." Jane breathed out the word like a sigh, her eyes dropping to their hands intertwined in the middle of the table. "I guess you could say I'm still a work in progress."

Nik remained silent, giving her space to say more.

After a moment, she lifted her chin, jaw set in resolve and determination in her eyes. "But I'm a lot closer than I've been in a long time. Maybe coming back here has helped me realize that I *can* be brave."

Nik sensed his opening, but before he could speak, someone approached the table on his left. *Damn it.*

"Hi," the server said, holding up a notepad. "Can I get you another brownie? Or some coffee?"

Jane slid her hand out from under Nik's and sat back in her chair. "Yes, please." She gave the server an extra wide grin, almost as if to counteract the sadness that had been in her eyes moments ago. "Coffee and another brownie would be great."

Nik ordered a cup of coffee, and once the server headed back across the café, he turned back to Jane. "Tell me about being brave..."

But Jane cut him off with a wave. "Oh, it's nothing. I'm probably feeling a little nostalgic being back here after all this time. My life really isn't that exciting." She shrugged, all traces of the emotion on her face wiped clean, a smile that didn't quite reach her eyes in its place. "I want to hear about what you've been up to."

"Jane..." Nik growled in frustration over her deflection. And then he leaned forward and said the thing he'd promised himself at the beginning of this coffee date, or *whatever* it was they were doing here, that he wasn't going to say: "What happened to us? How did we end up like this? Especially after..."

That night.

"Nik." Jane looked away. "I don't know what you want to hear."

"How about the truth, for once?"

She stared at the remains of the brownie on the plate. "The truth might..." She cringed like she hated to break it to him. "... disappoint you."

His eyes roamed over her, heart slowly sinking. Was it possible the night at the overlook hadn't meant as much to her as it had meant to him?

"Look." She sighed. "It was a long time ago. Can't we just catch up like old friends? Do we have to make this a whole thing?" Her voice was cold, distant, a tone he'd never heard from her before.

Was it possible that *none* of their relationship had meant as much to her as it had to him? His mother had suggested it when he'd spent that first summer after Jane had left lying on the floor playing sad songs on repeat. *Jane is a girl with big dreams. Maybe she needs to spread her wings and not be held back by teenage infatuation.*

But he'd known better than that. He'd known *her.* Or, at least, he'd thought he had. He wasn't sure about anything anymore.

The server came to drop off their drinks, an interruption

Nik was now grateful for, because he was trying to catch his brain up to the present when it was still swirling around in the past. He focused on stirring cream into his coffee.

"So, you ended up coming back to Linden Falls after college and med school?" Jane asked, cupping her hands around her mug.

Nik nodded slowly. *Something like that.*

"And you're a doctor now?" Jane prompted.

Nik took a sip of his coffee, wishing it were something stronger. "I'm in my third year of my residency at Linden Falls Hospital."

"Which department?"

"Emergency."

"Emergency?" she whispered, and he knew he wasn't imagining that tiny hitch in her voice.

Eighteen years ago, Nik's dad's heart had stopped when he was working at his job at an insurance agency over in Westbrook. His colleagues had called 911, but nobody in the small office of insurance salesmen had known enough about cardiac arrest to administer CPR. By the time the ambulance had arrived from across town, his dad was already gone.

It had been the worst day of Nik's life. He'd been ten at the time, and for a dark couple of months, he'd wished he could die, too. Jane had come over every day after school to sit with him on the porch swing until his mom got home from her new job cleaning houses. They didn't always talk—sometimes they'd listened to music, sometimes they'd just sat in silence—but she'd been there, through it all.

When he'd decided that he wanted to become an ER doctor so he could keep what had happened to his dad from happening to someone else, Jane had helped him research what he needed to do to get into medical school. And she'd been the one to grab the flyer about the EMT training from the police station bulletin board and encourage him to sign up.

She knew better than anyone how much this meant to him.

"You really did it." Her blue eyes shone with happiness. "Nik, that's amazing."

"Thanks," Nik said, with a sudden urge to tell her more. "This past year, I started a community outreach program that goes out to local schools and offices to teach them CPR." He felt his lips curve upward. "I just found out this week that I landed a grant to provide free AEDs—defibrillators—for groups that agree to do the training."

"You're going to save so many lives."

"I hope so."

Jane's smile slowly faded, overtaken by an emotion he couldn't quite read. "I'm so glad it all worked out exactly the way it was supposed to," she said, breathlessly. "The scholarship to Cornell. And now this."

Nik hesitated before answering. It was true that his volunteer work as an EMT back in high school had landed him a college scholarship from the Linden Falls town council. A full ride to Cornell. But it hadn't exactly worked out the way it was supposed to.

In fact, it spectacularly fell apart.

But if Jane wanted to keep secrets, then he could keep them, too. "Yep. It all worked out exactly the way it was supposed to," he repeated.

"Nik, I'm so proud of you." She bit her lip. "Maybe I have no right to say that, but..." She took a shaky breath. "I really am."

And damn it, here she was, stirring up all these emotions again. "I really love it," he confided in a low voice. "It feels like I'm doing exactly what I'm meant to, you know?" Maybe his life hadn't followed the flight path he'd mapped out a decade ago, but at least *this* part had landed in the right place.

To his surprise, Jane's eyes filled.

Nik cocked his head. "Hey," he murmured. "I didn't mean to make you cry."

Jane swiped at the moisture in her eyes. "I'm not crying."

"You definitely are. What's going on?"

She shook her head. "I'm just... I'm so relieved you're happy."

Nik blinked. *Relieved?* Had she worried that he wouldn't be happy? He hated not knowing what she was thinking—that, somehow, he'd lost the right and had no idea why. He hated this distance between them.

A tear trickled from her eye and, before he could stop himself, Nik reached out to gently wipe it from Jane's cheek. He half expected her to pull away, but instead, she leaned into him, turning her face into his palm.

And that's when he knew. Just a few minutes ago, when she'd implied that maybe he'd gotten their relationship wrong all those years ago... that he'd gotten that night at the overlook wrong...

She was lying.

The connection between them had always been as natural as pulling air into their lungs. That hadn't changed, and it wasn't in the past. Since she'd taken off without a word, it was like they'd been holding their breath. And he realized, as their eyes connected, that for the first time in a decade, they could finally exhale.

FOURTEEN

The minute Nik's thumb gently brushed her cheek, Jane knew that she should back away. She should get up and leave this café and never look back. Nothing good could come of his hand against her skin, the heat in his eyes, the gravitational force between them.

Instead she leaned in. And *Oh God*, it felt right—more than just about anything in her life had for so long. But then—

"Jane McCaffrey, is that you?"

Jane tore her eyes away from Nik's to find a tall, middle-aged man in a plaid apron framed in the doorway leading to the café's kitchen.

"Pete!" she said, pushing back her chair. Jane hadn't seen the café owner in a decade, but he was one of the people in the town she'd never forgotten. When she was a sophomore in high school, Pete had moved to Linden Falls for a quieter life after decades of working as a musician in New York. He'd opened the Grassroots Café in order to offer the town both good coffee and live music. Pete had heard Jane sing and play her guitar in church and had invited her to headline his weekly Saturday evening showcase.

Dad had agreed, as long as Jane got her homework done first. He'd enjoyed Jane's talent... when it suited him; when people stopped him on the street to congratulate him on his daughter's solo in the church choir or the folk song she'd performed at the café.

I played a little guitar in my day, too, had been Dad's standard reply. *That must be where she gets it from. Could have made something out of it but I decided to go to the police academy instead.*

Between Linden Falls, the neighboring towns, and the tourists who came in the summer to visit the wineries along the lake, the Grassroots Café had attracted a decent crowd. With Pete's mentorship, and encouragement from Nik, Hannah, and Ali, Jane had learned how to write songs and perform them up on that rickety stage with the battered guitar Nik had gifted her.

"I heard you moved out to LA to make it big," Pete said, giving Jane's shoulder a nudge.

"I haven't quite made it big, but I do live in LA."

"And you're still playing music?"

Jane lifted a shoulder. "Now and then." Hopefully, it came off as modest and not evasive. How could she tell this man who'd believed in her so completely that she hadn't picked up a guitar in a decade? That she'd left here to follow her dreams—or at least that's what so many people assumed—and had so little to show for it?

Pete slapped Nik on the back. "It's nice to have our girl back, isn't it?" And then to Jane, "We've had a lot of musicians come through here, but it's never been quite the same since you left."

Jane's heart squeezed. "Well, I haven't played anywhere this welcoming." She hadn't played *anywhere*, but even if she were headlining Madison Square Garden on the regular, Jane was confident that her statement would still be true.

"How long are you staying?"

"Just a week or so."

"Any chance I could book you for next Saturday?"

Jane felt her cheeks flush. "Oh, I really..." *Really couldn't.* She hadn't picked up a guitar in years. Hadn't sung a song that wasn't a lullaby to Scarlett. Jane was so far out of practice she wasn't sure she even remembered how to hold a note. "I'm just here to help my mom, you know, since my dad..."

Pete's smile faded. "I'm sorry for your loss."

"It's been hard on my mom, so I really don't know if I can get away."

"Well." Pete lifted the straps of his apron and pulled it over his head. "What about right now? Any chance I could get you to go up and sing something for us?" He waved a hand at the stage where a young man was setting up a stool and microphone. On a stand rested an acoustic guitar.

The noise from the patrons buzzed around her, and Jane realized the café had filled up considerably since she'd arrived a half hour ago. Tonight was the Saturday music showcase.

"I—" To Jane's relief, the phone behind the counter rang, granting her a temporary reprieve as Pete excused himself to answer it.

Nik shoved his hands into his pockets. "Are you going to play something?"

Jane eyed the guitar on stage. How could she possibly get up there after all this time? Would she even remember the basic chords? But how could she say no and let Pete down? And there was Nik. He thought she'd been working as a musician all this time. Surely someone who'd been playing bars and clubs for a decade in LA wouldn't be afraid to sing a folk song in their hometown coffee shop.

And then there was this yearning building inside her. Some of the happiest times of her life were here in this café, up on that stage. Getting lost in the notes, the lyrics, the energy from the audience. When else had she ever felt more like herself?

Jane wanted that feeling back, just for one moment. One song.

"I don't know." Jane twisted the sleeve of her shirt.

Nik cocked his head, understanding dawning on his face. "Are you nervous?"

"Of course not." Jane bit her lip. "Except... it's just... this town... you know?" She recognized at least a couple of faces in the crowd. Nobody she'd known very well, but well enough that they'd probably gossip about her later. "It's been a long time since I played here."

Nik paused for a moment, as if he were thinking that over. And then he leaned in, so close that his facial hair scraped her cheek and his breath whispered against her neck. "Jane," he murmured, and she shivered involuntarily. "They're going to love you."

A flush came over her, both at hearing the word *love* coming from Nik's mouth—so close that if she turned her head a little to the left, her lips would brush his—but also from the familiarity of the words. A promise from a lifetime ago. Nik had said those words the first time she'd ever played here, when her nerves had left her shaking so hard she could barely grip her guitar.

They're going to love you.

Like I do.

He hadn't said that second part out loud back then, but she'd felt it. On the long walk up to the stage. As she'd settled the guitar on her lap. When she'd taken a deep breath and sung her first note. He'd been there with her, just like always.

And he was telling her he'd be there with her now.

She glanced over at Pete, who motioned toward the mic in an *Are you ready?* gesture. Jane nodded. Pete finished his call and headed across the café to climb onto the stage.

"Ladies and gentlemen," Pete said into the microphone. "We have an extra special guest with us today. One of Linden Falls' own." He gave Jane a wink. "Jane McCaffrey."

Dozens of faces turned in her direction. A murmur went through the crowd. *Chief McCaffrey's long-lost daughter is back,* Jane imagined people saying.

Before she could change her mind, Jane straightened her shoulders and followed Pete onstage. She reached for the guitar, the fingers of her left hand wrapping around the neck as she slowly lifted it. The weight of it felt awkward, heavier than she'd expected, and it banged against the stool as she turned to sit down, vibrating through her solar plexus.

Jane cringed. "Sorry," she said into the microphone, and it came out too loud in the quiet room.

She sank down on the stool and gave the guitar a tentative strum. The G string was a little sharp. Even after all these years, she could still hear that slight bend in the note and, instinctively, she reached up to give the tuning peg a quick turn. One more strum told her the guitar was perfectly in tune now.

Maybe she could do this. It was like riding a bike, right? And then she made the mistake of looking up. Somehow, even more people had settled into the seats since she'd crossed the café and climbed up on stage, and they were all staring directly at her.

What the hell was I thinking?

She was supposed to be lying low. Her gaze skated across the café, past the tables peppered with coffee cups, the people shifting in their seats. Was it too late to get out of this?

And then her eyes landed on Nik. He gave her a slight nod, more of a hitch of his chin, really. A tiny gesture that meant everything.

They're going to love you.

Jane formed her left hand in the shape of a chord, using her right to strum down, up, down again. Her fingers stung a bit since she'd long ago lost the calluses that protected her skin from the texture of the strings. But after a few moments, she settled into the rhythm of the song. She didn't have the courage to sing one of her own—that was asking too much today—so she chose a song by one of her high school idols, an indie-folk singer who'd just been starting out a decade ago, but who had gone on to win a handful of Grammys in the years since.

Jane still remembered all the words, about a girl determined to live life on her own terms. Back then, she'd loved those angsty songs questioning everything and had internalized them in the way of a teenager with a lifetime of possibilities ahead of her.

Jane opened her mouth, and the sound that came from her throat was tentative, a tiny bit hoarse, but right on key. She closed her eyes, breathing into her diaphragm, singing the next line with more confidence, more clarity. At the chorus, she tried a slight deviation from the melody, ended the next line in a run. She opened her eyes now, looking out at the audience as she delivered the next verse. For the first time in years, the meaning of those lyrics came back to her, and she felt them deep in her soul.

Maybe I still have a lifetime of possibilities ahead of me, Jane thought, as the words rang out across the room. *If I'm brave enough to reach out and grab them.* And with that came a realization that something she'd thought was lost forever was still buried deep inside her, waiting to be found.

Jane came to the end of the song almost before she realized it, the last note of her voice carrying across the café, fading a beat after the guitar strings stopped their low vibration. For a brief moment, the room was silent—the people of Linden Falls, of her past, all staring up at her. And someone let out a whoop, another cheered, and the applause rang out, hands clapping at every table, a couple more high-pitched *wooohoos* cutting above the din.

"Thank you," Jane murmured, dazed, as she stood up and set the guitar back on its stand. "Thank you so much for having me."

She made her way back to the table where Nik sat with a proud grin on his face. He leaned in to be heard over Pete's announcement about the next singer. "You were amazing."

"I feel kind of amazing." Jane felt her lips curve into a smile. "Thank you for encouraging me to get up there. It's nice to be back on that stage."

And then her phone buzzed, and all the wind was knocked out of her. It was a text from Matteo. Jane flipped her phone face down on the table before Nik could see the name. "I really should go," she murmured. "My mom..."

Nik nodded. "I'll walk you out."

Jane quickly fired off a reply to Matteo while Nik pulled some bills from his pocket and dropped them on the table.

A cold wind hit them as Nik pulled open the door and they stepped out onto the sidewalk.

"Thanks for inviting me," Jane said, not really sure how to walk away now that they were standing here. Not wanting to walk away.

"Hey," Nik said, shoving his hands into the pockets of his coat. "I know it's silly, but I was wondering... Whatever happened to that old guitar I gave you?"

Jane froze. How could she tell him the truth? He'd saved for months to buy her that guitar from a pawn shop in Westbrook. It wasn't pretty—the body scratched, the resin worn off in patches—but he'd doodled over all the blemishes with flowers and vines and her favorite song lyrics. And the sound it emitted was deep and rich and textured, like it had wisdom and experience buried deep in the wood.

"I—" Jane stuttered. "Of course I still have it," she blurted out.

Nik's eyebrows rose. "Oh," he said. "That's great." But a

darkness crossed over his features, so fleeting that she wondered if she'd imagined it. And then it was gone, replaced by a smile that felt a little more detached than it had a minute ago. "Well, it was good to see you, Jane."

"You too, Nik." And then she turned and walked away.

FIFTEEN

TEN YEARS AGO

"Goddamn it, Kelly."

Jane flinched as Matteo's voice carried across the club. She looked up to find Kelly, a barback not much older than she was, crouching over a broken bottle that had slipped out of her hands and shattered on the floor. Kelly bowed her head, slowly picking up the pieces and dropping them into a dustpan.

Matteo stood over her, his arms crossed, face red. "What were you thinking? That shit is expensive." He let out another string of expletives. When he noticed Yolanda watching from behind the counter, he narrowed his eyes. "What are you looking at?"

Jane turned away and went back to wiping the tables before Matteo could notice her watching, too. She was slowly beginning to realize that Matteo's flash of anger on the day she'd met him a couple months earlier hadn't been a figment of her imagination. His temper tended to flare at the nightclub staff when they screwed something up, especially if that screw-up cost the bar money. Usually, it ignited quickly and then burned out before much harm was done. And once he'd calmed down, he'd always apologize. Well, except for that time he'd discovered one of the staff was stealing from him.

Jane shuddered at the memory of the blood spurting from the bartender's nose, but then she shoved it out of her head. It wasn't like Matteo had ever been violent or turned his temper on her. He'd snapped at her a few times upstairs in the apartment, but those were just normal arguments that all couples had. And he'd certainly never gotten physical. If she'd seen even a hint of violence from him, she would have been long gone.

It had been just a few months since Jane had started working at the club, and she and Matteo had been together for as long. She'd pretty much gone upstairs with him on that first night and then never left. When she took the job, she'd hoped to be able to move into her own place eventually, but it turned out that VIPs didn't always tip as well as that first table. Plus, she hadn't known then that she'd be expected to give a cut to the bar staff.

Matteo seemed happy to have her stay with him, and it was better than going back to that motel. Anything was better than that horrible motel. Matteo was nice to her—except for those arguments. But that was normal couple stuff. His place was comfortable, and she even enjoyed sleeping with him, though she would have preferred it if he used a condom. But he always pulled out, and he'd told her to get on the pill. She planned to, just as soon as she had a day off and could figure out the complicated bus system to get to the nearest Planned Parenthood.

Jane didn't fool herself into thinking she loved Matteo, or that she'd ever love him. But she felt comfortable with Matteo and lucky about how things had turned out. She shuddered every time she remembered pulling food from the trash can, every time she walked past the people sleeping in bus shelters. It could have gone so badly for her.

Jane was proud of how she was making it on her own, and grateful to be as far away from her dad as possible. She had her guitar—the gift from Matteo—and had been practicing as much as possible. Matteo had promised that, soon, he'd talk to his friends about having her play in their bars, and she wanted to have a set list ready.

So, if her life wasn't perfect, it was good enough.

Sometimes when she couldn't sleep at night, memories of Nik would drift in, and her heart would ache for him. When Matteo was in one of his moods, she'd fantasize that maybe she and Nik could be together again, someday. But he'd be in college for a long time, and four years felt like an eternity. Who knew what could happen? Maybe he'd meet someone. Or maybe he wouldn't want her anymore. So, lately when those thoughts of Nik drifted in, Jane had started digging her nails into her palm to stop them. That part of her life was over, at least for the foreseeable future, and the pain in her hand was nothing compared to the pain of knowing what could have been.

Jane pushed those thoughts out of her head now, focusing on a sticky spot on one of the bar tables. She sprayed an extra squirt of cleaner and scrubbed at it with a rag. The astringent lemon scent wafted up, and suddenly Jane's stomach lurched. She dropped the bottle on the table and made a run for the bathroom.

Jane had just finished emptying the contents of her stomach in one of the ladies' room toilets when she heard a voice on the other side of the stall: "Uh-oh. That doesn't sound good."

She exited the small space to find Yolanda leaning against the sink with her arms crossed over her chest.

"I think I must have caught a stomach bug a couple of weeks ago." Jane grabbed a handful of paper towels to wipe her mouth. "I just can't seem to kick it."

Yolanda's painted-on eyebrow rose. "Sorry, honey. But I don't think that's a stomach bug you've got in there."

Jane leaned over the sink to splash water on her face. "You think I have food poisoning?"

Yolanda snorted. "If that's what you want to call it."

"What do you mean?" Jane stood and reached for another paper towel.

Yolanda ripped it off and handed it to her. "You've been looking green for weeks. I have two babies and I've seen this a dozen times with my girlfriends."

Jane pressed the paper towel to her face, and then froze as Yolanda's words sank in. "Wait. Are you saying—"

"You're pregnant."

"No." Jane finished drying her face. "No, I can't be."

"You're sure about that?" Yolanda cocked her head. "Are you on the pill?"

"No." Jane turned away from Yolanda under the pretense of tossing the paper towel in the trash, but really it was so the other woman wouldn't see her reeling. "I was going to make an appointment."

Yolanda huffed. "Well, does he use condoms?"

Jane's nausea came back in a wave. "He pulls out," she blurted. *I can't be pregnant. Can I?*

Yolanda's face screwed up in an expression that said: *Men. What do you expect?* "Does he pull out every time?"

"Yes." And then after a pause, "I think so." Oh God. Jane wasn't sure. The truth was, she didn't have enough experience to know. Things down there were always a little... wet... after they had sex. But sex involved lots of fluids, didn't it? There was her own lubrication, and Matteo's, and the mess on the sheets and her thighs after he pulled out. Even when Nik had used a condom, things had still felt... damp down there. And since Nik had been her first time, she'd bled after. So how was she supposed to know what was normal?

Yolanda was looking at her sideways. "Oh, honey."

"Oh God." Jane slumped against the wall. "Do you really think I'm pregnant?"

"Only one way to find out."

Jane begged off work that evening, claiming a headache that was easy to fake when she was already pale and nauseous. Matteo wasn't happy about it, but Yolanda offered to cover for her, so he waved Jane off with a grunt.

Under the pretense of buying some Tylenol, Jane ran to the pharmacy three blocks away and then quietly let herself back into the building. She tiptoed up the back stairs to the apartment and headed straight for the bathroom, carefully locking the door behind her.

It took her a couple of minutes to read the directions and examine the accompanying diagrams. She didn't want to do it wrong and have to go and buy another one. Or worse, get a false response. But finally, Jane felt confident enough to uncap the plastic stick and pee on it. She set it on the counter and sank down on the edge of the bathtub to wait. Three minutes.

The longest three minutes of her life.

Jane sat frozen on the hard tile tub surround but her mind whirled. When had she gotten her last period?

I have no idea.

Those stressful, terrible first weeks after she'd left home came back to her in a wave. The pain of her injuries worsened by long hours in the car across Kansas and Colorado and Utah. And then she'd arrived in Los Angeles, and Kait had dropped her off at the motel, pausing before she drove off to ask if Jane was sure she wanted to stay here.

"Yes," Jane had insisted. But she hadn't been sure, not at all. And for those first weeks, her body had hummed with constant stress from the trauma of what had happened to her at home and the fear of how she'd survive. From literally counting her pennies and subsisting on ramen and other people's discarded food. She'd probably lost five pounds that first week. Ten by the time she'd been gone from Linden Falls for a month. Jane wouldn't have noticed when her periods stopped coming. That had been the least of her problems.

If she was pregnant, was it possible it had happened before she left Linden Falls? For one brief, unhinged moment, Jane's chest filled with hope. If she was pregnant before she'd arrived in LA, she'd have to tell Nik, right? He'd have a right to know. Just the possibility of dialing his number, of hearing his voice, comforted her. But then Jane shook her head. Nik had used a condom. And Yolanda had seemed skeptical of Matteo's pull-out method. Yolanda knew way more about this than Jane did.

The clock ticked down, but just as Jane was about to check the pregnancy test, there was a rap at the door.

"Jane?" It was Matteo. He knocked harder.

"Um." Jane grabbed the pregnancy test box and stuffed it in the garbage. "One second."

"What are you doing in there?"

"Nothing!" It came out sounding nervous. Too loud.

"Jane, open the door," Matteo barked.

"One second," she repeated. Jane wasn't sure why her instincts were telling her to hide this from Matteo. If she was pregnant, it was his baby, too, right? But maybe she just needed to have a chance to process it first. To figure out what she wanted to do.

But Matteo was rattling the doorknob now. "Do you have another man in there?"

"What?" Jane gasped. "No! Of course not."

He pounded harder. "Open the door, Jane. *Right. Now.*"

She cringed at that familiar anger in his voice. It had the same intensity as that moment downstairs when he was yelling at Kelly. Suddenly afraid, Jane twisted the lock and flung the door open, hurrying out into the bedroom.

Matteo glared down at her. "Don't think I fell for your sick routine. It was obvious you were faking to get out of work. Were you trying to sneak around behind my back?"

"Matteo—*no.*" But she was a terrible actress. Because she *had* been sneaking around behind his back—just not in the way he thought.

"Then what's in the bathroom?" He grabbed her and pushed her aside.

Jane stumbled, her shoulder knocking into the wall. Matteo stormed into the bathroom and flipped back the shower curtain as if she'd hidden a man in there. When he came up empty, he spun around, focusing on the counter by the sink. "What the hell is this?" He snatched up the pregnancy test and stared at the little plastic window.

Jane found herself praying like she'd never prayed before. *Please be negative. Please.*

Matteo flung the test in the sink and swung around to face her. "You're pregnant? You're fucking pregnant?"

Oh God. Oh no.

"How could you let this happen?"

Jane's mouth dropped open. "How could *you* let it happen? You were supposed to pull out!"

Matteo's face turned the same color red as it did when he caught the bartender stealing from him. "I told you to go on the pill."

Jane took a few cautious steps toward him. "I was planning on it, but I didn't have a chance yet."

"I'm trying to run a business, and you're my employee. Who the hell is going to take care of a baby?"

Jane closed her eyes as the reality of it sank in. Diapers and formula and crying at all hours of the night. Her friends were starting their freshman year of college, going to classes and parties and living the lives of normal eighteen-year-olds. And she was...

Pregnant.

How had she ended up here? And what was she going to do now?

"I—I don't know."

Matteo shook his head in disgust, pushing past her out into the living room. Jane trailed after him, pausing in the bedroom doorway to watch helplessly as he headed for the front door. A sudden terror seized her. What if he was so mad that he broke up with her and kicked her out? What would she do if she were back out on the street, pregnant and broke? "Matteo, wait. Let's talk about this."

He stopped walking and spun around in front of her guitar on its stand. But instead of calmly crossing the room to Jane, as she expected, Matteo reared back on one leg. Jane gasped as his foot flew forward with a terrifying amount of force, crashing into the center of the guitar. With a terrible, dissonant clang, the wood splintered, the neck cracked, and the instrument flew off the stand and into the wall.

And then he turned and stormed out of the apartment, slamming the door behind him.

Jane stared at the guitar pieces scattered across the floor, her heart cracking like the splintered wood. Unable to look any more, she turned back toward the bedroom, spotting her phone on the bed where she'd flung it when she'd arrived home with the pregnancy test.

She sank down on the mattress. Her first thought was Nik.

She'd ditched her phone with his number when she'd left Linden Falls, but Jane would never forget those ten digits. What could she say to him, though? *I'm a server in Los Angeles, pregnant with another man's baby. And I'm scared.*

Nik would probably come and get her. But could she ask him to?

Instead of dialing his number, she switched over to her internet browser and googled his name. He was probably in Ithaca, starting classes at Cornell right about now. The first link to pop up in her search was an article about his scholarship. The *Linden Falls Gazette* had featured Nik in a story last spring. They wrote about his volunteer work with the local paramedics, how he was the youngest person in the unit's history to earn his EMT certification, how he'd been chosen over all the other applicants for the competitive scholarship. The Linden Falls town council would pay his tuition, room, and board every semester of his undergraduate degree, as long as he kept his grades above a B average. Nik was well on his way to becoming the doctor he'd always dreamed of.

The questions hung in the air. *Was* she pregnant with another man's baby? Three months had gone by since Jane had been with Nik, and then she'd started sleeping with Matteo a couple of weeks later. Her nausea had started up maybe a month or two after that. How did the math work? Could this be *Nik's* baby?

Jane quickly dismissed the idea as longing rather than reality.

This was Matteo's baby, and there was no way she could call Nik. If her staying in Linden Falls would have ruined his life before, what would showing up pregnant do now? She'd gotten herself into this and she needed a plan.

Jane typed in the search bar again. How much does an abortion cost?

The first link to come up was the website for Planned Parenthood. She scanned the text. The average cost of a first trimester in-clinic abortion at Planned Parenthood is about $600. The average ranges from about $715 earlier in the second trimester to $1,500–2,000 later in the second trimester. Your abortion may be free or low-cost with health insurance.

Jane didn't have any idea what trimester she was in, and she didn't have that kind of money. Maybe she was still on Dad's insurance—she had no idea—but she definitely couldn't use it to get an abortion.

So, Jane did the only thing she could think of. She picked up the phone and dialed the one number she knew by heart other than Nik's. Mom picked up on the second ring.

"Mom?" Jane hadn't heard her mother's voice in months. Despite everything that had happened, it comforted her in a way that nothing else could. "Mommy, it's me."

"Jane. Oh, my goodness!" Mom exclaimed, but then she cleared her throat and dropped her voice. "Jane, where are you?" she whispered.

"Why are you whispering? Is Dad home?" Jane checked the time. It was early evening on the East Coast.

"No, but he'll be home any minute."

Jane could picture Mom clutching the phone to her ear, pulling aside the curtain to peer out the front window, braced for Dad's patrol car to come down the street.

"We were so worried about you."

"I left a note."

Mom's voice shook. "It didn't say anything about where you were going. Where *are* you?"

Jane hesitated. "California," she finally said. It was a big state, and she didn't think they'd be able to trace her to LA. She didn't rent an apartment, didn't have any bills in her name. Matteo paid her under the table and had given her the phone. "Mom." Jane scrubbed her sweaty palms on her pant leg. "Things aren't great here and I could use some help. Is there any way you could send me some money? I don't need a lot. Just a thousand. Maybe two." It sounded like a fortune to Jane, but it couldn't be that much for her mom. After all, her parents had an entire college fund they'd saved and wouldn't be using.

Jane listened to the silence on the other end of the phone. Finally, Mom cleared her throat. "Your father would notice if I took money out of the account."

"I know, but…"

"He's very angry you left."

"Mom, please." Jane felt tears welling in her eyes. "I need help."

"Well, Jane, you could come home."

"I can't come home. You *know* I can't." She grabbed a pillow and held it to her chest. "What if you left him and moved somewhere with me? We could go to Canada." Maybe she could get a bus out of Los Angeles and start fresh somewhere else. Vancouver, or if that was too expensive, maybe a small town in British Columbia. Mom could meet her there, far away from Linden Falls and Dad's control. If Jane went through with having the baby, Mom could take care of it while Jane got a job to support them.

"I don't see how I could possibly leave..."

"You could get a lawyer, right? You'd have a right to some of the money? Savings, or alimony, maybe. And I could work. I'm a really good server—"

"Dad would never let me go," Mom interrupted. "And no lawyer in this town would go up against Chief McCaffrey."

"He couldn't hurt you in Canada."

"It would never work."

"It would never work?" Jane repeated. "Or you're not willing to make it work?"

"Jane, you don't understand..." Mom began, but Jane hung up before she could hear any more of Mom's excuses.

Jane woke, disoriented, and in the dark. She sensed movement by her knee and sat up abruptly. The streetlamp shone in through the crack in the blinds, slanting across Matteo's face. Jane threw off the blanket and scrambled to the other side of the bed.

"Jane, wait." Matteo held out a palm. "Please."

She stopped, but still kept her distance.

Matteo hung his head. "I am so sorry, Jane. You have to know that."

She eyed him warily. "Do I?"

"There's no excuse for what I did." He took a deep breath and then blew it out slowly. "I thought you'd gone on the pill, and I just wasn't expecting this." A hint of an incredulous smile played on his lips. "I can't believe I'm going to be a father."

"You don't want this baby. You made that very clear."

"I do, Jane. I was in shock at first. I think that's why I"—he coughed—"reacted like I did. But when I left here, I realized I want it so badly."

Gingerly, Jane pressed her hand to the tender spot on her shoulder where he'd shoved her into the wall. "You know that's no excuse, right? There's *never* an excuse for what you did."

"I know. I'm sorry. You'll never know how sorry I am."

Jane wished the room was brighter so she could get a better look at his expression. But part of her didn't want to switch the lamp on. Didn't want to face her life in the harsh light.

Matteo got up and walked around the bed to where Jane sat. She slid back an inch. "I've been thinking about it all evening," he said. "I can hire another server at the club. You won't need to work; I'll take care of you and the baby."

Jane's first instinct was to shake her head. If she gave up her job, she'd be entirely dependent on Matteo, and she couldn't let that happen. But then she hesitated. If she said no, he could fire her and toss her back out on the street. Jane would be worse off than she was the first time around. She'd be homeless and pregnant. Jane clutched her abdomen. How had she let this happen?

Matteo reached out and took her hand. "Think of it, Jane. Neither of us has any family. But the three of us will be that for each other. A real family."

Matteo had only told her a little about his upbringing. His father was never in the picture, and he'd been close with his mother, but she'd passed away a few years ago. Jane had been vague about her own home life. Matteo knew she came from Linden Falls—he still liked to call it *East Bumfuck*—but she'd told him very little about her family. Only that they were estranged, and Jane wasn't in contact with them.

"You don't push someone you care about. You don't *break things*," she said accusingly.

Matteo leaned in, meeting her eyes, and Jane was stunned to see that they were red and rimmed with tears. "You're right." He slid closer, and in her shock, she let him. "I am so sorry," he repeated. "It will never, ever happen again."

"How can I believe you?" She could still feel the vibration of the broken guitar as his foot connected with it. Could still hear the wood splintering. Jane had been here before, and she'd be crazy to stay with Matteo. Wouldn't she?

"You have to let me make it up to you. You have to let me try." He reached across the bed to pick up a shopping bag he'd set on the side table. It was from the 24-hour pharmacy, the same one where she'd bought the pregnancy test just a few hours ago. How did it feel like days already?

"I got you some things." Matteo reached into the bag and pulled out a container of pills. He held it out to her so she could read the label. *Prenatal vitamins.* Next came a stuffed elephant. And then a handful of chocolate bars. "In case you have cravings." He gave her a crooked smile, and despite every part of her that knew better, Jane felt herself wavering.

Matteo cocked his head. "What do you say? Can we be a family?"

A family.

The sound of Mom's voice came back to Jane, telling her she couldn't help. She wasn't *willing* to help. Jane's family really was gone, and there was no going back.

"I'm going to be the best father to this kid you've ever seen." Matteo swiped at a tear on his cheek. "I can be a better man if you let me prove it to you."

Dad had never, ever apologized to Mom the way Matteo was apologizing right now. He'd doubled down and blamed everyone except himself. But not only was Matteo sorry, he was *crying*. She felt her own eyes well up. What if Dad had shown some remorse, some desire to be a better person? How would her life have ended up differently?

"What do you say?" Matteo asked, taking her face gently in his hands, brushing the tears from her cheeks.

"Something like today can never happen again," Jane said.

"It won't." Matteo leaned in to kiss her, and she let him press his lips to hers, let him settle her back on the bed. "I promise."

SIXTEEN

PRESENT DAY

The next morning, Jane woke to a text from Matteo, another version of the one she'd gotten at the café when she was with Nik. One of the servers had quit, and he was pissed they'd left him in the lurch right before the holiday. His message was a long rant about how he didn't have anyone to fill in.

Jane stared at the phone in her shaking hands. *Please, God, just don't have him tell me to come home to work at the club.* Though she'd quit when she was pregnant with Scarlett, Jane occasionally filled in as a server when one of the regular staff was out sick. Matteo didn't like it. Didn't like the men watching her in her low-cut T-shirt. Didn't like Jane forming friendships with Yolanda and the other bartenders. So, he'd rarely had her do it unless he was desperate.

Jane hoped he wasn't desperate.

She needed every minute she could steal before Matteo expected her home. It wasn't just the matter of Kait getting the car and paperwork together. Jane had hoped she'd have at least a few days to cross the border and get lost somewhere in the middle of Canada before Matteo noticed she was missing.

She typed a sympathetic message to Matteo and hit send, hoping that would appease him until he could find someone else to fill in. Sometimes that was all he needed: someone to complain to. Someone to take his frustrations out on.

Jane climbed out of bed with an enormous sense of relief that she wasn't there so he could take his frustrations out on her in person. With any luck, she never would be again.

Downstairs, she found Mom and Scarlett making pancakes again. After breakfast, they spent a quiet morning putting together a puzzle on the coffee table. It was a distraction from checking her phone for messages from Matteo, who'd texted twice more to complain about the server situation, but so far hadn't asked her to come home. Or Kait, who Jane knew wouldn't reach out for at least a few more days.

When Scarlett switched over to playing with her Barbie Legos that afternoon, Jane headed upstairs to take a shower. As she made her way down the hall toward the bathroom, she paused once again outside her old bedroom door.

If they couldn't take a Barbie Lego set with them, she definitely didn't have room for a guitar. So, what did it matter if it was in there or not? Her hand grasped the cold metal of the doorknob, remembering how that same hand had curved around the neck of the instrument last night. She hadn't played in a decade, but somehow it had all come back to her as if it was exactly what she was meant to do. Even now, as the thought floated through her head, her fingers twitched as if they were moving effortlessly across an imaginary set of strings.

Jane shoved the door open and was immediately hit with an assault of memories from her past. The green striped duvet on the bed, the shelf lined with old yearbooks, the posters of Lana Del Rey, Tegan and Sara, and the other musicians she'd loved in high school. Above the desk across the room, the bulletin board still displayed her old concert tickets and, next to them, photos of her friends. Nik showed up in most of them, of course. But so did Ali and Hannah.

Jane moved closer to get a better look, and she couldn't help but smile.

The four of them had become friends in ninth grade when they'd ended up sitting at the same lunch table. There was sweet, ethereal Hannah in her flowered maxi dresses and Birkenstock sandals. Jane never thought she'd miss those weird hemp-heart cookies Hannah used to bring to school every day but, over the years, she'd found herself craving them. It was really Hannah's calm, caring energy she'd craved.

And then there was Ali in her black jeans, matching black hoodie, and combat boots. On the surface, Ali had come off a bit like her clothing choices—dark and unapproachable—but it was only because she'd been too wrapped up in her latest art project to get involved in the usual high school activities and gossip. But once you were in her circle, she'd help you bury a body if you needed her to.

On one side of the bulletin board, Jane had hung a necklace that Ali had made for her in a metalwork class at the local art center. A single, delicate thread of silver twisted and manipulated into a treble clef and a series of musical notes. When Jane had thrown her arms around her in thanks, Ali had quickly extracted herself from the embrace. "Okay, don't get all sentimental," she'd mumbled. But Ali hadn't been able to hide the way her cheeks had turned pink with pleasure.

Jane unhooked the necklace from the bulletin board and tucked it in her pocket. Scarlett would love it.

When Jane had left for Los Angeles, she'd left Nik behind, but she'd left Hannah and Ali, too. Did they hate her for it? Or had they moved on and forgotten all about her? Jane told herself it didn't matter. Just like Nik and everyone else in this town, she'd pushed them out of her thoughts long ago, and once she and Scarlett were gone for good, it wouldn't matter what anyone thought of her. But she couldn't help but feel a pull of longing as she looked at those old photos of her friends with their arms around her, faces open and accepting, smiles stretching wide.

She'd never had a group of friends like she'd had in high school. Or any other friends at all, really. Matteo didn't like her hanging out with other people or focusing her attention on anyone who wasn't him. And he really didn't like anyone else knowing their business. The few times she'd formed a tentative friendship with someone—another mom at the playground, the bartender at the nightclub—Matteo had found a way to sabotage it.

Jane pulled a photo off the bulletin board and slipped it into her pocket to take with her when she left. Maybe she would never see her old friends again, but maybe she could get back to who she'd been when she'd had them in her life.

Jane closed her eyes, remembering the feeling of being up on that stage yesterday. The vibration of the guitar against her heart, the thrill of the song coming from deep in her chest. On that long, hard road between her childhood in Linden Falls and her life in LA, she'd lost so many little bits and pieces of herself. She'd stopped playing, stopped singing, even when she could have continued. Maybe she couldn't have performed professionally—Matteo wouldn't have allowed it—but in the shower, in the park. Just for herself. For the love of it.

Jane did a quick spin in the center of the room, searching for the guitar, but its old stand was empty, and there was no sign of the instrument's case under the bed. Maybe Dad really had made good on his promise to take it out to the quarry and burn it. If she spent too much time thinking about it—that beautiful gift from Nik... *gone*—she'd sink down on the bed and cry.

But the guitar, as much as it meant to her, wasn't what really mattered.

They're going to love you.

Yes, she'd lost so many little bits and pieces of herself. But maybe last night was one small step toward finding them again. Toward believing again.

Later that evening, Jane set the dining table and they ate a quiet dinner, but she didn't mind. The silence felt comfortable instead of tense. After dinner, Scarlett headed into the living room to watch Christmas specials on TV, and Jane and Mom wiped down the kitchen counters. As Mom slid the plastic containers of leftovers into the fridge, Jane heard her mutter, "Oh, darn it."

Jane looked up. "What's the matter?"

Mom sighed. "I promised Scarlett we could make pancakes again tomorrow, but I forgot we're out of milk." She shook the mostly empty carton. "Would you go over to Spring Street? The minimart at the service station will be open this time of night. All I need is a quart until I can get to the grocery store tomorrow afternoon."

"Sure. Would you mind if I walked?" Spring Street wasn't far, and Jane had a lot to think about.

"Of course. Take your time. I can put Scarlett to bed." Mom sounded genuinely happy about that.

Jane's heart twisted at the joy on Mom's face, the enthusiasm in her voice. Her excitement at spending time with Scarlett reminded Jane again of those times when Dad was out of town, and it was just the two of them. When they could pretend that everything was normal and safe and happy. But that's all they'd been doing back then. Pretending. When it really came down to it, Mom had chosen Dad.

Jane sighed, trying to tamp down her bitterness. She knew from experience that it wasn't easy to make a different choice.

How many times had she packed up their clothes, only to shove them back in the drawer before Matteo came home? How many times had she dialed the number of the women's shelter, only to hang up on the first ring? When she'd finally let the call connect, they'd told her they didn't have any beds available.

Call back next week.

Jane pulled on her jacket and peeked into the living room. Jane had to admit that Mom had made the space cozy and comfortable for them. Scarlett was snuggled on the couch, Lego Barbie in hand as she stared up at Charlie Brown and his sad little Christmas tree on TV. The soft pink blanket tucked around her looked new, as did the throw pillows with cats on them. There were more flowers on the table in here, and a vanilla-scented candle burning.

But then Jane focused on Dad's recliner in the corner. She'd been avoiding it since she got home. Why was it still here? Jane would have expected Mom to replace it with something less awful. Surely, she could afford to buy a new recliner, one where the acrid scent of smoke didn't linger.

Jane shuddered, sidestepping the recliner and sitting on the couch next to Scarlett. "Hey, honey, I'm going to take a walk to get milk for breakfast. Are you okay if Grandma puts you to bed?"

Scarlett nodded. "Yeah, I'm fine." She turned back to the TV. Charlie Brown threw up his hands, lamenting the materialism of the holiday.

"Are you sure?" Jane prompted, sliding closer. After all, Mom was essentially a stranger in a big old drafty house, and Jane had rarely left Scarlett alone with another adult before now. Not even Matteo. "I don't want you to be scared."

Scarlett shook her head, her blond curls bouncing. "I'm not scared. Grandma is nice."

"And you're okay if she tucks you in?"

"Yeah." Scarlett snuggled deeper into the blanket. "Mommy?"

"What, sweetie?"

Scarlett's wide eyes peered at her. "You left the door to your old bedroom cracked earlier."

"I did?"

Scarlett nodded. "I peeked in. It's really pretty. I like your old room."

In the apartment above the club, Scarlett had slept in a little alcove that was essentially meant to be an office. Jane had tried to make it nice for her, but she could see how Scarlett would be enamored by a room like the one upstairs.

"Can I sleep there tonight?"

Jane's eyebrows rose. "You want to sleep in my old bedroom?"

"I put clean sheets on the bed yesterday," said a voice from the doorway. Jane turned in her seat to find Mom looking at her as hopefully as Scarlett. Jane thought back to when she'd poked around the room earlier. It had looked the same as when she'd left it, and she'd assumed that Mom had closed the door and pretended that it didn't exist. But now Jane realized that the blinds had been thrown open, the surfaces dusted, the old stuffed animals lined up on the bed. Mom had gotten the room ready for them.

Jane turned to look at her daughter. For *one* of them in particular.

It was no wonder Scarlett loved it. She didn't have all the painful associations with this house that Jane did. She didn't know all the terrible things that had happened here. In fact, for Scarlett, this house probably felt like a sanctuary from her own painful memories and terrible associations.

"Maybe this house needs a few new memories?" Mom said, almost as if she could read Jane's mind. "Good ones, for once."

Jane looked at Mom standing in the doorway. She'd spent

the entire day playing with Scarlett, and her happiness was evident by the way the lines around her mouth had softened and her eyes looked bright. Had it really meant that much to her?

Yesterday, Mom had said that Jane and Scarlett were her Christmas gifts. But a gift was something you got to keep. And Mom wasn't going to get to keep Scarlett. *Or me.* Jane's gaze swung from the hopeful look on Mom's face to the one on her daughter's. They'd be leaving and they wouldn't be coming back. But maybe they could at least have these couple of days.

"Sure. You can sleep there."

"Yay!" Scarlett yelled, throwing up her hands.

Jane couldn't help but smile. "I'll peek in at you later, okay?" She reached for her daughter and gave her an extra big squeeze. Then she pulled on her shoes and headed out into the snow.

Most of the neighbors had shoveled their walks earlier— Linden Falls was the kind of place where people took care of things like that—so the walk to town was uneventful. Jane traced the old route from memory, picking up her pace at the turn that would take her past Mrs. Andino's house and again at the intersection that led up the mountain to Sand Hill Lane, where Nik apparently lived now.

As usual, the minimart attached to Butler's Garage was open late. Jane made her way to the refrigerator, slowing her steps past the door that opened to the autobody shop. She peered through the glass, looking for signs of Kait, but that side of the building was dark. A teenager stood behind the counter, barely looking up as she rang up Jane's quart of milk and slid it into a paper bag.

Jane headed back out onto Spring Street. She had to hand it to Linden Falls, they really knew how to do it up Hallmark movie-style for the holidays with wreaths, sparkly lights dripping from trees, and life-sized mechanical Santas waving from store windows.

Jane sighed, turning to head back the way she'd come and smacked face-first into a now-familiar blue Patagonia jacket. She staggered backwards as Nik reached out a hand to steady her.

"Jane." His eyes widened. "I didn't expect to see you here." His lips tugged into a smile that managed to look both happy and a little bit wary. "Did Hannah invite you?"

"Hannah?" Jane blinked. "Invite me where?"

Nik glanced at the sign over her head. *The Harp and Fiddle.*

Jane's eyes widened. This was the only bar in town. Her old friends were probably getting together for a drink. She definitely hadn't meant to show up and crash their party. "Oh, no. Nobody invited me anywhere. I was just out for a walk. And milk." She waved the paper bag in his direction.

Nik cocked his head. "I'm meeting Hannah and Ali. Do you want to join us?"

"I—" Jane stared down at her sneakers, chewing on her bottom lip. Her chest squeezed as she remembered those old photos of Hannah and Ali on her bulletin board. God, she'd missed them almost as much as Nik. "How are they? Hannah and Ali?"

Nik smiled affectionately. "They're really good. Hannah still lives in Linden Falls. She married a great guy she met in college, and she's a teacher at the elementary school. She has a six-year-old daughter named Amelia."

"Really?" Despite herself, Jane felt her face spread into a genuine smile. With the way Hannah used to mother them, of course she'd become a teacher. And she had a *daughter.* Jane pictured a little girl with wild red hair and a flowered dress.

"And Ali lives in New York City. She's the curator of an art gallery."

Jane's smile grew.

"Her mom is still here in town, so she makes it back every month or so. The three of us still hang out a lot. Why don't you join us?" Nik said. "I think everyone would be happy to see you."

Jane remembered that warmth she'd felt at the sight of the photos of her old friends. She would love a few minutes with Hannah and Ali. But it had been years. She might be nostalgic about the past, but they probably barely remembered her.

Before Jane could make up her mind, she spotted a tall, gorgeous woman hurrying down the sidewalk toward them. "Nik-o-las!" the woman said, flinging herself into Nik's arms. Laughing, he wrapped one arm around the woman, and used the other hand to push her long, shiny hair out of his mouth. "Jeez, Al, it's only been a couple of months."

"I missed you, dumbass," the woman said, leaning back to look at him. And then she shifted so she was facing Jane. Her smile slowly faded, and her eyes widened. "*Jane?*"

"Hi, Ali," Jane said, taking in her old friend. Ali still wore black, but instead of jeans and a hoodie, she had on wide-legged pants and a cropped top under an expensive-looking wool coat. Jane was suddenly self-conscious in her sneakers and jeans.

Ali stepped back. "Well, this is... yeah. A surprise." She shot Nik a glance that Jane couldn't quite interpret. "I definitely didn't expect to see you here."

Nik shoved his hands in his pockets. "We just ran into each other, and I invited her to come for a drink."

Ali's gaze swept over her. "So, you're... back from LA?"

"Just for a few days."

At that moment, they were interrupted by another woman hurrying down the sidewalk, her red hair frizzing, coat flying. *Hannah.* She looked exactly the same as Jane remembered her.

"Thank the Lord I finally made it. I thought I'd never get Amelia to sleep." Hannah reached over to give Ali a squeeze, and then she made her way down the line to Nik. Finally, she shifted to his left. "And you must be..." Hannah stopped, blinking rapidly. "You must be... Jane! Oh, my God."

The next thing Jane knew, she was wrapped up in a tornado of red hair, vintage fabric, and lavender-scented lotion. And, just like that, she was back in Hannah's room, lying on her back in a pink canopy bed flipping through their horoscopes in the *Linden Falls Gazette*.

"Hi, Hannah," Jane murmured, over the lump in her throat.

"Jane, I honestly can't believe it. Nobody told me you were coming." Hannah stepped back to look her over.

"Nobody knew," Ali said, her voice flat.

"It was a... last-minute trip," Jane said.

Hannah's face softened. "I heard about your dad. I'm sorry for your mom. I'm sure she's happy to have you here."

Jane looked down at her hands. "That's why I came. To help her out a little."

Ali huffed. "I'm surprised you did, especially after all this time."

Hannah gasped. "Ali!"

Ali turned to face Jane. "We thought something terrible had happened to you when you left."

Jane blinked. "You did?"

"Of course we did. You were our best friend. We hung out every single day, and we had all those summer plans."

Nik had wanted them to go camping at Randall Park and on a road trip to New York City. And she and Hannah were talking about applying for summer jobs at the ice cream shop.

"And then you just..." Ali held her hands together and splayed out her fingers. "Poof. Gone without a word. We literally thought you'd been kidnapped, because there was no way you'd leave without telling us where you were going."

It hit Jane with a jolt. She had been such a mess when she'd left, in such a hurry to disappear, she hadn't considered how her friends must have felt. And then, like she had with Nik, Jane had avoided thinking about Hannah and Ali once she got to LA. It had been less painful that way.

"Your parents just kept telling us you were fine, but nobody would say anything else. Finally, Hannah's dad went over one day to talk to your mom. She told him you'd gone to California to make it in the music business."

Jane nodded. Because what else could she do?

"Taking off like that was really messed up. Why couldn't you have just told us you were going? Sent an email once in a while or something?"

Jane had no idea what to tell her. No idea what to tell any of them. Through the window of the bar, the people of Linden Falls were talking and laughing, home for the holidays, and visiting with friends and family. *What am I doing?* Jane didn't belong here. Not in this town, and not with these old friends, pretending that anything about her life was normal.

How could she explain where she'd gone for the past ten years or what she'd been through? With any luck, in a week, she and her daughter would be in a questionably stolen car on their way to disappear forever. If she stayed here and hung out with them, what would her friends think when she just took off again?

"I'm sorry. I really am." Jane twisted the top of the paper bag in her hands. "But I should get going."

Ali shrugged. "We wouldn't expect anything less."

Nik nudged Ali in the arm. "Jane, you don't have to go."

"Yeah," Hannah agreed. "Don't go yet. I didn't even have a chance to tell you about Amelia." She pulled out her phone and clicked the side button. On the lock screen, a photo of a little girl of about five or six popped up. She had her mother's blue eyes and hair the color of maple leaves in fall.

Jane's heart pitched. "She's gorgeous."

Hannah reached for Jane's hand. "And I didn't get to hear

anything about you. How's the music business? Are you married? Do you have kids?"

A cold wind kicked up, blowing right through Jane's too-thin coat. She tugged it tighter around her and backed away from her old friends, panic rising in her chest. "I really wish I could stay. But—" Her foot caught on a crack in the sidewalk and she stumbled. Nik's hand shot out to steady her, but she pulled her arm away. "It really was good to see you all."

And then she turned and took off down the sidewalk.

SEVENTEEN

"Jane, wait!" Nik's voice called from behind her.

Jane kept moving, pretending she didn't hear, speed-walking down the sidewalk. God, it was freezing out now. Had the temperature dropped ten degrees in the last half an hour? Or was it that last encounter that had left her shaking?

"Jane, wait!" It was Nik's voice again, and then the thump of footsteps on the sidewalk behind her. "Where are you going?"

"Home." She walked faster, but Nik fell into step beside her, his long legs effortlessly matching her pace.

"You shouldn't be walking alone at night."

Jane huffed out an ironic laugh. Tonight's stroll through Linden Falls would be the safest she'd been in... well. Maybe ever. "I'll take my chances."

"Jane." He reached out to take her arm. "You're freezing."

"I'm fine," she said, through chattering teeth.

"Let me drive you."

Jane was about to refuse, but at that moment, a cold gust of air blew past, swirling her hair in her face and burning the exposed skin on her hands. She wasn't used to this weather.

"Okay. Fine." She sighed, realizing how ungrateful she sounded, and added, "Thanks."

Nik gestured across the street to a car parked next to the sidewalk. He drove a basic sedan, which didn't really surprise her. He probably wasn't making a lot of money yet, not that Nik was in the medical profession for the money. And Nik wouldn't buy a flashy car even if he could afford it. Not like the Tesla Matteo drove.

Jane shuddered. Matteo had wanted her to take the Tesla on this trip. He said it would handle better on the highways than the Toyota. Thank God she'd talked him out of it, told him she was afraid she'd scratch it. That Tesla was nothing more than a two-ton tracking device.

Jane turned her attention to the interior of Nik's car as they both climbed inside. There were no crumbs on the dash or food wrappers in the back seat. With a car this clean, he clearly didn't have kids.

Or maybe he did. What did she know?

Nik started the car and sounds of the local college radio station drifted through the speakers, the same station that had played all their favorites when they were kids. They used to spend hours calling that station and making requests. The DJ came on to announce the next song, and Jane could have sworn it was the same late-night announcer as when they were kids, too. His throaty voice was oddly soothing, and she leaned back against the seat and closed her eyes. "Nothing has changed in this town, has it?" she mused.

"Plenty has changed," Nik said, and the sharpness in his tone had her eyes flying open again. "I know it's not glamorous like LA, but Linden Falls isn't so bad, you know."

"I didn't say it was bad. And I didn't say LA was glamorous." *Not even remotely.*

"I know you wanted to get out of here the second you could."

"So did *you*," Jane said, sitting up in her seat and turning to look at him. "You always talked about leaving. You were just as excited to go to Cornell as I was. You could have been a doctor anywhere. So, why did you come back here? What are you still *doing* here?"

Nik fell silent for a moment, staring at the road in front of him. Finally, he turned to face her. "I actually never left," he said, in a voice so low she almost missed it.

Jane's head jerked up. "What do you mean, you never left? What about Cornell?"

"I didn't go to Cornell."

"You..." Her mouth dropped open. Was she hearing him right?

"I went to Westbrook Community College. And then commuted to Buffalo for medical school."

For a moment, Jane was speechless, and then she managed to choke out, "*Why?* You had a scholarship. You could have gone anywhere."

"Right. The scholarship." Something darkened across Nik's features, almost like he was angry about the scholarship. But that couldn't be right. He'd earned it with his volunteer EMT work. That scholarship had been his ticket out.

Why didn't he take it?

"I thought you wanted to leave here. Was it—" Jane remembered running into Mrs. Andino the other day. She'd looked great—healthy, like she'd barely aged at all. But what if she'd been sick? And Nik had been left to navigate that on his own. "Was it your mom? Is she okay?"

"She's fine. Better than ever."

Jane blew out a relieved sigh. "So, why would you stay here when you wanted to leave?"

Nik braked at a stop sign and turned to look at her. "*You* wanted to leave. *I* wanted to go where you were going." He blew out a breath. "Anywhere you were going." That darkness was back. "But that wasn't an option."

Jane looked away. "So, because I left and didn't end up going to Cornell, you just... *stayed* in Linden Falls?"

Nik stared straight ahead as he accelerated into the intersection. "No." His hands tightened on the steering wheel. "It's complicated."

Jane wanted to ask for details. *Tell me what made it complicated.* But she had no right to. And it wasn't like she'd ever be able to share her own reasons for doing everything she'd done for the past ten years.

Nik turned the car down Clinton Road, past the ice cream shop where they used to go on summer evenings. Was there any place in this town that didn't remind her of Nik? There were ghosts of the two of them everywhere she went. Jane peeked at his face, wondering if Nik ever felt that way, too. For a second, his gaze lingered on the shop's flashing neon sign, and she wondered if he remembered stealing her sprinkles or that face he used to make when she ordered mint chocolate chip. But then he looked away and kept driving.

Of course he wasn't haunted by the memories of this town the way she was. He lived here, he'd made plenty of new memories with Hannah, and Ali when she came back to visit. He probably took Hannah's daughter, Amelia, to the ice-cream shop for milkshakes and made silly faces at her. Maybe he'd made new friends at the hospital who he met for picnics in Randall Park and movies at the refurbished cinema on Spring Street.

Ahead, the old wooden sign for Pine Bluff came into view, the blue-painted letters so faded that unless you knew better, you'd think they read *Pin luff.* Jane was willing to bet Nik didn't even think of her when he passed that gravel fire road that wound up the mountain. He probably had a girlfriend now who he'd take up to the Pine Bluff overlook to watch the sunset.

The sign drew nearer, and Jane looked away, hoping that soon it would be behind her. But before she could register what was happening, Nik had jerked the steering wheel to the left, sending the car swerving onto the fire road. Jane looked from Nik's profile to the patchy gravel lines illuminated only by the car's headlights, and then back. "Where are we going?"

"For a drive."

"I thought you were driving me home."

"I will." He shrugged. "Eventually."

"You can't just—*kidnap* me." She peered into the darkness, shivering at the skeletal outlines of trees forming a canopy over the road. It wasn't that Jane was afraid of the darkness, or of Nik. It wasn't even the memories of what had happened ahead. It was the avalanche those events on Pine Bluff had triggered that still had the power to leave her battered and broken. "I need to get back." Jane needed *to get out of here.*

"What's the rush?" Nik took the curve in the road a little too fast, and Jane's stomach lurched. He swung the car around the next bend, and Jane's heart fell to somewhere around her knees. Because suddenly, the narrow road opened up to reveal a wide gravel clearing that dropped off abruptly at the edge of a steep cliff. Beyond it, the sparkling lights of the town spread out in all directions below.

Nik brought the car to a stop and shifted into park, but Jane could only stare out the windshield in front of her. That view hadn't changed a bit. Not that she'd been looking at the view last time.

Jane's cheeks flushed pink as she peeked over at Nik. Here in the darkness of the car, with his face cast in shadows except for the dim light of the dashboard, it all came rushing back.

The two of them in an old sedan not much different than this one. The melancholy guitar opening of a folk song playing on the same local radio station. His eyes boring into her with equal intensity.

"What are we doing here, Nik?" Jane said, her voice shaking.

"Do you ever think about it? That night we came up here together?"

The question took her breath away. *Do I ever think about it?* The night she'd leaned over, propping one arm on the center console, setting the other gently on his shoulder. They'd touched hundreds of times before that night, had hugged by her locker, snuggled under a blanket, tumbled together into a snow-bank. But never like that night at the overlook. She'd slid her hand from his shoulder to his neck, feeling the brush of his dark hair against her fingertips, the heat of his skin on her palm. He'd shifted in his seat, turning his body to face her, angling closer. And then their lips had touched, and the world outside had fallen away, the heat from the sun dropping beneath the horizon no match for the fire burning in that car that night.

They'd kissed until her lips were swollen and her cheeks raw from the razor stubble on Nik's jaw. Then he'd shifted his mouth to explore the sensitive skin of her earlobe and the curve of her neck before running his tongue along her collarbone. Desire had exploded inside her, a low moan escaping from the back of her throat. She'd woven her fingers into his hair, coaxing him to the swell of her breast at the neckline of her flowered sundress.

It wasn't long before that dress had ended up crumpled on the dashboard along with her bra and Nik's button-up shirt. They'd climbed into the backseat to escape the barriers of consoles and cupholders, so he could free himself of the rest of his clothes and she could wrap her legs around him.

"Jane," he'd murmured, brushing a lock of damp hair off her forehead. "Is this okay? Are you sure you want to do this?"

She'd never wanted anything more in her life. In the dark-ness, her eyes found his. "Yes," she whispered breathlessly. "I'm sure."

"I want to protect you." He'd reached for his trousers on the floor mat and fished a foil packet from the pocket. It had taken him a moment to get it open, and a few more to get the condom on. Jane had loved that he'd seemed a little bit flustered, a little unsure. This was his first time. He'd waited for her, just like she'd waited for him.

And in the next moment, he'd gently eased inside her, checking that she was okay all along the way. It had hurt, a sharpness followed by a dull ache, but she loved the feel of him on top of her, the strength of his arms around her, and soon the pain had faded, replaced by a throb of pleasure.

"Jane," Nik had murmured against her ear as his hips picked up speed. "Jane, I need to tell you—"

"Yes, Nik," she'd gasped, partly in response to his words and partly to encourage him to go faster, deeper.

"Jane, I love you."

She came apart then, her body tensing and releasing with the most intense pleasure she'd ever known. A moment later he followed, collapsing on top of her, the two of them in a heap of arms and legs and sweaty skin, naive hope and pure happiness.

And now, a decade later, Nik wanted to know if she ever thought about it.

"Or did you scrub it all from your memory?" he asked. "Like you scrubbed me from your life."

"I didn't—" Jane began, but then she stopped and looked down at her hands. Because she *had* scrubbed him from her memory and her life. She'd been in LA for a few months when it had dawned on her that there was no going back again. Matteo, the nightclub, and eventually, Scarlett... they were her future. After that, it had become too painful to think about Nik, to remember how safe she'd felt when she was with him. To accept that the night she'd hoped would be the start of the life she'd imagined had turned out to be the end.

"I used to drive up here after you left," Nik said. "I'd stare out at the view and wonder where you were. Were you okay? Were you happy?" He ran a hand through his hair. "And then I'd wonder if it was my fault that you left. If I'd done something that night to drive you away."

"*You didn't do anything.*" She reached out to grab his arm. "Nik, if you don't believe another word I say, please believe that none of this was your fault."

The fine lines around Nik's eyes deepened and his face looked strained. "You broke my heart, Jane."

Jane wrapped her arms around her midsection as if that would protect her from this pain. As if anything would.

"No, that's not true," Nik continued. "Breaking my heart would have been *kind*. You *crushed* my heart. You destroyed it. I spent a summer lying on the floor writing terrible poetry about you. I spent years after that—*years*—looking for you and agonizing over what had happened."

And with that, another crack opened up in her own heart. All this time, she'd told herself that he was fine. That she was the only one who'd come out of this battered beyond repair. But to hear the pain in his voice, to know that she hadn't been able to keep one more person she loved from hurting...

"I'm so sorry, Nik."

"Sorry? Really?" He gave a humorless laugh. "We had plans. We made promises to each other. And you poured gasoline on them and lit a match."

"I never wanted to hurt you."

Nik's eyebrows shot up. "That's great. But you know what that sounds like to me? A bunch of useless words ten years too late."

Jane felt a flare of anger. "If it's not an apology, what do you want from me?" She narrowed her eyes in his direction. "Or did you just bring me up here to torture me over the memories of everything we lost?"

He reeled back against the driver's side door. "Is that how you feel when you think about everything we lost? *Tortured?*"

"Of course I do, Nik. You think you're the only one whose heart was broken? You never knew me at all if you believe that."

"Oh, I knew you, Jane. I knew you better than anyone." Nik leaned across the center console, solidly in her space now.

She met his eyes, refusing to back up. To back down. But instead of fueling their anger, something else burned between them. That same heat that had stretched across a narrow space just like this one. How had it been ten years, and yet it felt like no time had gone by? If she inched forward, would he still smell like clean cotton flannel? Would his mouth still burn against her mouth, her cheek, her neck?

They'd been kids the last time, fumbling in the darkness with zero experience and an infinite amount of passion. What would it feel like now, to lean over and press her lips to his, to feel the scrape of his beard against her cheek, his solid arms around her?

Judging from Nik's sharp intake of breath, he was wondering the exact same thing.

He inched closer, the intensity of his stare pinning her in place so she couldn't move away even if she wanted to.

"Nik." She meant it to be a warning, but his name formed in her mouth like a plea.

Nik.

Please.

The cold wind whistled against the window outside, but she was burning up inside that narrow space. "What do you want from me?" she asked shakily.

He reached up and slid a hand into the hair at the nape of her neck, tugging her even closer. "I want to know how you could walk away from this. I want to know how you could disappear into thin air."

EIGHTEEN

TEN YEARS AGO

"Janie, look at this."

Jane tore her eyes from the endless row of diapers to find Matteo standing in front of her holding a tiny pair of knit booties.

"Can you believe how small the baby's feet will be?" He reached out to give her stomach a rub. "Especially with how huge you are."

Jane stepped away from him, pressing a hand to the top of her bowling-ball belly. "I'm not *huge*. This is what pregnant women look like." She focused on the shelf in front of her. Huggies and Pampers, what was the difference? *This is when I wish I could call Mom.*

"Don't be so sensitive," Matteo muttered, tossing the booties into the cart. "I'm just having a little fun."

Jane sighed. She probably *was* being sensitive. Her back hurt, her ankles were swollen, and yeah, she felt *huge*. While Matteo looked as fit as ever in his tight black jeans and T-shirt. She'd caught two other women and a man checking him out in this store alone—while nobody was going to look at her twice except to feel sorry that she had to endure being nine months pregnant in a Los Angeles heatwave.

"I'm sorry," she said, taking Matteo's hand. "The booties are adorable."

"Whatever," he said, wandering off.

Jane watched him disappear around the corner and her lungs squeezed with anxiety. She should chase after him and smooth things over. He'd been a perfect partner throughout this pregnancy. All of her fears that they'd have another incident like the one the day she'd gotten the positive test had turned out to be completely unfounded. Sure, sometimes he got a little grumpy when she didn't feel like having sex, and he expected her to clean and cook dinner every night, even though she could barely reach the stove around her midsection. But he'd been so excited, almost like a kid himself, buying baby toys and adorable little clothes, and making a list of names.

Jane tossed a package of newborn Pampers into the cart and followed it up with the same sized Huggies, and then she steered her cart after Matteo. She found him chatting up the pretty young woman at the checkout counter. *She's probably my age.* But the checkout girl's hair was glossy and her stomach flat.

"Hi," Jane said, sidling up next to Matteo.

"Jane, hey," Matteo said. "Vanessa was just telling me that most women only gain, like, 25 pounds during pregnancy."

Vanessa gave Jane a smirk. It was like she knew that Jane had gained more than that.

Matteo laughed. "I'm just messing with you." He wrapped an arm around Jane's shoulder. "You know I think you're gorgeous."

Jane forced a smile as she unloaded her baby items onto the counter.

. . .

That night, Jane's water broke. She woke up alone in their bed, the pain coming in waves. *What's happening? Where's Matteo?*

Jane sat up and looked at the clock. One in the morning. *He's at the club.* Jane grabbed her phone, hitting the button to call him. It rang six times and went to voicemail. She hung up and immediately tried again.

Voicemail again.

Jane hauled herself out of bed, stopping to grab the night table and bend over to breathe through a contraction. *I'm nine months pregnant. Why doesn't he have his phone on him?* She managed to get herself dressed and roll her suitcase out of the closet. Luckily, she'd packed it last week, just in case.

Panting heavily, she barely managed to wrestle the suitcase down the stairs, at one point nearly tipping forward and falling down half a flight. Inside the club, Jane fought her way through the crowd to the bar. She found Matteo pouring shots for a group of women in a bachelorette party, smiling, laughing, charming them with whatever story he was telling.

"Matteo," she gasped, shoving her way to the bar as another contraction overtook her. "My water broke. I'm in labor."

His eyes widened. "Oh, hell. Okay." He dropped the tequila bottle on the counter and rounded the bar to wrap an arm around her back. "I've got you."

Jane panted, leaning into his strong frame as he guided her out of the bar.

Matteo barked some orders to the bouncer and then they headed to his car down the street. Jane climbed in as another contraction hit. And suddenly, all she wanted was Mom. Her mommy, who'd spent hours on the bathroom floor, holding back Jane's hair and rubbing her back when she had a stomach bug. Who'd made her favorite soup and sat with her watching the entire first season of the *Gilmore Girls* when Jane had the flu. Who'd come in the middle of the night when Jane had a nightmare. This pain, this terror, it was like the worst nightmare coming to life.

I can't do this. I can't have a baby.

I need my mother.

"Breathe through it," Matteo said, repeating the words of the woman in the childbirth video they'd watched a few weeks ago. "You're doing great."

Jane gave him a weak smile. Mom wasn't there, but Matteo was.

Through the entire drive to the hospital, the elevator ride to the birth room, and finally, through twelve hours of labor, Matteo held her hand and coached her through the contractions with sweat beading his forehead and anxiety clouding his features. "You can do it, Jane. Push."

Later, while Jane held the baby against her chest, Matteo stood next to the bed and gazed down at them with a proud, tired smile. "You're amazing, Jane." He stroked her hair, and Jane closed her eyes, overcome with emotion.

The first few weeks were like a dream. Scarlett took to nursing right away, and she slept most of the time, so Jane was able to rest and heal from childbirth. Matteo went back to work at the club, but he'd stop in every few hours to check on them, to make sure Scarlett was nursing and that Jane had enough to eat.

Jane hadn't been in touch with Mom since her call all those months ago, but she sent a photo of Scarlett along with her phone number.

"She's gorgeous, Jane. I can't believe you have a baby." There were tears in Mom's voice when the call came through. "My baby has a baby."

"The doctor said she's perfectly healthy and right on track with weight gain."

"And your—" Mom hesitated. "The father of the baby?"

Jane told Mom a little about Matteo—how much he loved Scarlett, what a good father he was turning out to be.

"And he's nice to you? He treats you well?"

"Yes. He's wonderful."

Mom's relieved sigh carried through the phone.

"I'll send more pictures," Jane offered.

Mom was silent for a moment. "Maybe you shouldn't. I don't want your father to find them. Maybe we could just talk every now and then when Dad is on one of his fishing trips."

A wave of pain slowly rolled over Jane. "I understand," she finally managed to choke out.

But she didn't. And she never would.

When Scarlett was a month old, she started waking up every hour and screaming at the top of her lungs. Nothing Jane did would soothe her—not nursing, not bouncing her, not pacing back and forth across the living room.

"What the hell is wrong with that baby?" Matteo snapped, after the fourth night without any sleep.

"I don't know," Jane said, so tired she could cry. "The doctor said it's colic."

"Well, get her some medicine for that."

"There isn't any." Jane bounced Scarlett up and down in her arms. And then up and down again. She was so tired. "We just have to keep trying to soothe her."

"This is ridiculous," Matteo snarled. "I need my sleep. Some of us have to *work*. I can't just be lying around all day like you can."

"I don't just—" But Jane stopped. He was tired, they both were. Arguing would only start a fight.

The next night, Scarlett's crying seemed to intensify. Jane paced back and forth, back and forth across the living room, trying to shush the baby, to keep her from waking Matteo. He *did* have to work. "Please go to sleep," she whispered, over and over. But Scarlett just screamed louder.

Behind her, the bedroom door banged open. Matteo stormed into the living room. "You need to get her out of here." He waved in Scarlett's direction.

Exhausted and on the verge of crying herself, Jane sputtered, "What do you mean *get her out of here*? Where am I going to take her?"

"Just..." Matteo pressed a hand to his temples as if the noise was going to make his head explode. "Get. Her. Out." He grabbed Jane by the arm and pulled her across the living room.

"What are you *doing*?" She tried to break free, but his grip tightened. And then the next thing she knew, Matteo had opened the door and shoved her and Scarlett out in the hall. "I need my damn sleep."

Jane's mouth dropped open. "Matteo—"

But he'd already slammed the door in her face. The lock clicked into place.

Jane shook the doorknob, but the door didn't budge. He was joking. He had to be joking. She knocked once and then harder. Scarlett wailed louder, but Matteo remained silent inside the apartment. "Matteo," Jane screamed, pounding on the door, "let me in."

She kept knocking, kept shaking the doorknob, sure that any moment he'd let her back inside. Five minutes went by, and then ten, and finally exhausted, hoarse, and with her fist aching, Jane backed away from the door. She searched the narrow hallway for some idea of what to do now. Theirs was the only apartment above the club, so she didn't have any neighbors to ask for help. It was 4 a.m. and the club was closed. If she'd had her phone, she could call Yolanda, but Matteo had it locked inside. And she couldn't very well go walking around on the streets of LA with a crying baby and no shoes or wallet in order to find a 24-hour convenience store with a phone.

Jane slid down to the floor still rocking her wailing daughter. "It's going to be okay," she murmured, over and over. But at this point, she wasn't sure if she was saying it for her own benefit or the baby's.

Jane woke up on the floor, with Scarlett on her chest and Matteo standing over her. Dazed, she hauled herself to a seated position, trying not to disturb the baby, who had finally fallen asleep.

"Shit, Jane," Matteo said, his voice cracking. "I'm sorry." He raked a hand through his hair. "I was just so tired I wasn't thinking straight." He held out a hand to help her to her feet.

"How could you do that to me?" Jane mumbled, but she was too exhausted to put up much of a fight. Her neck hurt from sleeping at a strange angle, her arms ached from holding Scarlett for hours on end, and she was desperate to pee.

Matteo took the baby from her arms while she ran to the bathroom. When she opened the door a few minutes later, he was waiting there, rocking a sleeping Scarlett, a contrite look on his face. He shifted Scarlett to one arm so he could wrap the other around Jane. "You sleep as long as you need to. I don't have to be at work until eight. I'll take care of Scarlett."

When she woke, Matteo had given Scarlett a bath and changed her, and he had dinner waiting.

"You can't ever do that again," Jane told him.

"I know. *I know.* I won't."

Scarlett's colic seemed to improve, and Jane figured out that if the crying grew too loud, she could take the baby in the bathroom and close the door. Matteo started sleeping better, and another month went by as they settled into this new routine.

Soon, Jane grew more confident with Scarlett and began venturing out for short walks with the stroller.

On the way home from one of these walks, she passed Teddy, one of the club's bouncers, on his way to work. They'd always been friendly when she saw him at the club. Jane gave him a wave, and he fell into step beside her. "You're looking good, Jane. How's Mom-life treating you?"

"I think I'm starting to get the hang of it." She waved at Scarlett in the stroller, who was sleeping peacefully for once.

"She's an angel," Teddy said, which sounded so funny coming from a six-foot five former Division 1 offensive lineman that Jane had to laugh.

"Don't let her fool you," she said.

"Oh, I won't." He gave Jane a wink.

"What are you doing out here?" came a sharp voice behind them.

Jane whirled around to find Matteo standing in the doorway to the club, arms crossed over his chest, face red.

"Scarlett and I were coming home from a walk."

"You're home now," Matteo barked, "so go inside."

Jane felt her own face flush crimson. Why was he speaking to her in that tone? She glanced at Teddy, who just shrugged his enormous shoulders.

"*Now*," Matteo ordered.

Jane hurried inside, leaving the stroller at the bottom of the stairs and carrying Scarlett up to the apartment. She'd just gotten the baby settled in her crib when she heard the front door open. The next thing she knew, she was flying across the room, her shoulder slamming into the bedroom doorframe and her face burning with pain.

Oh, my God.

He hit me.

Jane gasped, one hand flying to her cheek, the other

grasping the door handle to keep herself upright as her head spun and nausea rolled over her.

"Don't let me find you flirting with my staff ever again," Matteo said in a low voice.

"I—" In her shock, Jane could barely form the words. *He hit me.* "I wasn't—"

"You weren't what?" He grabbed her by the shoulders and shook her so hard her teeth rattled.

"Stop!" Jane gasped. She wrenched free and made a break for the bathroom, slamming and locking the door behind her.

Her whole body shaking, Jane fumbled in her pocket for her phone. Though the moment played on repeat in her head, Jane couldn't quite believe it had happened.

He hit me.

She dialed 911. "Please help," she whispered into the phone. "Please."

Outside the bathroom, she heard Matteo curse under his breath. A moment later, the apartment door opened and then slammed shut.

Jane crept out of the bathroom to check on Scarlett, who was thankfully still sleeping.

Ten minutes later, two police officers arrived, both men—a fact that Jane became aware of when Matteo calmly brought them up to the apartment.

"She has postpartum depression," Jane heard Matteo say. "She locked herself in the bathroom. Thank God she didn't have the baby in there."

The officers turned to peer at Jane like she was an exhibit in the zoo. "Are you okay, miss?" one of them asked her.

"No, my boyfriend..." Jane still couldn't believe it. "He hit me."

Matteo turned to the officers. "I had to give her a shove to get the baby away from her. She was acting really crazy, threatening to hurt herself or our daughter. I was worried about what she might do."

One of the officers scribbled something in his notebook, and the other reached out to take Jane's arm. "Ma'am..."

Jane wrenched away. "Don't touch me."

The officers exchanged looks. Matteo was lying. Couldn't they see that?

"Should we take her in for a 5150?" one of them murmured to the other, under his breath.

"A what?" she gasped.

The officer hesitated. "Your boyfriend is worried about you. I wondered if maybe you wanted to talk to someone. A doctor. Psychiatrist."

Jane's gaze flew wildly from one officer to the other. How could this be happening when Matteo was the threat? *Not her.* "You can't take me—"

"That won't be necessary," Matteo cut in.

"He's the one—" Jane tried to explain, but Matteo's hand was suddenly gripping her shoulder.

"I've taken a couple of days off work," Matteo said, smoothly. "I can keep an eye on her and the baby. I also put a call in to her doctor." He tightened his grip. *Don't say another word.* She didn't, because nobody would believe her anyway.

That night, he brought flowers and her favorite Chinese food.

"I'm so sorry, Janie." Matteo hung his head.

Hands shaking, heart pounding, Jane told him she forgave him. Because what else could she say?

A week later, Jane went to the park, where she sat on a bench and stared at Scarlett in the stroller. Matteo had been a perfect partner since the incident last week, taking the baby for a walk so Jane could nap, rubbing Jane's shoulders after a particularly tiring night.

But the bruise was still bright purple on her cheek, and she could still feel her body flying into the doorway every time she walked past it. That morning, as she'd stared at her face in the mirror, all she could picture was Mom's face. The haunted, defeated look in Mom's eyes.

Jane adjusted the blanket over her sleeping baby. And then she fished her phone out of the stroller and googled *How do I leave my abuser*. She'd have to delete her search history later. Just in case.

The first few links that popped up were for domestic violence hotlines. Maybe she'd go back to those but, for now, she kept scrolling, and found a list of articles with headlines like "Why Victims Don't *Just Leave*" and "How to Get Out of an Abusive Relationship."

Jane clicked on the second one and scanned the bullet points telling her that it wasn't her fault and she didn't deserve the abuse. It helped, marginally, to see that. But what she really needed was some concrete information. She kept reading until she found the section about how to leave. There was information about how to find a domestic violence shelter, when to go, how to pack. Next came a section about safety.

The article detailed something called a protection from abuse order, or PFA, that she could apply for. It would be signed by a judge and state that Matteo couldn't contact her or come within a certain distance. *But*, the article warned, *if your abuser is only given a citation and not taken to jail, it might embolden them to pursue you further.*

And then Jane's eyes focused on the next words: *The time of leaving can be a very dangerous period for victims of abuse. Most women who are murdered by their abusers are killed after they leave, not before.*

Jane shuddered and closed the article. There was no way

she was going to be able to do this alone. She needed help. Before she could lose her nerve, she dialed the number for the domestic violence hotline. A woman picked up on the first ring.

"Um. Hi," Jane said. "I..." She looked at Scarlett for courage. "I need help leaving an abusive situation."

The woman was very kind, reassuring. She said all the right things. *It's not your fault. You're doing the right thing.*

"We can house you and your baby for up to six weeks," the woman explained. "From there, we can help you arrange transitional housing."

"What is that?"

"It could look like a lot of things. Do you have any family who might be able to take you in?"

Family. Jane remembered Mom telling her not to send any more photos. "No."

"Well, sometimes a spot opens up in one of the group homes. Or we can help you find an apartment share with another woman in our program."

Jane clutched the phone tighter. "How would I pay for that?"

"Do you have a job?"

Jane stared at Scarlett's tiny nose. Her eyes closed so peacefully. "No, I have a two-month-old baby."

"We can help you with training and applications to find a job."

"But..." A heavy weight dropped in Jane's stomach. "What about my baby? Who will take care of her while I work?"

"There are childcare vouchers you can apply for." The woman paused, and Jane could hear her shuffling through a pile of papers. "There is a waitlist, though."

The weight in Jane's stomach grew heavier. "So, what do I do? How do I start?"

"Are you in danger right now?"

Jane looked around the playground. "No. Not... right this

second." She heard more shuffling on the other end of the phone.

"We don't have any beds open right now, but we expect to in a couple of weeks. Can you call us back then?"

A couple of weeks?

Defeated, she hung up the phone and headed home. Outside the club, she spotted Teddy arriving for his shift.

"Hey," he called to her. "I'm sorry if I got you in trouble the other..." Teddy trailed off as Jane averted her eyes and kept walking.

A week later, Jane was heading home from the dry cleaners, Matteo's cleaned and pressed shirts draped over the handle of the stroller, when she passed a man sitting on a bench in front of a storefront. Something about him was familiar. As he leaned over to take a bite of his sandwich, his thinning blond comb-over flopped on his forehead. The man quickly reached up and smoothed it back into place. He looked up to find Jane watching.

"Do I know you?"

The sign in the window read *Morgan and Morgan, Attorneys at Law.*

"I interviewed for a job here once." She hesitated. "Well, not really interviewed. You just told me to go home."

The man swiped at his mouth with his napkin. "Tough break, kid. You ever find a job?"

She pushed Scarlett's stroller back and forth to rock her. "Sort of."

Mr. Morgan nodded and took another bite of his sandwich. A blob of mustard slid down his chin. While he wiped it away, Jane looked over his head to the younger version of his face on the sign. No comb-over yet. And then she focused on the words beneath the photo. *Free consultations.*

When women left their husbands on TV, they always hired kick-ass lawyers. Mr. Morgan was an ambulance chaser in a rundown strip mall. Jane had absolutely no faith that he was a kick-ass lawyer. But, in that moment, desperation and this man were literally all she had.

She took a quick glance down the sidewalk to make sure nobody was walking by who would overhear. "Can I ask you something? Can I get a—uh—consultation?"

"I'm kind of on my lunch break, here." Mr. Morgan lifted the sandwich.

"That interview made me late for my job and I got fired." *You owe me.*

Mr. Morgan sighed, stuffing the rest of his sandwich into the paper bag on his lap. "Fine. Do you want to sue your former employer for firing you?"

"No. I want to leave my boyfriend."

"Well... just leave."

"It's not that simple."

Scarlett fussed in her stroller, and Jane pushed it back and forth to soothe her until Scarlett stretched and fell back asleep.

"Ah. I get it." He nodded at the baby. "I don't do family law."

"But you"—Jane waved a hand—"you took some classes in law school, right? You can give me some advice." She looked at him beseechingly. "Please?"

Mr. Morgan sighed. "This is off the record."

"We need to get away. It's a... delicate... situation." Jane reached up to rub her shoulder. It still felt sore when she slept on it a certain way. "He's not going to want to let us go."

Mr. Morgan's eyes drifted over her. "There are shelters for this sort of thing."

"They're full. And once they have an opening, we can stay for six weeks, but then we need to find a place to go. I have a newborn so I'm not working." She pushed Scarlett back and forth again. "Is there any way that he can be made to pay child support or... something?"

"Sure. You can go to court. The judge will likely take your situation into account and order him to pay. But what he'll owe depends on the custody arrangement."

"Custody?" Jane's voice rose.

Mr. Morgan looked at her sideways. "If he's the father, he can potentially ask for fifty-fifty."

Jane's eyes widened. "But... what if he's dangerous? What if he's hurting me?"

"Do you have a record of that? Hospital stays? Police reports?"

Jane only had the one 911 call. And she couldn't imagine what the police report would say about her. "No."

"Does he have any history of harming the baby?"

"*No.*" Thank God. But it kept her up at night. What would she do if he turned his rage on Scarlett?

"Well, there's a very good chance he'll get at least partial custody. Unless he doesn't want it."

Jane grasped at that tiny bit of hope. Maybe Matteo wouldn't want custody. He was the fun dad who liked to play with Scarlett when she was dry, fed, and happy but as soon as she started crying, Matteo couldn't hand her off to Jane fast enough. "What if he doesn't want it? Can we get him to pay child support then?"

Mr. Morgan made a skeptical face. "You can ask. The judge will likely grant it. But that doesn't mean the guy's going to pay." He shrugged. "I'd never count on a deadbeat dad paying child support." His gaze swept over Jane. "But I wouldn't count on an abuser to let his woman go without a fight, either." He raised his eyebrows. "If you get my drift."

Most women who are murdered by their abusers are killed after they leave, not before.

"So, what should I do?" Jane kept pushing the stroller back

and forth, but her hands were shaking now. "If I were... your sister or something... what would you tell me to do?"

"I'd say get a job. Save as much money as you can. Document everything. And then as soon as you can, take your baby and get the hell out of LA."

Jane blinked to keep the tears from welling up. *Get a job?* What was she supposed to do with Scarlett? *Save money?* Without Matteo knowing about it?

Jane slowly turned and gave the stroller another push, and this time, she followed it down the sidewalk.

"Sorry," Mr. Morgan called.

Jane was sorry, too.

NINETEEN

PRESENT DAY

In the car, Nik stared at Jane's face, illuminated by the lights of the dashboard and the town glimmering out beyond the overlook. "What happened, Jane?" Nik repeated the question, searching her eyes for answers.

He'd told himself he wasn't going to do this. That he didn't care where she'd gone or why she'd left without a word. But somehow, he kept ending up here, leaning in, desperate for answers.

Desperate to take her by the shoulders and kiss her.

Jesus. He leaned back against the car door and balled his hands into fists. What was the matter with him? She'd walked back into this town forty-eight hours ago, and already he barely recognized himself.

Jane gazed back, her lips parted, almost as if his nearness had left her breathless. And then she closed her eyes, shook her head. "I need to get the hell out of here." And the next thing he knew, she was reaching for her door and yanking it open. She jumped out of the car and disappeared from sight.

"What the hell?" Nik muttered, pulling on his own door handle. The minute he climbed out of the car, the cold wind hit him in the face. Tugging the hood of his coat over his head, he turned to look for Jane. He spotted her maybe a hundred feet away, speed-walking down the gravel road back into town. "Jane!" He took off in her direction.

Nik had been running five miles a day for the past ten years, and it took him less than thirty seconds to catch up with her. He reached out and grabbed her arm, spinning her around. "What are you doing?"

"Isn't it obvious? I'm walking."

"All the way back to town? At this hour and in this weather?"

"Well, it's not like you're offering me a ride." She turned away from him and kept walking.

He matched her pace. "Jane, you're going to freeze to death. Get in the car."

"Don't tell me what to do. Last I checked, you were kidnapping me, so I don't think you get a say." She lifted her chin, and he remembered that stubbornness. He was almost tempted to laugh. Instead, he reached out and took her arm again, just as another gust of wind swirled around them. "Jane. Get in the damn car."

Something dark crossed over her features. "I'm not going back there."

"Where?" He glanced around. "To the car?"

"Yes. No. I'm not going back to the overlook." She kept walking.

He felt a stab of anger. "So, we're back to this again. Was it really such a terrible memory for you?" He took two big steps and swung in front of her so she had to stop walking. "That night with me? Is that why you left?"

She was shivering. Of course she'd gone out into the cold without gloves or a hat. She was from Los Angeles now. *Fucking Los Angeles.* He reached out to pull her against him, spinning around so his body shielded her from the wind.

"No, it's not a terrible memory, Nik. It's the opposite of a terrible memory."

"Then—*what the hell, Jane?* I just want to know *why*."

She shoved a forearm against his chest and looked up in his eyes. His heart nearly stopped when he saw the haunted look there.

"One of my dad's deputies was here that night," Jane said, in a low voice.

"What?" Nik blinked down at her. "*Here?*"

"Here at the overlook."

His surprise had him loosening his grip on her, but she didn't back away.

"That night that we..." He trailed off.

"Yeah, that night *we*..." Jane's gaze dropped to the zipper on his coat. "I'm sure you remember."

Of course he remembered. He'd been with other women since that night with Jane. But nothing had been like that first time. And nobody had been Jane. With her standing this close, leaning into him, his body reacted. It was more than a memory.

He put a hand on her cold cheek, tilting her head to look at him again. "What do you mean one of his deputies was here?"

"One of the deputies was patrolling the area and saw your car. Apparently, he approached, planning to knock on the window and tell the kids inside to go home. But then he realized that one of *the kids* was me. *The chief's daughter*."

Nik stared at Jane, her words slowly registering. The officer must have snuck up on them from the woods that night because, in his memory, the two of them were entirely alone on that overlook. But then again, they'd been so wrapped up in each other that they might not have even noticed if the patrol car had peeled in, lights flashing and sirens wailing. "He didn't knock on the window," Nik pointed out.

"No, he didn't."

"But I'm guessing he told your dad?" He imagined how

Chief McCaffrey might have reacted to one of his officers reporting that he'd found the chief's daughter making out in the back of a car at Pine Bluff. Except they hadn't been *making out*. What had the officer seen? And worse, reported back to Jane's dad?

"Yes, the officer told my dad," Jane confirmed.

"I take it your dad was mad about it."

Jane closed her eyes and shook her head, as if that would somehow erase the terrible memory.

"Jane?" His stomach churned. "What happened?"

"He was waiting when I got home."

It was amazing how such simple words could fill his whole body with dread. Nik could barely breathe. "You were eighteen. Legally an adult. He had no right to—"

Jane gave a humorless laugh. "You remember my dad. He didn't care about what he had a right to do."

"Did he expect you to never have a boyfriend? To never—?"

"It wasn't just about a boyfriend... I'd humiliated him, acting like a slut, having his officer catch me up on the overlook... and..."

When Jane looked away, Nik sensed there was something she didn't want to say. Something she was ashamed to say. And then it came to him. "It was me, wasn't it? He didn't want you doing that with *me*."

Nik had never been one of those clean-cut, popular kids, the ones on the football team sponsored by the police force. The ones who lived in the big houses they'd built on the old Baker farm on Route 8. His mother was a single mom who cleaned those big houses out on the old Baker farm. Nik had always known Chief McCaffrey didn't like him. When he was a kid, his mom had cleaned for the McCaffreys and she and Jane's mom had been friends. But then something had happened. He never knew exactly what, but one day his mom no longer went over to their house, and neither did Nik. When he saw Chief McCaffrey around town, the guy gave him the creeps.

Jane didn't talk about her dad much, but she always made sure she left Nik's house and got home in the evening before her dad did. Today wasn't the first time since high school that he'd wondered if he should have asked Jane more questions about him. Nik would forever be haunted by that terrified look in Mrs. McCaffrey's eyes that day she came into the emergency room.

"What happened when you found your dad waiting?" Another gust of wind blew up, and Nik wanted to shield Jane from so much more than the frigid weather. "Did he hurt you?"

Jane pressed her lips together and stared out at the lights in the valley. "He pushed me down the stairs."

For a moment, Nik wished Chief McCaffrey were still alive so he could drive over to his house and kill him. Without stopping to think about it, he pulled Jane against him, wrapping his arms around her. She held on, sliding her hands around his back.

"If I'd known any of this, I would have been there in five minutes to pick you up. You had to know that, right?"

She nodded against his chest.

"You know my mom loves you. You could have stayed at our house for as long as you needed." He remembered Jane and his mom giggling together in the kitchen. It had made him so happy that the two most important people in the world were so close. After losing his dad, Jane and his mom were everything to him. "You could have stayed forever."

Slowly, almost reluctantly, Jane pulled back. She turned her eyes to Nik's, and the pain he saw nearly did him in. "He said if I ever saw you again, he'd make sure you never got your scholarship. That he'd fabricate a drug arrest on your record, and that would be the end of college and med school."

Nik stared at her. Chief McCaffrey had known exactly what he was doing. He'd known how important the scholarship was to Nik, and he'd probably known how important Nik was to Jane. "But why did you keep that a secret from me?"

"I knew if I told you I couldn't see you anymore, you'd never agree to it." Tears pooled in her eyes. "You'd tank your scholarship yourself. And I couldn't let you do that. After everything that happened with your dad, I couldn't let you give up your dream to be a doctor for me. I couldn't let you get stuck in this town. And the only way I knew how to make sure that didn't happen was to go as far away as possible."

Nik's head spun. "But why Los Angeles? Why not go to Cornell like you'd planned? Were you afraid you'd run into me there?"

Jane shook her head. "My dad refused to pay for Cornell. After what happened, he said he didn't trust me, said I had to stay home and commute to Buffalo if I wanted to go to college." Her words were coming faster now. "I couldn't stay for four more years. I could barely make it another day in the same house with him." Jane took a gasping breath. "And with *her* letting him treat us that way. *He pushed me down the stairs* and my mom made excuses, asked me to let it go. So, the next day, I left. I ran." An icy tear slid down her cheek. "I thought I'd go away until you were finished with school, and they couldn't take your scholarship. Until my dad couldn't hurt either of us anymore."

Nik's body went hot and then cold. He'd told Jane that he never ended up going to Cornell. That he'd gone to community college instead. But he hadn't told her why. Nik had never actually received that scholarship. A few days after Jane had left, a letter had arrived from the Linden Falls town council. *Some new information has come to light that has caused the committee to reconsider the award.*

The pain he felt now was overwhelming. It wasn't about losing the scholarship. Nik didn't give a shit about that anymore.

He'd made it on his own. But Jane had run away to Los Angeles to protect his dream. And it had all been for nothing.

A haunted look crossed her face, and he realized the truth was dawning on her. He'd told her earlier that he'd stayed in Linden Falls and gone to community college.

Jane backed away from him, her eyes glued to his face. "Why didn't you go to Cornell, Nik? Why did you stay in Linden Falls?"

He reached for her. "Jane, it's freezing out. Let's get in the car."

She shook her head. *"Why are you still here?"* Jane was crying now, icy tears dripping down her cheeks. "Answer me, Nik."

"I like it here. I'm happy here."

She swiped at her eyes. "Maybe you do like it here. But that's not why you stayed. At least, it's not why you stayed ten years ago." Her voice rose with each word. *"What really happened?"*

How could he tell her? "Jane..."

"He took your scholarship away, didn't he? Even though I left and never saw you again. He took it anyway."

Nik hesitated and then nodded.

"Oh *God*." Jane paced across the road and sank down on a fallen log. She pressed her face into her hands. Her entire body shook.

Nik followed her across the road and crouched in front of her. "Jane, it's freezing out. Will you get in the car? Please?"

Her shoulders slumped, and wordlessly, she nodded. Nik stood and then took her hand, helping her to her feet. He kept her hand tucked in his as they headed up the road. Once he got her in the passenger seat, he rounded the vehicle and climbed in, cranking up the heat.

"I should really get home," Jane murmured, her voice flat.

Nik rubbed his hands together to warm them. "I think we should finish this conversation."

Slowly, she turned her head to look at him. "What else is there to say? It's over, it's in the past."

But we're here in the present. They'd missed out on ten years. He didn't want to miss out on ten more.

"My mom thought I was going out for milk." Jane grabbed the seatbelt and pulled the strap across her chest. "I'm sure she'll start to worry."

"You could text her and tell her you're with me."

Jane shook her head. "If she's asleep, a text might wake her up."

"If she's asleep, she won't be worrying about you."

"Well, there's no way to know, so I should get back."

Nik sighed. Why did he feel like she was still keeping things from him?

She was silent on the drive home. When he pulled his car in at the McCaffreys' driveway behind an older Toyota that he assumed was hers, he turned to face her. "I'm sorry I kidnapped you."

"It's okay." She gave him a lopsided smile, and his heart did a somersault. All he wanted was to keep that smile on her face. It killed him to think about all the reasons she'd run away. But she was back, and her dad was gone. And maybe... Hell, he didn't know. Maybe they could be friends again.

Friends.

Jane's nose was red from crying, eyes swollen, mascara smeared under her lashes. And still she was the most beautiful woman he'd ever seen. How many times in the last decade had he dreamed of that face? Dream of her body beneath his? And how many times did he wake up as aroused as a teenager?

He didn't want to be friends with Jane.

Nik took a chance. "I'm working the day shift tomorrow. Can I come by when I get off? We could get a drink or dinner. Talk more."

Jane shook her head. "I don't think that's a good idea." She glanced nervously up at the house, and a weight settled in his chest. He still didn't know anything about her life, really.

"Is there—someone? A boyfriend? Are you married?"

"No." Jane gave her head a hard shake. "There's nobody. Not like that. It's—" She reached for the door handle, almost as if she were getting ready to make a run for it. "I'm leaving, Nik. I'll be in Linden Falls for another couple of days, and then I'm... gone." She didn't meet his eyes.

Why did he feel like there was so much more to this story? She glanced at the house again. Why did she seem nervous? Nik shook his head. Why was he so adamant in unpacking this baggage? It had been ten years. He'd moved on. Or, at least he should have moved on.

"Okay. Well, if you change your mind, you know where to find me."

She hesitated for a moment. "I'm sorry, Nik."

He sighed. "Me, too."

Jane climbed out of the car and made her way up the porch steps. Nik waited only long enough to watch her unlock the front door and swing it open. And then he put the car in reverse, driving away before he could do something stupid like follow her.

TWENTY

The next morning, Jane stared at the light fixture on the ceiling while the events of the night before slowly came back to her. It was almost too unbearable to think of everything she'd given up when she'd walked away. *And it was all for nothing.* Nik had never received that scholarship. He'd never gone to Cornell.

It was impossible not to second-guess every decision she'd made back then.

Her dad had been a monster. Jane closed her eyes, remembering the fear and horror when he'd taken her by the arm, dragging her across her bedroom. She'd wrenched free and run past him, out the door and down the hall, but he'd followed. She could still feel him behind her, hear him panting, sense him closing in. She'd made it to the top of the stairs, and... a hard blow to her back. The twist of her ankle. The whoosh of air on her face as she fell.

She'd lain crumpled in the hallway below, stunned and gasping, when another blow came from behind. Her guitar. Nik's gift. Dad had thrown it after her.

He'd slowly descended the stairs, and Jane had scrambled to her hands and knees, crawling across the hardwood to escape.

But Dad had been finished with her. At least physically. That's when he'd told her she couldn't see Nik anymore. Couldn't go to Cornell.

And when he was done blowing up her life, he'd snatched up the guitar from the floor and left the house. Jane had watched helplessly from the porch as he'd descended the stairs, opened the door to his patrol car, and tossed in the guitar with such force that she could hear it vibrate across the yard.

That was when she'd turned to find Mom standing silently in the doorway.

Maybe Jane could have handled what had happened to her, could have stood up to Dad and stayed in Linden Falls to fight for her and Nik, except for what had happened next. As much as the pain of bruises and broken ribs had hurt, somehow the pain of Mom's betrayal had been worse. Mom had made excuses. Begged Jane to go quietly to her room. Cried and asked her to *please* not pour any more fuel on the fire.

Like it had been Jane's fault.

Like she'd deserved what had happened to her.

The next day, Jane had run. But what if, like Nik had suggested, she'd called him instead? What if he'd come and gotten her, and she'd gone to stay with him and Mrs. Andino?

But then he would have lost his scholarship, and Jane would have been the one to ruin his life, to crush his dreams. How could she have lived with that fact? But how could she live with it now, knowing that he'd lost his scholarship anyway, and her sacrifices were for nothing? She could have been with Nik this whole time, and everything that had happened in Los Angeles these past ten years would have been nothing but a bad dream.

She closed her eyes, remembering Nik's arms around her, warming her from the cold, offering comfort.

From downstairs, a giggle drifted up through the floor-boards, snapping her from her reverie. Mom and Scarlett were making pancakes again.

Jane rolled out of bed and headed downstairs. It would be too easy to fall back into Nik— which was exactly why Jane had had to say no when he'd asked to meet today. Jane *had* gone to Los Angeles, and the last ten years might feel like a bad dream, but they were very real. And now she had Scarlett to think about.

Downstairs, Jane found Mom and Scarlett standing at the stove, making pancakes just like the day before. Jane grabbed one from the plate on the counter, rolled it up, and took a bite as she sat down on one of the stools at the counter.

"Would you like a plate?" Mom asked, with slight disapproval in her voice.

Jane shook her head. "Thanks, but I actually need to run an errand. Are you okay with Scarlett for an hour or two?"

"Grandma said we could go out and play in the snow after breakfast!" Scarlett announced.

Jane was glad Scarlett was so excited about snow. They'd be getting a lot of it where they were going.

"Scarlett, can you run upstairs and get my slippers?" Mom asked. "These wood floors are so cold on my old feet."

As soon as Scarlett took off, Mom turned to Jane. "Have you heard from Kait? Is that what this errand is about?"

"Not yet." Jane had a list of things she wanted to pick up before they left for Canada, things she couldn't buy before they left LA for fear that Matteo might find them. Warmer coats for both her and Scarlett. A pair of haircutting scissors and dye in a basic shade of brown. A couple of baseball hats. "Kait said it could be a week or so."

"And you think you can trust her?" Mom frowned.

"She's literally the *only* person I can trust."

Mom flinched at that, but Jane couldn't bring herself to take it back. Sometimes the truth hurt.

"Did you think about my suggestion about hiring an attorney? I saw Martin Lefkowitz at the grocery store last week. I mentioned we might be needing some legal advice and he said to stop by anytime."

Jane's eyes widened. "You didn't tell him anything about me, did you?"

"No, he thought it was about Dad's paperwork. But the point is that I think he'd be willing to help you leave Matteo and get custody of Scarlett through the legal channels."

Jane shook her head. "Would calling a lawyer and going through the *legal channels* to leave Dad have worked for you?"

"It's not the same." Mom's shoulders drooped. "Dad was the chief of police in this town. And I didn't have anywhere to go. By the time I might have been able to consider leaving, your grandparents in Ottawa had already passed, and there was nowhere else."

Jane stared across the counter at Mom. The woman's voice at the domestic violence shelter came back to her, explaining her options. Or lack of options, it had felt like to Jane. Barriers at every turn. Mom's choices hadn't been any better.

"Just because he doesn't live here doesn't mean Matteo will ever let us go. If I tell him Scarlett and I aren't coming back, he'll show up here."

"Well, let him come," Mom snapped. "We can handle it."

Jane gaped at her. "*How?*"

Mom shrugged, busying herself with opening one of the kitchen drawers. "Well..." she finally said. "I think..."

Her voice trailed off at the sound of Scarlett's feet stomping on the stairs.

"I don't want to talk about this in front of Scarlett," Jane said, sliding off her stool. "For now, I think I'll stick to my plan."

TWENTY-ONE

Jane drove forty-five minutes south to a Walmart in Pennsylvania to pick up her supplies. The last thing she needed was one of the local busybodies shopping at Ford's to interrogate her about why she was buying brown hair dye and dark sunglasses in the middle of winter.

When Jane returned home, she parked her car and stepped out onto Mom's driveway. Immediately, a high-pitched wail carried out from inside the house.

Scarlett. Jane's heart slammed in her chest. *Oh my God, was it—? Could Matteo have—?*

Jane didn't stop to think, she just took off running up the porch steps and flung open the front door. In the hallway, she found Mom frantically throwing on her shoes while Scarlett sat on the steps clutching one arm with her opposite hand, a bleeding gash across her forehead, tears streaming down her cheeks.

Jane rushed toward her daughter, crouching down to look her over. Scarlett pulled her arm closer to her body and wailed louder.

"What happened?" Jane searched for an angry six-foot man,

but—*thank God*—there was no sign of him. She pulled a tissue from her pocket and pressed it to Scarlett's forehead.

"I fell," Scarlett gasped, the hitching in her chest turning the two syllables into five. "I bumped my head and my arm hurts."

"We were cleaning up the lunch dishes." Mom's voice shook. "I went upstairs for just a moment, and then I heard a crash. I ran back down and found that Scarlett had pulled a dining chair up to the kitchen counter and had climbed up to reach the chocolate chips."

"I'm sorry," Scarlett wailed.

"She slipped in her socks and fell off." Mom yanked her coat on. "We're going to the emergency room. I planned to call you on the drive." Mom's shoulders slumped. "I'm so sorry, I should have been watching."

Jane reached for Scarlett's boots and gently helped her daughter slide her feet inside. "It's not your fault. Scarlett has always been a chocolate monster. Right, baby?" She kept her voice upbeat, forcing a smile for her daughter so she wouldn't know how Jane's heart was pounding. "It's going to be fine."

"I'll drive, you can sit in the back with Scarlett," Mom said, swinging open the front door as Jane helped Scarlett to her feet.

Once Jane had Scarlett strapped in and they were on their way to the hospital, her heartbeat finally returned to normal. The gash on her daughter's forehead had looked worse than it was once Mom had handed her a box of tissues from the front seat and she was able to gently wipe away the blood. And Scarlett's wails had tapered to whimpers by the time they reached the hospital.

As Mom pulled the car door open and Jane helped Scarlett climb out, Jane couldn't help but think about how relieved she was to have a little bit of help. Though she'd been living with Matteo for a decade now, she was largely on her own when it came to parenting. Matteo tended to be the fun dad when the mood struck him, and then checked out when there was actual work to be done. If this had happened at home, Matteo would have blamed Jane for not keeping a better eye on Scarlett and complained about all the noise from the crying.

Mom steered Scarlett to a vinyl chair in the hospital waiting room while Jane checked her in at the front desk. The woman there typed some things into the computer in front of her, handed Jane a medical form to fill out, and then asked for Scarlett's insurance card. Jane hesitated. They had insurance through Matteo's job at the club. But what if it got back to Matteo that Scarlett had to be rushed to the ER? You never knew how he might react to something like that. He might blame Jane and demand they come home right away.

The front desk woman was looking at Jane expectantly, so she handed over the card. The insurance company usually sent a statement in the mail, but that would probably take weeks. With any luck, they'd be long gone by then. Still, when Jane sat down to fill out the forms, she scribbled the wrong building number and zip code in the address fields. Maybe that would slow down the paperwork. And then she spelled Scarlett's name with one T and fudged the line for her birthdate, too.

Jane had some experience with long waits at emergency rooms, so she was surprised when the nurse called Scarlett back to an exam room after only about five minutes. Just another way Linden Falls was an entire world away from LA.

"The exam rooms are small, so I'll wait here," Mom said, and Jane remembered that Mom had some experience with emergency rooms, too.

Jane and Scarlett followed the nurse through a sliding door and back to an exam room. The nurse got Scarlett situated on an exam table and directed Jane to sit on a chair on the opposite wall while he took Scarlett's vitals. Then he folded up a gauze square and handed it to Jane in case Scarlett's head started to bleed again. "The doctor will be in shortly."

Jane watched him leave. Though he was about her age, Jane

didn't recognize him from high school. Maybe he'd moved here for the job. The hospital appeared to be more modern, the equipment more state-of-the-art, than it had been a decade ago. Back then everything had seemed a little rundown and dingy. So, maybe the hospital was a draw for health professionals now.

And with that thought, Jane nearly jumped out of her chair. Because it was the moment she remembered that—

"Hello," came a voice from the doorway. It was extra buoyant in that way that doctors speak to make children feel comfortable. And it was familiar. "You must be Scarlett."

Jane spun toward the doorway just as Nik's tall frame filled the room.

"I'm Dr. Andino, but you can call me..." His voice trailed off as his eyes swung from Scarlett to focus on Jane. "Nik." He finally finished. "You can call me Nik." He took an audible breath. "And you must be..." His gaze darted to Scarlett and back to Jane. He blinked, rubbing his forehead as if he'd been the one to hit his head. "You must be Scarlett's mother."

TWENTY-TWO

Scarlett's mother.

Nik tried to wrap his mind around the words as a freight train roared in his ears. Jane had a child. And she hadn't said a word, not even after their conversation at the overlook yesterday. She'd kept it from him, just like she'd kept everything about her life for the past ten years from him. And so much before that, too. It shouldn't have surprised him anymore. But here he was.

Jane's wide eyes cut into him as she lunged to her feet and then stood frozen in the center of the room, her mouth open in surprise. "I—Nik. I forgot that…"

She'd forgotten that he worked here. What if she'd remembered? Would she have driven Scarlett twenty miles away to the hospital in Harrisville just to avoid seeing him? To avoid giving up her latest secret?

Nik focused on Jane's daughter. Her blond, wavy hair hung past her shoulders, blue eyes stared up at him. Scarlett looked—

Just like Jane. She looked like the girl he knew back when they didn't keep things from each other. And she looked hurt and scared.

That snapped him out of his stupor. He was the doctor here, and Scarlett was his patient. It didn't matter who her mother was or what kinds of secrets she'd been hiding. Nik headed to the sink to wash his hands. Then he turned to Scarlett, giving her a reassuring smile. "I heard you had a fall."

Scarlett nodded, still clutching her arm with the opposite hand. "I hurt my arm and my head."

"I can see that," Nik said in a low voice. He reached out a hand to Scarlett. "Is it okay if I take a look?"

Scarlett nodded. Nik took her by the wrist and gently worked it back and forth. "Can you do that on your own?" She flapped her hand in front of her with what looked to be the full range of motion, so next he held out a palm. "Can you press here?"

Scarlett pressed her little fist against the flat of his hand and let out a quiet gasp.

Jane's shoulder brushed his as she slid closer to her daughter's side, and Nik did his best to ignore the hum of electricity that kicked on the second she was in his vicinity. He shifted away from her, keeping his attention on Scarlett. "I heard you were going for the chocolate chips."

Scarlett sniffed and then nodded.

He gave her a crooked smile. "Those are my favorite, too."

"It was an accident." Scarlett's eyes filled with tears. "I didn't mean to fall."

"We know you didn't, honey." Jane slid an arm around her daughter's shoulder.

"Can I tell you something?" Nik tilted his head in Scarlett's direction. "I think your mom's been keeping secrets."

Beside him, Jane gasped. "Nik, I really don't think..."

He cut her off, still focused on Scarlett. "She didn't tell you that she almost ended up at the doctor after trying to steal a treat, too, did she?"

Jane blew out a slow breath.

Scarlett gazed up at him, wide-eyed. She shook her head.

Nik nodded. "We were baking special peanut butter fudge brownies, and your mom decided she couldn't wait until they were done. She reached in and burned her wrist on the roof of the oven."

Scarlett's mouth dropped open in surprise. "I know who you are," she declared. "You were her friend when she was my age. She told me about you."

Nik blinked. He'd always imagined that Jane had erased him from her thoughts when she'd taken off. But since their revelations last night, he didn't know what to think. *And what has she told her daughter about me?* It would be completely inappropriate to ask, though he was tempted. "That's right," he said. "Your mom and I grew up together." He couldn't help it now, and his eyes darted to Jane. She pressed her lips together and looked away. "That was a long time ago, though."

Nik cleared his throat and pulled an ophthalmoscope from his pocket. "I'm just going to use this to take a look in your eyes, okay?" Nik flashed the light at each of Scarlett's pupils. She squeezed her eyes shut and began to sway on the exam table. "How does your head feel?" he asked.

"It hurts," Scarlett whimpered.

Nik put a hand on her shoulder to steady her. "Does it hurt where you bumped it, or hurt like you have a headache?"

"Both."

"Anything else hurt?"

"My tummy." She turned to Jane, reaching for her mother. "Mommy, I'm going to throw up."

With three years in the ER under his belt, Nik was used to reacting quickly. He grabbed a plastic basin from the counter by the sink and spun toward Scarlett, getting it under her chin just in time. Jane pulled her daughter's hair out of the way while Scarlett leaned over, heaving, retching, and crying all at the same time.

"You're okay, baby. Get it all out." She stroked Scarlett's back, and Nik was sure that the girl wouldn't pick up on the tremor in her mother's voice or the worry creasing her face.

But he did. When Scarlett paused for a breath, and Jane reached for the basin to take over from Nik, he shook his head. "I've got it." He hitched his chin at Scarlett. "You just do what you're doing."

Jane wrapped an arm around Scarlett. The little girl leaned forward, tears streaming down her face, as she threw up into the basin again. "My head hurts..." she wailed, drawing out the last word into multiple syllables. In the next moment, more of her lunch came up.

"I know, baby. I know," Jane said. "You're going to be fine." Her eyes implored Nik to confirm her words were true.

He gave her a reassuring nod. "Nausea is common after a head bump." Nik leaned in to meet Jane's eyes, keeping his voice low. "We'll run some tests for concussion and maybe keep her overnight for observation. But she'll be fine. We see this all the time."

Nik didn't want to spend too much time analyzing the way his heart twisted when Jane's shoulders relaxed. Or the temptation he had to pull Jane into his arms when Scarlett finally stopped throwing up and lay back on the exam table to rest. Instead, he backed away, leaving the basin on the counter by the sink and heading out of the room.

Nik sat at the computer by the nurses' station and entered his orders for tests: an MRI to check for a concussion and x-ray for a possible forearm fracture. And then he began to type up his notes.

Nine-year-old girl admitted to the ER with forehead laceration complaining of headache, nausea, and—

Nik's hands froze on the keyboard.

Nine-year-old girl.

Jane had fled Linden Falls in the early summer ten years ago, the day after they lost their virginity to each other in the back of Nik's car at the overlook. And now she had a nine-year-old daughter. *Was it possible...?*

Nik closed his eyes, picturing Scarlett's long blond hair and blue eyes, searching his memory for any hint of his own features. All he'd noticed in that room was that she looked just like a younger version of Jane. But he hadn't been looking for more than that.

Nik grabbed the computer mouse and clicked around in Scarlett's medical form until he found her personal information.

Mother: Jane Allison McCaffrey

Father: Matteo DeLuca

Nik sat back in his chair, staring at the name. Ethically, he really shouldn't do what he was about to do. He was the doctor, and Scarlett was his patient. But if there was any chance that Jane had been keeping an even bigger secret from him...

Nik grabbed his phone and googled the name of Scarlett's father, and then added *Los Angeles* to the search bar. The first photo to pop up was of an attractive, smiling man in his early forties standing behind a shiny chrome bar. A neon-lit shelf lined with liquor bottles made up the background of the shot. Nik clicked on the link. Matteo DeLuca was the manager of a nightclub in Los Angeles. Nik zoomed in. Matteo had curly, dark hair, and brown eyes. His coloring wasn't that much different than Nik's. But nothing about his features ruled for or against him being Scarlett's father.

Nik focused back on his computer screen, clicking over to the information the receptionist had typed into Scarlett's medical record. He briefly skimmed the address—Los Angeles. At least Jane had been telling the truth about that. And then he checked Scarlett's birthdate.

August 2nd.

Nik slumped back in his chair. Scarlett had turned nine this past summer. Which meant that Jane would have been in LA for months before her child was conceived. So that was why she'd never contacted him. She'd met someone else, gotten pregnant, and moved on with her life.

It should have come as a relief that Scarlett wasn't his child. What would it have meant to learn that Jane had kept something like that from him on top of all her other secrets? How would he have ever forgiven her? But as Nik glanced at the handsome man smiling up at him from his phone, something knotted in his gut. Maybe Jane had left Linden Falls to protect him. But she'd run straight to this Matteo DeLuca in Los Angeles. Matteo had kissed her, touched her, been *inside her* mere months after she'd been with Nik. Mere months after she'd shared the most important moments of Nik's life.

And now Matteo had everything Nik had always wanted.

From the moment she'd walked back into this town, Nik had known. He still wanted Jane in his life, in his bed. He still wanted her laughter, her friendship. Her heart. But that guy in the photo and the little girl in the exam room next door meant he'd never have any of those things. Jane had a family and an entire life that he wasn't a part of. Hell, Jane had an entire life he didn't even know anything about.

Nik took one more look at Matteo's face and then closed the browser window. It was probably better he'd found out this way. Because this solved all the mysteries about where Jane had been and why she'd stayed away. And he could finally let her go and move on.

At that moment, the computer beeped, announcing a message had come in. Scarlett's test results. He clicked open the window and scanned the report. Scarlett had a distal radius fracture and would need to be fitted for a cast on her arm. He continued reading. The MRI had picked up some slight swelling in her brain. It was recommended they keep her overnight for observation.

When Nik entered Scarlett's hospital room to let Jane know the results of the tests, he found her lying in the bed, her back against the pillows, with Scarlett's head on her chest. Her eyes were closed, and the only sign she was awake was the way her hand gently stroked her daughter's hair. It hit him all over again that Jane had a child, that this was the reason she hadn't come back for the past decade. Somehow, he felt both happy for her—and utterly left out of her life.

Scarlett stirred, shifting on the bed and opening her eyes. "Mommy, I want to go home."

"I know, honey," Jane murmured, as if it took a supreme amount of effort to form the words. "It will just be a little longer." She looked so tired, so worn out, with dark circles under her eyes and a heaviness to her movements like she'd attached weights to her arms.

Nik stepped inside the room, rattling the curtain. "Hey."

When she spotted him, Jane slid her arm out from under Scarlett so she could sit up.

He waved a hand in her direction. "You're fine there, you don't have to get up."

"No, it's okay." Jane climbed out of the bed and perched on the edge.

Nik approached Scarlett. "How are you feeling?" They'd given her a wrap to secure her arm, and she looked exhausted but otherwise okay.

She shrugged and looked away, suddenly shy.

He looked to Jane. "Any more headaches or nausea?"

Jane shook her head. "The nurse gave her something that helped a lot. Now we're just ready to go home. Is there any news about the test results?"

"Well," Nik said, "the good news is that Scarlett is going to be just fine. She has a small fracture that will require a cast, and a little bump on her head. But we're going to have to keep her overnight to monitor that bump."

Scarlett let out a little whimper.

"It's just a precaution, I promise." He tried to keep his voice upbeat as he turned to look at Scarlett. "We have comfortable rooms upstairs, and they have nice big couches where your mom can sleep."

Scarlett stared wide-eyed, and Nik braced himself for the girl to start crying or at least to whine that she wanted to go home. He delivered a lot of news like this, and kids usually didn't take it so well. But though Scarlett's eyes filled with tears, she remained silent.

Jane stroked her daughter's hair again. "I'll stay here with you the whole time, okay?" She rubbed her temples like her head had suddenly started throbbing and turned to Nik. "So, what happens now?"

"The nurse will be in sometime in the next hour to get Scarlett fitted for her cast and then coordinate her admittance to the inpatient unit."

"Okay." Jane nodded. "My mom is out in the waiting room. I'll need to let her know she should go home." She hauled herself up from the bed, and then hesitated. "Scarlett, will you be okay for one minute? I'll be right back."

Nik checked his watch. He only had about a half-hour left on his shift, with an hour of paperwork to finish. But then his gaze slid back and forth between Jane's exhausted face and Scarlett's anxious one. "Take your time. I'll hang out here with Scarlett."

Jane hesitated. "Are you sure? I don't want to keep you from your other patients."

Nik tapped the phone on his hip. "They'll call me if they need me." Then from the pocket of his lab coat, he pulled out a pack of Uno cards. "While we're waiting..." He gave Scarlett a grin. "What do you say I beat you at Uno?"

Scarlett's eyes lit up and she sat up in the bed.

"You might regret that," Jane warned. "Scarlett is an Uno expert."

Something tugged in Nik's chest. Pete had kept an old pile of games on the shelf at the Grassroots Café, and Nik and Jane used to play Uno for hours at their table in the corner. Over the years, their matches had grown increasingly competitive. *Three out of five: Winner buys coffee. Loser has to declare the winner is the smartest, most beautiful person they've ever met.*

When Jane had been the winner, Nik had delivered his penalty with a goofy grin and a laugh to hide his true feelings behind the words.

Did Jane think about those old competitions when she was playing with her daughter? He sat on the chair next to the bed and pulled it closer, shuffling the cards. "You in, too?" he asked Jane, with a hint of a challenge in his voice. "We'll wait for you to come back."

She hesitated, glancing at Scarlett, who had rubbed away the tears and was smiling now. "Of course I am." Jane raised her eyebrows. "Same old rules?"

Nik looked at Scarlett with his head cocked. "Loser has to declare the winner is the smartest, most beautiful person they've ever met—?"

Scarlett giggled and nodded.

Nik shuffled the cards, his eyes drifting to Jane's. "Yep, same old rules."

TWENTY-THREE

Jane watched her daughter sleeping in the hospital bed. A bright green cast covered her arm from wrist to elbow, the billowy fabric of her hospital gown enveloping her small frame. Scarlett had eaten dinner and finally fallen asleep an hour ago, and Jane wished that she could do the same. She shifted on the vinyl couch that would be her own bed for the evening, and though her whole body ached with exhaustion, her mind was whirring with the events of the day.

Her thoughts inevitably drifted to Nik.

He'd looked so shocked when he'd first walked into the exam room and discovered that she was Scarlett's mother. But despite being blindsided, he'd been nothing but kind and compassionate, showing so much care for Scarlett, and to Jane when she was panicking over Scarlett's head injury. Maybe that was just his job. He was clearly good at it. But later, it hadn't been his job to hang out with them playing cards, cheering Scarlett up and taking Jane's mind off the situation. He'd done it because that was the kind of person he was.

Nik had been so good with Scarlett, teasing her about the card game, making her laugh with his sad faces when he lost a round. Scarlett had gazed up at him with adoring eyes. It was an expression she used to reserve for Matteo, but which had become less frequent as she grew older and began to understand who her father really was.

Over the years, Jane had imagined what it might have been like for her daughter to grow up with a man like Nik instead of Matteo. But it had only ever been a late-night fantasy that she never allowed herself to entertain in the light of day. Seeing them together, seeing how natural Nik was with Scarlett, Jane's heart ached with that old longing.

Jane glanced from her sleeping daughter to the clock over the TV. It was after eight, and Nik had probably gone home by now. When the nurse had come in to take Scarlett for her cast and admit her for the night, Nik had left to finish his paperwork. Jane knew it was better than having him hang around. The more he stayed here, getting to know Scarlett and making Jane feel like she wasn't alone, the harder it would be to leave in a few days.

So, when the curtain in front of the door rustled, and Nik stepped into the room, Jane didn't want to admit how glad she was to see him.

"How is she feeling?" Nik whispered from the doorway.

Jane stood on shaky legs but stayed where she was, on the opposite side of the room. "They gave her some meds for the pain in her arm, and it seemed to help the headache, too. She ate dinner and fell asleep about an hour ago."

"Good." Nik nodded. "I think she'll be fine by tomorrow."

Jane glanced at the clock again. "You're here late. I thought you would have gone home by now."

"I was on my way, but..." He shrugged. "You looked exhausted when I saw you earlier, and the nurse said you hadn't eaten, so..." Nik held out a paper bag. "I remembered you like Thai food." He gave her a crooked smile.

Nik had been running around taking care of people all day,

and then he'd played five rounds of Uno while they waited for the nurse. He certainly didn't have to go out of his way to feed her. He must be exhausted, too. Jane took in his messy hair and the way the dim overhead lights of the hospital room high-lighted the dark smudges under his eyes. "Have *you* eaten anything?" she asked.

Nik shook his head. "It's okay. I've got something in the fridge at home."

Jane crossed the room, taking the bag and peeking inside. She found a plastic container of pad thai and a handful of napkins and plastic silverware. "There are two forks here, and I'll never eat this all by myself. Do you want to share?"

Nik hesitated, his gaze sweeping over Jane's face as if he wasn't sure what to make of her. Finally, he nodded. "That would be great. Thanks."

The paper bag in Jane's hand crinkled, and Scarlett stirred.

Nik nodded toward the door. "There's a family waiting room across the hall. It's probably empty this time of night. Let's go over there."

Jane followed Nik across the hall to a small room with a coffee maker, vending machine, and a vinyl-covered couch. She settled at one end, placing the food carton on the coffee table while Nik sank into the cushions on the other end.

He reached out to take the fork she offered him. "I realize you turned me down for dinner tonight, so this wasn't meant to be me worming my way in."

Jane shook her head. "I would never think that." She bit her lip. "I guess now you know the reason I said no." She pulled the lid off the food container and stared at the swirl of noodles so she wouldn't have to look at Nik. "It's complicated."

The silence stretched, and she knew he was waiting for more of an explanation. But how could she sum up the last ten years? She couldn't, so instead, she stabbed her fork into the pad thai. "You were lovely with Scarlett today. I really appreciate it."

"She's a great kid." Nik smiled. "And just as competitive as her mom, I noticed."

Jane laughed, grateful to lighten the mood. "Yes, I've created a monster who can now destroy me." Jane had lost badly to both Nik and Scarlett at Uno. In the end, Nik had come out the champion, but Scarlett had put up a good fight.

"Does she take after you in other ways? Does she play music? I remember around that age you were constantly singing show tunes."

Jane shook her head. "I must have been so obnoxious."

"I always loved your voice." He gave her a crooked grin. "And thanks to you, I still belt out 'Defying Gravity' in the shower. Don't tell anyone."

"I would never." Jane handed him the carton of pad thai. "No, Scarlett doesn't really sing. She's more of a reader. And she likes to draw." Jane had encouraged quiet activities. She couldn't imagine Scarlett belting out "Defying Gravity" when Matteo was around.

"Since Scarlett will need to take it easy for a few days, I'll see what books my mom has lying around in my old bedroom."

He just kept taking care of them, and she didn't feel like she deserved it. Especially since she'd kept Scarlett a secret from him. "Nik, I'm sorry you had to find out about her like this."

Nik regarded her across the narrow space. "I wish you'd told me last night. But..."

"But what?"

He sighed. "I don't know. Now that I've met her, I get it. A decade has gone by. You have this whole other life, and you and I are basically strangers."

That was the thing. It didn't feel like a decade had gone by. And Nik didn't feel like a stranger. He felt safe. Familiar. Her feelings for Nik had grown slowly over time from best friends to something that could have been so much more. At eighteen, she'd loved him madly, desperately. Looking back on her life in Los Angeles, she'd managed to convince herself that she'd moved on. But now she could see it all so much more clearly. Her best friend had been the love of her life. She'd lost so much when she'd walked away.

"Is Scarlett's dad..." Nik waved a hand absently. "... in the picture? Does he know about Scarlett's accident?"

Jane bit her lip. "No. I didn't tell him."

"Can I ask why?"

Jane hadn't planned to say anything. But the exhaustion of the past week—the past decade—washed over her. And being around Nik made her feel safer, and more cared for, than she had in years. "I left him. We're not together anymore. Matteo isn't very interested in being a part of our lives." Every word was the truth. Matteo might have had a strong desire to control their lives, but very little actual interest in her or Scarlett.

Nik leaned forward and set the food container on the table in front of him. "I'm sorry." He shifted to face her. "Not that you left him. I'm sorry that you had to go through all that."

Jane stared down at her hands. "It's for the best."

Nik slid closer. "Is it?" He reached up and put a gentle hand on her cheek, rubbing his thumb on the spot where she knew her bruise was fading, but not quite gone.

He knows Matteo put that mark there. Nik had always been observant, especially when it came to her.

"It shows a lot of strength to decide you deserve better," he said.

Jane didn't feel strong. She felt terrified. But for the first time in a long time, maybe she didn't feel completely alone. Mom was waiting at home, and she'd texted twice to check in. Jane's gaze drifted to Nik. His shift had ended hours ago. He didn't need to be here. But he was. Bringing her food, checking in on her daughter, and making her long for all sorts of things that she never thought she'd ever have.

Their eyes met. If she leaned in a couple of inches, she could press her mouth to his. It was so tempting. To fall into him, to be encircled by the safety of his arms.

But Jane slid back in her seat, away from him, her face flushing. "I'm sorry. This isn't a good idea..."

Nik shook his head. "No, I'm sorry. You have an injured kid across the hall. I don't want to put this pressure on you."

"Nik..." Jane reached out a hand to touch his arm, but then she let it drop in her lap at the last second. "It's not that I don't feel this. But..." She bit her lip. "*I'm leaving.*" In less than a week, she would disappear from his life. How could she get involved and then put him through that again? How could she put herself through it again?

"Don't say anything now." He slid the carton of food into her hand. "You need to eat."

While they finished the pad thai, Nik filled Jane in on the Linden Falls gossip. He told her about the town council painting the water tower coral and accidentally turning it into a giant penis, and then about the senior prank where the football team hired a crane to move the principal's car to the roof of the high school. Lighthearted stories that made her laugh and distracted her from everything swirling around in her head. As she cleaned up after they'd eaten, and threw away the trash, she realized he'd known exactly what she needed in that moment.

They headed back across the hall to check on Scarlett. Nik bustled around the room, scrolling through a file on the computer to check the nurse's notes, glancing at the monitors on the wall. Jane stood back and watched as he rounded the hospital bed to grab an extra blanket from the cabinet. The dim light shone across his face as he leaned in to spread it across Scarlett and tuck it under the corners of the bed.

Jane studied his profile, taking in the slope of his nose, the sharpness of his cheekbones. Something familiar flickered in the back of her mind.

Nik leaned closer to Scarlett, smoothing the blanket.

Jane's gaze darted to her daughter's profile. To Scarlett's nose. Scarlett's cheekbones.

Jane blinked, over and over, as recognition slowly dawned. *Is it possible?*

She'd wondered... sometimes she'd even wished for it. But had she shoved this possibility so far out of her head that she'd completely fooled everyone, and especially herself?

Could Nik be Scarlett's father?

TWENTY-FOUR

Jane combed through her memories from a decade ago, trying to recall those weeks and months leading up to her pregnancy. It came back to her in a blur of emotions: the hopelessness, the shock, the fear, the sense of being utterly alone. But the specific details of that time floated just beyond her reach.

How long after she'd slept with Nik had she been with Matteo for the first time? A week or two? And then it was a couple of months later she'd discovered she was pregnant. Had she gotten her period in the time between? She'd been so young, so dumb about the mechanics of it all. Jane remembered that she'd wished Nik was the father more than she'd actually believed it. They'd definitely used a condom. She knew that much for sure: Nik had cared about her too much not to protect her. She remembered every detail of their first time together. Their only time.

But they'd been young and inexperienced. And condoms failed, sometimes. Had she convinced herself it was Matteo because she was three thousand miles from home, and being with Nik was impossible? Or was Matteo Scarlett's father all along, and now she was talking herself into believing it was Nik?

Jane watched Nik as he reached over Scarlett's head to push the button on a monitor. And there it was again. Their high, defined cheekbones. The straight line of their noses. And now she could see similarities in the arch of their eyebrows, too.

But then Nik bent over to untangle a cable, and the resemblance was gone.

This doesn't change anything.

Jane blinked and looked away. The notion that Nik had fathered Scarlett was nothing but half-baked speculation stemming from an overwhelming amount of stress. She and Scarlett were still leaving for Canada. It didn't matter who had contributed to Scarlett's genetic material. Matteo would never, ever let them go. Her only hope was running, just like she'd planned. Kait would come through with a car and, in less than a week, she and Scarlett would be safely across the border, as far away from Matteo as possible. They'd start a new life and Nik would never have to know she was having these unhinged suspicions that he was Scarlett's father.

Nobody ever has to know.

But as Nik looked up to flash Jane a smile, doubt curled in her abdomen. He'd been amazing with Scarlett earlier. Kind and caring and natural.

How could I leave, and take Scarlett away forever, without even considering finding out the truth?

If Nik turned out to be Scarlett's father, maybe Matteo wouldn't want to have anything to do with her. Maybe, legally, he wouldn't be *allowed* to have anything to do with her. Jane could take Mom's advice and hire a lawyer to help them. They wouldn't have to run, and Scarlett could know her father—her real father—the compassionate, thoughtful man that she deserved.

And then... maybe... someday...

Jane's attention drifted back to Nik just as he stepped into a narrow slant of light from the streetlamp outside. It was a far-fetched idea. A fairy tale. And Jane had never lived a fairy tale life. Wishes didn't come true, and there was no such thing as happily-ever-afters.

But, for the first time in a decade, Jane found herself starting to believe.

Scarlett woke early the next morning, just as the doctor came in to make her rounds before breakfast. Nik was no longer Scarlett's physician; he'd handed her case off to the attending on the inpatient unit, and Jane wasn't sure if they'd see him before they left. He said he'd be working in the ER that morning, but he was probably busy with patients. She wasn't sure if she was sorry or relieved.

The doctor checked Scarlett over, shining a light in her eyes and testing her reflexes before she declared the girl ready to be discharged. Jane helped Scarlett change from her hospital gown back into her street clothes, and they were about to head out when a message alert popped up from Matteo on Jane's phone.

Jane dreaded what he had to say. Matteo didn't like being home alone—he got bored, antsy, annoyed when he didn't have Jane to do things for him. Add that to the fact that he was having staffing issues at the club, and his messages were increasing in both frequency and urgency. It was only a matter of time before he started demanding that she come home. Which meant that the clock was ticking for her to finish putting her plan into place. She sent Matteo another soothing message, hoping he would hold off at least until after Christmas.

The nurse insisted that Jane take Scarlett out to the car in a wheelchair, and just as they were heading out into the hall, Nik stepped out of the elevator, a tote bag over one arm.

"Hi," he said, giving Jane a quick smile before he knelt down to Scarlett's level.

"Hi, Dr. Nik." Scarlett gave him a grin.

"How are you feeling?"

"Okay."

"How's the head? Still hurt?"

"It feels better now."

"Good. You're going to need to take it easy for a few days, okay? No running around."

Scarlett nodded.

"Your mom said you like to read, so I did some digging." He slid the tote off his arm and reached in, pulling out a small pile of chapter books. He set them on Scarlett's lap. "Have you read these Warrior Cats books yet?"

Scarlett's eyes lit up as she took in the colorful covers, each with a different cat's face. "No! Thanks."

"Let me know what you think, okay?" He hitched his chin at her cast. "Now, are you going to let me sign that thing?"

"Sure!"

Jane's eyes trailed after him as he grabbed a Sharpie from the nurses' station and came back to scrawl the words *Dr. Nik, Uno Champion* on the textured green material.

"Nooo!" Scarlett protested, laughing. "What happens when I beat you next time?"

Nik appeared to give it some thought. "Then I'll let you write *Scarlett, Uno Champion* on *my* arm. Deal?"

"Deal."

Nik held out a hand and they shook.

Still grinning, he came around to the back of the wheel-chair. "How are you feeling?" he asked Jane, leaning in. "Did you get any sleep on that couch?"

"Not much," she admitted, running her fingers through her tangled hair, self-conscious now that he was standing so close. The nurse had given her a small toiletry bag, so Jane had brushed her teeth and washed her face, but she'd been wearing the same clothes for twenty-four hours and didn't even want to think about the dark circles under her eyes she'd seen in the bathroom mirror that morning.

Nik nudged Jane aside so he could take over wheelchair pushing duties. Jane let him, her heart stirring at the small but thoughtful gesture. She was tired, he stepped in to help. Simple as that. But it wasn't simple to Jane, and her thoughts from last night went whirling again.

Mom had pulled the car into the loading zone, and when she saw them coming, she climbed out to open the door. Scarlett was a little unsteady on her feet, so Nik helped her into the back and reached over to click the seatbelt while Jane stood by and marveled again how much easier everything was with a little bit of help. When she wasn't trying to do everything on her own.

Nik closed the back door, and Mom gave a smile in his direction. "It's nice to see you, Nik. How is your mother?"

"She's great. Probably baking. It's her favorite thing to do this time of year."

"Oh, yes." Mom smiled. "I remember her famous Christmas cookies."

Jane could still remember the taste of Mrs. Andino's triple chocolate peppermint cookies. They might have been the single confection better than Pete's peanut butter brownies.

"What are your plans for the holiday?" Nik asked, looking back and forth from Jane to Mom.

"We're just going to have a quiet day," Jane said. She'd picked up one more gift for Scarlett on her errands yesterday and, knowing Mom, there would probably be pancakes. But they didn't have plans beyond that. Still, it would probably be the best Christmas they'd ever had.

"Why don't you join us at my mom's?" Nik asked.

Jane had so many happy memories from Mrs. Andino's

house. But Christmas was in two days. "Oh, we couldn't just show up at the last minute."

"Since I'll be helping her cook, I know we'll have plenty of food." He cocked his head. "And I know she'd love to see you and meet Scarlett." He turned to Mom. "And to see you too, Mrs. McCaffrey."

Mom's face creased with longing and, unexpectedly, Jane felt a lump in the back of her throat. *Mom is as isolated as I am.* She'd been alone raising a child... and then just *alone*, with Dad, for decades. She'd lost her family, her community, her best friend, too.

Before Jane could change her mind, she nodded. "If you're sure you have room for us, we'd love to."

On the way home, they stopped at the pharmacy to fill Scarlett's prescription, and Jane ran inside. She was headed down an aisle toward the back of the store when a tall man about her age stepped out of her path. His blue eyes and dark, curly hair looked vaguely familiar, but she didn't realize she knew him until he called out her name.

Jane turned around. "Martin?" They'd gone to high school together. She remembered him as tall and skinny, a bit nerdy. He'd worn glasses and braces and had gotten straight As in the honors classes.

He'd filled out in the past ten years, with broad shoulders and more muscle than she remembered. The braces were gone, obviously, and though he still wore glasses, they were the clear-rimmed, trendy kind. His tailored suit looked out of place in the aisles of the local pharmacy, though it fit him impeccably. "How are you?"

"Good." He nodded in Jane's direction. "It's great to see you. I didn't realize you were back in town."

"Just visiting." She shrugged. "I hear you're an attorney now."

"Did the suit give it away?" Martin laughed. "I don't usually wear one, but I was in court this morning."

"Actually, my mom told me. She said you practice family law. Divorces and custody cases." Jane hesitated, eyeing his suit. "Do you have reason to go to court often in a small town like Linden Falls?"

"You'd be surprised." Martin cocked his head. "Did your mom also tell you my door is always open? I offer a steep discount for old friends."

Jane might have been imagining it, but she felt his gaze shift to the bruise on her cheek. It seemed like overnight it had turned from purple to a hideous greenish-yellow color. That was good, it meant that it would be gone soon, but Jane couldn't help but feel extra self-conscious about it now. And since she'd slept in Scarlett's hospital room last night, she hadn't had any make-up to cover it up.

Did Martin know? Or at least suspect? He was clearly a smart guy.

For about the hundredth time that morning, Jane's thoughts drifted back to her revelation about Nik last night, and that same longing kicked her in the gut. What if it were true? What if Nik were Scarlett's father? And what if maybe there was a way out that didn't involve running away again?

She'd need the best lawyer in the business, someone who'd be willing to go up against Matteo, someone scary enough to get him to back down. Jane was pretty sure she wasn't going to find that kind of lawyer in Linden Falls.

As if he could read her mind, Martin pulled a card from his pocket and held it out. "Listen, Jane. I worked for five years at a firm in New York City on pretty much every kind of case you can imagine, and I saw just about everything. Opposing counsel might think I'm just a small-town lawyer in sleepy Western

New York. But I just use it to my favor when they underestimate me."

Jane took the card, studying the black font against the heavy cream cardstock. "Well, I should probably get going."

Martin nodded. "It was nice to run into you."

"You, too." Jane headed to the pharmacy window at the back of the store.

There was a garbage can near the checkout, and she almost tossed Martin's card in but, at the last second, she tucked it into her pocket instead.

Back at the house, Jane got Scarlett settled on the couch with Nik's books, and then she headed into the kitchen to make some breakfast. Mom was standing at the stove, pancake batter already mixed up, poured on the pan, and dotted with chocolate chips.

I could get used to this. With an exhausted sigh, Jane settled on a stool with a cup of coffee.

"I'm so sorry about the accident." Mom nudged the bag of chocolate chips, and Jane was reminded that this all started with Scarlett's sweet tooth. "I should have been watching her."

"It's not your fault." Across the counter, Jane met her mother's eyes. "I mean it. The same thing could have happened when I was here. You can't blame yourself."

"I should have protected her." Mom cleared her throat, her eyes filling. "I should have protected her, and I should have protected you."

Jane's mouth dropped open, but no words would come out. In all her years of living with Dad, Mom had never expressed regret over how she'd defended him instead of leaving. She'd certainly never acknowledged how it had affected Jane. But instead of that same old bitterness rising up, a new emotion took over, one triggered by old memories: Dad annoyed that Jane was out too late at

choir practice, and Mom mentioning that the mayor had compli-
mented Jane's beautiful voice. Dad grumbling about Jane's friends,
and Mom running to get Dad a beer. Dad angry about Jane's grade
on a science test, and Mom getting a slap across the face.

*Maybe it took eighteen years for Dad to turn on me because
Mom always stepped in to stop him.*

As a child, she hadn't realized it. But now it made perfect
sense, especially because now she knew what it was like to be in
Mom's shoes. How many times had Matteo been annoyed with
Scarlett, and Jane had feared he might hurt her? *You're in the
way, you're playing too loudly.* Jane had always made sure she
was there to step in, to draw his ire away. Had Mom silently
protected Jane by soothing Dad, by distracting him, and—when
that didn't work—by taking a punch?

"You did protect me," Jane whispered. "More than I ever
realized." Gently, she reached and touched Mom's wrist, the
one where she sometimes wore a brace.

Mom flipped her hand over and took Jane's, giving it a
squeeze. With the other hand, she brushed a tear from her
cheek.

The pan sizzled, and Mom turned away to attend to breakfast. "I know I keep dwelling on this"—she flipped the pancakes
—"but what if you were to stay here?"

Jane reached into her pocket and rubbed the edge of
Martin's card. He really did seem very competent. But all the
competence in the world wasn't going to stop Matteo if he
didn't want to be stopped. "I don't think Matteo would ever let
us go."

Mom took a deep breath, almost as if she were debating
whether to say something. "There are ways to deal with
Matteo."

"Like talking to a lawyer?"

"Well, yes. For one thing. Or—"

A knock at the door cut off her next words, and Jane's mind flew to Matteo. He'd texted her about staffing at the club less than an hour ago. He wouldn't show up here now. *Would he?* The fear always lingered in the corners of her mind. That fight-or-flight response always turned slightly up.

Jane ran for the door, swinging it open, and found Hannah standing on the porch along with a little girl of about six years old.

Jane's shoulders relaxed. "Hannah! Hi."

"Hi," Hannah said, giving her a tentative smile and nervously adjusting the beanie hat she'd tugged over her hair. "I'm sorry to just show up like this. I don't have your number anymore." Hannah lifted her mitten-covered hands in a shrug. "I wondered if you were free to grab some coffee or something? I'd love to catch up a little before you leave town."

It was so like Hannah to reach out and make a gesture of friendship, even though Jane didn't deserve it. Jane's gaze drifted to the girl by her old friend's side, and a wistful smile tugged at her lips. She looked so like how Jane remembered Hannah as a girl. "You must be Amelia."

The girl nodded shyly.

"I recognize you from your photo, and because you look exactly like your mom."

"I really wanted you to meet her," Hannah said, smoothing a wayward curl from her daughter's forehead.

Behind Jane, a voice drifted from the living room. "Mommy? Who's at the door?" A second later, Scarlett appeared in the hallway, clutching her cast to her chest.

"Did she say..." Hannah's eyes grew wide. "You have a daughter, too?"

So much for keeping Scarlett a secret. Jane wasn't worried about Hannah spreading rumors all over town. Far from it. But every connection with someone she'd cared about from her past was making it harder to think about leaving without a trace again.

Hannah was still standing in the doorway, though, and the words were out of Jane's mouth before she could stop to think about what she was saying. "Would you like to come in?"

"Only if you're not busy."

"We're not. My mom just made coffee and pancakes."

Hannah and Amelia stepped inside and hung their coats on the rack. Hannah turned her attention back to Scarlett. "I guess I didn't need to ask if this is your daughter. I see the resemblance."

"This is Scarlett," Jane said.

Hannah's face broke into a huge smile. "Hi, it's so lovely to meet you. How old are you?"

"Nine."

"This is my daughter, Amelia. She's six."

"Scarlett," Jane explained, "this is my old friend Hannah. I've known her since she was a little older than you."

"Like you knew Dr. Nik?"

Hannah's eyebrows rose. "You met Nik?"

"At the hospital."

Hannah's green eyes drifted over Scarlett's cast.

"Scarlett," Jane said. "Why don't you take Amelia into the living room and show her your Legos?"

Scarlett eyed the other girl. "Do you know how to play Uno?"

Amelia shook her head.

"Come on, I'll teach you." The girls headed into the living room.

Hannah beamed. "It's sweet to see our daughters together, isn't it?"

Jane peeked in at Scarlett and Amelia as they settled on the couch. Scarlett was attempting to shuffle the pack of Uno cards

Nik had given her, and then she began counting them out. "You get seven and I get seven," she explained patiently to Amelia.

Jane realized now how lucky she was to grow up in Linden Falls, where kids could roam freely—even if Dad had kept the whole town in his grip. Jane had been allowed to hang out with friends and participate in local activities. It was new to her to see suddenly how much protection that had offered her, how she'd been able to avoid the sort of isolation that many kids in her situation would have experienced. Kids like Scarlett.

There were no kids roaming their neighborhood in LA. Where would they have gone? The strip malls and night clubs? Scarlett's school was huge, underfunded, and full of kids who had a lot more problems at home than Scarlett did. There were no slumber parties, no playdates in their neighborhood in LA, no after-school activities. It was easy to go unnoticed, and Scarlett and Jane mostly kept to themselves.

She smiled as Scarlett's voice drifted out, its hint of older-child authority evident as she explained the rules. Amelia hung on every word.

Jane leaned into the room. "Just Uno, okay, Scarlett? No running around. You're supposed to be resting."

Scarlett nodded and went back to her game.

Hannah looked concerned as they walked down the hall to the kitchen. "Was she in the ER with Nik? Is she okay?"

"She fell yesterday, but she's fine. She fractured her wrist and has a little bump on her head."

"Oh, no. That's so much for you to handle on a trip away from home." Hannah glanced up the stairs to the floor above. "Is her dad here to help?"

"No, he's back in LA." Jane hesitated. "But my mom has been really helpful." She said it partly to change the subject, but as the words came out of her mouth, she realized that leaving Mom behind again was getting harder to come to terms with.

Mom, alone in this big house. And she and Scarlett miles away in Canada. It didn't make any sense.

They entered the kitchen and found Mom setting the kitchen island with two plates of pancakes and two mugs of coffee. Hannah and Mom exchanged hugs and pleasantries, and then Mom headed for the doorway. "I'll let you girls talk."

"Thanks for this," Jane said, nodding at the food and drinks Mom had made for them. "And for your help earlier today."

Mom's lips curved up in a smile that Jane couldn't help but notice was a little wistful. "Anytime." With a wave she exited the kitchen.

The sound of giggling drifted in from the next room. Scarlett and Amelia seemed to be having fun. Jane and Hannah exchanged a smile as they settled on their stools at the counter.

"Thanks for having us." Hannah wrapped her hands around her mug. "I didn't mean to intrude or anything."

"You're not intruding at all. I want to apologize for taking off the other day." Jane knew she owed Hannah an explanation for her strange behavior in front of the Harp and Fiddle. And even more than that, for taking off a decade ago. If it had been Nik, Hannah, or Ali who'd disappeared without a trace, Jane would have been frantic. At the time, she'd been so wrapped up in her own desperation that she hadn't realized what they must have gone through. But she had no idea where to even begin, especially with so much of her future still up in the air.

Luckily, Jane didn't have to figure out what to say because the girls chose that moment to come into the kitchen and request hot chocolate.

"Sure," Jane said, hopping off her stool and pulling open the fridge to get the milk. The girls ran back to their game and Jane quickly changed the subject to Hannah. "So, you're a teacher now?"

Hannah nodded, her red curls bouncing. "I teach fourth

grade at Linden Falls Elementary. And my husband is on the police force here in town."

Jane's head jerked up from where she was pouring milk into two mugs. "So, he worked for my dad?"

Hannah pulled her plate of pancakes closer and picked up her fork. "Not for very long. Ed was in the military for four years after college, and then he joined the police force about a year and a half ago." She twisted the fork in her hands. "They weren't... close or anything."

Jane focused on stirring the hot chocolate mix into the milk, relieved she hadn't revealed anything about leaving Matteo. Hannah's husband might not have been close with her dad, but he was still a cop.

More giggles drifted in from down the hall and, for a moment, Jane wondered if she should tell Scarlett to take it easy so she wouldn't end up with another raging headache, or worse, back in the ER. But when she stopped by the living room to deliver their hot chocolate, Jane couldn't bring herself to tamp down Scarlett's happiness. It was so rare for her to get to play with other kids.

Maybe when they found a place to live in Canada, Scarlett could finally have a normal childhood. She could have friends and sleepovers and there would be no tiptoeing around. And maybe they could even find a house with a space to play outside. But Jane's mind couldn't quite form a clear picture of it. Instead, her attention was drawn out the window to the yard in front of Mom's house. It had snowed again last night, just an inch on top of the foot that had been there previously, and the drifts were fluffy and white, just waiting for a kid to run out and build a snowman.

"A couple of decades ago, who would have thought our daughters would be playing together?" Jane mused, once she returned to the kitchen and sat on a stool next to Hannah.

"I would have," Hannah said, with a crooked smile. "Or I

would have hoped it, anyway. You know I've always been a small-town girl, so my dream was that we'd all end up back here someday." She shrugged. "I'm lucky that Ali's mom is still in Linden Falls, and they're close so she comes back to visit a lot. And, of course, I got Nik full time, which I never expected."

"Was it awful when he lost the scholarship?"

Hannah pushed a bite of pancake around on her plate. "That whole time was hard for Nik. But I think it worked out in the end. He's doing amazing, really important work at the hospital and in the community." She shot a glance in Jane's direction. "And I think he's happy here. Linden Falls isn't the backwoods town it was when we were kids. It's come a long way."

East Bumfuck.

When Matteo had first started calling it that, Jane had laughed. That was back when she still hoped LA was a place where her dreams could come true. She stared at the mug wrapped in her hands. The handle was chipped, the blue glaze faded, but still, it felt warm, comforting against her skin. This whole kitchen felt that way, with the heat coming from the oven where Mom had left the pancakes to warm, the smell of maple syrup mingling with Hannah's familiar lavender perfume, the sound of the girls laughing over a game she used to play with Nik.

Her dreams were so much simpler now.

Almost as if she could read Jane's thoughts, Hannah said, "I'm not sure why you left without a word all those years ago, but I know it must have been a good reason." She looked at Jane with an intensity that left Jane wondering if there was more to her statement that Ed and Dad hadn't been close. Did Ed know who Dad really was? Did Hannah?

"But we're here for you," Hannah continued. "Even Ali. She puts on a good show, but she still cares about you."

Jane's heart ached as she stared down into her mug of

coffee. All those years ago, she'd been desperate to get out of here, terrified Dad would destroy her and the one person she'd cared about the most. But Dad had done exactly what she'd feared and stolen Nik's scholarship anyway. Except it hadn't destroyed him. Nik was still a doctor, maybe even a better one for how hard he'd had to fight for it.

It turned out that Dad had never had all the power after all. What if, a decade ago, she'd stayed and leaned on the people who loved her? Like Hannah and Ali. Like Nik. What if she stayed *now*, and leaned on the people who loved her?

Maybe it was time to stop running, to stop giving another abusive man more power over her life. She thought about Mom cooking and playing with Scarlett, so eager to be a part of her granddaughter's life. And Hannah showing up here, after all this time, ready to give Jane a second chance.

And then she thought about Nik, crouching down next to Scarlett's wheelchair to make her laugh. His eyes meeting hers across the crowded café. *They're going to love you.*

What if she called Martin and asked for his help, and then opened up to Hannah, Ali, and Nik about her past in LA? What if, instead of spending her life running, looking over her shoulder, isolated and alone, she surrounded herself with people who cared for her and would protect her?

Jane looked up from her coffee and met her old friend's eyes. "That means a lot, Hannah. You have no idea how much."

TWENTY-FIVE

Jane glanced over her shoulder at the door to the apartment before she swiped to answer the FaceTime call. It was a busy night at the club and unlikely that Matteo would stop up here to say goodnight to Scarlett. But it was her ninth birthday, so he could surprise them.

"Hello?" she said, once she'd confirmed that there wasn't any sign of him. Jane wasn't hiding Mom's call from Matteo, exactly. But he didn't like Jane talking to her, and he'd roll his eyes and sigh until she finally hung up. It wasn't like it was a regular occurrence. They talked maybe twice a year.

Jane held the phone up to Scarlett so Mom could see her.

"Happy birthday, Scarlett!" Mom said buoyantly, waving at the camera. In the background, Jane could see the living room wall with its old family photos, and a corner of brown fabric that was probably Dad's recliner. Jane wished Mom would FaceTime from the kitchen so she wouldn't have to look at it.

"Thanks, Grandma," Scarlett said, shyly.

"How was your day?" Mom asked.

"Good," Scarlett replied. She was always shy on these calls. Jane couldn't blame her. In the past nine years, Scarlett had only seen Mom a handful of times, and only over FaceTime. Mom only called when Dad was away on his fishing trips since he had no idea they were in contact at all.

Jane couldn't imagine what he'd do to Mom if he knew.

Mom chatted with Scarlett for a few minutes about her birthday—Jane was taking her to see the new Disney Princess movie tomorrow since Scarlett was just getting over a cold—and then Jane told her she could go watch TV in the bedroom.

"So," Mom said, as Jane swung the camera away from Scarlett and in her own direction. "Scarlett is nine. I can't believe it."

Jane couldn't either. Almost a decade had gone by since she'd left Linden Falls, since she'd moved in with Matteo and gotten pregnant and—

Jane pressed a hand to the latest bruise on her cheek. Almost a decade since she'd been living with this. Sometimes she couldn't believe she was still here. Somehow, she'd managed to keep putting one foot in front of the other. But she'd looked for a way out—so many times—and she was starting to despair of ever finding one.

Jane peered at Mom through the small phone screen. After that day she'd asked for money and Mom had turned her down, she'd never asked again. She'd never let Mom know that her life was anything other than fine. Jane could handle these once-in-a-blue-moon calls so Mom could see Scarlett. But she couldn't handle Mom knowing she needed help and refusing to give it. So, Jane had never told her the truth.

But when she pulled her hand away from her cheek, she realized her mistake. Mom's eyes widened, and she gasped. "Jane, what happened to you?"

Jane swore under her breath. She'd forgotten to hide the mark with make-up. They hadn't gone anywhere today, so she hadn't done her usual routine of cover-up, foundation, and powder. The ugly purple bruise was right there in the open.

"Um..." She searched for an excuse. "I ran into a cabinet."

But Mom's face screwed up suspiciously. That was the kind of excuse Jane remembered her using when Dad had left similar marks. "Did Matteo do that to you?"

"Mom, I have to go."

"Jane." Mom cut her off. "How long had this been going on?"

"It hasn't. It was an accident. I have to go."

"I thought he was such a good man. I had no idea..." Mom began, but Jane hung up before she could finish the sentence.

Six months later, Jane answered another FaceTime call from Mom. She looked at the phone buzzing in her hand, and then reflexively glanced at the door to check that Matteo wasn't around. Mom usually texted her before she called, and Jane considered letting it go to voicemail. Now that Mom knew Matteo had hit her, she'd called four times in the last six months to check up on Jane. She'd even asked if there was any way for Jane to leave him. That was ironic.

With a sigh, Jane swiped to answer. She might as well get it over with and tell Mom to butt out once and for all. But when Mom's face came onto the screen, Jane forgot everything she was going to say. Because Mom's face was bright red and splotchy, her nose swollen, eyes wet with tears.

"Are you okay?" Jane gasped. It still had the power to gut her, seeing her mom like this.

"It's your father," Mom said, her voice wobbling so much Jane could hardly understand her.

Jane stood up straight. "Did he hurt you?"

"No." Mom held up a tissue, wiping her eyes and then blowing her nose. "He's—your father is dead."

Jane reeled backward, her calves hitting the couch. Slowly, she sank down into the cushions. She opened her mouth, but no words would come out. First came the shock, but it was followed by a feeling she couldn't quite identify. A loosening of her shoulders, a heaviness lifting from her chest.

Oh God, it was *relief.*

Jane was relieved, and it was terrible, and true. Dad would never hurt Mom again. He'd never hurt anyone. She closed her eyes, and a long-buried memory came back to her. It had felt like time had slowed down with each jolt of the staircase hitting her body, leaving cracks and bruises on her skin and bones and somewhere deep inside her.

"Jane," Mom said, her shoulders shaking with sobs. "I need you. I need help. Can you come for a visit?"

Jane's breath caught. "You want me to... come *home*?"

Mom gave a teary nod. "Just for a little bit. You and Scarlett."

Home. Jane turned that word over in her mind. She never thought she could go back. But it was safe now. Finally. And with that came another thought. A wonderful revelation, like a cool breeze blowing in off the Pacific Ocean.

Was this finally her chance to be free?

TWENTY-SIX

PRESENT DAY

As soon as Jane walked into Helen Andino's home, she was surrounded by memories. The furniture had changed since she'd last set foot in the house, the shabby well-loved couch replaced by a newer, less sagging model, a coat of paint in pale cream on the walls. But the layout was exactly the same, and even with the scent of Christmas dinner roasting in the oven, Jane could still detect a faint hint of vanilla from Helen's baking.

Nik strode down the hall with a smile. And that was familiar, too, the way his eyes used to light up when he swung the door open and found her standing on the welcome mat. She stepped inside and he reached for her, a quick hug to say hello and merry Christmas, and a spark ignited the moment her body pressed against his. She stepped back, just an inch, but couldn't bring herself to move farther away. And, for a split second, it was just her and Nik in that familiar living room, the two of them on the couch under the window sharing a pair of headphones, the cord so short their shoulders bumped when they leaned in to choose another song from Nik's old iPhone.

Behind her, Jane felt Mom and Scarlett step inside the

house, and she quickly turned away to help Scarlett with her shoes. They made their way farther into the living room, and as Jane crossed in front of the fireplace, she realized the photos over the mantel were the same as she remembered, too. They were a timeline of Nik growing older: as a baby, a toddler, then a little boy. Jane was in some of those photos, the two of them grubby from playing in the creek behind the house, covered in flour after a failed attempt at baking brownies in Helen's kitchen.

Did elementary-aged Nik resemble Scarlett in those old photos? And would anyone else notice? Jane wanted to examine each one, hold it up next to Scarlett to scan for similarities.

"Hello! Welcome!" called a voice from behind her, and Jane spun around to find Mrs. Andino wiping her hands on the apron tied around her midsection as she made her way from the kitchen. Her wide smile swept around the room until it settled on Scarlett. "Oh...this must be Scarlett." Was it Jane's imagination that Mrs. Andino froze for just a moment when her gaze landed on Scarlett's face? Or was she just being paranoid?

"Yes, this is my granddaughter," Mom said proudly, sliding an arm around the girl's shoulder.

Was Scarlett Mrs. Andino's granddaughter, too? Jane was starting to spiral now.

"Hi," Scarlett said shyly, clutching Mom's arm.

"It's very nice to meet you." Mrs. Andino blinked down at Scarlett, and something Jane couldn't identify momentarily crossed her features. "Did you know I've known your mom since she was even younger than you?" She plucked one of the photos off the mantel. "See? You look just like her." Mrs. Andino held up the image of Nik and Jane with their arms wrapped around each other, and Jane held her breath.

She finally exhaled when Mrs. Andino set the photo back on the mantel and turned to Jane, a welcoming smile on her face. "I'm so glad you could make it." She crossed the room to wrap Jane in her familiar vanilla-scented embrace. "What a delight to get to see you twice in one week."

Jane did her best to shake off her worries over Scarlett's paternity. She didn't know that Nik was Scarlett's father. In fact, he probably wasn't. But the more time she spent thinking about it, the more she wanted it to be true. Maybe a little part of her had been hoping that Mrs. Andino would grab that photo from the mantel and declare Scarlett a carbon copy of Nik. But the older woman was already making her way to the front door to swing it open for her next guests.

Hannah stood on the doorstep, stamping the snow from her boots and ushering Amelia inside. "Hi, everyone," she said buoyantly, giving a wave as she tugged at the scarf around her neck. A tall, lanky man with blond hair and a wide grin followed close behind.

"You're not at your parents' today?" Jane asked around Hannah's wild hair as her friend threw her arms around her. Had something happened to Hannah's parents? She'd missed so much.

Thankfully, Hannah stepped back and gave her a wry grin. "My parents take a cruise in the Caribbean over the holidays. We come to Helen's every year now. It's tradition." She tugged the man closer. "Ed, this is my old friend Jane."

Jane held out a palm. "It's so nice to meet you."

Ed bypassed her hand and reached out to give her a hug, his eyes sparkling with warmth. "Hannah has told me so many stories about you all as kids. I'm glad to finally meet you, Jane."

Jane liked him immediately, and she felt her chest expand with hope that her friend had been lucky to meet a good man. He'd probably heard that Jane had run off without a word. Still, he welcomed her without hesitation.

"I heard you're a police officer," Jane said.

"I am, yeah. I knew your dad." He avoided her gaze. "Sorry for your loss." He cleared his throat like he'd had to force that last part out, and something about his tone gave Jane the feeling he was saying it more out of obligation than genuine feeling.

When Jane was growing up, all the officers on the police force seemed to be part of an old boys' club, and Dad was their leader. He could do no wrong in their eyes. Jane remembered the officer who'd come when Mom had called 911. How he'd stood awkwardly in front of the house, backing away slowly while Mom cried. But Ed seemed uncomfortable with this conversation, almost like he hadn't been a fan of Dad. Maybe in his later years, Dad's cracks had started to show on the surface.

The front door swung open again, and this time it was Ali on the welcome mat, in a black dress under her elegant black coat. Next to her stood a tall, dark-haired woman in equally stylish attire. It was obvious they were a couple by the way the woman held on to Ali's arm as she stepped into the house.

Jane felt a burst of happiness for her friend. Ali had come out to their group in high school, but she'd kept it a secret from her parents and everyone else. Linden Falls was a small town, and Ali had worried about people accepting her. But Ali was clearly out now, and Jane suspected that most people in town were just fine with it. She thought about Dad terrorizing Kait at the autobody shop, and then looked over to see Ed giving Ali and the other woman a warm greeting. Maybe this town really had changed.

In a bustle of hugs and casserole dishes being handed over, Jane somehow ended up standing across from Ali and her companion.

"Hi, Ali," Jane said. "It's good to see you again."

"Jane. Hey." Ali looked vaguely uncomfortable, but her eyes didn't radiate the same anger from the other night. "This is my wife, Lexi."

"It's so nice to finally meet you," Lexi said, warmly.

"It's so nice to *finally* meet you, too," Jane said, her lips tugging as she remembered back to their dramatic teenage conversations when Ali used to lament that she'd be single forever because she was never going to meet a girl in this town. Jane's eyes met Ali's, who seemed to be holding back a hint of a smile, too. Maybe she was looking back on the same moments.

At that moment, Scarlett came running over. "Mommy, can I have the Legos we brought? Mrs. Andino said Amelia and I can go upstairs and play in the guest room."

"Whoa, you have a kid?" Ali blurted out, her dark eyebrows raised.

Jane slid an arm around Scarlett's shoulder. "This is my daughter, Scarlett."

Scarlett peered up at Ali. "Your picture is hanging in my room at my grandma's house. Were you my mom's friend, like Hannah and Dr. Nik?"

"Yep, I sure was." Ali's dark eyes drifted over Scarlett. She blinked in surprise. "That's a nice necklace you're wearing."

Scarlett beamed, reaching up to run her fingers over the twisted silver that Ali had shaped into musical notes over a decade ago. "It was my mom's. She said it was her favorite." Scarlett hadn't taken the necklace off since Jane had given it to her the other day.

Ali's face softened.

"I guess I should go get those Legos," Jane said, swallowing down a lump in her throat.

"Sure," Ali said. And then she added, "We'll talk more later."

Jane found her purse and fished out the bag of Legos, handing them to Scarlett. "Just clean up when you're done, okay?" But Scarlett was already running off to find her new friend.

Jane headed into the kitchen, where she found Mom and Mrs. Andino putting the finishing touches on dinner, laughing over glasses of wine. Mom's eyes were bright, happy. Jane had so few memories of seeing her this light and carefree. The crease of anxiety was gone from her forehead, and her eyes didn't dart to the door, worried that Dad might walk in. She was finally free of the dark cloud that had hung over her for the past three decades.

That's what I want, too.

The freedom from fear, from looking over her shoulder.

The thought stayed with Jane throughout the holiday meal as the laughter and warmth of her old friends surrounded her. She didn't have to hold her breath, or censor herself, or worry that something might set someone off. When Scarlett reached across the table and knocked over her glass of grape juice, nobody even blinked. Nik simply got up and grabbed a towel, tossing it on the stain and remarking that he'd always thought the tablecloth would look better tie-dyed anyway. Scarlett's shoulders had immediately relaxed.

This could be our future.

At home, Jane's spine would have stiffened, automatically, out of habit. Her nervous gaze would have flown to Matteo's face turning white, jaw twitching. Later, he would have made sure she knew he blamed her for Scarlett's carelessness. But the worst part would have been watching Scarlett react. Her posture tense, her eyes clouding with fear.

We don't have to live like that anymore.

TWENTY-SEVEN

Nik lifted the half-empty bowl of mashed potatoes and followed his mother into the kitchen. Everyone around the table had offered to help clean up, but Helen wouldn't hear of it. They were guests, she'd insisted. "Sit and enjoy your coffee."

As soon as he set the bowl on the counter, though, Nik began to suspect why his mother wanted him to be the only one to come back to the kitchen with her.

"It's wonderful that Jane could come," she said, getting right to the point.

Nik squinted at his mother across the butcherblock counter. She knew how much it had hurt him when Jane took off a decade ago, and he suspected she was trying to feel out how Jane's sudden presence in Linden Falls was affecting him after all this time. Still, she wasn't usually one to meddle in his personal life.

"Sure." He raked a hand through his hair. His emotions had been on a spin cycle since he'd realized Jane had a kid... And she'd left Scarlett's father... And this magnetic pull between them had never gone away.

And hell, it probably never would.

"And Scarlett," his mom continued, filling a pot in the sink with water. "What a lovely little girl."

Nik gave a curt nod. "She's a good kid."

"You two seem like fast friends."

He hadn't missed his mom poking her head in the guest room when he'd gone to deliver some more Legos from his childhood bedroom to the girls and got roped into helping them build a car for Barbie and Ken. "I was her doctor. We met the other day."

His mother turned away from the sink and picked up a dish towel. "It's more than that. You have a lot of patients, but you and Scarlett seem to have a... special bond."

Nik watched his mom twist the cloth in her hands. After everything he and Jane had been through, was his mom playing *matchmaker,* trying to get them together again? And using Scarlett to make it happen? "What is it you're trying to do here?"

"Nik." She sighed, tossing the dishcloth on the counter in frustration. "Has it really not occurred to you?"

He stared at her. "What?"

"Scarlett."

"What about..." But he knew. It *had* occurred to him.

"She's *nine,* Nik." His mom crossed her arms. "Jane left here ten years ago and has a nine-year-old daughter. Now, I know I'm making assumptions about what you two were up to back then. But I'd be surprised if I was wrong."

Nik sighed. If he didn't want to talk about his personal life with his mother, he really didn't want to talk about his sex life. But she'd obviously gotten herself worked up about this. And he couldn't completely blame her. "You're not wrong. Jane and I did..." He waved a hand. "Anyway, you get the point."

"So, Scarlett *could* be yours, Nik."

"She's not."

"If there's any chance she is, you've got to find out. You have to stop Jane from going back to LA."

Nik sighed. "Scarlett's father is a nightclub manager named Matteo."

His mom blinked. "Did Jane tell you that?"

Nik pictured Matteo's smiling face on his phone. Peeking in Scarlett's medical records and googling the guy probably wasn't the most ethical thing he'd ever done. But it wasn't like he could have asked Jane. "I saw her medical forms. I was her doctor, remember?" Telling his mom Scarlett's personal information probably wasn't the most ethical thing he'd ever done, either. But she wasn't going to let this go if he didn't. "Matteo was listed as her father. And Scarlett's birthdate was on the forms. She turned nine this past summer."

Helen cocked her head, trying to work out the math.

"Jane left Linden Falls in the summer. Scarlett was born in August, over a year after Jane took off. I'm not an obstetrician but I'm pretty sure that if I were Scarlett's father, Jane would have had the longest pregnancy in the history of pregnancies."

"Oh." His mom's shoulders slumped. "Oh," she repeated. "Well, I guess that answers that."

He studied her across the counter. "Are you disappointed?"

"Are you?" Her face softened. "If you went looking, you must have had some... feelings about it."

Hell, he didn't know. If he was Scarlett's father, and Jane had kept that from him, the betrayal would be unbearable. But... he remembered their eyes meeting across the couch cushions. The brush of his hand on her cheek. The hitch in her breath as she leaned closer. If Scarlett were his, it would be a reason for Jane to stay.

From the dining room next door, he could hear Ali's voice telling another story from high school, followed by a burst of Jane's laughter. She was happy here, surrounded by family and old friends. Her shoulders had finally relaxed, as if she'd stopped scanning the exits for a place to run. He'd never forget that haunted look in her eyes when he first spotted her in Ford's

General Store. The edge to her voice when she'd said she'd left Matteo. Nik's chest filled with rage when he thought about that bruise on her cheek.

Jane didn't belong in LA, in the same vicinity as that asshole. She would have never gone there in the first place if she hadn't been protecting him. And she hadn't given him one good reason why she should go back.

Jane appeared in the doorway holding a stack of plates. "Hi." She blinked from Nik to his mom and then back. "Am I interrupting something?"

He smoothed a hand over his face and let his lips curve into a smile. At the sight of her, it wasn't hard.

"Not at all." His mom waved her inside.

Jane set the plates on the counter. "I felt bad leaving all the cleaning up to you. You two did all the cooking. Please let me help."

His mom gave Jane a wide smile. "Well, if you insist, you can help Nik finish up in here while I take dessert out to the dining room." And before he knew what had happened, his mom had picked up a pie and tray of Christmas cookies and was heading for the dining room. "There's no rush, we'll save you some." And with that, she disappeared out the kitchen door.

Nik watched her go with a shake of his head. "Damn."

"What is it?" Jane asked, moving to his side of the counter to set the plates in the sink.

He could smell her shampoo as she brushed past, something light and fruity. Green apples, maybe. He grabbed a bowl from the counter to keep from pulling her against him and burying his face in the side of her neck. Nik cleared his throat. "She's matchmaking."

"Who?" Jane's head jerked up. "Your mom? And *us*?"

"Yep." He leaned his hip against the counter.

"Oh." She left the plates in the sink and turned to face him. "And, um... how do you feel about that?"

"How do *you* feel about it?" he countered, feeling like he was twelve and passing her a note. *Do you want to be my girlfriend? Check yes or no.*

"Well, she's just trying to help." Jane pressed her lips together, but a hint of a smile broke through. "She always liked me. And you always had terrible taste in women."

His mouth dropped open as a laugh escaped. "What do you know about my taste in women?"

"Well..." Jane pressed a finger to her lip like she was remembering back. "There was that Kelsie in third grade. You had a huge crush on her, and she was such a bully."

"I like assertive women." Nik leaned closer. "Besides, what about *you*? That guy who took you to the ninth-grade dance? What was his name—Jeremy? He had more muscles than brains and spoke three words the whole night."

"He was the strong, silent type."

Nik huffed. "I think he was just silent."

"It was my dad who liked him, not me." She rolled her eyes. "If I recall, Jeremy left the dance with Shana Smith, and you and I ended up in an Uno battle at the Grassroots Café."

"Just like we always did."

She nodded slowly, smile fading. "Just like we always did."

He looked down into her eyes, so close now that he could almost feel her sharp intake of breath. How many times had the two of them stood in this same spot in this same kitchen? How many times had he been tempted to lean in and kiss her? Back then, he'd held off, taken it slow, convinced that they had all the time in the world. But now he knew better.

"I didn't really have bad taste in women," Nik murmured. "I was just biding my time with Kelsie until you finally noticed me." He reached out a hand and cupped her cheek. "I'm still just biding my time until you notice me."

"Nik," she whispered. "I always noticed you. And I think I'm realizing that I always will."

From the dining room, the voices rose, and laughter erupted, but there was no place else besides this narrow space between them, no one besides Jane. He reached out to pull her against him just as she took a step forward and came crashing into his chest. Their mouths collided, desperate, almost bruising. He parted her lips, sliding his tongue against hers, tasting her, familiar after all this time. She wrapped her arms around his neck, pulling him closer, but it wasn't close enough. It could never be close enough. He shifted his weight, lifting her off her feet and onto the counter so he could settle between her thighs, tangle his hands in her hair, run a trail of hot kisses down her neck.

"Nik," she gasped, tugging on his hair to tilt his face back up to hers.

He was sliding a hand under her shirt just as another peal of laughter from the dining room finally yanked him back to his senses.

"*Damn it.*"

They were in his mother's kitchen with their friends and family in the next room. And all he wanted was to be alone with her.

Jane took a shaky breath and climbed off the counter, back onto her feet. "I guess this isn't the best time for this."

He slumped against the cabinets, raking a hand through his hair. "Probably not."

Jane's gaze slid down to the zipper of his jeans, where he was sure it had never been more obvious that he was turned on. "I'll go grab some more dishes and let you finish cleaning up in here." She gave him a sideways smile, her eyes bright and cheeks flushed.

This wasn't the right time, but soon, they were going to find a time that was right. There was no denying that this was happening between them, and nothing was standing in their way. Jane had left Matteo and she'd said there was nobody else.

Maybe she had a life in LA, a job, Scarlett's school to get back to, but they could talk about it. They could work it out. He only had a year left in his residency program. If he couldn't convince Jane to move back to Linden Falls, he could get a job out there. He was willing to do anything to put the past behind them and convince her that wherever they were, their future was together.

Nik was never going to lose her again.

TWENTY-EIGHT

All Jane could think about for the rest of the night was Nik's mouth pressed against hers, his hand sliding down her spine... the truth that she would have had her clothes off and on the floor in about two seconds if it weren't for their friends and family in the next room. She felt like a giddy teenager with a crush all over again, her face flushing and butterflies taking flight in her stomach every time Nik walked into the room.

Even a phone conversation with Matteo the next morning couldn't take away her happiness. He barely muttered an obligatory "Merry Christmas" before he started complaining about the staff at the club. Jane made all the right noises to soothe him, agreeing that it sounded incredibly stressful. But maybe it was the thousands of miles between them, or maybe it was the memory of being surrounded by her old friends last night, because she just didn't feel the same anxiety when he started getting worked up. His anger didn't have quite the same power over her.

We don't have to live like that anymore.

She ended the call as quickly as possible and headed to the living room, where Scarlett was drawing in the sketchpad that

Jane had given her for Christmas, and Mom was reading the newspaper. Or at least Mom *had* been reading the newspaper. Now it appeared that she was glaring at Dad's old recliner. "I hate that thing."

Jane took in the ugly brown color, the worn spot on the arm where Dad liked to rest his drink and the remote control, the sag in the seat cushion. Jane had always hated it, too. That chair had been Dad's favorite, it was where he used to sit when he got home from work. Though he hadn't smoked in the house, the tobacco scent had seeped from his clothes into the fabric, and she'd always thought that the chair smelled like the bottom of an ashtray. Nobody had sat there since Dad had died, and it almost seemed like they all gave that chair a wide berth. Even Scarlett made a face when she walked by it. Maybe the scent of it reminded her of the stale tobacco smell that lingered on Matteo.

"It's ugly," Jane said.

"And old," Mom added.

"And it *stinks*." Scarlett held her nose, confirming Jane's suspicions.

"It definitely stinks," Jane agreed, glancing over at Mom. "Why don't you get rid of it?"

Mom eyed the chair for so long that Jane wondered if she were getting sentimental and missing Dad. But then Mom stood, brushing off the front of her pants. "You know, I think I will." She set her hand on the back of the chair and gave it a shove, as if she were testing how sturdy it was.

Jane raised her eyebrows. "You're going to get rid of it right now?"

Mom shrugged. "No time like the present." She gave the chair another shake. "The garbage men come tomorrow. I think we ought to have that chair on the curb for them when they arrive."

Jane looked at Scarlett, whose mouth twitched in a smile.

"Okay." Jane mirrored her mother's movement, standing up and brushing off the front of her leggings. "Let's do it."

"Yay!" Scarlett yelled, jumping to her feet.

Getting the old recliner out to the curb for the garbage men proved to be more difficult than anticipated, though. For one thing, it weighed about five hundred pounds and was impossible to lift. Together, Jane and Mom managed to shimmy it inch by inch across the living room and through the doorway into the hall.

Jane eyed Mom, who was panting heavily. "Are you sure this is a good idea? Maybe it's too much for you." She remembered Mom's old wrist injury.

But although Mom looked tired, her eyes shone brightly. She shook her head. "Are you kidding? I'm just getting started. Only a little farther now."

By the time they got it to the front door, they were both red-faced and gasping. And then they hit upon the next problem. The chair wouldn't fit through the front door. They tilted it to the left, then right, and then Jane tried to lift one end to slide it diagonally through the frame. She nearly threw her back out and almost dropped it on Mom's foot.

"This is not going to work," Jane grunted, setting it back on the floor as gently as she could.

"We started this," Mom panted. "I want that chair out."

Jane shoved her sweaty bangs out of her face. "Maybe we should call someone to help? A moving company?"

"That will take days to arrange." Mom gave the chair a kick. "I'm not moving it back into the living room."

"What about that high school kid down the street?" Jane propped her hands on her hips.

"I have an idea." Mom brushed her hands together. "Come on, Scarlett, you can hold the door." She moved down the hall into the kitchen, and Jane heard the basement door open. A moment later, Mom appeared back in the hallway, limping under the weight of the sledgehammer she was carrying. Scarlett skipped beside her in excitement.

Jane's eyes widened as she put the pieces together. "Are you sure this is a good idea?"

"It's a great idea." Mom held out a palm. "Scarlett." Scarlett slapped a pair of safety glasses into Mom's hand, and Mom slid them on her face. "Stand back."

Jane grabbed Scarlett around the shoulders and tugged her out of the way of Mom's wind-up. Mom took a deep breath, wrapped both hands around the handle, reeled back, and took a swing. The hammer came crashing down into the back of the chair with a loud crack. Jane yanked Scarlett back farther, just in case, but though the wooden frame of the chair buckled, it didn't break. With a grunt, Mom swung again, landing the hammer in the same spot, and the wood cracked a little more. She bounced on the balls of her feet, and swung again. And again, it cracked against the wood, but the frame stayed intact.

By this point, Mom's chest was heaving, the hammer hanging by her side.

Jane took a step forward. "Let me try."

Mom passed the sledgehammer to Jane and took her place against the wall next to Scarlett. Jane eyed that chair, picturing Dad sitting in it, yelling at Mom to get him a beer. She pictured Matteo sitting there, too. The burnt tobacco smell was stronger now, probably from the years of dust that had settled in the old cushions and was now kicked up into the air. Jane hated that chair. She wanted that chair out of this house, out of her sight. Just like Dad. Just like Matteo.

She reeled back, swinging the sledgehammer with a strength she didn't know she possessed, letting out a guttural yell as she brought it down as hard as she could into the chair back. This time, the wood cracked, then splintered, tearing a hole in the worn brown fabric as the hammer sliced the back of the chair into two.

"Yeeees!" yelled Mom, pumping her fist in the air as Scarlett jumped up and down with her hands raised like a boxer who'd won a fight.

Jane handed the sledgehammer to Mom again, who took three or four good whacks at the side of the chair back until it entirely broke off and slumped backward toward the floor. Then Jane got to work on the seat, hammering at the frame until it collapsed inward. Mom ran to get the kitchen scissors and they cut the fabric, pulling out the cushions and tossing them onto the lawn. It took almost an hour of hammering, cutting, and tearing at the chair until all that was left in the hallway was a pile of dust, splinters, and crumbled bits of cushion filler.

"Well," Mom said, rubbing her shoulder as they stood on the porch and surveyed the garbage on the lawn. "I can't say I'm sorry to be rid of that."

Jane grinned. Her whole body ached, and it had never felt so satisfying. So much more than an old chair had gone out the door.

An older woman with a small black dog on a leash made her way down the street. The woman and the dog wore matching Christmas sweaters, and as the woman came to a stop on the sidewalk in front of Mom's house, Jane registered who she was. Mrs. Swanson. Her face displayed that same pinched, critical expression that she'd had at Ford's General Store that first night Jane had come home. But this time, she directed her disapproval in Mom's direction.

"My goodness, Diane. What happened here?" She wrinkled her nose at the pile of cushions, fabric, and splintered wood.

Mom shrugged. "Oh, we were just getting rid of some old furniture."

"Was that the chief's chair?" Of course Mrs. Swanson knew it was Dad's chair. She liked to stop by each house to personally ask for money for the church fundraiser. It was harder to say no when someone was sitting in your living room. Plus, then she could peek around people's houses and get her fill of gossip.

"Sure was," Jane called over the porch railing. "But it's garbage now."

Mrs. Swanson sucked in an audible breath through her nose, her eyes bugging as she surveyed the mess. "I assume this was your idea, Jane? It's disrespectful to treat your father's favorite possessions like garbage, don't you think?"

Jane remembered her guitar crashing down the stairs after her. The body had probably cracked, the neck snapped, the strings broken. Not that she'd ever gotten to open the case and confirm it. Dad had said he was going to burn it, and since Jane hadn't found it anywhere in the house, she could only assume he had.

"I think this chair and my father have gotten all the respect they deserve."

Mrs. Swanson's mouth dropped open, but before she could say a word, Jane spun on her heel and swung open the front door.

"Well, I hope you plan to clean this up!" the older woman called as Jane ushered Scarlett inside and stepped in behind her.

Mom gave a wave toward the lawn. "Nice to see you, Mrs. Swanson." And then she followed Jane inside and slammed the door behind her.

Jane's phone rang, and she ran to answer it, hoping it wasn't Matteo again.

It was an unfamiliar number with a Western New York area code. Maybe it was Kait coming through with her car. But the possibility that her ticket out might be on the other end of the phone didn't spark the same joy Jane had expected. In fact, it filled her with a different kind of dread. So when Jane answered and found Hannah on the other end, she sighed with relief.

"I hope it's okay I called," her old friend said. "I texted your mom for your number."

"Of course it is."

"I wondered what you're up to today. Would you and Scarlett like to come over? We've had so much snow lately, the girls can play outside. And we can chat some more. I've missed you."

Jane looked over at Scarlett, who was sitting on the floor near where the recliner used to be, building her Lego house. Jane was tired of seeing her daughter playing all alone, tired of refusing to allow Scarlett to make friends, tired of being afraid all the time.

"We'd love to come."

When Jane opened her car door in Hannah's driveway, she was immediately hit by the sound of shrieking and laughter coming from somewhere in the vicinity of the backyard. She and Scarlett peeked around the side of the house and found at least half a dozen children on colorful saucers and sleds, gliding down the long slope that ended in the neighbor's backyard.

Scarlett looked up at Jane with shining eyes. "Am I allowed to go play with them?"

Jane's heart squeezed. There was no going alone to do anything in downtown LA, let alone play with other children. It wasn't safe. But here—her gaze swept over the backyards lined up in a neat row, dotted with swing sets and snow forts and the tracks of children moving effortlessly from one yard to the next—here Scarlett would be more than safe.

A woman stood on the back porch of a neighboring house, helping her child into his mittens before sending him off with the other kids. She spotted Jane and gave a wave. Jane waved back.

"Just be careful of your arm," Jane said, adjusting her own

daughter's mittens. "No sledding this time. But you can build a snowman, okay?"

Scarlett nodded eagerly, and Jane had the feeling that she would have agreed to anything.

With one more glance at her daughter, Jane headed back around to the front of Hannah's house. There were two cars in the driveway, so Jane assumed that in addition to Hannah, she'd see Ed when she got inside. But when the door swung open, she found Ali on the threshold.

"Ali," she said, surprised. They'd talked last night at dinner and Ali had been perfectly nice. Friendly, even. But that was with everyone sitting around the table. Was her old friend still mad at her?

Ali cocked her head. "Well, come in then."

Jane stamped her boots and stepped inside. "I'm glad you're here."

"Yeah?" Ali gave her a crooked smile. "Me, too."

They made their way back to the kitchen where they found Hannah arranging some of Mrs. Andino's leftover Christmas cookies on a plate and pouring hot water into mugs. She set down the kettle and ran over to give Jane a hug. "I'm so glad you could make it." She hitched her chin out the kitchen window. "The girls seem like they're having fun already."

Through the glass, Jane spotted a group of kids at work constructing a giant snowball. Scarlett blended right in with the others in her winter coat and hat, hauling handfuls of snow to the pile and patting it into place. Jane turned back to the room and gave her old friend a smile.

Hannah's kitchen was just like her: warm, inviting, a little bit disheveled. Soon Jane was seated at the island with a cup of tea and a plate of cookies in front of her. They talked about Hannah's teaching job and Ali's work at the gallery, and then about Ed and Lexi and married life.

"So, Jane," Hannah said, refilling her mug with tea, "I don't even know what you do for work."

Jane opened her mouth to say she was a server, but she didn't want to talk about Matteo or the club. And she didn't want to keep lying. "I'm kind of between careers right now. I guess you could say that my job is to be a single mother to Scarlett."

"Single mother?" Ali took a sip of her tea. "So, Scarlett's dad is—"

"Out of the picture," Jane said, quickly.

Hannah slid onto a stool, propping her chin on her hand. "That's a lot to deal with."

"Believe me, it's for the best."

Hannah's face creased with sympathy. "Well, then, I'm glad he's out of the picture."

"Do you still play music?" Ali asked. "We all heard you headed out to LA to make it in the music business."

Jane wished she could at least say she'd tried. But somehow it didn't hurt like it used to. She'd been in a terrible position, and she'd done what she needed to survive. She'd done what she needed to do to care for her child. Jane peeked over Hannah's shoulder, out the kitchen window, and saw Scarlett and another little girl from the neighborhood laughing in a pile of snow. Maybe Jane didn't have a lot to show for a career, or any of her life in LA, but despite everything they'd been through, her daughter was going to be okay.

Jane's hand slid to her cheek. The bruise was almost completely gone now. Anyone would have to squint to spot the last yellowing remains near the corner of her eye. But inside her, the pain remained. The bruises buried, hidden, secret. She'd been so isolated and alone for so damn long. Matteo had made sure of it.

If she moved to Canada, it would be more of the same. She'd still be alone, still looking over her shoulder, still tensing up every time she heard a car outside or a knock at the front door. Jane regarded her old friends across the island. They had been everything to her. What if she'd told them the truth back then?

What if she told them now?

"I ran away to LA to get away from my dad," Jane said, quietly. "He was abusive."

Hannah gasped and Ali's eyes went wide.

"Oh, Jane." Hannah's voice shook. "That's awful."

"I knew your dad could be kind of strict." Ali's face clouded over. "We were all afraid of him. But we had no idea he was..."

"It wasn't physical at first." Jane stared into her mug of tea. "At least not with me. Though the way he treated my mom was a different story. He was mean, and I was terrified of him. But then—that day before I left... that day, he got violent." It felt so good to say it. To admit it. To stop being the only one holding this secret.

Ali cursed under her breath.

"I—well, I won't get into the details. But it was bad. And I packed a bag and took off," Jane said.

"Why didn't you tell us?" Hannah's eyes filled with tears. "We would have been there for you. You had to know that, right?"

"I was afraid. He was the police chief. I didn't think anyone could help." Jane looked down at her hands. "So, I ran away."

"Jane, I'm so sorry we weren't there for you then. But"—Ali slid off her stool and rounded the counter to stand in front of Jane—"I hope you know that we're here for you now. If there's anything you ever need..." She reached out and brushed a hand against the fading bruise on Jane's cheek.

Hannah nodded. "Things aren't the same as they were back then. Ed is on the police force. They arrest abusers now. They can't get away with it."

Jane looked at her old friends. Maybe she couldn't have

leaned on them back then, but they weren't kids anymore. And maybe she wasn't alone anymore.

"Did Nik know about your dad? What happened that night?" Ali asked.

Jane shook her head. "He didn't know back then. But now he does." She glanced out at Scarlett playing in the yard. Jane studied her daughter's face, looking for signs of Nik's features. Maybe Nik didn't know *everything*. But hopefully soon she'd have more answers.

Hannah's face softened. "He loves you, you know. He always did."

Last night in the kitchen came back to her again. Nik's mouth against her, his hand hot against her skin. She loved him, too. She always had.

The sound of laughter drifted in through the window, and Jane realized the sun would be setting soon. "I should probably get Scarlett home for dinner. She's going to be starving. She's never played so hard in her life."

Hannah peeked out the window. "They're having so much fun. Why don't you let her stay? She can have a slumber party with Amelia, and we'll order a pizza."

Jane considered it. Slumber parties were another experience Scarlett had never gotten to have. There was nobody Jane would have trusted to keep Scarlett overnight. And Matteo wouldn't have allowed it anyway. But Jane knew she could trust Hannah with her life.

"If you're sure?" Jane asked.

Hannah nodded. "Go and enjoy your night off. I'll bring her back tomorrow."

Jane said goodbye to her friends and waded out into the snow to call Scarlett over. Scarlett's shoulders slumped as she slowly dragged a snow shovel across the backyard. "Do we have to go, Mommy? All the other kids are staying for another hour."

"Actually," Jane said with a grin, enjoying being the bearer of good news for once, "you can stay. Hannah invited you to sleep over with Amelia. Would you like that?"

The happiness on her daughter's face filled Jane's heart. Scarlett deserved to be a regular kid, without fear, without constantly running away.

Jane got in the car, but instead of heading home she turned left at the sign for Sand Hill Lane. Nik's mother had said that Nik had a place there. It was a winding country road, just outside of town, with large sections of woods between properties. Jane slowed as she passed each driveway, checking out the cars parked there, the houses nestled between the trees. A couple of miles down the road, she spotted a gray sedan parked in a driveway. The car looked to be the same make and model as the one she rode in with Nik a few days earlier, and the one parked at Mrs. Andino's house at Christmas.

Jane took a chance, pulled into the driveway, and climbed out of her car.

The house was more of a small cabin made of long wooden planks stained a deep caramel color. A wide front porch stretched across the front, furnished with red-painted Adirondack chairs. She heard a rustling sound and spotted Nik emerging from around the back of the house in a flannel jacket and hiking boots, carrying a stack of logs.

He stopped on the driveway and blinked. "Jane. I didn't expect to see you here."

"I was—uh." She gave him a sideways smile. "I was in the neighborhood?"

Snow swirled around them, landing on his shoulders and making his dark hair shimmer like a halo. He grinned back. "Well, come in then."

TWENTY-NINE

Jane followed Nik into the house. The front door opened to a large living room with a worn gray couch draped in a plaid blanket and set in front of a fireplace. Nik had lit a fire, and it crackled in the hearth. The kitchen was set off to one side, separated from the living room by a long counter. On the other side of the main room, Jane could see a short hallway with what looked to be two bedrooms and a bathroom. It wasn't large and there was nothing fancy about it. The wooden coffee table was marked with scratches, and she was pretty sure the couch had been in Mrs. Andino's house when they were kids. Jane could imagine Nik buying his mom a new one and taking the old one for himself. But the cabin was warm and comfortable. It felt like Nik.

It felt like home.

"Can I get you anything?" Nik asked, dropping the wood in his arms next to the fireplace. "Tea? Wine? Something to eat?" He stuffed his hands in his pockets like he wasn't quite sure what to do with them now that they were empty.

Jane shook her head. "I just came from Hannah's, and we ate all the cookies your mom sent home with her."

"Yeah?" He grinned. "I'm glad you guys are hanging out."

"Ali was there, too. It was... nice." Jane went back to looking over the room. She wanted to see everything, know everything about him. On either side of the fireplace was a built-in shelf with rows of medical textbooks, novels, and cookbooks. Alongside them, he'd set several framed children's drawings that had to have come from Amelia, and a handful of oddly shaped rocks and pinecones she imagined he'd found in the woods. She stepped closer, and her knee bumped against something that emitted a slightly low, off-key vibration in E minor.

Jane looked down to find a guitar resting on a stand. She blinked at it. Had Nik started playing? He hadn't mentioned it at the café that night. Jane leaned down to get a better look.

And then she gasped.

The chip in the pickguard. The worn marks on the body where her pinkie finger had dragged against the lacquer. The pictures and song lyrics Nik had doodled across its body to hide the worst of the scuff marks. They were all there.

My guitar.

"I was sure it was gone. That it was lost forever. Where did you get it?"

The firelight flickered on his face, his eyes dark and unreadable. "I stole it."

Her eyes widened. "From my dad?"

Nik nodded. "It was about a week after you left, and I ran into him outside of Ford's. He told me I needed to come with him, and he dragged me to the police station."

"Did he arrest you?" She knew Dad had made up some charges about Nik being arrested for drugs, but had he actually gone through with the whole charade?

Nik shook his head. "No, but he made it clear that I'd better go with him, so I did. He took me in his office and asked me a whole bunch of questions—had I talked to you lately? Had we been hanging out? At the time, I just thought he was being a dick, and he wanted me to stay away from you because he'd heard the rumors that I'd lost my scholarship. I figured he didn't want you associating with me." Nik stepped closer. "Now I can see that he was probably trying to find out if I knew where you'd gone."

"How did you get the guitar, though?"

Nik cocked his head, remembering. "It was in his office, on a chair in the corner."

"He took it from me," Jane said. "He locked it in his patrol car and said he was going to take it out to the quarry and burn it."

"I heard him tell one of the other officers to get rid of it. I didn't know he'd taken it from you. I figured that when you left, you didn't want it anymore." Nik stared at the guitar. "I couldn't let one of your dad's minions sell it at a pawn shop or throw it in the trash. So, once your dad let me go, I hung around the front desk with Mrs. Swanson. When I saw him leave his office on a call, I snuck in and..." He shrugged. "I stole it."

Jane slowly reached for the guitar like it might turn to dust or disappear into a cloud of smoke. "I can't imagine how you must have felt." She picked it up gingerly by the neck, and it was so familiar, so completely right in her hand. And then her gaze flew to his. "You asked me if I still had it. The other day at the café. But you knew I didn't. Why?"

"I don't know. I guess I just wanted to see your face. To see if you were sorry it was gone. If you were willing to tell me something that was true."

And she'd lied to him. She'd said she still had it. When all along it was here. "I'm sorry, Nik. I just couldn't admit to you what had really happened to it. Or at least what I *thought* had happened. It was too heartbreaking. And I didn't want you to think I'd just ditched it. I *never* would have done that." Jane ran her hand over the well-loved wood, the scuff marks. The strings vibrated under her touch. "These strings look new. Do you play now?"

"No." Nik shook his head. "But I took it to the music shop the other day. They tuned it up and put on new strings."

"Why?" Jane's left hand automatically formed a chord, her right hand gently strumming the strings. "Why did you keep it for all these years?"

Nik raked a hand through his hair. "You *know* why, Jane. Because I love you, and I've always loved you. Because it was my connection to you." He dropped his hands to his sides. "Because I've been waiting for *ten goddamn years* for you to come home to me and play this guitar again."

Jane froze, her eyes glued to Nik. The man who had filled her dreams for a decade was finally there in front of her. *And he loves me.* With very little grace, Jane set the guitar back in the stand and moved in his direction, closing the narrow space between them. He was waiting for her, dark eyes full of desire, and as Jane fisted her hands into the fabric of his shirt to pull him closer, he was already wrapping one arm around her waist to yank her against him. His other hand tangled into her hair, tilting her head, holding it steady as his mouth crashed down against hers.

She pushed up on her tiptoes, opening her mouth, sliding her tongue against his and pressing her body against the solid length of him. He was already hard for her, the evidence straining against his jeans, pressing into her abdomen, and it sent a flare of desire through her.

Their first time together had been slow, cautious, with the gentle fumbling and nerves of teenagers. But after a decade of waiting for this, their movements were impatient, purposeful, urgent. Within seconds, Jane had unbuttoned Nik's flannel shirt and was shoving it off his shoulders to discard on the floor at the same time that he gripped the hem of her sweater and pulled it over her head.

Jane stood back for just a moment, taking him in. The hard planes of his chest. The taut muscles of his arms. Nik had changed physically since she'd last been like this with him, but the look in his eyes, the care he showed her, the assurance that she was utterly safe, and the love—they were the same as they'd always been.

Nik dipped his head, tasting the skin of her neck, her collarbone, the top of her breast. He unhooked her bra, tossing it onto the growing pile of discarded clothes on the floor while his mouth returned to its place, skimming his tongue against her nipple, tugging it into his mouth.

Her body went weak, neck unable to support her head, and she floated back against the bookshelf. Nik moved lower now, bracing his hands on her hips as he slid to his knees, pressing his mouth to her stomach, tugging at the waistband of her leggings.

All the heat in Jane's body gathered between her legs. And once Nik had rid her of the rest of her clothes, he found that place, first sliding a finger inside her, and then two. Her body clenched around him, pressure building as she gasped in pleasure, gripping his shoulders to hold herself upright. And then he followed his hand with his mouth, and the fire that he was stoking finally ignited, spreading through her bloodstream, blazing in her core and exploding through her limbs. "Nik," she whispered, weakly. Her legs finally gave out, and she slid to the floor beside him in a heap.

She'd never come like that, not with a man who cared about giving her pleasure. Not with anyone besides herself, alone in her bed late at night while Matteo was at the club and Nik was possessing her thoughts in a way that she'd never, ever allow in the light of day. She wanted more. She wanted every fantasy, every moment she'd longed for and that they'd missed out on for the past ten years.

"Nik, I need you inside me." She grasped for the button on

his jeans, fumbled with his zipper, tugged the denim down over his hips. "Now."

"Jane," he murmured against her hair. "Wait." He reached for his jeans, now on the floor, dragging his wallet out of the pocket and tugging a condom from the folds. He put it on while she climbed on top of him. As soon as he took his hands away, Jane sank down on him, their heat, their breath, their bodies finally moving together, exactly where they belonged.

THIRTY

Afterward, they lay on the couch wrapped in a flannel blanket, Jane's head resting on Nik's chest, his arm wrapped around her back.

"I can't believe you're really here," Nik mused, pressing a kiss to her forehead.

Jane snuggled closer. "It feels like the most beautiful dream. I don't want to ever wake up."

"Maybe you don't have to."

Jane leaned back to look up in his eyes.

Nik gently shifted so she slid beneath him. He leaned over her, elbows braced on either side of her head. "Jane." He ran a hand gently against her cheek. "Who put that bruise on your face? And don't tell me you ran into a cabinet. Was it Scarlett's father?"

Jane hesitated and then nodded. "Matteo."

"Does he—" Nik cleared his throat. "Does this happen often?"

Jane nodded again.

Nik swore under his breath. "When did it start?"

"There were red flags before we had Scarlett. He had a temper and would snap at the bar staff. But it really escalated after she was born. I was so vulnerable then. No job, no money, nowhere to go, and he knew he could do whatever he wanted."

"And you lived with this for ten years?"

Jane closed her eyes, the gravity of that statement settling on her chest, heavier now that she finally had some distance from that terrible place and time. Now that she was back here with Nik. *How could I have stayed for ten years?* "He went through phases—sometimes he could be sweet and thoughtful. Sometimes he really seemed to be trying. He was sorry. He wanted to be a better man."

Jane remembered how *relieved* she'd felt during those times of remorse. How hopeful that everything was going to be okay. "Once he bought a book about anger management. Another time, the bartender at the club, Yolanda, recommended a good therapist."

But Matteo never read past chapter three in that book, and he never called the therapist. He never *changed*, not on more than a surface level, and never for long. But each time he gave the appearance of trying was a reprieve for Jane. The calm, the peace, they were enough to trick her into staying for a while longer. And in the darkest times, it was the terror that had gripped her.

Most women who are murdered by their abusers are killed after they leave, not before.

Staying was safer than leaving.

In the darkest times, Jane believed Matteo would kill her.

"I know how it sounds, believe me. When I was a kid, I never understood why my mom didn't just leave. Just... *leave.* How hard could it be?" Jane stared over his shoulder. "I had no idea how hard. How an abuser gaslights you into thinking it's your fault. You think you did something wrong or you're imagining what's happening to you." She twisted the throw blanket in her hands. "And then you become so isolated, so alone, that you can't imagine where you'd go or what you'd do, even if you could manage to get out."

"I wish..." But then Nik trailed off, shaking his head.

"What?"

"It doesn't matter. It's in the past. What matters is that you're here now and you're *not* alone." He pulled her closer. "You'll never be alone again."

"I wanted to call you, Nik. I wanted to so badly. But I was eighteen and traumatized and had just given birth to Scarlett. And I was terrified of ruining your life, and so scared for my own. And for my daughter's. When you're in a situation like that, you can't see anything clearly. You're just moving dirt around in your little hole and you don't even have the energy to look up and see if there's sky overhead." Jane took a shaky breath. "I couldn't come home. My dad was still here. I'd fled from him in the first place. And, after a while, I convinced myself that nobody would want me anyway."

"I want you, Jane. And so do Hannah and Ali. And I know you have a lot to work out with your mom, but I saw her with Scarlett, and I saw the way she looks at you. She's so happy you're home."

"I know she is. And I know she was in the exact same situation I was. I hope that someday Scarlett will be able to forgive me." With that thought, Jane hesitated. She hoped Scarlett would forgive her, not just for staying with Matteo. If Nik really was her father...

But she couldn't say that to Nik. Not yet. Not until she figured out what to do.

"You said you left him." Nik searched her face. "But it's more than that, isn't it?"

Jane nodded. "I told him Mom needed my help cleaning up

Dad's paperwork and convinced him to let us go. But he thinks we'll be back on New Year's. He doesn't know we're running away." She met his eyes. "My plan was to move to Canada. You remember that I'm a citizen? Matteo doesn't know that."

Nik was very still. "Your plan *was* to move to Canada?"

"It was. But then... we got here, and Scarlett is so happy. Happier than I've ever seen her. I don't want to be looking over my shoulder all the time. And I don't want to be alone anymore." Jane swallowed hard. "I ran into Martin Lefkowitz, the attorney?"

Nik nodded.

"He says he can help me."

"He's a really smart guy."

"But you don't know Matteo. I don't know if he'd ever let us go."

"Jane." Nik shifted to face her. "This isn't Linden Falls from when we were kids. The police force isn't your dad's police force. And you aren't alone anymore."

For the first time in a decade, Jane felt a glimmer of real hope. Could she really leave Matteo? Not just to flee to Canada where she'd be looking over her shoulder for the next several decades, but to stand up, stay, and fight for the life she and Scarlett deserved, with the people who cared about her?

At the thought of Scarlett, though, Jane's confidence faltered. Nik was here, he was all-in now. But what would he do if he found out Scarlett might be his daughter? Jane hadn't meant to keep this from him—she hadn't known herself—but would he ever see it that way? She'd taken off and disappeared for a decade without so much as a text or phone call. Why would he believe her? Her heart folded in on itself. It was unbearable. The years they'd lost. The time they could have had. And now—with her suspicions that Scarlett might be Nik's —the loss of the time Scarlett might have missed was unbearable, too.

But Nik still loved her after all this time. She had to believe that he would forgive her. Tomorrow, she'd go talk to Martin Lefkowitz and find out what to do about Matteo. Once she'd gathered the information she needed, she'd tell Nik everything.

Jane looked up and found only love radiating from his eyes. She could do this. She was ready to start the rest of her life.

THIRTY-ONE

Jane's momentum was stalled slightly, the next morning, when she got in her car and it wouldn't start. Nik opened the hood and peered inside, a move that made her smile. She had a feeling that unless the car had lungs and a spleen, Nik would have no clue what to do with it. He confirmed as much when he closed the hood and offered to drive her home.

She'd call Kait later about towing the car. Maybe by then Jane would have talked to Martin and gotten an idea of her next steps. Maybe she could tell Kait she wouldn't need to trade it in for a nondescript sedan to get them across the border to Canada after all.

When they pulled up to Mom's house, though, there was a car parked out in front that exactly matched the description of the sort of vehicle she'd asked Kait to get for her. A small white Nissan hatchback with New York plates. Had Kait dropped the car off? Jane was surprised that the other woman hadn't texted or called to do the switch at the garage where Mom's busybody neighbors like Mrs. Swanson wouldn't be peering out their windows, wondering about the unfamiliar vehicle in their driveway.

Nik glanced over as he pulled up next to the Nissan. "Looks like your mom has a visitor."

Jane shook her head. "I think it's the car Kait got me to take to Canada."

A dark cloud crossed Nik's face.

Jane reached out to weave her fingers through his. "I don't think I'll be needing that now."

"You won't." He turned to face her. "Jane, promise me that you won't go running again and shut me out. No matter what, we're in this together."

Her eyes met his, and she was overwhelmed by the love she saw there. How could she ever go back to being on her own? "We're in this together," she repeated, pressing a kiss to his lips.

When she pulled away, Nik leaned back to look her in the eye. "I'll call Kait about towing your car in front of my house. You worry about talking to Martin."

With that, Jane felt another weight lift. She didn't have to do everything on her own. Mom was here to help with Scarlett, and Hannah and Ali were back in her life. And so was Nik. For the first time in so long, Jane had people she could trust. People she could count on. "Thank you," she whispered, leaning in to kiss him again before she hopped out of the car.

Jane climbed the porch, and with one last wave, she turned and opened the front door. She was still smiling when she stepped inside the house and bent over to kick off her boots. And then, suddenly, she heard a loud crack. Her head snapped back, and a burning pain seared across her face. From somewhere far away, she heard a shrill, terrified female voice call out, "*No! Stop!*" right before another blow had her flying across the hallway and slamming into the wall.

Jane bent over, gasping as her head spun and her vision blurred. What had just happened? But at the same time, she knew. This feeling, this moment, was so familiar. She'd been here, hugging a wall, her body aching, terror filling her lungs, more times than she could count.

She clutched a hand to her burning cheek and slowly lifted her head. "Matteo," she whispered.

He towered over her, holding his right fist in his left palm. "Surprised to see me?"

"I—" Jane's brain felt like it had rattled around in her head. *Focus. You need to focus.* "What are you doing here?"

He crossed his arms over his chest. "I came to see my girlfriend and my daughter. Aren't I allowed to do that?"

Scarlett. Jane's eyes swung wildly around the room, past Mom, who stood shaking in the living room doorway. Scarlett wasn't here.

And then she remembered. *Scarlett is staying with Hannah.* Her friend had said she'd drop her off today. Jane's gaze swung to Mom's stricken face. Almost imperceptibly, Mom gave a shake of her head. Jane closed her eyes in relief. *Oh, thank God.* Scarlett wasn't here, and Mom hadn't told Matteo where to find her.

"Imagine my surprise," Matteo said, in a low, eerily calm voice, the one that Jane knew meant more trouble than the yelling. He took a slow step toward her. "When I got here..." Another step. Jane shrank as far away from him as possible. "... and saw you making out with some guy in the driveway."

And then like a predator who'd been stalking his prey, Matteo pounced, reaching out and grabbing her by the shoulders. "Who the fuck is that guy?" He shook her so hard her head smacked against the wall. "Who is he?"

"Stop!" Mom yelled, grabbing one of Matteo's arms and trying to pull him off. But Matteo barely flinched. Instead, he just waved a hand and flung Mom away, sending her reeling back across the hall where her shoulder crashed into the coat rack.

And that was when Jane knew for sure. The ominous look

on his face, the emptiness in his eyes, the ease with which he used violence on anyone who crossed him. He'd never let her leave him to live here in Linden Falls. He'd never let her take Scarlett.

He would stalk her for the rest of her life.

And he would kill her.

Jane's head spun, but she had to get it together, she had to focus. "Why did you come here?"

Matteo crossed his arms over his chest again. "One night, when you were gone, I started googling. I wanted to see about this East Bumfuck place that you were so eager to come back to after all these years. What was the big damn deal?"

"And...?" Jane said, cautiously.

"You'll never guess what I found."

What could Matteo have *possibly* unearthed in an internet search about this town? The Linden Falls town council webpage? A review of the wineries out by the lake? None of that had anything to do with her.

"I found a video of my girlfriend singing at some café. Someone had posted it on the East Bumfuck Instagram page."

Oh God. The musical showcase at the Grassroots Café. Someone had been taking a video? "So, I sang one song. It was a favor for the old friend who owns the café."

"Are you fucking him, too?"

"What? No. Of course not. You *know* I used to sing and play guitar. Why is this such a big deal?"

Matteo pulled out his phone. "Maybe you want to take a look at the video." He scrolled around for a moment and then held it out.

Jane peered at the small screen, watching herself climb on the stage and pick up the guitar. She cringed again as she watched the replay of how she'd accidentally banged it against the stool. Her mind whirred, fast forwarding through her memories of that night. What could possibly be on this video that would upset Matteo? The song was by a well-known artist, there was nothing objectionable about it. Maybe her singing had sounded terrible, and she hadn't realized it. Was he *embarrassed*?

Jane watched herself settle on the stool. And then she watched herself freeze up. Her face had gone white, her brow pinched. Was this it? Was this what was upsetting Matteo? The video kept playing... Jane scanning the room and then stopping on someone in the crowd. And then—oh God.

Oh no.

The camera slowly panned away from her and across the crowd of people sitting at café tables. And then it stopped.

On Nik.

He must not have noticed he was being recorded either, because... Jane remembered his face so clearly that night, and now she watched it play out again... His eyes were locked on hers, an intimate smile tugging at his lips. The camera panned back to her, capturing the matching half-smile on her face.

Jane closed her eyes.

"You see the big deal now?" Matteo shoved the phone closer to her face.

"I—" How could she explain this in a way that would appease him? How could she talk her way out of it? "He's just an old friend." It sounded just as bad coming out of her mouth as it did in her head. And with her voice shaking like that, she sounded guilty.

"I'm taking you and Scarlett home with me." His grip tightened around her arm, but his voice stayed calm. It was worse than if he'd yelled at her. Yelling meant he'd react quickly. A slap, a kick. Calm meant he was planning something.

This was an absolute nightmare. She needed more time. *A plan.*

"Come on." Matteo yanked harder.

Jane wrenched her arm away. "No." She stumbled backwards, back into the doorframe leading to the living room. "You can't force me to go with you."

Matteo laughed and backed up, holding up his hands like he was surrendering. "Fine. I can't force you." He paused, looked at her sideways. "But I am taking my daughter."

Jane's heart hammered in her chest. She could barely breathe. "No."

Matteo shrugged. "Either you both come, or Scarlett and I are going alone."

"You can't take her."

"The hell I can't."

"I won't let you." *Thank God Scarlett is at Hannah's.* But Scarlett couldn't stay there forever. Matteo would find her, and he would take her. He'd done it before.

"She's my flesh and blood, and you kidnapped her and took her across state lines. I could have you arrested."

And then it came to her. The only way out.

Jane stood up straight. "She's *not* your flesh and blood."

Matteo's head jerked back like she'd been the one to hit him. "What the fuck are you talking about?"

"She's not your flesh and blood. You're not her father."

"Well, then who the hell is her—" And then Matteo's gaze slid past her, to the front door. And that's when Jane heard Nik's voice.

"Jane?"

Jane closed her eyes. "Oh God." She'd never had a chance to close the door before Matteo had hit her. Nik must have heard the yelling. Nik must have heard *everything.*

Matteo looked from Jane to Nik and back again, and the disbelief on his face would have almost been comical if her whole life weren't imploding.

"You've got to be fucking kidding me," Matteo grunted. He waved a hand in Nik's direction. *"This* guy?"

Jane slowly turned around to find Nik standing in the doorway, his face as pale as she'd ever seen it.

"Is it true?" he choked.

"Nik, listen—" Jane began, but then stopped. How could she explain this to him? And with Matteo standing right there. This was a nightmare.

"*Tell me,*" Nik barked.

Finally, Jane nodded. "I don't know. But I think you could be." Now that she had seen the similarities on their faces, she couldn't get past it. Every time she looked at Scarlett, she saw Nik's cheekbones, his nose, the arch in his brow.

"Fucking hell," came Matteo's voice from behind her now. "Why should I believe any of this?" He balled his fists. "I'll get a lawyer. I'll get custody. I want proof that she's not mine."

"That's a great idea," Mom stepped in, agreeing readily. *Too* readily. "You'll get your proof. We'll get a DNA test." She bustled over to the entry table and yanked open a drawer. "I'll give you my phone number, and we'll arrange it for tomorrow. In the meantime, there's a motel out on Route 8. You can check in there."

Jane gaped at her. She didn't want Matteo in a motel on Route 8. She didn't want him anywhere near her or Scarlett. What was Mom thinking?

Matteo's gaze swung from Mom, who was holding out a scrap of paper with her phone number on it, to Nik, who had stepped in front of Jane and crossed his arms protectively. Finally, Matteo snatched the paper from Mom. "Fine."

He headed for the door, and though it was a wide hallway, he intentionally veered left, invading Jane's space as he brushed past her. Jane's body tensed, an automatic reaction. It was like she'd egged him on because in the next second, Matteo's broad shoulder slammed into her collarbone, sending her flying back into the doorframe and knocking the wind out of her again.

Nik covered the space between them in three strides, grabbing Matteo by the shoulders and yanking him away from her. From somewhere far away, Jane heard him tell Matteo to stay the fuck away from her, and then a scream, probably from Mom, as Nik flung Matteo across the hallway and toward a vintage mirror that hung by the coat rack.

Matteo put a hand up to stop his momentum and his palm hit the mirror, cracking it into pieces. A jagged shard sliced through his skin. "Fucking hell!" Matteo yelled, grabbing a scarf off the coat rack and wrapping it around the bleeding gash.

Still dazed from her second collision with a doorframe, Jane could only watch in horror as Nik took another step toward Matteo, his hands curled into fists. But then—*thank God*—Mom ran in between the angry men.

"That's enough." She held up her phone, waving it at Matteo. "My husband was the police chief in this town for over thirty years. If I make a call, we'll have every deputy within fifty miles at my door in five minutes."

"And then what?" Matteo snarled. "Are you going to have me arrested?" He hitched his chin at Nik. "I'll have *him* arrested."

"Nobody is going to be arrested if we can all behave like adults," Mom snapped. "Now, you have my number, and we have a plan for a DNA test."

Matteo headed for the door, this time keeping a wide berth. But as he passed, Jane could hear him mutter under his breath. "You know this won't work out for you, Jane. This *never* works out for you."

Jane shivered, knowing he was talking about the one time she'd tried to leave him. She'd thought about running away a lot over the years, but there had been one day when she'd finally packed up their things and bought bus tickets to San Diego.

A shelter there had had a couple of beds open. If they took the 8 p.m. bus while Matteo was working at the club, they could have made it there before he noticed they were gone. But she hadn't counted on Teddy, the bouncer. He'd spotted her trying to lug her suitcase and four-year-old Scarlett down the block. He'd wanted to help, he'd said, so he'd called inside to Matteo and offered to take a short break so he could drive them.

She'd ended up in the hospital, and Matteo had refused to bring Scarlett to see her. Jane had been frantic, desperate to see her daughter, to know she was okay, but Matteo wouldn't tell her anything. And when Jane came home in a cab a couple of days later, Matteo and Scarlett were just... gone. *Gone.* She'd called the police, but since Scarlett was with her father, they said there wasn't much they could do.

Matteo had rolled in three days later, Scarlett by his side in a princess dress and Mickey Mouse ears, like they'd planned a trip to Disneyland all along. Jane had played along for Scarlett's sake, but inside she'd been screaming. Matteo had never done something like that again, but he hadn't needed to. The message was clear to Jane that he'd use any means to control her, even their daughter. Jane had never tried to leave again.

But if Scarlett wasn't biologically his, would that make a difference? Could Jane keep him away from her for good? She truly didn't know. Scarlett could well be Matteo's. And not knowing for sure was tearing her apart.

She watched from the front window as Matteo climbed into his Nissan and drove down the block. And then she turned to face Nik.

"Are you okay?" He took her by the arm and looked her over.

"I'm fine," she said.

"The hell you are."

He strode down the hall to the kitchen, and Jane could hear him rattling around in the freezer. A moment later, he came back with a bag full of ice wrapped in a paper towel and pressed it to her cheek. "Mrs. McCaffrey? Did he hurt you?" He turned to check Mom over.

"Don't worry about me," she said.

"We should call the cops." Nik adjusted the ice on her cheek. "At the very least, you should have a record of this. A police report."

"But what about you?" Mom wrung her hands. "If we press charges against him, he'll do the same to you."

"Don't worry about me."

"Of course we're worried about you. You could lose your job. And if you really are Scarlett's father, we need you *here*. Not in jail."

"Nik..." Jane began. But she didn't know what to say. How to explain this. "We need to talk about Scarlett."

Nik stepped away from her and headed back down the hall. For a moment she thought he was going back into the kitchen, but then he spun on his heel to face her. "I could get over you taking off for LA without a word. I even understand why you did it. But *this*. How am I supposed to forgive you if you kept my daughter from me?"

"Nik, you have to believe me that I didn't know." Her eyes filled with tears. "I *don't* know for sure."

"But you suspect it, at least enough to tell Matteo that I'm Scarlett's father. Or were you just saying that to get him to go away?"

Jane hesitated. What if she said yes? What if she said it was just a story she'd made up to protect Scarlett from Matteo? Maybe if she did, Nik would stop looking at her like this, like she'd betrayed him in the most unimaginable way. Like she was shattering his heart. But Jane couldn't lie to him anymore, couldn't keep him away from his daughter if that's what Scarlett truly was. "Yes, I think it's possible."

He slowly shook his head as if he were trying to process that. "And how long have you suspected?"

"Just a few days." Jane swiped at her wet cheeks. "When I came home and saw you and Scarlett together... when I saw your baby picture at your mom's house again... That's when it started to come together."

"I don't know what to say to that. What to think. How could you get this wrong?" Nik raked a hand through his hair, turning to pace down the hall and then back again.

"Please, Nik. You have to understand what it was like for me back then... I was living in a shitty motel in a strange city. I was out of money and hadn't eaten anything but ramen in days. I didn't even notice my periods until suddenly I was puking in a night club toilet. Matteo didn't like condoms. And I was just a kid. I assumed..."

Nik whirled around. "I was just a kid, too, Jane. I didn't know what the hell I was doing with that condom. You don't remember that?"

Jane shook her head slowly. So many terrible things had happened right after that night. All she remembered was how Nik had made her feel safe, loved. She'd hung on to that feeling for a decade.

"Were you ever going to tell me?"

"Yes," Jane whispered. "I know you have no reason to believe me. But when I realized the possibility a few days ago... I knew I couldn't keep it from you." Jane's voice broke, and suddenly, she was crying. Sobbing over the heartbreak of everything she'd lost, that Nik had lost. And Scarlett. To have grown up with a man like Matteo instead of Nik. "I was going to talk to Martin and figure out a plan."

Nik inhaled a sharp breath, and the next thing Jane knew, his arms were around her. "Hey," he whispered against her hair. "Come on." He steered her to the living room couch. "Where is Scarlett now?" he asked, brushing her hair off her wet cheeks.

"Still at Hannah's. I need to text her and ask her to keep Scarlett another night."

Nik nodded. "I'll sleep here on the couch tonight." He

looked at Mom. "If that's okay with you. Just in case he comes back. And then tomorrow..."

"I'll look into DNA tests," Mom said. "Jane will go meet with Martin, and we'll figure out where to go from there."

Jane looked from Mom to Nik. Nik might be sleeping on the couch, but he was staying, and he had his arm around her. And Mom... she couldn't believe how Mom had talked to Matteo. She'd never stood up to Dad like that. But she had now, finally. Maybe they could face this together. Maybe everything would be okay.

THIRTY-TWO

"I need your help," Jane said. She'd been sitting on the bench in front of the Lefkowitz Law Offices for the past hour, waiting for Martin to arrive after his court appearance that morning. He wore a dark gray suit this time, with a vest and pocket square, and Jane had to admit that he looked like a high-powered New York attorney. The thought reassured her. "Did you win your case?"

Martin scoffed at her. "Of course I did." He unlocked the door and waved for her to go inside. "You said over the phone that this is about custody of your daughter? And protection from"—he dropped his briefcase on the desk and when he turned to look at her, his eyes widened—"oh my Go..." He trailed off, shaking his head. "Protection from whoever did that to you."

Jane's hand flew to her cheek. As soon as the bruise on her face had healed, Matteo had put another one there. But this one would be the last. "Yes."

He nodded for her to sit. "Okay, start from the beginning."

She laid it all out, her history with Matteo, living in LA, the abuse she'd suffered. Martin nodded, took notes, stopped her and asked to go back to clarify a point. And then she told him about Nik, and how she suspected he might be Scarlett's father.

Jane leaned in, trying to get a look at his notes. "So, knowing all of that, can you keep Scarlett away from Matteo forever?"

Martin sat back in his chair and met her eyes. "I want to be honest with you. If this guy really wants to make this hard for you, he will."

Jane blinked. "But... I thought you were the best."

"Oh, I am. But I need you to know this isn't going to be easy."

"Nothing is ever easy. I don't expect it to be."

Martin gave her a long look. "Did you put Matteo on the birth certificate? Did he act as the child's father for a significant part of her life?"

Jane's chest filled with dread. "Yes."

Martin scribbled something else in his notes. "Then it might not matter what biology says. He probably has custodial rights."

Her mouth dropped open. "But he's an *abuser*."

"Has he physically abused Scarlett?" Martin checked his notes. "I thought you said he hadn't."

"No." But that didn't mean he wasn't capable of it. Dad hadn't physically abused Jane until one day... he had. "But who knows what he'll do to punish me."

"I'm afraid a judge won't necessarily go on speculation. They may allow him to see her."

"How is this fair? How is this right?" Jane shouldn't have been surprised. Hadn't Mr. Morgan, the lawyer in LA, told her the same thing? But, somehow, she'd allowed herself to believe that it could be different. That somewhere, somehow, women like her had a chance. "The system is rigged against victims and their children."

"It often seems that way." Martin leaned in with a sharp nod of his head. "It's fucking terrible. And I'm going to fight like hell for you. But I need you to know what we're up against. This could be long and drawn out. We may not be able to keep Matteo away from Scarlett in the meantime. It's going to get ugly." He looked at her sideways. "Are you prepared for that?"

On the drive home, Jane's phone rang with a Western New York area code. She pulled the car to the side of the road and quickly swiped to answer it.

"Jane?" came a female voice through the phone. "It's Kait. I have your car."

Jane opened her mouth to thank Kait and tell her that she no longer needed it. But something stopped her. Martin's words, coming back to her. *We may not be able to keep Matteo away from Scarlett in the meantime. It's going to get ugly.*

Was she naive to believe that Martin could help her? That anyone could help her? She'd promised Nik that she'd stop running. That they were in this together. But what if she couldn't protect Scarlett? What if nobody could? If Matteo had a right to see Scarlett, Jane would have no control of what he might do. He could hurt her. He could *kidnap* her. Jane had heard the stories, seen the news articles about the women who did everything legally in their power, and still their abusers used their children against them. Matteo had done it before.

He'd do it again.

Jane cleared her throat. "Is the car ready now?"

In the background, she could hear the whir of drills and hydraulic lifts. "Give me until tomorrow morning to get the license plates and paperwork together. Then you can come by and get it."

Tell her no, a voice whispered. *You promised Nik. Tell Kait you don't need the car.* But Jane's mouth wouldn't form the words. And finally, she managed to choke out, "Thank you. I'll see you then."

THIRTY-THREE

The minute she turned down Mom's street, Jane's heart slammed in her chest. Matteo's car was back. She pressed on the gas and accelerated into the driveway, barely taking the time to throw the car into park before she ran into the house.

Jane stumbled to a stop in the doorway to the living room where Matteo sat with his phone in his hand. He looked up, and her stomach curled in fear.

"Where's Scarlett?" he barked at her.

"I—" Jane's terrified eyes darted down the hall toward the kitchen. What had Mom told him? "I was just about to go pick her up."

Matteo leaned back against the couch cushion, arms stretched wide. "I'll come with you."

Jane almost argued with him, but then he'd double down and definitely insist on coming. She needed to think of a way to get him to agree to let Scarlett stay at Hannah's house without leading him over there. "Okay," she said, calmly. "Let me just check in with Mom first."

Jane turned and hurried down the hall to the kitchen. She

found Mom standing at the stove, swirling a wooden spoon in a large pot. The scent of cumin and onions filled the kitchen.

"What is he doing here?" Jane hissed.

Mom grabbed the handle of a frying pan and gave the contents a toss. Ground beef and spices sizzled. "I told him he could come back today."

"Why did you let him in the house?"

"If I didn't, he would have come in anyway, just like last time." Mom rubbed her shoulder.

Jane felt awful that Mom had to go through this. Her husband was finally gone, her abuser out of her life. And now another monster was down the hall, terrorizing them. But Mom just went calmly back to stirring the pot on the stove.

"What did Martin say?" Mom added salt to the pot. Was she really making chili at a time like this? Maybe she'd finally gone numb to the trauma. Jane wondered if that would ever be her someday.

"He said it's going to be a long fight." Jane lowered her voice, glancing nervously at the kitchen doorway. "He said we might not be able to keep Matteo away from Scarlett. He said even if Nik is the father, Matteo might have custodial rights. Mom," she hissed, "if Matteo gets custody of Scarlett, he'll kidnap her. I know he will."

Mom faltered for a moment. But then she seemed to shake it off, grabbing a spice jar from the counter and shaking it into the pot. "We'll never let that happen."

Jane glanced at the doorway again. "I talked to Kait," she whispered. "She can have our car ready tomorrow. I just need to figure out a way to stall him until then. And then figure out how to get away."

In her original plan, they would have swapped cars with Kait and then had days to head to Canada. How could she pull it off with Matteo watching her every move? "Maybe we can sneak away at night." It was only a couple of hours to the border. But she wouldn't have any kind of head start.

It all felt so futile and hopeless.

Mom's voice cut into her thoughts. "There are other ways, Jane."

"Like putting all my hopes on Martin Lefkowitz?" Hands shaking, Jane held on to the counter for support. She couldn't fall apart now. "He's a good guy and a good lawyer. I can see that. But the system can't help women like me. We need to take matters into our own hands."

Mom tapped the wooden spoon on the side of the pot and set it on the counter. Then she turned to look at Jane. "I couldn't agree more."

"So, you'll support me in going? You'll help?"

Mom turned back around and picked up the spoon, plunging it back into the chili. "We never discussed the day Dad died."

Jane looked at her sideways. Did this really matter right now? Maybe Mom had hit her head yesterday. Or was this her way of processing the trauma? "Mom, Matteo is waiting in the living room. I'm not sure this is the right time to talk about—"

"Your father, he never took very good care of himself," Mom interrupted, as if she hadn't heard Jane. "So much red meat all the time. Barbecues with the guys. And then the smoking." Mom slowly shook her head. "Two packs a day for thirty years. It was only a matter of time before he went into cardiac arrest." The beef sizzled in the pan. Mom gave it another toss. "Matteo reminds me of your father that way. He's a smoker, too, right?"

"Yes, but..." Jane's heart hammered. "I can't wait around for Matteo to keel over and have a heart attack," she hissed. "Dad was sixty-three."

"No, you can't wait," Mom agreed. She paused, cocking her head. "Did you know that a very high level of nicotine in your system can cause cardiac arrest?"

Jane stared at her. "So, what are you saying? I'll just hope Matteo smokes a bunch of these at once?" She yanked open the drawer where Mom had been keeping Dad's cigarettes, but it was empty. At least Mom wasn't holding on to them anymore. The drawer still smelled though, a little like the man out in the living room. Jane shuddered and slammed it shut.

"Of course not. It takes far more nicotine than you could smoke in a couple of minutes to cause cardiac arrest." Mom picked up a bowl on the back of the counter, next to the sink. She spooned some chili into it and gave it a good stir. "Excuse me one moment."

Jane heard her footsteps tap down the hall, followed by Mom's voice offering Matteo some lunch. Her voice was so pleasant, so soothing, so like the way Jane had learned to talk to him over the years. Calm, so as not to upset him or set him off.

Matteo grunted his thanks, and Jane heard the clink of the spoon on the side of the bowl.

Okay, so maybe the fact that Mom was serving food in the middle of this crisis made sense after all. Hopefully, it would stall Matteo for a few minutes. Jane could catch her breath, think of a plan.

Mom returned to the kitchen empty-handed. "Your father, he loved chili, too." She sounded sad now, almost wistful. "I sent some with him in the thermos on the day of his fishing trip."

Jane stared at her. Why was she making chili if it reminded her of her dead husband?

"It has a strong flavor, my chili. I make it extra spicy. Men like your dad and Matteo can handle the spice. It makes them feel manly."

This conversation was getting weirder. "Mom, maybe you want to go and lie down?"

"Oh no. I'm perfectly fine." Mom gave the pot another stir. "All those spices, they can hide a lot of secrets. If you burn the meat or buy the wrong kind of beans. Nobody will notice if you make it nice and spicy."

Had Mom burned the chili? From down the hall, Jane could hear Matteo's spoon scraping against the bowl. He'd certainly make it known if the chili didn't taste good.

"No," Mom mused. "It's not possible to smoke enough in one sitting to cause cardiac arrest from nicotine."

And now they were back to the smoking again. Jane eyed the kitchen door. What if she snuck out the back? She could go and get Scarlett and make a run for it in her own car. It was risky, Matteo could call the police. But then she remembered what Hannah had said about Ed and the other officers. Maybe they'd at least be willing to give her a head start.

"But," Mom cut into her thoughts again, "you could concentrate the nicotine down into a liquid. Boil it and let it condense. All you need is a bunch of cigarettes with the filter torn off. And then you could put the liquid in something with a strong flavor." She picked up a sponge and began wiping the counter. "Something like chili."

Jane's gaze flew to Mom's face.

Mom kept wiping the same spot on the counter, over and over. "One bowl of spicy chili and a couple of minutes is all it would take."

"Mom..." This was hypothetical, right? There was no way that Mom was suggesting that—

"They didn't even bother doing an autopsy with your father. Someone in their sixties, out of shape, who smoked two packs a day. Why bother? And I didn't want that, of course, as his widow. Cardiac arrest, they'd ruled it right there. And that was the end of it."

"Oh my God." Jane gripped the counter, her vision blurring. "You *poisoned* Dad?" she hissed.

"That day I saw you on a video call with all those bruises on your face." Mom closed her eyes as if she couldn't bear to remember it. "I had no idea you'd been in that situation for all those years. You had nowhere to go. No way out. And neither did I." She set the sponge in the sink. "I realized in that moment that it would go on forever if I didn't stop it. There was only one way to get you out of there—you had to come home."

Jane stared at her mother, her whole body shaking. This couldn't be real. Could it? Could Mom really have poisoned Dad's chili so Jane could finally come back home?

"How do you even *know* about this? Did you *google* this?"

"I forgot to bring a book the last time your father wanted me to come to the lake with him, so I read one of those Graham Smith thriller novels he had in his bag. That's where I first learned about it. And then later, I looked it up on one of the computers at the community center to see if it would really work. They don't require an account or login at the community center."

Jane heard the clink of a spoon on a bowl down the hall. Her gaze swung to the pot bubbling on the stove and then to the empty drawer where the cartons of cigarettes used to be. "The chili you just gave to Matteo..." Her eyes widened.

Mom nodded slowly. "They didn't do an autopsy for your father. But someone who is young, in their early forties—they might investigate a death like that." She shrugged. "But all they'd find in his system is nicotine."

"*Oh my God.*"

"And if he were a heavy smoker..." Mom shrugged. "According to the medical journals, that would make it harder to detect foul play."

The clink of Matteo's spoon against the bowl sounded louder now. Like an alarm in her head. Would Mom have really done this? Jane had to do something. Run down the hall and stop Matteo from finishing that bowl.

But Jane just stood there, frozen.

Matteo's words came back to her. *You know this isn't going to work out for you, Jane.*

And then Martin's warning. *We may not be able to keep Matteo away from Scarlett. It's going to get ugly.*

The spoon scraped against the bottom of the bowl.

You know this never *works out for you.*

He would never let her go. He'd never let Scarlett go. And if Jane tried to run, and Matteo caught her...

Most women who are murdered by their abusers are killed after they leave.

Jane sank onto the bar stool, her breath shallow.

And she waited.

Mom began loading the dishwasher. Jane's mind went still. Down the hall, the spoon clattered into the bowl. And then came a thump.

Mom calmly wiped her hands on a towel and headed down the hall. Jane knew she should get up and follow her, but her whole body was shaking, and she didn't think her legs would carry her.

A moment later, Mom reappeared in the doorway holding the empty bowl of chili. Calmly, she crossed the kitchen to the sink, rinsed the bowl, and set it in the dishwasher. "We should call 911."

Jane swayed on the stool. "Is he—?" She couldn't even choke the words out.

"It was too late by the time we found him."

THIRTY-FOUR

"Be sure to follow up with your primary care physician on Monday, Mrs. Banerjee," Nik instructed the older woman as he led her from his exam room. "And no more shoveling icy sidewalks. From now on, call one of those teenage boys who live down the road."

"Yes, young man," Mrs. Banerjee said, holding her newly casted wrist to her chest as she shuffled down the hospital hallway next to him. "Thank you."

Nik was just handing Mrs. Banerjee over to the woman at the front desk for discharge when the call came in.

"This is Ambulance 81 en route. Forty-three-year-old male experiencing sudden cardiac arrest. VF, no pulse. CPR in progress, six shocks, two adrenalines. ETA four minutes."

Three years in, Nik was so used to the drill that his pulse barely even picked up speed when an emergency call came in. But as the ambulance driver called out the patient's age, his hand clutched the phone just a little bit tighter. Forty-three. Not much older than his dad had been. That thought galvanized him into action. Nik washed his hands, grabbed a pair of gloves, and headed toward the ambulance bay just as the paramedics were wheeling the patient in, pumping a manual ventilator and performing CPR. The paramedics repeated the patient's stats and treatment, and then handed him off to Nik and the rest of the ER team.

Nik took over chest compressions—up, down, up, down, like a kickdrum—as the nurses wheeled the patient into a treatment room. Once inside, Nik rested just long enough to press the button on the defibrillator to take a rhythm analysis.

"Charging."

The machine let out a long, high-pitched beep.

"Clear."

Nik and the other medical staff stepped back, and the machine delivered a charge. The man's arms and bare chest lifted off the stretcher and then dropped back down again. When the patient's heart didn't respond, Nik ordered a cocktail of medications for the nurse to administer in the IV the paramedics had started.

"Come on, man," Nik muttered, returning to the patient to continue chest compressions. *Up, down, up, down.* He used all the strength of his shoulders and back as his attention narrowly focused on the man's muscular abs and chest see-sawing with each shove of his body into the stretcher. "You can do it."

The nurse stepped back from inserting another IV, and with a deep breath of air, Nik paused for another rhythm analysis. "Charging... clear."

This continued for several more rounds—*up, down, up, down,* then, "Charging... clear!"—when suddenly the ECG machine let out a high-pitched beep and the line indicating the patient's erratic heartbeat had gone flat.

"Administer one milligram epinephrine," Nik barked, steeling his muscles to resume chest compressions. "Come on," he murmured to the patient... *up, down, up down...* This guy was young. Did he have a family? Kids? Nik usually didn't think about anything beyond the body parts in front of him, the outcome he was trying to achieve. *Pulse... heart... charging... clear...* But sometimes the thoughts slipped through.

Nik continued chest compressions through another round of epinephrine, and then another, but the ECG continued to show that the patient was flatlining and not responding to treatment. With a deep, sorrowful breath, Nik knew it was time to call it. He dropped his hands from the patient's chest and checked the clock for the time of death.

Damn it. He always hated losing a patient, but knowing this guy was so young was an extra kick in the gut. The next part would be the worst... letting the family know. Would they be anxiously pacing the waiting room right now? Nik lifted his gaze from the patient's lifeless body to his face. The man's nose and mouth had been obscured by the ventilator, but now the nurse slowly detached the plastic parts and dropped them by his side on the bed.

Nik blinked. In a small town, there was always a chance he'd know his patients personally. This man, he looked familiar. Handsome face, dark hair, slightly crooked nose...

Nik's own heart almost stopped beating.

Matteo.

Nik reared back, crashing into a hospital cart. The high-pitched clang of metal hitting the tile floor ricocheted in his head, bouncing around like a pinball. *Matteo.* The smiling man in the photo. The man brimming with violence and hatred in Mrs. McCaffrey's hallway yesterday. This was Jane's Matteo.

And he was dead.

Nik scanned the room, searching for a patient file, for some evidence of what had happened for the man to end up here. *Like this.* But of course Matteo didn't have a file. He'd been brought in on a stretcher.

And with that realization came the most terrifying moment of his life.

Jane.

What if Matteo had attacked her, and she'd fought back?

Nik charged out into the hallway and found Elise, the other doctor on duty.

"Sorry about your patient in there," she said. "It's rough. Are you okay?"

"Was anyone else brought in with him?" Nik demanded. "A —woman?" He could barely choke out the words. Had Jane picked up Scarlett from Hannah's house yet? "Or a kid?"

Elise slowly shook her head. "No."

"Are you sure?"

She gestured down the hallway, where a single nurse sat calmly typing into a computer. "We've got an older man with food poisoning in room four, but that's it."

What if they hadn't been brought into the ER because they were already—

Nik nearly bent over from the horror of it. *Don't think that way. You can't think that way.* "I need to go, I—" He yanked off his white coat and crumpled it into a ball. "It's an emergency."

"Okay." Elise blinked at him. "Of course. I've got this."

Nik ran for his car in the parking lot and broke just about every traffic law on his way to the McCaffreys' house.

He pulled up just in time to see Ed climbing into his police car. At the sight of the red lights flashing on the roof, Nik almost stopped breathing. He yanked the steering wheel to the right and jumped out of the car without even bothering to turn off the engine.

"Hey," Nik called, running across the street to intercept the police officer. "What happened? Jane... Scarlett... are they...?" His lungs deflated before he could get the words out.

Ed climbed back out onto the sidewalk. "Jane and Mrs. McCaffrey are both fine, and Scarlett is still at my house playing with Amelia."

Relief flooded through his limbs, and Nik closed his eyes,

leaning against the police car. "Thank God." But he quickly blinked them back open again. "What happened here?"

Ed shook his head. "911 got a call about a man collapsing. It sounded like cardiac arrest. Turns out it's a friend of Jane's from California. I guess he flew in yesterday." He let out a heavy sigh. "I hope he's okay. I was on my way over to the hospital now to check in."

Nik swallowed hard. "I just came from there. He didn't make it."

"Damn. Did you know the guy?"

"No." Nik pressed a palm to his forehead with the sudden memory of Matteo standing in the McCaffreys' hallway, fists clenched, voice low and threatening. The bruise on Jane's cheek. Matteo's limp form on the stretcher. Nik could still feel his own body rocking from the hundreds—maybe thousands—of chest compressions he'd administered, trying to save the man's life. He'd done everything he could.

But would he have if he'd known who he was trying to save?

Nik's blood pounded in his ears. Thank God he hadn't known. Thank God he'd never have to find out.

"What do you think happened?" Ed's voice cut into his thoughts. "Did you see any signs of drug use when he came into the ER?"

That explanation would make sense. These rural areas saw their share of heroin, fentanyl, pain pills. Clubs in LA probably did, too. But then, Matteo had been the same age as Nik's dad when he'd died, and maybe their causes of death were similar. An undiagnosed coronary artery abnormality and a whole bunch of really shitty luck.

"Nothing immediate, but..." Nik trailed off.

"Mrs. McCaffrey said he was staying in the motel on Route 8. I'll send a deputy over there to gather up his belongings. See if that will tell us anything." Ed looked Nik over, his face creasing with concern. "You look pretty shaken up. Are you okay to deliver the news to Jane and her mom, or do you want me to?"

Nik stared at Ed, trying to wrap his mind around those words.

How do you tell the woman you love that her abuser is dead? That you tried to save him but couldn't. Nik didn't want anyone to die—ever—on his watch. Hell, he'd gone into this profession for the exact purpose of saving lives. But right now, part of him wanted to throw a fucking party. Jane's nightmare was over. Every time he thought about what she'd endured for the past ten years, he wanted to punch a wall. Or Matteo's face.

But though one nightmare might be over, a new one could be starting. She'd spent a decade with the guy, had raised Scarlett with him. A part of Jane must have cared about him. Loved him, even. Nik's stomach clenched at the thought, but he couldn't just shove it aside. How was she going to take this news that Matteo was dead?

And how was she going to tell Scarlett?

"Nik?" Ed's voice came from somewhere far away. "Maybe I should be the one to tell them?"

Nik shook his head. "I'll do it."

THIRTY-FIVE

Jane sat on the couch, too stunned to move or speak. Matteo had left in an ambulance half an hour ago, unconscious and with barely a pulse. She had no idea if he was okay or if he...

She squeezed her eyes closed.

Ed had shown up moments after the first responders, and once Matteo was in the back of the ambulance on the way to the hospital, he had asked her and Mom some questions, but he'd only seemed worried about them, not suspicious. And why would he be suspicious? Never in her wildest dreams would she have imagined that Mom would be capable of poisoning her husband.

Poisoning Matteo.

Every part of her wanted to reject the thought. There had to be some other explanation. But given Mom's admission in the kitchen, Jane had no idea how it could be anything else.

She finally managed to turn her head to glance over at Mom, who sat calmly beside her, hands folded in her lap. "Is it true?" Jane whispered. "Did you really do this? Did you really —" She coughed. "—*murder* Dad?"

Mom's hands tensed, the white skin on her knuckles the only sign she was affected by the question.

"And—" Jane could barely get the words out. "Did you really try to do the same to Matteo?"

Mom remained silent, her head nodding almost imperceptibly, as if she were running through a dozen responses in her head, trying them out until she landed on one that felt right.

Jane waited, breathless.

Finally, Mom turned in her seat and looked Jane straight in the eye. "What choice did I have?" She paused, straightened her shoulders, and continued. "What choice do any of us in that situation have?"

Jane stared at the worn indents on the floor where Dad's recliner used to rest. Those marks were probably permanent. They should have ripped out the whole damn carpet. Set fire to it on the lawn.

"Could I have found a way to run?" Mom gave a slow shrug. "Maybe I could have. But I would have spent the rest of my life living in fear. Every time I left the house, I would have worried that he was there. Waiting. Every time I turned off the light, I would have wondered if that was the night he would finally find me."

The words were as familiar as those old family photos lined up on the mantel. How many times had she thought of leaving Matteo, only to spiral through the exact same thoughts?

Most women who are murdered by their abusers are killed after they leave.

"Your father took everything from me. My independence, my dignity, my self-worth." Mom took a breath, and the slight hitch at the end finally gave away a hint of emotion. "He took three decades of my life and, eventually, he took *you*. My daughter. *My baby.*" Her voice shook now. "Do you understand that there was only one way to take it all back?"

Jane slowly took in the steel in Mom's eyes and the rigid set of her spine. And, just like that, Jane's whole life shuffled and then slotted into place like those puzzles they used to do right there on the coffee table. She'd had no idea how strong her mother was, how much courage it took to say *no more*.

A series of loud thumps carried in from the porch outside, followed by the swoosh of the front door. And then Nik appeared in the living room, his chest rising and falling with each breath. "Jane." He kneeled on the ground by her feet as his gaze raked over her. "Are you okay?"

Jane froze at the sight of his wrinkled blue scrubs, face mask hanging around his neck, Linden Falls Hospital ID badge swinging on a clip by his hipbone.

Though Nik had wanted to call in sick and stay with them that morning, Mom had insisted that he go in to work at the hospital. It all made sense now. Otherwise, how would Mom have gotten Matteo alone? But now Jane realized, in horror, that it meant Nik must have been at the ER when they'd brought Matteo in. That he might have been the one to treat him.

"Jane, I need to tell you something," Nik said, the tension in his voice confirming her suspicions. "It's about Matteo."

An entire lifetime of emotions hit her in a single breath.

Fear. Hope. Terror.

What if Matteo was still alive?

What if he wasn't?

"Jane." Nik leaned in, taking her gently by the shoulders. "Matteo came into the ER in cardiac arrest."

She nodded. She knew. Of course she knew.

"He didn't make it."

And then came a wave of relief so seismic it nearly pulled her under. "Oh my God." It was all she could manage. "Oh my God." If she weren't already sitting, if Nik hadn't been holding her up, she would have collapsed.

"Jane, I'm so sorry."

Sorry. Jane turned that single word over in her head. Sorry.

That was right. That was what she should feel. She should feel *sorry*. Matteo was dead. The man she'd cared about and slept with and spent ten years of her life next to. The man she'd called the father of her child. He was... gone.

But all she could think was that he would never hurt her again. He would never take Scarlett away. They were finally safe. Really and truly safe.

It's over.

"Are you okay? Are you hurt?" Nik slid a hand across her cheek, his eyes seemingly searching her face for signs of bruises.

More bruises, Jane thought, remembering staring in the bathroom mirror at the purple marks blooming under her eye. *The very last bruises.* They would fade, and heal, and soon, those bruises would be in the past.

Just like Matteo.

"I'm not hurt," Jane said. Not anymore.

Nik turned to Mom, who shook her head. "I'm fine," she said.

"Can you tell me what happened?"

Jane took a deep breath and looked at the man kneeling in front of her. The man she'd loved for her whole life. They'd lost so much. The years they could have been together, the life they might have had. And Scarlett.

This will be the last secret I ever keep from him, Jane vowed. *The very last secret.* "Matteo just—" She lifted a shoulder. "He collapsed." She felt movement to her right as Mom slowly reached over to squeeze her hand. "We called 911," Jane continued. "And the ambulance came right away."

It's over.

The pain, the terror, the decades-long nightmare. *Over.* From now on, there would be no more fear. No more running. Her shoulders would never tense when he walked in a room, her eyes would never search his face to gauge his mood, her heart would never slam in her chest at the first sign of his anger.

She hadn't wanted Matteo dead. But if it hadn't been him, it would have been her. Or Scarlett.

Dear God, it might have been Scarlett.

He took everything from me, Mom had said. *There was only one way to take it all back.*

Jane's only regret was that Nik had been the one in the ER when they brought Matteo in. That he had to go through the trauma of losing a patient to cardiac arrest, his worst nightmare. But... *sorry*. No, she wasn't sorry. She'd never be sorry.

Her gaze found Nik's. "We did everything we could."

THIRTY-SIX

"Is Daddy here?"

Nik's head jerked up at the alarm in Scarlett's voice as the little girl stepped into the house. After hearing about Matteo, Hannah had volunteered to bring Scarlett home. But Nik knew that Hannah wouldn't have breathed a word about him to Scarlett.

So, why would the little girl think Matteo was here? Nik glanced around the room, looking for some evidence the man had been in the house and finding none. Matteo's boots had still been on his feet when they'd wheeled him into the ER, and his jacket had been crumpled at the end of the stretcher where the paramedics had tossed it after they'd cut it off him. Nik had vaguely registered their presence as he'd taken in Matteo's lifeless form on the stretcher, after he had died.

With that thought, Nik steeled himself against that clutch of grief he felt every time he lost a patient. It came automatically from years of doing this work and decades of dealing with his dad's untimely death. But then he took in Scarlett's wide-eyes and the way her arms wrapped tensely around her midsection.

"Your bruises, Mommy. You have new bruises." Her voice shook.

And with that, the rage crashed in, displacing any bit of regret that might have lingered over the loss of Matteo.

"No, Daddy isn't here, honey," Jane said, holding out a hand to lead Scarlett into the living room. The way Scarlett's shoulders relaxed at that news wasn't lost on Nik, either.

Mrs. McCaffrey followed, sitting on the couch on the other side of Scarlett, placing a comforting hand on her knee. Nik lingered in the doorway, torn between his desire to give them space and his need to be here for them.

"I have something to tell you about Daddy," Jane said, turning on the couch to take her daughter's hand. "There's no easy way to say this, but he died this morning. He had a heart attack. It happened really fast, and he didn't feel anything. He didn't suffer."

Scarlett stared at Jane, blinking once, then again. And then her blue eyes filled with tears and her face crumpled.

Jane's arms flew around her. "I'm so sorry, baby."

Scarlett pressed her face into Jane's chest. "I don't want him to be dead."

"Of course you don't, honey." Jane shot the briefest of glances at Nik. "None of us do."

"I want him back," Scarlett wailed, her shoulder shaking with sobs. "I want Daddy."

"I know." Jane's voice wavered, and with that, she was crying, too, tears rolling down her own cheeks as she held Scarlett against her.

It nearly did Nik in to see Jane sobbing like this. Rationally, he knew her sorrow was for Scarlett's pain, and she was crying over the complicated emotions of this entire fucked-up situation. But he had to wonder if Jane had loved Matteo. Would she ache for him now that he was gone? Would she miss him?

Scarlett's cries grew louder, and he had to admit that hurt, too. It hit him suddenly how much he'd lost if he really was Scarlett's father. The three of them could have been a family for *ten years*. Instead, Matteo had been given this gift, and he'd... tossed it aside. *Literally tossed it aside*, Nik thought, his hands curling into fists as he remembered the man sending Jane flying into the doorframe.

Across the living room, Jane rocked Scarlett back and forth as they sobbed together, lost in their own world of heartbreak. Mrs. McCaffrey ran her palm up and down Scarlett's back, murmuring soothing words, and Jane reached for her other hand, pulling her into the embrace.

From his place on the outside, Nik backed away slowly and then turned and headed down the hall to the kitchen. Mrs. McCaffrey had scrubbed it spotlessly while they'd waited for Scarlett to get home. He settled in to wait.

Nik had barely even had a chance to process the revelation that he might be the one who was Scarlett's father. He had no idea if he was or not. All he knew for sure was that when he'd believed Matteo might have hurt her, the terror had lodged in his chest like a thousand shards of glass, deflating the air from his lungs. He hadn't cared about a DNA test or all the secrets that had piled up until they threatened to topple. All he'd cared about was that Scarlett was safe.

All he'd known, with complete clarity, was that he wanted to be a part of her life.

It *should* have been him for all these years, not Matteo.

But as Nik sat there at the gleaming kitchen counter, the sounds of cries from the room down the hall mingling with the slow drip from the faucet and low hum from the refrigerator compressor, the doubts settled around him. Was it too late? After everything they'd been through, could he and Jane navigate this together? Could Scarlett accept him in her life? Could they finally move forward together, or had they lost too much to ever have a chance at happiness?

. . .

It took hours for Scarlett to calm down, and even then, it wasn't so much that she settled as that she passed out and Jane put her to bed. By that point, it was after dark and Mrs. McCaffrey had gone to bed, too.

It was three hours earlier on the West Coast, and Jane had to call the club to let them know Matteo wouldn't be coming home again. She broke the news to someone named Yolanda. Nik could hear the woman on the other end of the phone, her voice deep and raspy but hitching with sobs at the same time, calling Jane "honey," telling her she would be okay. Jane cried too, silently, so many tears spilling over her cheeks and dripping onto her T-shirt that Nik filled a glass with water and put it in front of her just to help her rehydrate.

Jane and Yolanda talked about all the people they'd need to tell—names Nik had never heard before. A whole world that he knew nothing about.

Nik got up from the counter, needing to move, to have something productive to do. Since Jane hadn't eaten in hours, he made her a piece of toast smeared with strawberry jam—one of her favorite snacks from when they were kids. When she finally hung up the phone, her eyes were swollen into slits, and the purple smudges of exhaustion under her eyes nearly blotted out the bruises on her cheek.

He slid the food in front of her and she picked it up, but then put it back down on the plate, uneaten. Nik shoved his hands in his pockets, watching her from across the kitchen. The room had gradually grown dark while he'd been sitting there, as he hadn't switched on the overhead light. A single bulb over the stove illuminated the corner of the room, casting Jane's face in shadows, making it impossible to read.

"Jane, tell me what you need. I want to be here for you, but if you need a little space, I can go."

Jane stared at him for so long, exhaustion tugging on every feature of her face, that he began to wonder if she'd heard what he said. And then she slid off the stool and slowly crossed the room until she was standing in front of him. "I don't want you to go."

He released a breath.

"I want you to take me to bed." She took his hand, tugging him toward the hallway. "Right now."

Wordlessly, he followed her, stepping carefully so the creak of the old wooden staircase wouldn't wake Scarlett or Mrs. McCaffrey. It had been years since he'd been on the second floor of the house. He remembered how nervous he used to feel when they hung out in her bedroom, the intensity of knowing she'd let him into her most personal space. He used to perch on the edge of the green-striped bedspread, keenly aware that Jane slept there every night. Nothing had ever happened there—not in her bedroom anyway—but that bedspread had starred in more of his teenage fantasies than he could count.

And now, so much had changed, and nothing had changed at all. They weren't kids anymore, and this wasn't a fantasy, but he was filled with that same anticipation, that same need for her.

She led him into a dark room at the end of the hallway. Vaguely, he could make out a queen-sized bed against the far wall, flanked by two side tables. She didn't turn on a light, just closed the door and pulled him over to the bed. He sat down, facing her, and she climbed on his lap, her legs bent and straddling him, breasts pressed against his chest.

His hand automatically reached for her hip, but he forced himself to stop there. "Jane," he murmured, "are you sure that after everything today—"

Jane leaned even closer. "Please, Nik," she whispered against his mouth. "You're the only person in the world who can make this okay. Please let me feel something that's real and right and beautiful." And then with the slightest tilt of her head, she was kissing him, sliding her tongue along his bottom lip, grazing it with her teeth.

Giving in to her need, to his need, he tumbled back onto the bed, pulling her on top of him. In a flurry of hands and mouths and clothes peeling off, he rolled over and slid inside her, savoring the way her eyes closed and lips parted as she exhaled a low moan. He moved slowly and then faster, following her cues, pouring all of himself into giving her the joy and pleasure she deserved.

Afterward, as she lay across the sheets in a slant of light shining through the window from the streetlamp outside, a tear trickled down her cheek.

"Hey." Nik rolled to his side, feathering a hand across her shoulder. "Are you okay? Did I hurt you?" He'd tried to be careful, conscious of her injuries. He looked at the freshly mottled skin on her arms, and a jagged red line along her collarbone from what looked like a surgery incision from a broken bone.

"No, you didn't hurt me. You could never hurt me." She bit her lip. "But... Nik, I do have scars." She grasped her wrist with her opposite hand, running her thumb absently over a faded crosshatch of lines. More stitches, probably from another surgery or broken bone. "And I need you to understand that I'm not the girl you knew ten years ago."

His heart ached. "Jane," Nik whispered. "You're the most beautiful woman I've ever seen." He leaned forward and pressed a trail of light kisses across the scar on her collarbone. "Each one of these scars is a place where you healed and grew stronger. And the ones inside you, too. I'm in awe of your incredible bravery. I don't want the Jane that I knew a decade ago. Believe me, I loved her. But I only want the woman that you are right now."

Another tear spilled over. "But can we move past all the pain? The secrets?" she asked, echoing his fears from earlier.

"And Scarlett. If we find out she's yours, how will you ever forgive me?"

Nik shuddered, remembering the shot of pure terror when he'd discovered Matteo on the stretcher and feared the worst about Jane and Scarlett. "Jane, I love you. When I was in the ER trying to save him, before I even knew it was Matteo, I just kept thinking about my dad. How he was around the same age when he died. How that could be me in ten or fifteen years." Through the darkness, his eyes found hers. "I *hope* Scarlett is mine."

Jane's chest hitched and another tear spilled over.

"But if she's not, it's just DNA. I want you both in my life, and I'm not about to waste any more time." Nik slid a hand to her cheek to wipe away the dampness. "So, are we in this together? Finally? Forever?"

And the next thing he knew, she was in his arms, her mouth pressed to his. He fell back against the pillows, his hands roaming over her bare back, her shoulders, feathering across her scars.

Jane paused, pulling back just far enough to look into his eyes, a hint of a smile tugging at her lips. "Finally. Forever."

EPILOGUE

NINE MONTHS LATER

"Can I get you anything before my shift is over?" Jane propped a hip against the table in the back corner of the Grassroots Café, pen and paper in hand.

"Just a peanut butter brownie for my girlfriend."

"I already put in the order," she said with a grin, leaning down to press a kiss on Nik's mouth. He snaked an arm around her waist and pulled her down on his lap.

"Ew. Gross!" came Scarlett's voice from behind them. "Mom! Nik! *Please.* One of my friends might see you."

Jane looked up to find her daughter pressing her hands to her eyes as if she didn't want to be blinded by their public display of affection. Jane couldn't help but laugh. Scarlett was in fifth grade at Linden Falls Elementary and, at ten and a half, she suddenly found everything about her mother to be deeply embarrassing. *Especially* if her friends were around.

Jane rolled her eyes at Nik but she slid off his lap. "I'll go and close out," she said. "And then Nik and I will go someplace where we won't *mortify* you anymore."

Nik gave Scarlett a grin. "Can you at least sit and tell me about your day?" He hitched a chin at the opposite chair.

Jane's heart warmed as Scarlett dropped into the seat and began chattering with Nik about the *super hard* math test she had coming up. As Jane crossed the room to close out her tabs, she watched Scarlett pull out her math book and slide it to Nik so he could talk her through a problem.

It was these little moments that made her the happiest. Seeing them study together when Nik came over for dinner. Watching them out in the backyard throwing a ball.

They hadn't told Scarlett that Nik was her father yet. The DNA test had come back a couple of weeks after Matteo's death, but everything was too raw back then. It still was. A decade of trauma couldn't be erased in a few months. Maybe it couldn't ever be erased. They'd agreed to wait a year and then revisit the conversation. In the meantime, Jane had found therapists for both herself and Scarlett. And Nik was being patient with her.

Jane still lived with Mom, and there was a lot of healing that needed to happen in that relationship, too. But they were working on it, slowly. They took long walks together while Scarlett was at school, talking about what it was like for Mom when she was with Dad, and for Jane with Matteo. They weren't that different, both of them trapped in the cycle of abuse. But they were going to do everything in their power to make sure it never happened to Scarlett.

Over the register, Jane watched her daughter and Nik. Every day, Nik was demonstrating to Scarlett what a healthy relationship looked like. How a man was supposed to act. He glanced up and saw her watching, and his eyes softened. And, just like it always had, her heart slowly turned over in her chest.

He tilted his head toward the door. *Hurry.*

Jane laughed. On Fridays, she and Hannah took turns watching the girls so the other couple could have a date night. Since the only place to eat out in Linden Falls was the Grass-roots Café, and Jane worked there as both a server and host of the Saturday music showcase, she and Nik usually spent their "date" back at Nik's place, wrapped in a blanket on the floor in front of the fireplace.

She hurried, finishing up at the register and heading out to the car with Scarlett and Nik. They dropped Scarlett at Hannah's, where Jane's chest filled with a familiar gratitude that she had friends she could trust, and Scarlett had a community looking out for her.

When they arrived at Nik's cabin, she didn't waste a single moment, moving into his arms almost before he could close the door. These times they had together between his intense hospital schedule, her job, and parenting Scarlett always felt precious and far too rare. Jane knew that Nik would have loved for her and Scarlett to move in with him, for them to be a family in every sense. Jane felt closer to being ready for that every day.

So, when he stepped back from her embrace and whispered, "I have something I want to give you," her heart turned over in her chest.

He looked at her sideways, a grin tugging at his lips. "It's not an engagement ring... *this* time." The raise of his eyebrows told her, *soon.* "But it *is* something for your next chapter."

Her next chapter? Jane followed him into the living room. Nik stopped at the fireplace mantel and picked up an enormous package, holding it out to her. If Jane's lungs hadn't been filling with emotion, she would have laughed out loud. The gift was wrapped in bright red paper and tied with a silver bow, but it couldn't have been more obvious what was inside. The package was shaped exactly like a guitar case.

Now that they had plenty of space at Mom's house and Jane's old guitar back again, Scarlett had expressed an interest in learning how to play. Jane had been teaching her and found she enjoyed it. She'd just started classes at the community college last week, taking the prerequisites she'd need to eventually transfer to one of the local universities to major in music education.

Jane slowly unwrapped the paper and then lifted the lid of the case. Inside, she found a brand-new Martin guitar in a rich, gleaming mahogany. "Nik," Jane gasped, pulling it out of the case. "*Thank you.* It's beautiful."

"Now that our daughter is learning to play on your old guitar..."

Jane's breath caught. *Our daughter.*

"... I wanted you to have your own," Nik continued.

Jane settled on the couch, pulling the guitar to her chest, strumming a couple of chords, feeling the vibration of the notes as they moved through her. Or maybe that wasn't the guitar at all, maybe that was just what Nik did to her.

He sat down next to her. "I thought you might miss all the doodles and drawings on your old guitar, so I left you a little something on the back." He hitched his chin at the instrument, and she flipped it over.

Right by the neck, he'd doodled a small vine with flowers woven around two simple sentences.

They're going to love you. Just like I do.

Jane looked up, tears in her eyes. Nik didn't need to have an engagement ring. She was *always* going to marry him. From that first day when their mothers had enrolled them in preschool together, there was never any doubt. Never going to be anyone else for her but Nik. And when he finally asked her—*soon*—she was going to say yes.

A LETTER FROM MELISSA

Dear Reader,

I want to say a huge thank you for choosing to read this book and for coming along on this journey with Jane and Nik. The topics addressed in this book are not easy to read, but please know that I did my best to treat them with sensitivity. If you would like more information or support for domestic violence, please see the following resources.

National Domestic Violence Hotline (USA)
1-800-799-SAFE

National Coalition Against Domestic Violence (USA)
ncadv.org/get-help

National Domestic Abuse Helpline (UK)
0808 2000 247

Women's Aid (UK)
www.womensaid.org.uk

I would love it if you'd keep in touch. Please reach out over social media, email me from my website, or sign up for my newsletter using the link below to receive information on my latest releases. Your email address will never be shared and you can unsubscribe at any time.

In addition, I always appreciate a short review, which helps new readers discover the book.

www.bookouture.com/melissa-wiesner

Best wishes,

Melissa Wiesner

www.melissawiesner.com

 facebook.com/MelissaWiesnerAuthor

 x.com/melissa_wiesner

 instagram.com/melissawiesnerauthor

ACKNOWLEDGMENTS

Love and Other Lost Things was not an easy book to write, and I know that it was not an easy book to edit. To my editor, Ellen Gleeson, please accept my sincerest gratitude for your patience, kindness, encouragement, and calm in the face of my meltdowns during the making of this book.

To Sharon M. Peterson, thank you for every single message you sent, in all caps, yelling some version of *YOU CAN DO IT*. This book would be nothing but crumpled tissues and candy wrappers without you.

To my agent, Jill Marsal, I am so fortunate to work with you. Thank you for your incredible skill in navigating this business so I can focus on writing.

To the entire team at Bookouture, thank you for creating a rare and wonderful environment for authors to thrive. Thank you to the Bookouture crime thriller and mystery writers who were an unbelievable fount of information on methods of murdering someone without evidence. And an extra special thanks to author Graham Smith for pointing me in the direction of nicotine poisoning.

Thank you to Sena Thompson and Chris Hannigan for fielding my questions about music.

To my local writer friends, Lainey Davis and Elizabeth Perry, thank you for entertaining and encouraging my slightly unhinged ideas and for the many brainstorms that eventually led to this book. I value your feedback so much.

As always, thank you, my wonderful family. And very

special thanks to my husband, Sid. You are always incredibly supportive when I'm working on a book, but this one required a heroic amount of stepping up, and I could not have done it without you.

And finally, my most sincere gratitude to my readers. I appreciate every single one of you.

PUBLISHING TEAM

Turning a manuscript into a book requires the efforts of many people. The publishing team at Bookouture would like to acknowledge everyone who contributed to this publication.

Audio
Alba Proko
Sinead O'Connor
Melissa Tran

Cover design
Emma Graves

Commercial
Lauren Morrissette
Hannah Richmond
Imogen Allport

Data and analysis
Mark Alder
Mohamed Bussuri

Editorial
Ellen Gleeson
Nadia Michael